Mob Princess

The O'Rourke Brotherhood

Sabine Barclay

OLIVERHEBERBOOKS

All that glitters isn't gold.
For those who are more than people expect.

Find me writing Historical Romance as Celeste Barclay.

Happy reading,
Sabine

Subscribe to Sabine's Newsletter

Subscribe to Sabine's bimonthly newsletter to receive exclusive insider perks.

Have you read *The Syndicate Wars?* This FREE origin story novella is available to all new subscribers to Sabine's monthly newsletter. Subscribe on her website. www.sabinebarclay.com

The O'Rourke Brotherhood

Mob Boss

Mob Star

Mob Princess

Mob Saint

Mob Bride

Mob Knight

Chapter One

Sean

I've been to way too many funerals for a thirty-one-year-old. I've stood beside weeping parents. I've carried coffins. I've sworn revenge, and I've gotten revenge. Today, I can only do one of those. I'm a pallbearer to the most influential man in my life who isn't family. He was a graduate school professor who offered me opportunities no mobster should ever have. He did it at the risk of his own career. And now, after he did so much that jeopardized his reputation, I can do nothing to defeat the cancer that stole him from so many of us.

The Arlington weather is offensive in its cheeriness on a day so somber. The sun is shining. The birds are chirping. And the flowers sway in the light breeze. Yesterday would have been a better day for a funeral. It poured from sunup to an hour before everyone arrived at the church for the service this morning. The bright light is jarring against the crowd of somber black.

I glance down at my black suit with the charcoal gray

button down and steel gray tie. I've been wearing suits since I could walk. Thank you, Christmas and Easter at Catholic Churches. Or really, thank you, Mom, for making sure your three sons always appeared like properly brought up young gentlemen. At least until we each turned fourteen and turned into mobsters. I normally don't mind a tie around my neck; but today, it's a noose. It's suffocating me when I think about all the missed opportunities I had to express my gratitude to my late professor. All the doors he opened and all the nudges he gave me in directions a man with my family name never should have received.

I say the final Amen and make the sign of the cross as an ingrained habit. One that I still believe in, even if lapsed is putting it lightly. I've been aware of everyone in front of me. I'm standing outside the group of mourners because I don't like people standing behind me. It makes me uneasy when I let people get that close, but I can't see them. However, in a crowd of innocent people, I'd rather have my back exposed than put someone else in the line of fire if an enemy decides it's time for me to join the dearly departed.

I drop my single white lily on the coffin as a woman standing across from me does the same. Our gazes meet, and it's like I've been pole-axed. I've taken pipes to my ribs before, and that's hardly a pain I relish. This is more extreme how she steals my breath. Her hair is so sun-bleached it's nearly white. She's definitely not a bottle platinum blonde. Her eyes are a deep amber I don't think any colored contacts could replicate.

If I couldn't see the resolve in her eyes, I would fear a gusty wind would blow her away. She's 1990s model thin. Waifish. But she's elegant, and her clothes give the appearance she just stepped off a runway. I only know one woman that slim who pulls it off in just as sophisticated a style—Anastasia Kutsenko, Niko's wife. I'd take one Ana over a dozen of her douchey husband. Fucking— *fecking*—I am at a funeral after all—bratva.

The knockout turns away from me, and it's as though someone robbed me. But I'm uncertain what they took. She's headed toward the line of black town cars. Amongst them is mine. It's just under an hour-and-a-half flight down from NYC, so I'll head home tonight. But I have a car service while I'm here. Baltimore Washington Airport is in neither Baltimore nor Washington. Pain in the arse, but private planes can land there.

My arm shoots out and wraps around the blonde beauty as she jerks back and stumbles as her heel hits the curb. I practically haul her off her feet as I pull her away and twist to protect her from the spray of muddy puddle water that's just soaked my entire left side. Fucking arsehole limo driver.

So much for not swearing.

"Are you all right?" I keep my voice low since my lips are beside her ear. Did she just shiver?

I have no chance to find out because she's pushing my arm away as she takes a step forward. She spins around, clearly displeased I manhandled her. But when she recognizes me from only minutes ago, her mouth snaps shut. She nods as her gaze darts to the limo with the professor's family driving away from the cemetery. Deep sadness flashes in her eyes, and it matches what I feel but refuse to show anyone.

"I'm fine. Thank you. He pulled out as I stepped down. I didn't expect him to speed up so soon."

"He should have paid more attention."

"You're soaked. You didn't have to do that."

"Yes, I did."

Her brow furrows, and we're staring at each other again. She's clearly waiting for me to explain. I'm the douche now because I want to make her ask. I want to know if she's curious enough to acknowledge her confusion.

"Chivalry isn't dead. Thank your mother for me." She adjusts the fascinator with the birdcage veil, putting it back in place from where it slipped along her hair. I only know what the thing is called because of all the funerals I've attended with my mom and aunts.

Men who trained me. Men I trained. Men I went on missions beside. As painful as those are, they're understandable in my line of work. My grief floods back, and I swallow. She must see my Adam's apple bob because her expression softens.

"I'll be sure to let my mom know the lessons stuck. And my aunts. They're just as strict." I flash her a smile that's barely more than half-hearted but genuine.

It's my dad and uncles as much as it's my mom and aunts who ensure they drilled chivalry and civility into my brothers, cousins, and me. Old-fashioned by most people's standards, but we aren't all blood and guts just because we are *the* Irish mob in New York City. Hell, on most of the Eastern Seaboard. My dad and uncles would skewer me if I abandoned the manners my mom and aunts engrained in me.

I extend my arm, and she doesn't hesitate to accept. "I'm Sean."

She either doesn't notice or doesn't care that I didn't offer my last name because she doesn't drop a beat. "I'm Nicolina."

Little Nicole. I wonder if that's her full name or a nickname. I speak way more Italian than any of the Mancinellis realize. My entire family does. It pays to understand your rivals, so we all speak Spanish fluently, along with Italian and Russian pretty proficiently. None of the other families have bothered to learn Irish Gaelic. Works for us.

"It's nice to meet you. Were you one of Dr. Carmody's students?" A good Irish last name most people wouldn't know comes from the motherland.

"I was. I graduated from the master's program three years

ago." That likely makes her twenty-six or twenty-seven to my thirty-one. Not a bad age difference, but why am I thinking about that?

"I finished seven years ago."

Her expression would be impassive to most people, but I spend my life reading what people don't want their facial and body language to show. It's speculative, and it makes my cock think about twitching. Not what I need right now.

"Cybersecurity?"

I shake my head. "Security Studies." It's a graduate major at Georgetown. "You?"

"Same actually."

"Do I strike you as a computer geek?" I grin. This time she doesn't hide her assessing gaze.

"Appearances can be deceiving."

And how! More so than she would ever guess. I could pass for a stockbroker or a fed when I'm at home. In the DC area and Baltimore, I can pass for a fed or a diplomat. I know because I've pretended to be all three.

She shifts her gaze to past my shoulder where I already know they're shoveling dirt over our professor's coffin. That same sadness flares. She's young and gorgeous, so I could wonder if she's mourning a former lover. But I've been to so many of these, I can decipher the different degrees of loss. He was a friend to her just like me.

"Are you headed to the reception? You're going to be miserable and cold. Thank you again for shielding me."

Always. "I am, but I'm traveling, so I have another suit I can change into."

My thoughts are growing more and more disconcerting. She has an aura that's drawing me in like the Sirens who nearly led Odysseus to his death. That got morbid fast. I don't need to develop a crush on a woman I'm never going to see again.

Only two town cars remain in what was once a long line of black sedans. One is mine, so I suppose the other is hers. I didn't think about how she would leave. I suppose I assumed a taxi or ride share service. But the driver is standing near the back door and watching her just like my driver is doing the same to me.

"Is that car waiting for you?"

She turns her head enough to see over her shoulder. "Yes."

"I'll walk you to it since mine is behind it."

She's in sensible shoes for walking across grass, but it's slippery from last night's rain. When her foot goes out from under her, I wrap my arm around her waist again, my free hand catches her forearm as she raises it to keep her balance. She doesn't need to turn toward me, but she does. It presses her against my dry side. I don't let go, and her right hand comes to rest on my chest. But her left hand is just above my waist and precariously close to the gun holstered at the small of my back. There's no one close enough to see the outline that surely appears as she presses my suit coat against my back.

"You're my knight in shining suit. Thank you." She blushes. I'm not certain if she's embarrassed that she nearly fell in front of me, or if it's our nearness.

"I'm glad I've been here to help." And to have the hottest woman I've ever met cling to me.

I can tell she's as slim—thin—as I suspected. But I also feel the muscle beneath her clothes. This is simply her stature and not an issue of being malnourished. I've never had a type. I've fucked women of all different builds, and the few I've dated have been a variety. But Nicolina—I don't want to let go. I want to strip her and devour her. I've *never* had this visceral a reaction, and there have been women I've desired to distraction.

We exchange a lingering look before I steer us toward her waiting car. Her chauffeur appears less than impressed with me. He's definitely looking down his nose. *Fuck you, buddy.* I saw him step forward when she nearly slipped, but he stopped when I did nothing more than keep her upright. I step aside as she climbs in. She offers me a warm smile that is in stark contrast to the grief I noticed earlier.

"I'll see you in a bit." Her voice is soft as her driver closes the door and steps to block my view. Bodyguard? Definitely possible near DC.

I watch the car pull away before going to my own. My driver pops the trunk for me, and I unzip my garment bag. Perfectly dry-cleaned suits and perfectly starched shirts await me. Seems counterintuitive that I'll be squirming around the backseat as I change. It's hardly the first or last time I've changed in the back of a car.

I'm usually going from a suit to black cargo pants, black turtleneck, black boots, and black beanie. Even in summer I wear the infernal thing because my shock of red hair is far too recognizable. The bane of being an O'Rourke. We all share it. Three sisters with red hair married three brothers with red hair. The only dominant gene was the recessive one.

Since I've been wearing suits for nearly thirty years, I can tie a tie in my sleep. I can even do a bowtie without any thought. My filthy clothes are folded and will have to go in a plastic bag. They definitely aren't going next to my fresh ones. I can already tell they stink.

My town car pulls up behind hers. I recognize the license plate, but she hasn't gotten out. Her driver waits beside the door, his palm resting on the handle. As I walk past, I hear the light tap. That's when he opens it. Ah. The same system we have. No one opens a back door until the passenger signals. We do it because we're often on calls no one outside our family needs to hear. There are six cousins who run our syndicate.

My oldest brother, Finn, is second in command. Dillan, our

boss, is only a few months older than him. My twin, Shane, and I are a couple years younger than them. We're basically the same age as our mutual cousins Cormac and Seamus. They're seven months apart because Seamus was a preemie. He's a month older than Shane and me. My twin is three minutes older.

Fecker has always been the impatient one between the two of us. I enjoyed a room of my own after nine months of him hogging all the space. God bless our mother for giving birth to two monsters. She went all the way to her due date, and we were both exactly seven pounds, eight ounces. Ginormous apparently.

I hear the tap of Nicolina's heels on the sidewalk behind me. Maybe I've let my mind wander to my family to justify not hurrying to the door. Maybe I need that justification because I want to let Nicolina catch up. I see her reflection in the hotel's door. The family's holding the gathering in a banquet room. Not because there are swarms of us. Dr. Carmody was a private person, so I know he would have loathed people pouring into his home.

I'm certain there are things in his home he'd rather no one outside his family sees. I think he pictured himself much like an uncle to me, and I definitely saw him as someone similar. I've been in his home a handful of times. That's why I have no doubts he'd prefer other people not see the collections of foreign antiques; original Soviet era maps of the USSR, China, and Vietnam; and the U.S. satellite and weapons designs he acquired over four decades of working in national security.

"We meet again." How cliché am I as I hold the door open for the blonde bombshell?

Her amber eyes bore into my emerald ones. "Once is an accident. Twice is on purpose."

She steps past me, and I don't know if she's admitting she

orchestrated it, or she's accusing me of forcing her to see me. I can usually read people better than this. I could tell her emotions earlier.

She's like me. She only lets me see what she wants me to. If I'm not more careful, she's going to see me trailing after her like a lost puppy, the kind she patted once and now wants to be hers.

Hell. I'd like her to do a shite ton more than just pat me. I want more than her scratching behind my ears. Though my leg might shake if she did.

"You don't sound like you're from Virginia. You have a hint of New York." She looks at the button panel once we're on the elevator.

"And you have a hint of French. I grew up in Queens."

"I grew up in Montréal."

There's the French accent. It's soft, but the way she says her hometown gives it away in what's a mostly neutral accent. She did it on purpose that time, but I caught a trace of it earlier.

"Do you live there now?" She's curious.

"Yes. But not in Queens. I'm in East Harlem." Not that I expect her to know where that is.

But when she shifts her gaze to my hair, then back down to my eyes and grins, I'm certain she knows East Harlem is also called "El Barrio." It's one of the best places in all five boroughs to get Latin American and Caribbean food. Before that, it was an Italian stronghold. Chaps the Mancinellis' arses that I have a luxury condo there. It's technically still Manhattan, but I only considered Finn as a Manhattanite since he used to live in SoHo. He and his wife are in Queens now. My cousin Cormac is two blocks from me.

"I went to Barnard before Georgetown."

"Did you know an Anastasia Andreyev?" The bratva wife

she reminds me of—now Anastasia Kutsenko—is about the same age, same build, and same hair color as Nicolina.

"No. Why?"

"She went there, and you resemble each other, so I wondered."

The elevator pings; I hold the door back with my hand. She steps off and could go in her own direction. But she hangs back. There are people here I'm guessing were former students. Many are professors I recognize, and I can tell many are from the intelligence community. They likely work for the NSA or CIA. Perhaps the FBI, but they don't have the arrogance that usually comes with being America's top cops. The slang "pigs" comes to mind when I think of them. Oink, oink, motherfuckas. My family's had some recent trouble with them, so they aren't on my list of friends.

"Sean, you made it." I turn toward the voice and wish I could melt into the floor.

"Hi, Amanda." I went on three dates with her and slept with her for six months during my first year of grad school. She wanted way more than I was willing to give. Now she's looking at me like I'm a full seven course meal. If I hadn't met Nicolina half an hour ago, I might return the appreciation.

"Excuse me. I see some people I know." Nicolina's voice is soft, but I hear her. I don't want her to go. Fuck me. I wanted to give her my number. I never do that. Ever.

"It's been a long time, Sean. It's good to see you."

"Same. How's your husband?"

"We're divorced. Neither of us was ever home long enough to consider it a marriage."

She and her ex-husband are collectors for the CIA. They go places I shouldn't know about and collect human intelligence. Those forbidden locales are where my family does a lot of our business. I've kept track of her, her ex-husband, and a lot of our former classmates to ensure they don't get in the way or get caught in the crossfire.

"I'm sorry to hear that."

She shrugs. "I don't see a ring." She looks over at Nicolina.

Does she think Lina's competition? *Lina.* She's not mine to come up with pet names for, yet it fits. It sounds Scandinavian, and she's super blonde. I doubt she goes by that. It's why I like the idea I might have something of her I don't share. Possessive as fuck to say I've known her for a hot second.

"I'm not married."

"How long are you in town?"

"I leave when this is done." I don't. I hadn't planned to leave until tonight, but I'm not giving her the impression there's time for dinner or a fuck.

"What a shame."

"Mmm. I see some people I know as well. Excuse me." I make the noncommittal sound as I search for someone—*anyone* —I know and can escape to. The only problem is, Amanda knows the same people I do.

When I step toward four men I recognize as being in the program a year ahead of Amanda and me, I try to make a beeline for them. But Amanda comes along. I sweep my gaze around the room, and it lands on Lina. I knew it would. But I looked around anyway on the off chance I could find someone else to mingle with. Our eyes lock as they have each time we've seen each other. She gives a woman a quick hug before approaching me.

"Honey, do you remember me mentioning Samantha and Tony? They're both in doctoral programs now." Lina slides her hand into mine and leans against me as my arm sits in the valley between her tits.

"Didn't you share an apartment with Sam?" I fall into the

roleplay with ease. Though it's not the roleplaying I'd like to do with her. That involves blindfolds, handcuffs, and a flogger.

"No. That was Lisa. But Sam and I took nearly all the same classes together." She beams at me before shifting her gaze to Amanda. Her left hand is in my right, so she extends her free hand to Amanda. I can tell my former fuck buddy isn't pleased. Oh, well. It's been eight years. Life moves on.

"Hello, I'm Amanda Garrison."

"Hi, I'm Nikki."

She sounds casual, and she has the nickname I suspected. But she didn't offer her last name this time either. Does she ever? Is she being cautious since I'm still a strange man? Does she want Amanda to think there's no need since she shares mine? I drop my focus to her as she looks up at me. God, how I want to kiss her. There's a conspiratorial gleam in her eyes that makes me giddy.

"You must be a lot younger than us. I don't remember you." Bitch. Amanda just has to take a dig.

"A bit. People say I still look young enough to be in college. Never mind I finished grad school three years ago." Her smile is nothing less than patronizing. She knows it. I know it. And Amanda sure as fuck knows it. She deserved the jab in return.

"Sean, how did you meet?"

"At a fundraiser in Montreal about two years ago." I did attend an event back then. It was to elect a city council member favorable to a very open border for the goods my family ships down the St. Lawrence River.

"I didn't realize you live in Canada now."

"We don't. We live in East Harlem." Lina chimes in, unwilling to be snubbed. I like her assertiveness. I let go of her hand, and she doesn't stop me. But it's only so I can wrap my arm around her waist. What the fuck possessed me to do that?

It feels so right to touch her and have her against me. I want to drag her out of here and into somewhere private. I want to pull her modest dress up to her waist and sink into her. I want to taste every inch of her and make her scream my name as I come inside her. I want a lot of things with her, but I can't have any. There are so many reasons why.

I was always the best at playing make believe.

"Lina, we have to get going. We don't want to miss our flight, *cailín*."

Chapter Two

Lina

The devil must have possessed me because there is no other reason to explain why I just slipped my hand into the one belonging to the hottest man I've ever met. Sex appeal pours off him like a waterfall in Hawaii. Its power is so strong it threatens to suck you under. It's the devil telling me to step closer to him as he wraps his arm around my waist while we pretend to be a couple.

I can tell myself I came to his rescue because he already saved me twice. But that's not it. At least, not entirely. It's actually only a sliver. I want him to notice me as more than some klutz. I want to feel his chiseled pecs under my hand again. I never needed to touch him to regain my balance. It was an impulse that's left my panties wet. If the car ride hadn't been between a cemetery and a funeral reception, I would have gotten myself off a few times. I want to rub myself against him like a kitten he can make purr.

"You're right, honey. I've already said my 'hi's and byes.' Is there anyone you want to talk to?"

I hope it sounds the way I intend it. He didn't want to speak to this woman. It was clear she ambushed him. They have a past. A sexual past. I walked away because I wanted to claw her eyes out the moment I saw her. But Sean looked so desperate as he searched for a way out. I said a hasty goodbye and went to him as though we're opposite pole magnets.

"Remember what I said, Sean."

What the fuck was that?

"Yes. Such a pity about your divorce."

Before Amanda can say anything, he nods and turns us toward the door. When we pass through, I expect him to release me. Instead, he moves along faster. He reaches out and tests a door handle. It's unlocked. He swings me inside but doesn't shut the door. I nod, and it practically slams closed. He's pressing me against it as his mouth descends to mine. I cup his jaw and neck as I try to give as good as I get. But his kiss is hungry and dominant. When he grasps my wrists and pulls, I let go immediately. When he lifts my hands over my head and pins my wrists in one hand while his free hand grips my hip, I give myself over to the kiss and him entirely.

I've never relinquished complete control to any man in anything. Not to my dead father. Not to my asshole brother. Not to past boyfriends. Not even my mom. But I do with Sean. In an instant without hesitation or reservation. He accepts what I offer and presses his entire body against me. I feel how hard he is as he keeps me sandwiched between the door and him. I can feel how long and stiff he is. The temptation to drop to my knees and suck him off crashes over me with a strength I've never felt before. I've never minded BJs, but I've never lined up to offer them. But I want to taste Sean. I want to make him stark raving mad with desire just like he's doing to me. I must be losing my mind.

I press my hips into him and arch my back, so only my head and shoulders rest against the door. I shift to open my legs, and he takes the invitation. He slides his thigh between mine. It's freaking titanium. I have enough self-restraint not to grind against it to get myself off. But I want to. I need to. But I know self-denial, and I know I can survive it. Just barely. I've never wanted a man like I do Sean. I squeeze his thigh between mine, and he groans. It only encourages him. His hand slides from my hip to my ass and squeezes. He's tightening his hold in tiny increments. It hurts, but not enough.

"More, Sean. Harder."

He obliges, and it makes me go onto my toes. I didn't expect that much strength in his hand. I tug at my wrists, and he immediately lets go. I bring my hands to his chest and let them roam over his pecs and abs. I slip my fingers into his belt and tug. He obliges, and I can go nowhere. He's careful not to hurt me, but I'm truly pinned now. I thought I was before, but his hand resting on my throat eradicates any thoughts of leaving or that I'm in control.

"More, Sean."

"Short of me fucking you in here, Lina, there's not much for us."

"You've done that before. I go by Nikki. Why do you call me Lina?"

"Because I can, *cailín*."

"What does that mean?" I feel like I've heard it before, but I can't place where.

"Little girl in Irish."

We're looking at each other, so I'm certain he sees something change in my gaze because his hips rub against my pussy. I fist his suit coat and practically maul him. Those two words

16

do something to me I never imagined. They make me feel safe. They make me feel precious. It's been a long ass time since I've felt either of those.

"Lina, if we don't stop now, we're going to fuck. And as much as my cock is telling me we should, you are not a one-night stand kind of woman. You deserve better than against a wall in a storeroom."

"And if I'm not?"

His hand tightens just enough to make me raise my chin. His entire expression hardens, and I'm looking at a Dom. I wonder if he is in real life or if that's just his personality.

"You deserve the best of everything. Never settle, little girl. Never accept less."

"But I won't see you again. I don't want to wonder what might have been. I want to know. I want to tuck that memory away for a freezing Canadian night."

"Then let me take you out on a date. If you still feel this way, then we'll talk about it."

"You live in New York. I don't."

"If you say yes to going out with me, I will make it happen."

I want to say yes. I want to scream it. But my life—my family—makes it virtually impossible for me to date.

I don't answer fast enough because he steps back. He doesn't let go entirely. His hands rest on my waist, but his body isn't touching mine. It chills me to have that space after the furnace that held me in place a moment ago.

"I'll give you my number. If you want to text me after you think about it, I'll be sure to answer. If you change your mind and want to go on that date, I will make it work."

"Okay." I sound so brainless.

I look down to where I dropped my purse at some point. He steps back even farther as I bend to pick it up. My lips go past his cock and balls, and I nearly lick them—him. I get my phone out and hand it to him once I unlock it. He programs his number in. When he hands it back to me, I send him a message.

ME

The clumsy Canuck

He must feel it vibrate because he pulls it from his pocket. He grins when he sees my message. I feared it was lame. I watch him type something. Maybe it's just my first name. We still don't know each other's last name.

SEAN

The neighborly New Yorker

He sends a smiley emoji right after he pokes fun at himself. Our gazes settle on each other's lips. But we know better than to start another round. He opens the door and looks up and down the hallway. He waits thirty seconds—I counted because I'd be doing the same thing if I were in the lead—before he steps out. He calls the elevator, and our hands brush against each other. Once it's moving, our hands wind up with our fingers entwined. But it's over too soon. The moment we get to the exit, my driver's door opens. So does his. We let go.

"It was nice meeting you, Lina."

He makes it sound so final. Like he doesn't expect to hear from me again. We reach my car, and I shake my head at my driver. He scowls, and I shoot him a warning glower. I know he's going to run straight to my brother and bitch. Fuck them both.

I reach for my door, but Sean's arms are longer. I move out of the way as he opens it for me. I turn toward him.

"It was nice meeting you too, *nounours*."

He chuckles. Fuck. He understood.

"No one has called me a little anything let alone a little teddy bear since I was six."

He watches me for a moment before his expression turns predatory. He leans forward to whisper in my ear, but he presses a kiss just beneath it first.

"*Je préférerais être ton loup.*" I'd prefer to be your wolf.

Merde. Shit. He speaks French.

"*Peut-être.*" Maybe.

I kiss his cheek and turn away from him. I slip into the car, and he closes the door. I lean back and close my eyes for a moment. It's been an unexpected past two hours. I nearly had— desperately wanted to have—sex with a virtual stranger. I've had a few one-night stands. But that's not what I want from Sean. The reasonable part of me knows it would have broken my heart to fuck him once, then never see him again. I glance at the phone in my hand where it rests on my lap.

ME

What's your favorite color?

SEAN

Cornflower blue. You?

The response is immediate. Just the time to dictate, not even type.

ME

Lavender

SEAN

What's your favorite food? Don't tell me poutine.

ME

LOL not every Canadian likes fries with curdled cheese.

SEAN

Cheese curds

He sends me the green face emoji.

ME

Agreed. Bacon but the proper kind not the burnt stuff you have in America

SEAN

Do you mean Canadian bacon?

Now it's the eyes squeezed shut laughing emoji. Nothing about the self-assured, suave man I met made me think he'd use emojis when he texts. It makes me grin like an idiot. Thankfully, I'm alone, and no one can see me laughing at nothing but my phone.

ME

Sure. What's yours?

SEAN

With my red hair don't expect corned beef and cabbage. Steamed carrots with butter, salt, and pepper. That's probably the real reason for my red hair. I ate pounds of it as a kid.

His red hair. I wanted to run my hand through it and see if it's as soft as it looks. Yet it stayed in place despite the breeze. It was as though it didn't dare move out of place. That it wouldn't make him look anything but perfect. It's definitely not carrots, but neither is it russet. It's a rich red that fits perfectly with the greenest eyes I've ever seen. A deep emerald like Irish grass after it rains. With red hair, freckles, green eyes, and a name like Sean, it didn't take him mentioning corned beef to know he's Irish. Like probably recently Irish. Maybe a generation or two since his family lived there. He called me *cailín* and said it was Irish.

I have a couple Nova Scotian friends. Maybe they could teach me some Gaelic. What the fuck, Nikki? Teach you Gaelic? Like you're going to see him again. Like he's going to care.

> **ME**
> What's your favorite pastime?

And even though I know this is going nowhere, I'm still asking questions. Fucking glutton for punishment. Masochist.

> **SEAN**
> Sailing

> **ME**
> Sailboats? Catamarans? Yachts?

> **SEAN**
> Sailboats mostly. I can sail catamarans. And yes, I've spent time on yachts.

Of course he has. There is no doubting the man is rich as sin.

> **SEAN**
> You?

> **ME**
> TBH I love sailing too. Catamarans mostly but I know my way around sailboats. And yes, I've been on yachts before too.

I try not to be too flashy with my clothes and jewelry. But if he has an eye for custom-tailored suits, I'm certain he could tell my dress wasn't off the rack at Nordstrom or Macy's. It's obvious we both have wealth. I came to mine later in life—all things relative since I'm twenty-six. I don't know if Sean comes from it or earned it. But he's not poor either.

SEAN

> I have a call coming in and I'm about to go through the Fort McHenry Tunnel. I'm going to lose you and I have to call my brother back. I'm glad we met, cailín.

ME

> Me too nounours. Or was it loup?

SEAN

> Both Bye

ME

> Bye

At least he didn't just leave the conversation dangling. But I feel hollow now. I stare at my phone. He responded to me and went along with my banter. I doubt it'll be anything more than this. And that blows.

I wish I were going home to Montreal, but I'm not. My home's now in Boston, and I hate it. Not Boston, per se. It's the reason I'm in Boston. Guilt. Plain and simple manipulated and manufactured guilt. My life had enough fucked-up parts to it growing up with a grandfather who heads the Irish mob in Quebec. But having a father who was a shitty leader of the Boston Irish only compounded every complication I faced as a teenager before my father bothered to be a father.

It's not like my paternity was a state secret. I've known my entire life that Rowan O'Malley was my dad. He acknowledged me, and his name is on my birth certificate. But I don't have his last name. I'm the product of a one-night stand.

Considering that's how I came into the world, you'd think I'd never have one. But I've had a few. And I would have gladly included Sean on that limited list.

My dad got a woman pregnant when they were sixteen. My half-brother Ewan is twenty-seven. My dad's parents and hers forced them to stay together, but the moment he turned eighteen, he dumped her. He thought he could do whatever he wanted because he was an adult. His dad was so pissed he sent him to meet my uncle to arrange some shipment exchange. While he was in Montreal, he hooked up with my mom, who was twenty. Apparently, he hadn't learned his lesson about being careful. Turns out, my mom was on antibiotics to get over a sinus infection. She didn't know they decreased her birth control pills' efficacy. Along I came nine months later.

My dad was not only back together with Ewan's mom, but they were also married. He knew full well he had another child on the way. His wife knew he'd impregnated another woman. My mom knew he wound up married to someone else. I know he loved my stepmother and always had. But he was an arrogant and self-centered man at eighteen and not any better at forty-five when the O'Rourkes killed him a few months ago.

He'd dumped my stepmom to spite his father and hers. He slept with my mom because he could. He'd planned to get back together with my stepmom all along. That was a convenient detail he didn't mention to my mom. She never would have looked in his direction if she'd known.

He always acknowledged me as his, and he would visit whenever he came to Montreal. He'd make an effort to come up there at least once every three months. It was like I was a quarterly tax he had to pay to keep my grandfather from gutting him. I spent a few Christmases and Easters in Boston, too. I spent several weeks each summer. But I was a guest, not a family member. Ewan and I are so close in age that he says he doesn't remember a time before me. He's known his entire life that he has a sister. He just didn't know why I didn't live with him until he was ten and I was eight.

"Nikki?"

"Yeah. I'm here." I slide my coat off as I close Ewan's front door.

I'd taken my coat off in the car between the funeral and reception yesterday. I'm glad I did because it made it way easier to feel Sean touching me. I was wearing it now because it was one less thing to carry.

"Come out to the backyard." Ewan's grilling from the smell of it.

My brother and I overheard our dad talking to Uncle Riley that Christmas. He and I were building a model airplane together at the dining room table. Uncle Riley suggested I come back in four months for Easter. Dad said he was only obligated to have me for one family holiday a year. Since he had a trip to Montreal planned for February that would force him to see me, he said he saw no reason to have me visit any sooner than the next Christmas.

I know now my grandfather pissed him off, so it was more about them not getting along than me. But Ewan and I stood staring at each other in the dining room, a bottle of glue in my hand and tongue depressor looking things in his. That was the day I swore I would never cry in public again. If I could keep myself from crying when I was eight, I can keep myself from crying now. Ewan wasn't a hot-head, but he had no qualms about standing up to Dad even back then. He dropped the wood pieces on the table and stormed into the kitchen.

"Welcome home, Nik." Ewan shoots me a smile as he hands me a beer. He has the same expression as he did when we were kids.

Ewan told Dad and Uncle Riley that we heard everything

while we worked on the model airplane. He told Dad he should be ashamed of himself and if he was the man he claimed to be, then he didn't pick on little girls. That he wanted to be nothing like Dad if he couldn't love both his children equally since neither of us asked to have him as our father.

I remember standing there like a fish flopping on a dock. Eyes popping out and mouth hanging open. I didn't know what to expect, but I was ready to bolt. I was wholly unprepared for Dad to pick me up and carry me into his study. He sat me down on his lap and just hugged me for like ten minutes. Then he apologized. It was the only time in my entire life I heard the words "I'm sorry" put together in a sentence. I heard him say plenty of other people would be sorry.

That was the night I learned how I came to be. At least, in a way an eight-year-old could understand. After that, he was much nicer to me. I was welcome for all holidays and during the summer. I didn't see him much during those visits as I got older, and Ewan wasn't around that often, either. But my step-mom, Maureen, is kind, and that made up for a lot. Especially once I got to college, and Dad turned all those decent memories into guilt.

"Thanks. It was a short flight both ways, but those three days were long. It was fun seeing friends on Thursday. But Friday blew, helping Cynthia pack up her husband's office of thirty years on campus. Yesterday just sucked." Except for when I was with Sean.

I stare at Ewan and think about the argument my brother and I had before I left. He looks so much like Dad. Our father loved to tell me how I owed his side of the family allegiance. That I should support his side of the family since he'd welcomed me into his home and paid for college. That I'd walked away from my mom and her side of the family when I came to the U.S. for college. I didn't walk; I flew. But I will always consider myself far more a Tremblay than an O'Malley.

"Do you need tomorrow off, or can you start the project?" Ewan barely glances at me as he flips burgers for the ass hats lounging around his pool.

How fucking generous. The "project" is what caused the argument with Ewan before I left.

And now Dad's dead thanks to some guy named Finn O'Rourke, and Ewan's the one laying the guilt trips on me. That if I'd done my part to help gather intel, then Dad and Uncle Riley would have been prepared and not ambushed. That if I cared about my brother, I would help him now. I didn't go into intelligence analysis to help my mobster families off their rivals.

I went into it because global security interests me. My maternal grandfather paid a fuck ton of money to the Canadian government to turn a blind eye to his involvement in organized crime. He made a convincing argument that I have no interest in domestic security, so I wasn't a homeland danger. I only want to focus on other parts of the world.

A whole lot of good it did him or me.

Dad laid the guilt on as soon as I graduated from George-town. He deposited a hefty amount—three million dollars—into my bank account as a graduation gift. It was to make me indentured. He expected me to work that money off by slipping him information about what goes on in Montreal.

Ewan started guilting me the moment he told me Dad was dead. That was not one of the times I had to hold back tears. I would have been more upset if he told me one of my favorite TV shows got cancelled. But Dad and Uncle Riley fucked around and found out, leaving Ewan to clean up the disaster. And by that I mean, left him to recruit me to tidy up.

"Do we have to talk about this right now?" I take a swig of beer.

"I offered you tomorrow off."

As though that's supposed to give me time to grieve and get shit together since I moved down here two weeks ago. The project is gathering intel on the O'Rourkes for whatever Ewan's going to do to get back at them. His face has healed from the beating he took from some guys they sent up here. But I know his shoulder still hurts whenever he moves the wrong way. His broken ribs are still keeping him from lifting and running. That's the real reason he's a fucking ogre. He gets cranky when he can't work out. Like a kid who missed his fucking recess and has energy to burn off.

"I meant do we need to talk about this while everyone else is here. You promised you'd keep my involvement a secret. I thought you don't want Jimmy pissed that you have me digging since you don't think he can get it done. And I thought you were going to hide that you need me since I'm a girl."

I cross my arms with my beer still in my left hand. Mob business is supposed to be for just the menfolk. We little women are supposed to stay home, tucked away and none the wiser. Except Rowan O'Malley had a daughter who runs circles around the knuckle draggers he put in charge of gathering intel. Beating the shit out of people to make them talk is not the way to get deep dark secrets. Hacking encrypted networks and clouds is the way to get what Ewan needs. If I learned how to hide nuclear secrets and discover enemy hideouts—in theory, not in practice since I no longer have my government intel job—then I can figure out what the fuck the O'Rourkes are up to.

"None of them are listening."

I stare at him before shifting my gaze to sweep across the backyard. There are a dozen men here, some with wives or girlfriends. They all appear occupied eating and drinking. A few are in the pool. But they're mobsters who've lived long enough to enjoy this barbeque. They didn't do that by not being situationally aware.

"You're a fool if you believe that. You aren't naïve, so pull your head out of your ass, Ewan. I don't want to die for this shit."

"And who's being melodramatic?"

"If Jimmy finds out you don't trust him and you went behind his back to get your little sister's help, he's going to lose his shit. He can't do a damn thing to you, but he can do plenty to me."

Ewan puts the tongs down and fully turns toward me. "He will never touch you and live."

"A fat lot of good that does me if I'm already dead. And he has plenty of ways to get to me without ever touching me. We both know the only reason he headed up Dad's intel gathering is because he's the best enforcer."

"Are you scared of him?"

"Of course." I'm about to say more, but my phone vibrates in my pocket. I pull it out far enough to see the screen. I force myself not to grin.

"Who is it? Some guy?"

I look up at Ewan. "And if it is?"

"Then I want to know who he is."

I laugh. I laugh hard. I laugh hard in his face.

"Now you want to be my big brother. You're worried about who I'm fucking, but you aren't worried one of your men could squeeze the life out of me with one of his ham hock hands. Your priorities are fucked."

I don't wait for him to respond. I walk inside and leave my beer on the counter. I jog up the stairs to my room. I cannot wait to find an apartment and move out. But I'm safer here than on my own. Until I'm certain Ewan can keep his men away from me and that Jimmy can play nice, I'm better off under Ewan's roof than my own.

SEAN

Did you make it home safely?

He probably thinks I live in Montreal again. I never told him I moved to Boston. The only time I said where I lived was when I pretended to be his girlfriend. I said we lived in East Harlem.

ME

I did. You?

SEAN

Yeah. It was nice meeting you. It made a bad day a lot better.

He's sweet.

ME

It really did. I'm glad I met you too. I never asked which of Dr. Carmody's classes you took.

SEAN

All of them. But I enjoyed open-source intel, and lies and disinformation the most.

The exact things Ewan expects me to use.

ME

Same. People put more info out there than they realize. It's there if you just look.

SEAN

And what people are willing to believe is on them.

ME

True

It is, but I don't know that I would have said it outright. Is he testing me?

SEAN

My brothers just pulled up so I gotta go. But I'm glad you made it home safely.

The weather out of DC was crap this morning, but it's beautiful in Boston right now. I doubt that's what he means, though. I bet he means the distance between the DC area and Montreal. Did he think I went home yesterday after the funeral or today?

ME

Brothers?

SEAN

Yeah. Two. You?

ME

One

SEAN

Older or younger?

I know he has to go, but I don't think either of us wants to stop chatting.

ME

Older. You?

SEAN

Baby of the family

He sends me that grinning, eyes squeezed shut emoji. There's nothing about him that makes me think he's the baby of anything. He's all alpha male all the time. Just thinking that makes my cunt ache. I wish we had fucked in that storeroom.

SEAN

TTYL Have a good day

ME

You too

I started the text conversation yesterday when we were in our cars. He picked it up today. Do I say more tomorrow?

"Nikki!"

For fuck's sake.

"Yeah. I'm in my room. Hold on. I'm getting changed."

I slide off the trousers and blouse I'm wearing and grab a pair of shorts and a tank top. If there weren't a bunch of guys in the backyard I barely know, I'd grab a bikini and lay out. I don't need them staring at how thin I am. I know I'm flat chested and bony. I'm fine with it because it's just the way I'm made. But I'm hardly what most guys want when they see a woman half naked. I don't need them staring at my flat ass any more than they would if I had a fat one.

Though Sean seemed to like what he felt yesterday. He made it seem like he couldn't get enough. He didn't make me feel too tall or too gangly. He made me feel desirable. He pinned me against the door, but I never felt trapped. Even when he exerted dominance, I never feared him. Just the opposite. I felt—treasured. I've never felt that way with a man before.

I glance down to see my nipples are hard. Great. I need a different bra. It's definitely not cold out. I strip off my clothes and pinch my nipples to the point it hurts. I close my eyes and picture Sean's hands on me instead of my own. I remember how it felt to have his thigh between mine. What I wouldn't give to feel that again.

"Nikki!"

"I'm coming! Hang on!"

Nothing like your brother bellowing at you to ruin the mood. I toss on my clothes and head downstairs.

"What?"

"Your hot dog's ready."

I look down at the plate he fixed me. Not only is there a hot dog with mayo and ketchup, there's macaroni salad, a brownie, and Doritos. He offers me a lopsided grin as I accept the plate. It's all the stuff I like. He tries, and I have to give him credit for that.

Turns out, though, it's not so altruistic as I hoped.

"You're going to New York in two days."

Chapter Three

Sean

Finn and Shane just pulled into Dillan's driveway behind me. I texted Dillan when I turned on his street to let him know we were almost there. Now that he's married and can't keep his hands off his wife, the open-door policy to his house slammed shut. We make sure to give them a heads up before we come through the gate. Finn's the same with his wife. They moved into a house two streets over.

Among the many fucked-up things in this world, all the married syndicate couples live in the same two neighborhoods. My parents and my aunts and uncles live near Nicoletta and Massimo Mancinelli, who live a block from Massimo's second cousin, Domenico, and his wife, Carlotta. Their neighborhood is around the corner from the one all the Kutsenkos and younger Mancinellis moved into. Dillan's on the corner of the two neighborhoods, and Finn is six houses down and two streets behind.

The neighborhoods are Switzerland. We see each other,

but we keep our eyes forward. At least, we supposedly do. There isn't a moment we aren't watching for who's in front, beside, or behind us. But there are children in these families now, so no one will risk taking a shot with one or more kids being in a car. Outside the neighborhood, when we're certain it's only the men? Fair game, bitches.

"Hey. Welcome back." Shane is my absolute mirror image except I have a freckle on my throat, and he doesn't. The freckles on our face are so damn similar, they're of no use for people to tell us apart.

"Thanks." I knock before punching in the code for the front door.

"Dillan? Mair?" Finn calls over my shoulder as I step across the threshold.

"Mair's at the office. I'm in the kitchen."

Dillan's voice carries in the mostly furnished home. They made sure they set up all the bedrooms as soon as they moved in. We all have our own room. It's that way at all the parents' homes. It's that way at Finn's. Dillan and his wife are taking their time to furnish the family room and living room. They have similar taste, so it's not because they can't agree. They just aren't in a hurry to settle. Finn and Ally merged their belongings.

My cousin looks up from the sandwich he's making. There are already three others waiting on plates. "How'd it go?"

I shrug. "How does any funeral go?"

I grab a plate and move to the kitchen table. Shane and Finn do the same, and Dillan joins us once he puts everything away.

"Did you have a chance to see any friends?" Shane speaks before he takes a bite. I haven't filled Shane or Finn in yet, either. Finn and I talked about other stuff when he called yesterday, and I had to stop texting with Lina.

I got home the night before last, and I spent yesterday catching up on work. I know Lina got home yesterday, so I used her flight as an excuse to text her.

"I saw Taylor Hamilton for breakfast before we headed to the funeral separately. There were a few people I wanted to say hi to at the reception, but Amanda cornered me."

All three of them have matching disgusted expressions. Shane warned me away from her, saying she was trying to sink her fangs in because I'm rich. I am. We all are. Like billionaire rich, even though the rest of the world thinks we're scraping by as just barely millionaires. We like our net worth to appear far smaller than it is. And not just for the tax advantages. Let the Diazes, Mancinellis, and Kutsenkos gloat. None of us could give a flying fuck. We own shite for a rainy day that would make their heads spin.

"How'd you escape?" Shane's smirk matches the one I'm usually wearing when we talk to Dillan and Finn. It's fecking annoying seeing my reflection directing his patronizing as feck expression at me.

"I ran into someone who was close to Dr. Carmody, too. They distracted Amanda." *They.* Not her. I don't want to hear about it from them.

"Does *they* have a name?" Dillan appears casual as he takes a sip of iced tea, but his tone irks.

He's probably already planning to run my unnamed woman's background check, get surveillance on her, and dig into her bank accounts. He loves Mair more than anyone else, but they had a rocky start. They probably wouldn't be together if he'd run a full background check on her, but it would have made life a little easier.

He ran a full check on Finn's wife, but Finn asked him not to say anything to him. My brother wanted to get to know Ally on his own. Life might have been a little easier if Dillan told

Finn the one big thing he discovered. But it worked out in the end, and that one big thing is dead now, anyway.

"Nik. We didn't talk much. Just long enough to extract me from Amanda."

No one needs to know Nik isn't what Nicolina goes by. No one needs to know I think of her as Lina. For now, it's not a lie, but it sounds masculine. I have too much to sort out in my head about why I want her so much. I don't need the peanut gallery chiming in.

"Anyhow. Did anything turn up about Ewan's plans for the rugs we wound up letting them have?" His father and uncle are dead, in part, because they fucked us over and stole rugs that had nano chips woven into them.

We took our stolen shipment back but decided on second thought to let Ewan and the Boston Irish have them to keep them doubly indebted to us. They might run Bean Town, but we run the Eastern Seaboard. If this were the Middle Ages, we'd be their feudal overlords. They'd be vassals who can do what they want, but only to a point. If they stay out of our way, then we give them freedom.

Rowan and Riley flexed, and we reminded Ewan and his band of Merry Men that they exist at our largesse. If we don't want them in Boston, they won't exist. Ewan's other debt is we offed his father, so he didn't have to commit patricide.

Finn shakes his head. "They're tighter than a nun's arse in church. Someone's taken over their networks. I need your hacking skills because this exceeds mine."

Shane practically snorts his soda. "A nun's arse? Be sure to let Mom hear that one."

Finn's scowl only makes Shane laugh harder. In my head, I roll my eyes.

"What's different? You're as good a hacker as Lorenzo. What can't you crack?"

Lorenzo Mancinelli is their family's accountant like Finn is ours. They both have backgrounds in computer science because they're forensic accountants along with the regular shite they do and day trading. Enzo's cousin Carmine is pretty good too, but that's because he's always been a nosey fuckwad.

Between Enzo's and Finn's skills and mine are Sergei Andreyev and Anton Kutsenko. The bratva shites went to UPENN, and you can tell. They might not wear the sweatshirts anymore, but they're smug motherfuckers. Sure, they went to an Ivy, but so did I. And right now, my alma mater's computer science program is still ranked higher than UPENN's.

Ithaca might be fucking miserable in winter, but my education made up for the dreariness. Sergei's one of the best hackers I've ever met, and Anton's a whizz at programming. But the two of them still don't touch what I learned between Cornell and Georgetown. There's plenty all of us have learned over the years, mostly self-taught.

Joaquin Diaz is the Cartel's intel gatherer. He's probably the smartest of all the families' computer geeks, but he's lazy as shite. And not like how my family likes to be underestimated. He truly has the attention span of a goldfish. He went to MIT, so he's not incapable of finishing things. He just doesn't have the patience to dig all the way to the Earth's core like Sergei and I do. What he does, he does well. He keeps the Colombians looking like their noses are clean, and he keeps an eye on the other families like we all do to each other. But he's not going above and beyond. Overachiever has never been said in the same sentence as his name.

Finn sits back and looks at me. "They must have someone new. This is more than some fancy firewalls. It's more than just encrypted. This is your CIA spook level shite. I've tried all my programs that usually get me into everyone else's shite. I even created a new program update, but I can't get in. They have their info buried deep."

I reach into my laptop bag, which I put down beside my chair. I move my plate out of the way and open it. Talk about encryption. Our networks at our homes are tighter than a virgin's arse in a whorehouse. Pretty sure our mom wouldn't appreciate that one either. I'm not worried about hacking while I'm here.

I pull up the program I created that studies, analyzes, then runs algorithms to crack encryption codes. I get into the O'Malleys' encrypted bank account the same way I always do. Then I hit a dead end. I can't see any transactions like I usually do. It's just blank as though nothing exists at all. Interesting.

I set my program to work, assured it'll pull up something within the next couple seconds. But that turns into a minute, which turns into three. It's still blank. That's not the way it's supposed to fucking be. I exit out of that bank and move to some offshore accounts they have.

They believe these offshore ones are invisible, but Rowan did some money transfers four years ago in the middle of the night on an unsecure server. I had my program running as usual to monitor our rivals among the other syndicates and our mob rivals from other cities. That's how I know where to look now.

They're duds too. I move over to their investment portfolios. I get into those because they can't hide those transactions when they go through the New York Stock Exchange. I try to leapfrog to the trades they buried under shell corporations or forced others into trading for them. Their shell corp ones are gone. Fucking hell.

I look up at my brothers and cousin. "This isn't good. Whoever's doing this must have the text already encoded at least once before putting it into encryption programs to adopt the secret coding. They could use pig Latin for all I know, then run it through their algorithms to hide it. I'm certain they've scrubbed past information, too. It's going to take me a while to find where their codes changed and then try to replicate the first few changes they made. I have some other tactics too, but they're going to take time to test. I may not get it the first try. Whoever did this isn't just a hacker or programmer. They have national security level skills. Fortunately, I have those skills too."

It automatically makes me think of Lina. Someone like the two of us did this. Someone with the same training we have. Amanda? She might spite us, but what connection could she have to the Boston mob?

"Once I have the scrapers running, I'll dig to see where graduates from the top ten Homeland Security and International Intelligence programs are working and who they're related to. That's going to take hours."

Dillan's brow furrows. "Do you need to be in front of your computer for that?"

"Ideally, but I don't have to watch the data scroll on my screen. I can set alerts. Why? What do you need me to do?"

"Cormac and Seamus have court today. Finn's got payroll, and Shane's got city inspectors going to three sites. I'm meeting with Haruki Nishida this afternoon. Can you take Mair to a doctor's appointment?"

"Of course."

I'm certain Dillan would much rather be with his wife than meeting with a *yakuza oyabun*. But we have a big deal going down between them investing in four pharmaceutical labs and us transporting products they want to bring in through Washington state and take down the coast to Mexico. It means our truck drivers going through a lot of ganglands and into Cartel territory when they cross the border. The only way we'll accept that risk is if they pony up the money for the labs.

All six of us are the majority shareholders of a pharma company. The labs keep the company legit, but we'll be refining the heroin they send us and blending it with synthetic shite to make it go further. They'll get the same number of kilos to Mexico as they sent, but we'll also have plenty to sell at the street level. We provide goods and services. It's not on us when people buy. Personal responsibility is the cornerstone of capitalism.

Even I can't say that with a straight face.

"Thanks. Can you meet Mair at her office in three hours?" Dillan glances at his watch as he speaks.

"Sure. That'll give me time to work on this stuff. Can I stay here rather than going all the way back home?"

In theory, East Harlem to Midtown takes about the same time as where Dillan lives in Forest Hills to Midtown. That's assuming there's no major traffic jam. Then all bets are off. But I don't want to go back to northern Manhattan from Queens just to go to south Manhattan. It's a waste of time in the car when I could run the programs in a place that has jammers to prevent anyone knowing where I'm cruising the information superhighway.

"Of course."

"Cool. I'll use my room."

The four of us talk about the cases Seamus and Cormac have right now. One's corporate—Cormac's—and one's criminal —Seamus's. Both are higher profile than any of us want. But we aren't worried about the outcome. And Mair's making sure not too much is going in the press since she's a journalist at the city's largest newspaper. But that doesn't stop other news outlets from wanting details she's helping to make sure aren't available.

Once my brothers are gone, Dillan heads to his office, and I head to my room. I don't stay here often. But there are times when we're all here late, planning in Dillan's office. It's nice to crash here instead of going home. Sometimes we're headed out so early in the morning or even in the middle of the night, it makes the most sense for all of us to already be here when it's time to go.

I've just arranged my pillows behind me with my portable monitor and mouse propped on pillows too. I'm picturing the sequences I need to unravel this mess. I hear my phone buzz where I put it on the bedside table. I expect it to be one of my brothers or cousins. I can't help the smile when I see Lina's name appear in the message bubble.

LINA

What's your favorite sport?

Random. But I'll take it because it means we're chatting.

ME

Rugby. You? Curling or hockey?

LINA

LOL Neither. I row and like to watch crew, swimming, or soccer

ME

Starboard or port

LINA

Starboard bow

She's tall, but with how slender she is, it wouldn't have surprised me if she'd said she was a coxswain—the person who steers and commands the pace. No, coxes don't scream "stroke, stroke, stroke"—but she's a rower.

> **ME**
>
> Port stroke

From a rower's perspective, since we move backwards, the person in the bow is the last rower. The person who rows stroke is the first one and keeps the pace. Again, since rowers move backwards, starboard is to the left, and port is to the right. It's all reversed.

> **LINA**
>
> Rugby is your favorite sport but you rowed?

> **ME**
>
> Rugby is the sport everyone—men and women—play in my family and the universal one we all enjoy watching. Both my brothers played lacrosse. One cousin swam and played water polo, another wrestled, and another played soccer. I only have one cousin who played rugby competitively through college.

Despite what most would assume looking at Seamus and Cormac, it was Dillan who wrestled. Cormac swam and played water polo, and Seamus played soccer. Shay and Cor are built like ox. Most assume they're meatheads with nothing between their ears but air. At best, people think they're pro athletes. Few believe they're lawyers until they see my cousins in suits and hear them speak.

Dillan's sister, Colleen, was the rugby player. She was so damn good. Fearless. Agile. Competitive—way more than any of us guys. She was our ringleader growing up. She was also a vet who specialized in rescue animals. Like the depressing ASPCA commercial rescue animals. But being part of my fucked-up family got her killed.

I don't want to think about that while texting Lina.

LINA

Sounds like there're a lot of you.

ME

Yup. Always someone to play with growing up. Always someone breathing up your arse as an adult.

LINA

I only have one brother and I know what you mean about someone breathing up your arse.

ME

What's your favorite movie?

LINA

It's a toss-up. Misery, Primal Fear, or Silence of the Lambs. I know. Pretty effing dark but I love psychological thrillers.

ME

Maybe I shouldn't tell you The Princess Bride is my fave.

LINA

Is it?

ME

No. Da Vinci Code and anything like that. Mysteries.

No, it's not fucking *The Godfather* or *Goodfellas*. They're fucking Mafia. Douchey Italians. And *The Princess Bride* is among my favorites. Colleen teased me mercilessly. If I asked her to do anything, she'd always respond, "as you wish."

Fucking hell. I don't want to think about Colleen right now. I picture the way Lina looked after I kissed her. How she felt against me. Well, now I have a fucking tent pole in my pants.

ME

Night owl or up with the chickens?

LINA

I lean toward late nights but I have no problem getting up early.

ME

Same. Snooze button?

Why am I asking that? Is she going to think I'm wondering whether I'm going to hear her alarm go off over and over one of these mornings? I wouldn't object.

LINA

Definitely no snooze

ME

I'd rather sleep until the last minute than get woken up every nine minutes.

LINA

Exactly I don't see the point. Coffee?

ME

Yes and strong enough to stand a spoon up.

LINA

Ew! I can lick mud for free.

ME

You just haven't had it made properly then.

LINA

You cannot put enough milk and sugar in it to convince me coffee tastes good.

ME

So no coffee flavored ice cream? No chocolate covered espresso beans? No tiramisu?

LINA

Gag. God bless my mother but she bought a tiramisu cake for my birthday three years ago. She knows I loathe coffee. She's had a nine month advantage on anyone else who knows me and she still got it. She just wasn't thinking. Everyone else had cake but me.

ME

That stinks. Red velvet, chocolate, yellow, lemon, or carrot?

LINA

YES! But cake is just a vessel for frosting.

ME

Cream cheese, whipped, buttercream, or fondant?

LINA

Fondant is disgusting. Looks pretty tastes gross. Whipped is pretend frosting. Cream cheese or buttercream all the way.

ME

You could lose a finger in my family if you try to take someone's corner piece. We all love frosting. Guilty pleasure.

I can think of another guilty pleasure I enjoyed. Her. I'd love to have several more helpings.

LINA

What's your fave cake?

ME

YES!!! I haven't met a cake I don't like. Brownies?

I give her the same answer she gave me when I asked her what her favorite is. I don't have one. I'll take any cake offered to me.

LINA

Definitely. With or without frosting?

ME

That goes without saying. Fudge frosting all the way and no nuts

LINA

If I'm going to have brownies why would I go and have something healthy like nuts? I'll eat an apple later.

ME

Caramel covered apples?

LINA

Meh

ME

Same. Homebody or nightlife?

LINA

The older I get the more of a homebody I become. I like to go out dancing and can still hang. But I prefer to be home reading or watching something streaming. How about you?

ME

Work keeps me out some nights but I prefer being home.

I'm treading dangerous ground if she asks what I do. I'm testing the water.

LINA

Obviously we both just traveled but do you like to?

ME

Yes. A lot. But preferably warm places. I can ski, snowboard, and ice skate. But I can live without them.

46

LINA

Sacrilege! We're born with skates in Canada. Do-ncha know?

ME

Bien sûr.

Of course.

ME

Do you enjoy those?

LINA

I learned to skate before I turned four. I can ski and snowboard but I'm more of a chalet and hot cocoa kinda gal.

I'd keep her warm. Fuck. My dick aches. I should be working. I shouldn't be wanting to wank off. I never text women beyond agreeing to a time and day to meet at the BDSM club I belong to. And that's only three women. The same three I've been with off and on for years. I don't fuck anyone else at or outside the club. If I'd had sex with Lina, she would have been the first new partner in five years.

ME

Brandy or Schnapps?

LINA

Either if it's already poured in but I wouldn't ask for it. You?

ME

Whiskey if I think I'll never be warm again—I don't like winter. But usually just hot choc.

LINA

Don't like winter? You wouldn't survive Montreal.

ME

I've been in winter many times. You have an underground city and the hotels are heated.

There isn't an entire underground city, but there are plenty of shops, hotels, office buildings, residential and commercial complexes, and the metro that connect down there like a rabbit warren. Brilliant. All cities should have that if their windchill drops below minus twenty. That's Celsius for the Canucks.

LINA

You just need a hat and good coat. It's not so bad.

She adds the sideways laughing so hard it's crying emoji. I'd noticed she left her coat in the car between the funeral and the reception. It made it much easier to grab and hold her arse. And what a fine, fine arse it was. It fit perfectly in my hand. I'm certain her tits would, too. I want to hold both while she rides my cock, while I fuck her against a door, fuck her on a table, fuck her in a pool, fuck her on a St. Andrew's Cross. Fuck her anywhere and everywhere. I could be the Dr. Seuss of sexual locations.

ME

If you could go anywhere where would that be?

Her response isn't as immediate as it has been. I wonder if she got called away. We were going back and forth pretty fast, so I don't think she got bored.

A photo pops onto my screen.

LINA

Seychelles absolute bucket list place. You?

Maldives. We both like it hot and sandy.

Again, there's a pause. Then a GIF pops up of a guy in boardshorts with sunglasses on a beach. No red hair, but the guy's built like me. Ripped, if I do say so myself. I search and find a GIF of a woman in a bikini. I'm in two minds whether to send it. Does it cross a line she won't want? Is it that different to send her a bikini GIF than her sending me one of a guy in shorts? Am I overthinking this? Or am I not thinking about this enough?

I don't fucking know. There. Done. I sent it.

LINA

I'd need a sunhat. I'm a bit fair. Do you burn?

A bit fair. She's not pale, but her hair is so light that you'd expect her to be. She has a tan, but I doubt she gets as dark as I do.

ME

Nope. I've spent most of my life outdoors so it's pretty rare. Despite the red hair and freckles no one in my family burns.

LINA

I don't burn easily but I am careful.

Can I offer to smear sunblock all over her? Offer to be her cabana boy?

ME

Have you been to the Tulip Festival?

LINA

Many times. It's next month.

49

ME

I know. I have meetings in Ottawa and Quebec City that week.

Legit business in Ottawa. Finn and I are venture capitalists. There's a company I'm interested in acquiring in Ottawa. I'm supposed to meet with a senior member of the Montreal mob, but I refused to do it in Montreal. I didn't want to be obvious. Now I'm thinking I should reschedule.

LINA

You'll love it. Ottawa, Quebec City, Montreal —you can't go wrong. I wish I still lived there.

She doesn't live there? I guess I assumed she went back to Canada after grad school. I don't know why I did. But she never said where she lives. We don't even know each other's last names. If I ask her for her last name, then she'll ask me mine. I haven't offered mine because I'm enjoying just being Sean. I don't know whether she would recognize the O'Rourke name, but it would only take a single google to find a shite ton of unfavorable things about my family. Most of the accusations are true, even if they haven't been proven. We're good at making sure they aren't.

ME

Do you go back often?

LINA

I've always gone back every few months. Never too long between trips.

ME

You have the best of two worlds.

There's a pause. Her response doesn't come as fast as it has been. It's nearly a minute—I watch my phone clock—before she responds.

LINA

Most days. I just got a call from my grandfather. I need to take it.

ME

TTYL

LINA

Bye

"Sean?" Dillan knocks on the door as he says my name.

"Yeah?"

He opens the door. I'm glad my computer is still on my lap to hide my boner. Just texting her does that.

"You making any progress?"

"I've been dealing with something else. But I'm nearly done. I'll see what progress I can make before I take Mair to the doctor."

"Thanks. I'm headed out for my meeting."

He's watching me, and I know he suspects something. I just don't know what he's assuming. I watch him walk out, closing the door behind him. I wait until I hear him walk away, then I lie back and reread the texts.

I made no progress before taking Mair to her appointment yesterday. It fucking chaps my arse that I haven't cracked this shite yet. Whoever did this knows my family has someone with their skills. Why else would they make it this complicated? I almost take it as a personal challenge, and therefore, a personal insult. I've been working on this all day, and I'm nearly cross-eyed. I sit back at my desk in my home office. I'm annoyed and tired. I have a headache.

I glance over at my phone. With a deep inhale, I accept there's only one thing that'll make me feel better. I reach for it and unlock the screen.

ME

Did you have a favorite pizza place?

Such a fucking random and stupid question.

I hold my phone for a minute, but no response comes in. I set it aside and click on my email. I'm about to respond to the second one when my phone pings.

LINA

Three Brothers from Sicily in Queens

Of course. Fucking Marco Mancinelli's place. He bought it the summer after his freshman year in college to eat for free. Eat his own profits. Fucking numb nuts.

ME

I've heard of it.

I'm not going to say I've heard good things, even if I have. No need to be effusive about those douches.

LINA

Do you?

ME

Paul's Place in Brooklyn

Finn owns it. He has a bunch of bars and restaurants. The six of us jointly own a slew of strip clubs and night clubs across the tri-state area.

ME

Favorite bar

LINA

That's easy. McGinty's

Does she know a mafioso owns her favorite pizza place? Does she know a mobster owns the other two places? Do I admit my brother owns them?

ME

That's my favorite too.

It is. I loved the Dubliner more, but revenge is a bitch. The bratva made it look like a gas leak and blew it sky high. McGinty's is special because it was our nana's place. She gave it to Finn right before he turned twenty-one.

LINA

What's your sign?

She includes three astrological emojis.

ME

Capricorn. You?

LINA

Pisces. Were you a Christmas baby?

ME

No mid Jan. St Patty's Day baby?

LINA

LOL no Ides of March rather inauspicious.

ME

I hope Julia wasn't on your parents' short list.

LINA

No. Neither was Julius if I'd been a boy.

ME

If you'd taken a national security advisor job for a senator it would be kinda ironic.

LINA

I nearly named a dog Brutus.

Born the day Julius Caesar was stabbed in the Senate with his best friend leading the charge. The first syndicate in the U.S. might have been the Irish, but the Italians have been fucking shite up since the Ancient Romans.

Damn it.

"Hey, Cor. What's up?" My cousin would call now.

"The Kutsenkos just busted up an underground poker ring. Stole seventeen grand right off the table. Dillan wants you, me, and Shay to head over there."

Wonderful. Cormac and Seamus will make sure I get answers to my questions. I know where Cormac's talking about. I could handle it myself, but it'll go faster with the two of them backing me up.

"And after?"

"Knock off a couple of their liquor stores. But we can get a few of the guys to do it."

"Give me twenty to get to you."

"Shay and I are on our way to you."

"See you in a few."

Motherfucker.

ME

I'm sorry. My cousin called. We're headed out to a show. I gotta go.

It'll be fucking entertaining watching the Kutsenkos from a distance when they arrive to check out what we do to their stores.

LINA

No worries. Have fun. I hope it's something good. TTYL

ME

Me too bye

It's been three weeks of trying to break this goddamn code. In all fairness to me, I've been distracted. The shite with the gambling ring led to more shite with a fencing ring we run. We discovered a few of our guys decided to freelance for the Cartel. We did a little late spring cleaning. I spent a few days at the station.

When I left after those four days, I turned on my phone and saw I missed texts from Lina. My heart sank. I know she thought I ghosted her. I didn't have a good way to explain why I didn't have my phone on. We haven't talked about work, so I don't know what she does. She hasn't asked me, so I haven't had to lie. At least not until I left the station.

Since we studied the same thing, it's reasonable to believe we have jobs in the national security fields that require discretion. I told her I was at a conference where we couldn't use unsecured lines. She bought it. One of umpteen lies I'll tell her if this goes anywhere.

Except for those four days, we've texted every day. We've shared stories about our childhood, and I have plenty of happy ones to tell her. I'll never tell her the ones about how my grandfather trained me to be a mobster. The things my dad had to watch my grandfather and uncle force me to do. The things my dad taught me. The physical training I endured to know exactly how to torture someone.

They say if you can explain something, then you really

know it. My uncle and my mom's cousin definitely knew plenty about coercion. They also say nothing teaches you better than firsthand experience. They're right. My brothers, cousins, and I caught on right snappy. It only took a few broken fingers and arms, bruised ribs, and dislocated shoulders to get the hang of internalizing every emotion we have. We also learned fifty different ways to inflict the same injuries on others.

Besides remembering those days, my text conversations with Lina have been awesome. She's hilarious and easy to talk to. We enjoy a lot of the same books and TV shows. We often dislike the same foods and discovered she's way more adventurous than I am with new foods.

We've discussed philosophy, physics, linguistics, calculus—who knew that could be sexy—and tons of other things I've never bothered to talk about with women in my past. Hell, not even most of my friends.

Our conversations last for hours sometimes. I want to see her again, but she hasn't hinted at wanting to see me. I have to imagine she does since we keep chatting. That or she loves having a pen pal.

We've shared some photos from vacations. Even the ones of her snowshoeing make me hard. I've jerked off to them as many times as I have ones of her in bikinis and sundresses. I'm ready to the climb the walls.

ME

> My trip to Canada's been postponed indefinitely. I'm going to miss the festivals.

LINA

> That's a bummer. You should go up just for the hell of it and enjoy yourself.

ME

> I thought about it but it's a long way to go for a day or two to see flowers.

LINA

Seize the opportunity. Take a weekend off and smell the roses or rather the tulips.

ME

Tempting. It's been a few months since I've been anywhere besides DC.

I'm so fucking tempted to invite her to come with me.

LINA

I'm actually going to be in NYC tomorrow.

Was she testing the water with all of this before telling me? Was she not planning to tell me at all and just decided to?

ME

How long will you be in town?

LINA

I arrive tomorrow morning. The plan is to leave the day after tomorrow. But nothing's set in stone. I was supposed to go right after the funeral. Things got moved around and delayed.

ME

I'd like to take you out.

To breakfast.

LINA

I'd like that. I have meetings at eleven and three. Other than that I'm free.

ME

Which works better for you? Lunch or dinner?

LINA

Both. I like brunch too.

Does she mean...?

57

I hit the call button before I think twice.

"Hi, Sean."

"Hi, Lina."

There's a pause. I called, but I don't know what to say.

"I hope I'm not keeping you from getting work done. I didn't think about whether you'd be in the middle of something when I texted. I don't want to disturb you."

"*Cailín*, I would have told you if I needed to go. I like texting, but I like hearing your voice more."

Little girl. It's not because of her build. Nothing about her makes me think of a child. But my heart ached for her the times I saw the sadness at the funeral. I wanted to shelter her and make everything better. I want her to turn to me. And that's ludicrous.

"I like your voice. Just a touch of New York without sounding like Danny DeVito in *My Cousin Vinny*. 'The two yutes.'"

"Vinny Gambini. That's because I'm not a Guido. I don't think I look that Italian."

"No. You look very Irish."

My chest tightens. We're getting into even more dangerous ground. Did she look me up? She'd need my last name for that. Does she already know it?

"Haha. At least the green eyes ensured I never got pinched on St. Paddy's Day."

"Do green eyes count as wearing something green?"

"When you're half a head taller than most of your class-mates all the way to graduation, it counted if I said so."

"You are rather tall."

I'm over six feet. Somewhere between six-two and six-three. Depends on the haircut.

"It has its advantages."

"Mmm."

Is she remembering how well she fit with her head just beneath my chin? How tall is she when she doesn't have heels on? They were probably about two-inch wedge looking things, which would still make her tall. But she'd come to my collarbone.

"Which works better for you? Lunch or dinner? I'll probably be free by twelve-thirty if you prefer lunch."

Now she's offering me a choice. She said both earlier.

"How about one? Do you want to meet somewhere? Or—or I could pick you up. I could send a car."

Did my voice just crack? What the fuck. I sounded like a fifteen-year-old asking a girl out for the first time.

"I'll be in Midtown for the morning meeting and the Upper East Side for the afternoon. If it's not too inconvenient, you could pick me up."

"I'll be in Midtown too. Send me the address."

I hear Finn walk in my front door. "Sean?"

"Hang on a sec, Lina. It's my brother." I hit the mute button. "In the living room."

"Hey, do you have the contracts for the new construction? Shane said he left them here last night by accident."

"Yeah. I figured either you or he would be over. Here." I hand a stack of papers to my brother.

"You on a call?"

"Yes."

"I'll let you finish. This is all I needed. Thanks."

"You're welcome."

I watch Finn walk to the front door, when I'm certain he's gone, I unmute the call.

"Sorry about that."

My brother was here for like three minutes, and I'm annoyed. It's not his fault. Mob stuff will always come first. But I want to finish making plans with Lina. I'm practically giddy!

"It's all right. I have to go. I gotta get some stuff done before I leave in the morning. I'll text you the address once I find it in my emails."

"Sounds good."

There's another pause. Should I say more? Is it her turn to talk? I've doubted myself more on this call than I have since I went on my first mission. I was terrified I'd fuck up and not only get myself killed, but my brothers and dad.

"I'm looking forward to it, Sean."

"So am I. I'm glad you texted me."

"Me too. Bye."

"Bye, *cailín*."

We both linger before we hang up. I wake my computer screen. I need to figure out what the fuck is going on with the O'Malleys. I look at my phone. There aren't too many people with the skills to do what this invisible person did. Lina is one of them, and so are our fellow classmates.

I work on the encryption some more for two hours, creating and running a program to undo whatever this mystery person did. Then I pull up the alumni portal and type in Nicolina.

We've been chatting for nearly a month, and neither of us has shared our last name. I'm not in a hurry to give mine because I've gotten to know someone new without my mob affiliation hanging over my head. I haven't asked her since she's a single woman who hasn't volunteered it. I don't want to scare her.

She pops up immediately. Not surprising since I doubt there's another Nicolina who went through our major.

Nicolina Tremblay.

No. *No. NO!*

Son of a bitch.

Chapter Four

Lina

Should I be this nervous? I sent Sean the skyscraper's address where I'm stuck in an interminable—or is it infernal—meeting. We've been going around and around for an hour and a quarter. I thought we'd finish in forty-five minutes. An hour tops. If I don't wrap this up, I'm going to be late to meet Sean. His response to my text with the address and saying I was looking forward to seeing him was less than effusive. I didn't want to read into it, but it didn't feel as warm as our conversation had a few hours earlier.

"Mr. Nishida, I understand you have other things to consider before you agree to invest in our pharmaceutical company, but we're breaking ground in three months." *Shit or get off the pot.* "We have other potential investors, but you've been partners with my family for many years. We wanted to give you first right of refusal."

I'm certain he's playing my family. I'm certain he has something going on with another syndicate. I just don't know who. I know he's invested in Mancinelli casinos in the past. Perhaps it's them. I dug yesterday, but I found nothing conclusive. If he's negotiated anything or said anything, it wasn't recorded digitally.

"You're far from home, Ms. Tremblay."

I wait for him to say more. It was an observation, not a question. I have nothing to say back. I mean, "you too" seems lame. We stare at each other.

"I didn't know your brother does business in New York now."

"We knew you were flying in. It's a quick flight for me. It meant not another one for you. We do business in Boston."

"We. It was your father until two months ago. Now you've joined your brother. What does your grandfather think?"

That when this blows up—which it inevitably will—he'll say I told you so.

"He believes family comes first."

Which is completely true. He just wishes half my family weren't O'Malleys. From what I know, it was a disaster when my mom told her parents she was pregnant because we're Catholic. If she'd been married, they could have all believed it was immaculate conception. But she wasn't even dating my dad. We don't discuss sex. As far as my family is concerned, we're born virgins and die virgins. My mom having a baby with no father in the picture screamed she wasn't a virgin. It's obvious my father wasn't her first, but I sure as shit will *never, ever, ever* ask who was. Ew. Gross.

"His family first. It surprises me you're here."

For fuck's sake. This is how the conversation began. I'm going to be late. It takes all the restraint I can muster not to look at my watch.

"Like I said before, he believes in family first. The O'Malleys are my family. Ewan asked me to meet with you, and we wanted to be considerate of your time. I know your time is limited, so we'll move forward."

Let's see if my positive assumption pisses him off or nudges him.

His grin makes me doubt myself.

"Yes, Ms. Tremblay. We will move forward. Your brother can expect the first deposit tomorrow. When he secures the shipping route, I will send the rest."

He wants Ewan to move heroin down the entire West Coast. It's not like we have a fleet. But he wants his product to go by boat rather than truck. It's safer in many ways. Less likely to be pulled over. It's faster. It's also more expensive and requires more risk since we don't have loyal men out there. We can send them, but none of them can captain or crew a ship. Nishida is testing us.

I stand and thrust out my hand. But I reach less than halfway across the table. Let them think my arm is too short. When he grins again as his hand clasps mine, I know he recognizes what I did. I forced him to meet me more than halfway.

"A wise man would be wary to get caught in your crosshairs."

"Patience ensures there's nothing in the way."

Let him assume whatever he wants. He's hinting at my ambition. I had plenty, but it was for the career I gave up. I have none for this life I've been dragged into. Maybe he believes I'm hinting I'll last longer than my grandfather or my brother. That my patience will ensure I wind up on top with nothing in my way. As though I want to lead the family. However, I mean that if I wait until this is done, I have no reason to come back.

Sean's a reason.

I can't get the man out of my head. I shouldn't be nervous, but I am. There. I answered my own question. What was I thinking to say I'm available for lunch and dinner, *and* I like brunch? I may as well strip naked and twirl in front of him.

I know the Japanese envoy—the *oyabun* came with six men —waits for me to walk to the door. I shake my head.

"I have another appointment soon."

I won't be seen walking out of a building with the head of a Tokyo *yakuza* beside me. That's suicide. An association with him alone is enough to get me killed. But to meet with him in NYC? I'm still fucking pissed Ewan insisted I do this.

I don't fear Ewan physically. I know he would never touch me, and he wouldn't let his men do it either. But he would fuck with me. He could ensure I never get a legit job again. It wouldn't take much for him to ruin my professional reputation. He could cause trouble with my grandfather and get my mom caught in the middle. He could do plenty of other things. None of which I want to imagine right now, but I'm certain he already has.

I wait ten minutes until it's twelve-twenty-six. Four minutes to get down to the ground floor. I know Ewan worries about me personally as much as he does my work for him. He's not entirely a sociopath. He insisted I bring bodyguards. I refused. The less attention I bring to this trip the better. I flew commercial. I have my ultra-blonde hair in a bun. It lightens to platinum every summer and darkens a shade or two in winter. I spend as much time outside as I can, so my hair is already lightening. It's recognizable, so I have it up to try not to make it so noticeable.

I look around the lobby as I step off the elevator. I spot Sean immediately. Fuck. He's hot. Like so incredibly hot my panties are soaked already. It took one glance. His physical features— height, build, face—are striking. But put it all together with the well-earned self-confidence, he's a magnet to me. I'm certain he's a magnet to anyone with a pulse and likes to fuck.

"Hi, *cailín*." He steps close to me, and I wonder if he might kiss at least my cheek. He doesn't.

"Hi. Thank you for meeting me. I hope I didn't keep you waiting."

"Not at all. Just people watching."

Is he telling me something? Did he recognize Nishida?

"I find that fascinating. My brother and I used to try to guess where people were going or what they did for work. The more outlandish the better."

"How much older is your brother than you?"

"Nearly two years."

He seems to tuck that away. He rests his hand at the small of my back as he guides me to the door. A man opens it for us, and Sean lets me pass first. I sweep my gaze over our surroundings. I glance up at Sean, and I know he just did the same. Is he checking for viable threats? The way he walks with his shoulder slightly behind mine—so he could step behind me to protect my back or encircle me and cover my whole body—makes me think he's used to danger. That or he's paranoid.

"Have you heard of La Petite Fleur?"

I fully look up at him as we reach a black town car. "Only in passing."

"My brother owns it. It has a fantastic menu, and I can be sure you aren't late to your next meeting."

"Thank you."

I slide into the car, noticing the privacy glass is up, and I'm still not sure what to make of Sean. He seems so much more distant than he did when we met and on the phone yesterday. He shuts the door behind him as I reach for my seatbelt. I get my hand on it, but that's it when he cups my nape. Once again, I'm looking up at him. His entire expression has morphed into something predatory. He leans forward and presses his mouth to mine. I open without hesitation. I sigh at the feel of his tongue against mine.

Then I'm off my seat and straddling his lap. Fuck. What I wouldn't give to unbutton his pants and push them down, so I can ride his cock. When he pulls my hips flush to him, I fear leaving a stain. I try to scoot back, but his grip on my hips tightens.

"Sean, I'm too wet."

His chuckle is pure sin. "Good."

His hands skim up my calves and over my thighs to dip beneath the hem. He grasps my hips again, his bare skin on my bare skin. He tugs a third time, and I give in. But only for a moment. During that brief flash of time, I revel in the feel of him where I've ached since I met him.

"Sean, everyone is going to know you've had a woman riding your dick if you don't let me back up."

He flips me onto my back and kneels beside the seat on the floor. It must be awkward with how broad he is and how long his legs are, but he's able to face me and my pussy. He pushes my skirt up, then waits for me to object. I do nothing but watch him.

"Then let me make sure none of the cream spills."

He lowers his head as he pushes my thong aside. I close my eyes at the first feel of his tongue pressed flat against my cunt. He swirls his tongue before dipping it between my pussy lips. He draws it up and flicks my clit before sucking it.

"Fuck, Sean. Yes."

I reach for him, but he snags my wrist and pushes it down. My other hand grips the side of the seat. He encircles that one too. He holds my arms in place. I try to lift my hips, but he releases my left arm and presses down on my belly. He sucks again, and I can't stop my cunt from wanting to get closer. He nips my clit, and I cry out. The spark of pain surprises me, but I'm more aroused than I've ever been in my life.

"Give me more, Sean. Now."

The assertiveness loses something as I moan. It's more of a plea. He pulls away, and I whimper. His hand comes down, slapping my pussy. I buck.

"You do not command me, *cailín*. I decide what you get, how you get it, and when you get it. I decided you aren't coming yet."

Can I come just from words?

"Yes, Sir."

His emerald eyes spark as he pinches my clit and presses two fingers into me, using both hands. He already knows I'm soaked, but he also knows two fingers aren't nearly enough. He's taunting me, and I can barely stand it.

"If you want to share dessert tonight, little one, I'll make sure you're starving for brunch."

"Yes!" It comes out a choked sob as he thrusts a third finger into me.

I cross my wrists and raise my arms over my head. I grasp the end of the seat, knowing he saw me. He knows I've already submitted, but I offer the clear sign this is what I want. He returns his mouth to my pussy, working my clit as he works three wide fingers inside me. He finds my g spot, and I squirm.

"Right there. Please, Sir."

He presses his free hand down on my belly right where his fingers stroke the inside of my cunt. His tongue and lips keep a steady, torturous rhythm as they lavish attention on my clit, which is growing more and more sensitive.

"Sean, I'm not going to last. Please, may I come? Please."

"No."

I wail. I'm so close, but he stops moving. He doesn't pull out. Thank God.

"I told you. You will come when I decide. You will wait until I'm inside you." His gaze bores into me. "And that won't be until tonight."

"You're going to edge me?"

"Both of us, little one. Don't doubt I'm ready to explode."

"Sean, I can't do this. I ache so much it's painful. I need you."

He shifts and moves me to sit in his lap as he returns to the seat. I'm not straddling him this time, so my legs fall open. He trails his fingertips up my right thigh. He cups my pussy, the heel of his hand rubbing circles on my clit.

"Shh, little one. Rest against me. I promise I'll take care of you, but I'm not fucking you for the first time in a car. I sure as fuck am not having our first time be a quickie."

"Then why do this? Why drive me crazy?"

"Why should I suffer alone?"

He grins before he gives me the softest kiss I've had in—well, forever. I'm not ready for this tenderness. It's like sub drop happens, but I'm not his sub, and we haven't done enough to get that many hormones pumping through me. At least, I didn't think we had. I curl with his hands still between my legs. I burrow against his chest, and I suddenly have this over-whelming need to cry. Part of it is sexual frustration.

A greater part is that I feel safe and taken care of. Yes, he's denying me. But he's doing it to give me pleasure. I like delayed gratification, even if I hate it right now in the moment. He's giving me what I really need. I don't want our first time to be a quickie. I don't want it to be in the backseat of a car. I don't want to rush into this because I got myself so worked up dreaming about him that I make an impetuous leap I regret by the time lunch is over.

His hand moves to cup my ass, and I sigh. I'm truly content right now. I don't want to move, and I almost cry again when the car comes to a stop. I feel it shift into park, so we aren't at a stop light. I realize he still has his hand up my skirt and scramble to get off his lap.

"I decide. My driver won't open the door until I knock. I heard you do the same thing for your driver. Sit here for a moment longer and let me hold you."

"Sean, are you going to decide everything?"

"No. But for today, when it comes to pleasuring you, I am. This is for you. I want you more than I know how to explain. And a large part of that is wanting to see you come because I'm the one who did it."

"That's possessive."

"I know."

Our gazes have been locked since I tried to get off his lap. He's been confident until this moment. He has a moment of uncertainty. He fears he's gone too far.

"I want to reciprocate, Sean. I don't want this to just be about me. I feel the same way about you as you do me. I want to watch you come and know I'm the one who made you. If I thought any of this was too much, I would have stopped you. If I thought you were too possessive or controlling, I would already be out of the car. Instead, I want to curl up again and hide from the world. I want to suck you off and taste you. I want to watch you mark me with your cum." I take a breath. "I can't believe I just said all that."

I'm embarrassed I admitted more than he did. I showed my hand too soon.

"Lina, something is between us. I don't think it's just physical, but maybe it is. You called me Sir twice. I'm dominating our physical intimacy right now, but I am not your Dom, nor do I want to be. That isn't the dynamic I want."

"I don't know how well suited I'd be to being a submissive beyond what we're doing together. I know people who are. I know people who are subs purely in sexual relationships and others who are in romantic ones. If that were what you wanted, I don't think I'd be the right person."

"You're my equal, *cailín*. In all things. Even when I say I control what we're doing, you have the ultimate say. If you want something to stop, it does immediately. I will never question your limits. I will never guilt you for stopping."

"I called you Sir twice, but I also called you Sean. Are you all right with that?"

"Absolutely. Use my name whenever you want. I like hearing it."

"I like hearing you call me Lina."

I want to keep hearing him call me that along with *cailín* and little girl. We just established I'm not a submissive. At least, not anymore. I definitely am not a Little. I know a couple of women who are and one guy. I've been part of the BDSM world in Montreal for years. I will submit during most scenes, but I don't want that kind of relationship. I swap just as often, sometimes being a top and sometimes being a bottom.

As I smooth back my hair, I think about my membership. I can't imagine being with another man and feeling like I just did. The array of emotions. The intensity of them. But I also don't want to go unsatisfied when I inevitably leave NYC tomorrow. I've considered two clubs in Boston, and I've applied for membership at both. I won't join two, but hopefully, this guarantees at least one. I'll find someone to fuck Sean out of my mind.

No, you won't. That's complete bullshit. You're more likely to call a man the wrong name.

He taps on the glass once I'm seated beside him, and the door opens. He offers me his hand once he's standing. When we look at each other, something shifts in his eyes. It's like he came out of whatever trance he was in while we were alone in the car. His demeanor shifts back to what it was when I met him in the lobby. Is it because we're back in public? Does he not believe in letting even his face show some PDA?

"Let's go in. My brother has a table for us. I don't want to make you late for your next meeting."

His tone has changed along with his expression. It hurts. A lot. We just shared one of the most intimate moments of my life, and he's so detached you'd think he wasn't a part of it. I wait for him to put his hand at the small of my back when we get to the door, but he just holds it open.

The hostess smiles at him, and he returns it. I want to claw her eyes out. It's not anything sexual. But why does she get warmth when he's turned frigid with me? The possessiveness I felt in the car when we talked is flaring into a blaze. It's unsettling.

He pulls the chair out for me and stands until I'm seated. That wasn't for me. I'm certain it was drilled into him. I feel myself withdraw as I look at the menu.

"I'd offer a recommendation, but everything is good here." Some of the ice just chipped away. But it's probably because he's thinking about his family.

A different waitress comes over, and she's just as friendly. But she looks a bit like Sean. I must have stared a little too long when I watched her walk away.

"That's Katie. She's my third cousin or something like that. The woman at the door is her sister, Mary Beth."

"Is all of your family that close?"

"Yeah. Both sides."

I was so close to looking him up on the alumni site, but I forced myself not to. I want him to volunteer it. When I think about what we just did in the car, and we don't know each other's last name, it makes it feel all of this has been a protracted one-night stand. I don't like it.

I smile because he does when he thinks about his family again. There are no lines around his eyes or mouth when he isn't smiling, but they appear when he does. It makes him look boyish and at ease. Seeing him like this makes me realize how intense he's been the two times I've been around him. He tilts his head a little before he speaks again.

"What about you? Are you close to your family?"

"I am. Both sides, but I grew up with my mom's side."

"You said your brother is a little less than two years older than you. Irish twins?"

Was there something in his tone when he said those last two words?

"Not that close. But I come from Irish families on my mom's and dad's side."

"Was it hard leaving Montreal to move to New York?"

"It was hard leaving my mom behind, but—besides the weird accents—it didn't feel any different." I grin, hoping he'll smile again. Success.

"How you doin'?" He sounds like Joey on *Friends*.

"Well, doncha know." I don't draw it out quite like I did when I texted it.

Was our first and only phone call really only a day ago? The meeting with Nishida felt like an eternity. It dragged so much it's like yesterday was a lifetime ago.

"What about you? Was it hard to leave New York to live in DC for two years?"

"No. I went back and forth a lot. I knew all the train conductors by the time I graduated."

"Did you come back every weekend?"

"Most. I worked for my family, so I still had commitments up here."

Was that a veiled comment? Is he hinting at something that

he wants me to ask? Or just the opposite? Is it a warning not to pry?

Occupational hazard of working in intelligence. There are ten questions to everything before it becomes a fact.

"Does Amtrak have loyalty points or something? You could have racked up the frequent flyer miles."

"They do. But the perks aren't quite as nice as most airlines. Did you go home often or just during breaks?"

"I have family in Boston. My dad lived there, so I went there sometimes."

"Did he move?"

Was that too casual? Like he's testing me?

"No. He died two months ago."

Our gazes lock with intensity that doesn't need to be there. I don't get it.

"I'm sorry for your loss."

Is he, though? Talk about a perfunctory response. It almost sounds like the exact opposite.

"Thank you."

"That must be hard on you and your mom."

"My parents aren't—weren't—together. It's complicated, but my brother has a different mother. My stepmom is kind to me. I get along with her well. It's been rough on her."

"And your brother?"

I shrug. "He's not the most emotionally communicative. He was a lot closer to my dad than me. They worked together."

Shit. I shouldn't have brought that up.

"Oh, what did they do? What does your brother do?"

"A bit of this and that. My brother now has some companies they owned. How about your family?"

"Same."

He leans back as the food arrives. But he doesn't lean

forward once the waitress leaves. I don't understand what's happening.

"Ewan's never had a head for numbers. Is that why you're here?"

I sit and blink. I eventually swallow as a sinking feeling drops from my throat into the pit of my stomach.

"You're an O'Rourke."

"And you're a Tremblay by way of an O'Malley. Double the fun."

"Have you known all along?"

"No. I resisted the temptation to look you up. I found out last evening. You didn't look me up?"

"No. I wanted you to tell me. I knew if I brought it up, I'd have to tell you mine. I was scared you'd google me. I guess that's rather moot."

I don't know what to do next. I feel nauseous. What started as a fantastic lunch date just went to shit. I guess Ewan'll be happy. I found an O'Rourke. Now what the fuck am I supposed to do?

Chapter Five

Sean

I toyed with her, and now I'm the arsehole.

She's maintaining a neutral expression, but I can tell she feels anything but. It's the slight strain in the muscles in her neck when she realized who I was. It's like her body vibrates because it's gone so stiff. I felt her feet pull back under her chair.

"What do you want from me, Sean?"

"To finish lunch and figure out where we're having dinner."

"Why?"

"Because you told me you were free for both. And I'm certain I told you I plan to make you hungry for brunch."

She turns her head in each direction to see who's near before she lowers her voice. "Are we going to hate-fuck?"

"Hate-fuck?"

"Yeah. You hate my family, and my family hates yours. Are we going to fuck thinking we're fucking over each other's family?"

"We are going to fuck because I've never wanted a woman more than I do you. We are going to fuck because I can't walk away even though this is likely to blow up in our faces. We are going to fuck because if I don't feel your pussy wrapped around my cock within the next eight hours, I'm likely to go stark raving mad. But I'm taking you out tonight because you've intrigued me since the moment I saw you. I'm taking you out tonight because as fecked-up as this is, I want to get to know *you* better. I'm taking you out tonight because tomorrow I'm going to have to deal with you being an O'Malley, but tonight, I want a reprieve from being an O'Rourke."

"I—"

Her phone buzzes in her purse. We hear it because the phone must be next to the chairback. She ignores it.

"I want that—"

It buzzes again. It must have gone to voicemail, and whoever it is called back immediately. I cock an eyebrow, but she shakes her head.

"I want that, too. I want—Motherfucker." She mumbles the last word as she twists to get her phone.

She mutes it and drops it back in her purse, but it buzzes a fourth time.

"Answer it. Whoever it is needs to speak to you."

"Hello."

I see her finger press the button to lower the volume. She doesn't want me to hear who it is. Ewan or her grandfather, Jean-Peter. A combination of French and English, but both apostles. His family touts being good Catholics because they're more Irish than Canadian when it's convenient. He heads the mob there, after all.

"I'm busy right now... No. That'll have to wait. I'm in the middle of lunch... Don't worry about that... Don't worry about it."

Is Ewan asking who she's with? She hasn't looked away from me since she answered. It's almost unnerving to be honest.

"It went fine. I'll fill you in when I get back... No, I have plans later... I lived here for four years. I know a lot of people in the city. I will not cancel. I've been looking forward to this since I made the plans."

Her body relaxes as she admits that. Knowing she's going to be with me puts her at ease. That or she knows she's lying, and knowing she's not seeing me tonight makes her feel better. I could be a professional body language interpreter. It's a skill I've honed since I was eleven and got in my first fight.

Juan Diaz pushed Shane, so I knocked him out. His cousin Alejandro saw it but did nothing. At least, that's what he wanted Shane and me to think. But I saw it. The twitch of his pinky five minutes later, just before he struck. I was ready. I kicked him in the balls. Neither of them got up for half an hour.

I honed that skill working at the abandoned underground train station in the Bronx. It's where we take care of things no one needs to know about. We did some redecorating. It has a bunkroom, kitchen, and showers. We're often there for hours at a time. It's where I was when I couldn't talk to Lina for a few days. Reading people's reactions allows me to know when to whale on them and when to let them think they're getting a reprieve. It's how I know when I've reached their limits and when I can push them to the brink.

But this isn't torture. At least, not for Lina. I don't know her well enough to understand all her tells. So, I'm conjuring various scenarios and how I'll react to her acceptance or rejection. Occupational hazard of working in intelligence. I have contingency plans for ten different outcomes. My family thinks Dillan's the one who comes up with the most backup plans. He does because he thinks of consequences and contingencies for his contingencies. I only go to the first level unless I need more.

I'm more of a don't beg for trouble where there is none. I don't worry until there's a reason to. Have I gotten to the worrying stage now?

"Bye." She hangs up and drops her phone in her purse before looking back at me.

Neither of us says anything. I don't know if I should ask, and I don't think she knows if she should volunteer. I watch the anxiousness creep up her neck as the muscles tighten and stand out with each swallow.

"*Cailín*, if you want to call off to—"

"No. Absolutely not. I—I—don't know what we're doing. I know it's likely to blow up in our faces. But you still came, even though you know who I am. I think you were testing me, but I think you were also giving me a chance to tell you more about me. I didn't know you were an O'Rourke, but I wanted—want— to know more about you."

"Will he hurt you when he finds out?"

"Who says he's going to find out?"

I spotted her bodyguard the moment he came in. I'm certain she doesn't know he's here. He left the office building right after us. I saw him get into a car that pulled up ten feet behind my town car. He came in and got a table with another guy who looks more like an informant than a bouncer. The second one's the one who's going to tell Ewan. I've kept them both in my peripheral vision. Neither has used a phone.

"Lina, to your four o'clock, there's a man who followed you out of the building and got into a car a quarter of the block down from us. Now he's here. He's your bodyguard. The man sitting with him is likely your brother's informant. Neither of them has gotten out a phone, but the second guy is the one more likely to tell your brother. That's if the first guy didn't do it in the car."

"What?" She lifts her chin and looks into the framed

picture on the wall. The light reflects off it—Finn insists everything be spotless—so she can see the men.

"Do you know them?"

"Yeah. The big guy is Justin, and the rat-looking guy is
Haydon. They both work for my brother. Haydon got a job in
the city planner's office about a month ago. He's supposed to
fuck things up for your family's construction projects. Justin is
one of Ewan's oldest friends. I told my brother I didn't want a
guard. I wanted to blend in. Justin might have come on his own.
He's been protective of me since we were kids."

"Does he love you?"

Her brow furrows. "No."

"Are you sure?"

"I've never had any reason to think he does."

"Then why would he volunteer without even telling
Ewan?"

"He doesn't like the way Ewan lets some of the guys talk
to me."

She snaps her mouth shut when she sees my expression
darken. I want her to know I'm not okay with that. I want her to
know that isn't happening again.

"Who, Lina?" My voice is deceptively low.

"No. You aren't putting a hit on them." She whispers as she
leans forward.

"I don't need to."

I'll motherfucking kill them myself. I've never felt this
anger in defense of someone who isn't part of my immediate
family.

"Sean, please don't. I don't want you going to Boston
unless it's to visit me. And I don't want you to visit me, so you
have an excuse to deal with them. Stop. I know you can
protect yourself. That isn't what I'm worried about. And I
don't give a shit about the assholes you're already angry about.

I don't want more trouble between our families. I'm here to fuck you over."

She closes her eyes as her head tilts down. I see the color rising in her cheeks. Ewan sent her to the meetings that will screw my family over. She doesn't have to say it out loud.

"Lina, look at me, please."

She shakes her head.

"Look at me."

I infuse the same command into my voice that I did in the car. Her head jerks up. I don't want to bully her, but I want her to listen not just hear.

"Little one, I won't do anything you don't want me to. Not when we're alone and not about this. But that promise is only absolute for one of these. You will not convince me to compromise or back down if someone is a threat to you or makes you uncomfortable for even a moment. *No one* is exempt from that."

Her eyes widen, and tears brim. Fuck. I pushed too hard because she knows I meant Ewan and her grandfather. I haven't forgotten about him. He leads the fucking Irish in Montreal. I'm supposed to meet with him soon. Wonder-fuck-ing-ful.

"I won't cry, Sean. It's not because I'm scared for my family. No one but my mother has been that protective of me."

"You are mine to pleasure. You are also mine to protect."

"Until I go home."

"No. Until you tell me to leave. Boston. Montreal. Here. Wherever. Until you say we're done, you are mine to take care of."

"Do you have any idea how hot you are—like—all the time? Do you realize how even hotter you are when you say stuff like that?"

"Thank you for thinking I'm attractive. But I've never said that stuff to any woman but you."

I want her to know she's special to me. Like I can't describe it, but I already know I'm on the same road Dillan and Finn paved for me. There's no point in fighting the current because these feelings are already sweeping me away.

We're quiet for a few minutes as we eat. That shite got heavy fast. I'm uncertain what she's thinking about, so what she says next surprises me.

"Can we get through tonight together as just normal people? Then I'll tell you what I can about Ewan."

"*Cailín*, I don't expect you to share family secrets."

"Even though you wish I would. You don't expect it because you don't want me to expect the same in return."

"I'll admit to the first part, but it isn't because of what you'll expect in return. I won't ask because I hate that you're already in the middle. It's a dangerous place for you to be."

"You said I'm yours until I tell you to leave. I will leave if this puts you in danger."

"So, you're going to keep one foot out the door and ready to run. You know the danger I'm in since you've stayed for lunch and still want to see me for dinner. If that danger gets inconvenient, you can bolt."

"No." She glances over her shoulder. "Is Ewan going to put a hit on you the moment he finds out? Will my grandfather?"

"I don't know." It's true.

"Now that I know who you are, I know there's always danger surrounding you. I meant if the threat is credible and impending. I won't lead them to you and serve you on a platter. I will leave before that happens. I don't want you to die like my—"

She presses her lips between her teeth. She's just

connected another set of dots. She knows I had something to do with her father's death. She just doesn't know what.

"I need to know what you know about that, Lina. But we can't talk about it here."

"I know." She sounds morose as she goes back to her food.

I want nothing more than to hold her like I did in the car. Just have her in my arms, so I can comfort her. I won't promise that everything will be all right because it absolutely won't be. But I'll do my damnedest to make most of it all right.

I've lost my appetite, but I don't want her to feel like the meal is over. I won't rush her through it, so I finish most of mine. It really is delicious. My brother is the best cook of the six of us. Our parents made sure we can cook because they said the cafeterias closed when we moved out. No more sweeping through their houses and expecting to find food ready for us. Finn likes to ensure there's good food wherever he goes. Seamus and Cormac might be the biggest of Finn, Shane, Dillan, them, and me, but Finn can eat the most. The man is a stomach that happens to have arms and legs.

Lina pushes her food around a bit but eats most of it. She finally lays her knife and fork down. She meets my gaze, and I have the surge of protectiveness course through me again.

"I think I'm going to cancel my next meeting." Her voice is barely more than whisper.

"Do you not feel well? Do you want me to take you to your hotel?"

"I feel fine, but I'm tired. I don't know where I want to go, but it isn't to the meeting."

Her left hand is resting on the table, and the inside of her thumb is swiping over the tip of her index fingernail. She doesn't seem aware. I wonder if that's an unconscious nervous habit or just something for today.

"Sean, how on earth can this possibly work? I want to tell

you everything for a few reasons, but I can't tell you anything. I can't betray my family. They don't deserve that from me even if they've been shitty to you. I don't want to draw you closer to an enemy and put your head on a chopping block. It's not just about Ewan and Granddad. Anything I tell you endangers everyone connected to the O'Malleys and the Tremblays. That includes my mom and stepmom. I said I'd tell you everything, and I still want to. But I can't."

"And I don't expect you to. I told you that."

"I appreciate it. But it doesn't put me any less in the middle. It's going to piss your family off when they find out you hooked up with me. And it's pretty much inevitable both of our families will know. With Justin and Haydon here to confirm it, the town criers are already out."

"I didn't hook up with you, Lina. We didn't have and won't have a one-night stand. We aren't becoming fuck buddies, either."

"I'm going to cancel the meeting this afternoon. I want to see you tonight through to tomorrow morning. But I have to go back to Boston. I can't stay here any longer, or Ewan will shit a brick."

"When you get home, I don't want this to be over." Do I sound like I'm begging? It feels like it.

"It won't be. Can we keep texting and talking on the phone?"

"I'd like that."

"Me too. Do you have meetings this afternoon?"

"No. I was going to do some research, but it's not pressing."

Her lips draw back between her teeth, and she sighs. "You were going to see if you could crack my encryption."

I neither confirm nor deny.

She closes her eyes, and she appears drained. I feel the way she looks.

"I can't tell you the code because that would fuck over my family. But I hate keeping this from you. If it were any other family, I know I would confide in you. I just know I would."

"Shh, little one. Do you want to take a nap before dinner?"

"Yes." She looks like she wants to say something, but she holds back.

"You're going to sleep in my arms this afternoon because I don't plan to let you get any sleep tonight."

We walk through the suite to the bedroom. The living room doesn't appear like anyone's checked in. The bedroom has a small roll aboard suitcase on the folding suitcase rack. It's closed, so I don't know if she fully unpacked. I can see a pair of jeans and two shirts hanging in the closet as we walk past. The bathroom is just beyond.

When we come to the bed, I slide my arms around Lina's waist. I held her during the car ride here after she called someone when we stepped outside the restaurant. I gave her space to cancel her meeting, but it left me staring at Justin and Haydon when they stepped out. They must not have realized we were on the sidewalk. None of us said anything. We just sized each other up. I glowered at Haydon, hoping it would get him to wait at least five minutes before running off to tattle to Ewan. I watched Justin, and he watched me. He's definitely in love with Lina. He hid it, but that body language reading I do— it was obvious he isn't pleased I'm where he wishes he could be.

"*Cailín*, I invited myself over. If you'd rather have space and be alone, I—"

"No. Don't go." She spins in my arms. "I was so relaxed in the car."

She shakes her head and looks down. She's so conflicted

right now. Reality is crushing her, and she doesn't know which way to turn. I draw her closer to me, and she sags against me. I don't know what it is about me to her and her to me. It's something elemental.

"Sean, why doesn't any of this bother you?"

"It bothers me a lot. Lina, I rarely show emotion. Not even with my family. It doesn't mean I don't feel them. I've just— learned not to show it." I was taught and not with kindness and patience.

"Okay. So, you feel bothered, but you're still here. Aren't you worried about what your family's going to say when they find out?"

I unzip the back of her dress, but I don't push it down. I let her decide if she wants to be even partly nude in front of me. She hesitates, then kicks off her shoes and lets the dress fall off her shoulders.

"Do you have pajamas?" I practically croak each word.

Hurt and embarrassment flash across her face. She steps back, but I don't let her go farther than that. I snag her wrist and jerk her back to me. My hands grasp her arse and squeeze until she presses harder against me to get away from my hands. I rock my cock against her before I lift her and guide her legs around my waist. I walk the six steps to the closest wall and trap her between me and it. With one arm under her arse, I yank down her left bra strap. Her tits make my mouth water. I'm ready to devour them in one bite each.

I lean forward and take her left one in my mouth, tonguing her nipple. I suck on it before letting it go. I attach my lips to the inside and suck as hard as I dare. When I'm certain I've left a hickey, I squeeze until she whimpers. I move to the outside of her breast and leave another hickey. She hasn't stopped me, so I move to her right side. When I put my mouth to the top of her tit, I look up. Her gaze is passionate and hungry. She doesn't stop me as I leave one after another close to her nipple. There are five spread out across the top and sides.

I pull the hair tie from her bun and let her hair tumble down her back before I fist it. I hold her head pulled back as I rake my teeth along the side of her neck until I tug on her earlobe.

"I am going to hide us away for a week. I am going to mark you everywhere and anywhere I want. And that means your neck. I will see them and know you're mine. They are for my eyes only. I won't embarrass you with them where anyone else can see them. But I will do it and enjoy knowing I can. You thought I didn't want to see you naked. I don't, but not for the reason you think. I'm about a hair's breadth from tying you to that bed and fucking you every way I can think of. If you don't put some clothes back on, I will."

I lower her to the floor and step away. She slips past me, and I turn to watch her. She unfastens her bra and lets it drop to the floor. She pushes down her panties, and I pounce. I have to watch my strength. She's so light that if I'm not careful, I will hurt her. I wrap my arm around her waist and haul her backward until I can lift her onto the bed. If I wasn't careful, I would have flung her.

I push her legs wide and have a far better view of her cunt than I did in the cramped backseat. I mark a line up each thigh. I see her breathing grow more rapid. I see her get so wet she's dripping. When I move to get off the bed, she reaches for me. I roll her onto her belly and land a slap across her arse before rolling her back.

"Do you not remember already? I decide. I will put you exactly how I want you. It isn't with your hands out to hold me. Cross your wrists and put your hands above your head."

I pull my tie loose as I toe off my shoes. I'm way too much of an expert at restraining people's wrists. When I have them secured, her arms straight above her head, I press a kiss to her cheek.

"Baby, what's your safe word?"

She looks at me. "Tulips."

The flower festival. I freeze for a moment when I realize how fast that came to her.

"Sean, I've been picturing us like this since the funeral. It probably makes me a shitty person because I wanted this before we even left the cemetery. I've had time to come up with what I'd use with you. I have never used that with another man."

"But you understood what I meant and already knew to have one."

"I belong to a BDSM club in Montreal. I have applications out to two clubs in Boston. I'm into the lifestyle."

That makes me pause.

"Do you have a Dom?"

"No. Not since grad school. I scene with certain people, but I haven't been in a formal arrangement in years. Do you have a sub?"

"I did until six months ago. She wanted more than I was willing to give. She wanted me to feel for her what I already feel for you. We had an arrangement for a little over a year."

"You've shown me lust, possessiveness, protectiveness, politeness, kindness. Didn't you feel those things for someone you were with for more than a year?"

"No. I didn't want to, and it didn't come naturally. I liked what I had with her, but nothing about her or any woman in my past made me feel what I do for you. They may have gotten lust and politeness, but that's about it. I didn't hold them while they slept. I tended to their aftercare, and I did it without reservation. I liked it. But it wasn't with affection."

Is there any intimate subject we aren't going to discuss today? A prostate exam would be less revealing.

"I feel those things toward you. It's been a long time since I've been curious about a man. You piqued my interest the moment I saw you. I enjoy texting with you and getting to know you. I haven't wanted to do that with anyone in ages. I don't like to fall asleep with people because it makes me too vulnerable. Not emotionally. I mean physically. You know both sides of my family are mob. I've been aware of the danger since I was fifteen. I feel safe with you. I want to fall asleep with you holding me."

"What are your limits?"

"Just the real taboo. No body fluids."

"What else? Impact? Temperature? Denial?"

She watches me as I strip. She seems to weigh her words.

"Sean, I'm terrified of what's going to happen when Ewan and Granddad find out I've been with you. Been around you. I'm torn between what feels right—telling you everything—and what I believe is right—keeping my family's secrets secret. I don't know if this is the one and only time we'll be together. I want everything we can come up with. I want it hard and rough. I need that."

"You were scared that I didn't find you attractive the moment you took off your dress. You're scared this is our only chance together. You're scared I don't want this as much as you do. You need me to show you I want you as much as I say. I need to show you I do. And that's for my sake, not because of you. I'm bigger than you and stronger than you. I will always be careful with you, but if it goes from hurt to harm, and you don't tell me, I won't forgive either of us."

"Sean, I get why you're worried. I'm scrawny and bony. I look like a twelve-year-old boy. But I—"

I pick her up and turn her over. I don't fully drop her onto the bed, but I'm not gentle like before. My hand cracks down on her arse over and over. I pay close attention to my strength and where each spank lands because she's so slender. She doesn't have much padding over the bones. She's also supple and feminine.

"Speak poorly about the only body I've ever craved, and the first time we fuck it'll be in your arse. You will discover just how much I like it when my cum is in you."

She won't because I'll have to wear a fucking condom. That's a reality check that makes my balls angry. I've never gone bareback. Ever. I roll her over more carefully, but I pinch her right nipple until she claws at the air.

"Sean, I know I'm extremely thin, but I won't break. I know you'll be careful. Even when you think you're on the brink of no control, your conscience wouldn't let you hurt me. I believe that to my soul. That's why I trust you like this. Why I don't need or want limits. I know I'm safe with you. At least when we're like this."

But she's already in danger in the real world.

I widen her legs and rub her clit. She watches me as I stroke my cock. Her arms flex, and I know she's fighting not to reach for me. I want her hands on me. Her mouth. Her cunt. But I'm denying us both. Delayed gratification.

"I think we reached one of my limits, Sir."

I stop immediately. I sweep my gaze over her, terrified I've hurt her already.

"Shh, Sir. My limit is I can tell I'm about to get really upset watching you pleasure yourself. It's bothering me more than I expected. I can handle orgasm denial, but you not—letting me touch you."

"That isn't what you were going to say. Tell me, Lina. Say it."

I'm pushing her. Normally, I wouldn't insist she share her thoughts. They're hers to have. But I'm certain what she's avoiding saying.

"You not needing me or wanting me to touch you."

"Open your mouth. Keep it open."

I move her, so her head is at the edge of the bed. She's perpendicular to me. She knows what I want, so she tilts her head back off the side. I slide my cock into her mouth, careful not to shove it down her throat—despite the consuming temptation.

"You really think I don't want you to touch me. You really think I don't need you to touch me. You are going to swallow all my cum, little girl. Suck me."

I close my eyes as she works my cock. Fucking hell. I'm coming already. I have never gotten off this fast. It's embarrassingly fast. She'd watched me. She knew I couldn't last. She licks me as I pull out. I shift her again, propping pillows under her head in case the angle she was in hurt her neck.

"I didn't want you to know how soon I was going to come if you touched me. But now you do. If you want me to last long enough to fuck more than your mouth or hand, you'll understand why I won't let you touch me when I'm too close to coming."

"Sean, please don't hold back. This isn't about how long or short this lasts. I still don't want you pleasuring yourself. I get now that it's not about your feelings toward me. But it makes me feel—" She shrugs.

I help her sit up before I sit on the edge. She twists, and I hold her upper body.

"It makes me feel empty. Hollow. Separate from you. It felt amazing having you rub my clit, but I couldn't concentrate on that because of how badly I wanted to be the one touching you. I don't get why my emotions are swinging from one end of the pendulum to the other over and over when I'm with you. I don't know how to deal with this. Why are we like this?"

Chapter Six

Lina

I've shared more about myself, my thoughts, and my feelings, than I did at my first confession. I went to the priest with a list. If I was going to be absolved, I wanted to be *absolved*. Now I'm confused, scared, nervous, and horny. That is a powerful but wholly negative state to be in.

My question hangs in the air, and I would swallow it if I could. But I can't. This entire situation intimidates me, but my most immediate fear is that I've finally pushed too far, wanting Sean to explain his feelings more than he's willing. He said he doesn't show emotion even if he feels them. I'm not just asking him to show me. I'm asking him to explain them.

"I don't know, *cailín*. I don't know enough psychology to understand primal attraction, but I think that's what I feel. Maybe it was pheromones or something that drew me to you. But everything I've learned since then makes me want to get to know you more and more. It doesn't help that whatever this is that we share also brings more danger than either or both of us already lives with. I think it's heightening all our emotions."

"I only found out who you are an hour and a half ago. You've known since last night. I know I wanted you before we had lunch. I still want you. But what about you? Does knowing I'm a Tremblay and an O'Malley change how you feel about me? Not the situation, but me."

"About you? No. I'm still as physically attracted as I was before I saw your last name. It's not that lust is my top priority, but I just proved I desire you. There's no point in ignoring the obvious. I didn't keep our lunch date to toy with you. Everything about you impresses me. The way you maneuvered Amanda into a corner and came to my rescue. The way you make me relax when I'm talking to you. Yes, you do. I swear." He cuts me off before I object. "And the skill and intelligence it takes to keep me out of files I've perused countless times is as arousing as it is incredible. But I have been angry and frustrated that we are who we are. I've doubted you and me. Doubted this. I didn't know what I was going to do at lunch. When I arrived to pick you up, I didn't know how I would feel when I saw you."

He stops, and I want to know more. I wait for him to continue, but he remains quiet.

"Sean, what did you feel?"

"I saw Nishida leave before you. I knew what that meant the moment I spied him. It pissed me off. I'm angry Ewan put you in danger. Who knows who saw you coming and going from the same building within minutes of each other? I'm angry that Nishida is doing business with your family when my cousin met with him weeks ago. I'm certain he's playing both of our families. I'm angry that I'm in a position where what I want and what I should do are so vastly different. I'm angry that when everyone discovers which one of those I chose, they're going to have a meltdown that I'm going to have to deal with."

He runs his hand through his hair and takes a deep inhale. I know there's more, so I say nothing.

"I was suspicious about whether you really knew who I was and were stringing me along. I was suspicious that you were using me to get to my family. I was suspicious that you're making me a target for either side of your family. Then we were alone in the car. I didn't stop myself from going after what I want. But reality slammed back into me when we got to the restaurant, and I remembered you had a bodyguard following you. I didn't know if you'd told him to watch me, so he could tell Ewan."

"Earlier you said, 'which you *chose.*' What does that mean?"

"You. I chose you."

"And if that turns out to be a mistake? That we aren't compatible after all? That our families shit mountains of bricks?"

"Then I live with it. I'm thirty-one-years-old. In all the years I've been aware of sexual and emotional attraction, no one has affected me like you have in the weeks since we met. You can guess why dating is difficult. You know there are things I can never share. Not even with you. But if I'd really wanted to —if I'd met someone in the past—I would have figured it out. But I've never met anyone who even tempts me. I don't need to date to have sex. I belong to a BDSM club, too. I have for years. I have standing arrangements that are over now. I won't go back to them. I didn't miss emotional companionship either because, until four months ago, my brothers, cousins, and I were insepa-rable. I have a twin. I've never truly been on my own since my conception. You make me want something that held no interest for me before I met you."

"What's that?"

"A relationship."

Those two words hang in the air. Not because they anger me or repulse me. They unnerve me. He told me he wouldn't leave until I told him to. That hinted at a relationship, but it could have been purely sexual. I don't think that's what he means. So that shocks me. I didn't think he'd be interested in a romantic relationship once I knew who he was. I hoped before I did, and I hope so again. But the moment I realized he's an O'Rourke, I figured that ship had sailed. Fuck. The moment he realized who I was, that ship should have taken on water and gone under.

"I want that, too."

I watch him, but his expression turned inscrutable when he started explaining. It hasn't changed since. He's guarding his emotions. He's vulnerable, but he'd rather I not realize it. Or at least, he'd rather not make it obvious. We're laying shit bare. I don't want him to hide from me.

"Sean, you said we wouldn't be fuck buddies. I don't want that either. There's a shit ton that's against us already. I don't know that I can or that we should enter a relationship yet. Not anything official. But I want to work toward that. I want that to be the goal."

"I feel that way, too. A relationship is what I want. But I don't think it's going to manifest because I put it out there to the universe. I want to make my intentions clear."

"And they're so honorable." I grin. He's so serious that he sounds a bit old-fashioned. I like it.

"Lina, we have today and tomorrow morning. I want to spend all the time with you I can. When you go back to Boston, I'd like to call and text like we've been doing."

His jaw tightens, and he looks away. Once again, I wait, not wanting to put him on the spot. But he volunteers nothing.

"Sean?"

"I'm not considering whether to hide this from you. I'm figuring out if there's any good way to put it. There's not. That trip to Canada that got postponed is back on. I have a meeting with your grandfather in a couple weeks. He'll know by then that we've been together."

"And that's bad for business."

He goes rigid. His gaze hardens as he looks down at me. "No. That's bad for you. I couldn't give a flying feck about the business end of this. Your grandfather likes money way too much to turn down a deal with my family. I'm worried about how he's going to treat you."

Feck. I thought I heard him say fecked-up earlier, but then I assumed I misheard. He's said fuck plenty of times, but always in the sexual context. Won't he swear in front of me?

"He'll be as angry with Ewan as with you. It'll piss him off that Ewan used me for more than intel. He won't like that Ewan made me do something in person. It'll piss him off that you're anywhere near me, especially to have sex."

"To date. Sex is part of that. But that isn't why I want to be with you."

I can honestly say we've gone on a date already but haven't had sex. We've come close three times, and we've gone down on each other. But the date was perfunctory to get to the sex. He made it sound like we wouldn't have sex until after dinner, so I guess that counts as two dates before penetration.

"And it isn't why I want to be with you. But considering my father got my mother pregnant, then walked away, he won't be very welcoming. He's not an idiot. He'll know we're having sex if we say we're dating."

He stares at me for a long moment, mulling something over. It's definitely not what I expected. "If it'll make it easier for you, then we won't have sex."

"What? No! My grandfather doesn't decide who I have sex with or when. He *will not* be the third person in this relationship. He has no say, and I won't let either of us worrying about his reaction make us change who we want to be as a couple."

"I won't do anything that puts you in the path of your grandfather's temper. I've seen it."

"So have I, but he's never directed it at me, my mom, or my grandma. He just wouldn't. He's like you—he'd go apeshit if someone spoke badly to me. He won't do it."

"Maybe not chew you out, but he can make your life difficult. He could make Ewan's life miserable, which would make him take it out on you. That's not something I'm willing to risk."

"I am. Sean, I want tonight. I want whatever comes of it, and if that includes sex, then I'm down for that. I want to continue to get to know you in person like we said we would. After that, we figure out what comes next. But there will be a next."

He cups my jaw as he gazes down at me. His expression is open and tender. He brushes his lips against mine before pressing more firmly. I open to him as he pulls the tie from my wrists. I don't think either of us noticed they were still bound. Once they're free, he lifts me to straddle him. His cock is between us, and he's hard as a fucking post. I rub my pussy against him, coating him with how wet I am again.

"There will be a next, *cailín*. Your fierceness is yet another turn on. I'm glad you want this as much as I do."

"I do, *nounours*."

He chuckles when I call him teddy again. His hands rested on my ass after lifting me onto his lap, but now they squeeze as he helps me rock against him. I ache to feel him inside me. To satisfy my longing and curiosity. There's so much I still want to know about him and discover with him. I pull back when we come up for air after our next kiss.

"I'm on the pill, and I tested for my membership applications. I can show you the results."

"I believe you. It's standard for applicants to send those in. I saw the birth control pack on the counter when we walked past the closet. I could see into the bathroom."

The stupid circular pill holder. It screams birth control since there aren't any other medications I can think of that come in a wheel like some types of the pill.

He's quick to reassure me I'm not the only responsible one. "I have my results on my phone. I can show them to you. I tested a month ago. I've been with partners since then, but I've never had sex without a condom. Not as a teenager, not in college. You know I wouldn't at a club."

Besides the obvious reason that people often have more than one partner—sometimes in a single visit—many require the use of condoms if the people aren't in a committed relationship and members together.

"If you don't have anything, I have one in my purse." I don't know if he wants to use a condom or not. For the first time, I don't think I want a guy to. I've had boyfriends who used condoms to doubly ensure I didn't get pregnant. It wasn't about fear of catching something.

"I have one in my wallet."

I bite my top lip before I smile. "That's only two. Um... Only twice?"

He dives in and nips at where my shoulder meets my neck. He flicks my earlobe before sucking. He keeps his breath light, just enough to make me shiver. He stands, and I wrap myself around him as he walks to his pants. I cling to him as he bends over. I know he won't drop me, and he has an arm around my waist. But it's still disconcerting for him to lean forward with me hanging on. He pulls out his phone and walks back to the bed. I watch him pull up a food delivery app. He taps on a drug store.

He scrolls to what he wants and taps on the box of condoms' image. He grins at me, watching me, as he taps his screen three more times. He just added three thirty-six-count boxes of Magnums to his shopping cart. He cocks an eyebrow at me.

"You think we're going to have sex a hundred and eight times between now and when I fly out tomorrow? A hundred and ten if you include the condoms we already have here."

"It's an investment in our future." He waggles his eyebrows.

I put my hand on his wrist because that makes me think of yet another thing we haven't discussed but probably should before we bang.

"I'm headed back to Boston tomorrow. You live here. If I come back down, Ewan will want to know which friend I'm seeing. I don't feel obligated to tell him anyone's name—friend or otherwise. But he will ask. He'll assume it's you because Justin and Haydon probably already told him. If you come to Boston, he'll find out. It's not like Montreal is neutral either. Are we going to see each other?"

"Of course. There are any number of places we can meet in Boston or New York that wouldn't be obvious. We can meet somewhere else. Somewhere in the middle or far away. My family's jet is at any of our disposal. It doesn't belong to only one of us. I can get you, or we can meet somewhere and fly wherever we want."

"Your family will want to know where you're going, especially if you take the jet."

He brushes hair back from my shoulder. This time his kiss is gentle when his lips meet my skin. I tilt my head away from him, and he trails feather-soft kisses up my neck. Both hands cup my jaw as he gives me a kiss that makes my heart ache.

"Little one, my family will ask, and they will also understand. My brother's wife and my cousin's wife have family connections to the mob that made dating difficult. But through all of it, the one thing that was always certain was my family's acceptance. No one in my generation or my parents' or even my grandparents' chose to be in the mob. We were born into it. We're in no place to fault someone for who their family is. For better or worse, no one picks who they're related to."

"But they pick who they date."

"We come from mob families, which automatically means not only do we get each other's families, but the branches we belong to. That's why my brothers, cousins, and I never planned to marry. Now Dillan and Finn are. I want to date you. My family accepted Mair's and Ally's unexpected ties to the mob. They'll accept yours too. You are not your grandfather, your father, or your brother. They trust my judgement. If I'm with you, then you're someone they'll trust. They'll welcome you because we've chosen each other. Feck. I can already hear the guys teasing me that you're too good for me. They aren't wrong, but it'll be annoy—"

I cover his mouth with my hand.

"We're about to see if I can roll you over fast enough to spank you. Do not finish that sentence, Sean. Do not say you're not good enough for me. It'll piss me off and fast. You don't want to hear my negative thoughts about my body because you don't agree. I don't want to hear your negative thoughts about your worth. I won't have it. If you were shit, I wouldn't want to be with you. I'm naked, on your lap, discussing how the hell we deal with our families, and we've only had lunch together. You are worth whatever is about to happen."

I pull my hand away and replace it with my mouth. I'm

aggressive. I rise on my knees and press my weight against his chest. He only falls back because he lets himself. I feel the tip of his cock press into my pussy. I sink down an inch. I wait for him to stop me. Our gazes lock. His hands grip my hips as he presses down and thrusts his hips up. I drop onto his cock without his help.

"Shite, Lina. You feel fucking perfect. Goddamn. I might never fucking pull out."

"Holy fuck, Sean... Fucking hell... Fuck this feels good."

We lie connected for a moment, marveling at how we fit together as though his cock and my cunt were made to be matching parts.

"*Nounours*, nothing has ever felt like this. You're—you're—"

I don't even know what to say. Part of me wants to savor the lingering sensations of him sliding into me. Another part of me wants to ride him hard and fast. I rub my clit against him as the initial pleasure gives way to feeling full to the point of pleasurable pain. My hips are narrow to go along with my thin frame. But I'm muscular from being a long course swimmer.

I've been with endowed guys before, and it's never felt like I couldn't take them. Sean is longer and thicker than I realized. He feels big enough to split me in two, and I love it. I'm so fucking wet that he slid in without trouble. But his groan as I rock on his dick makes me wonder if I'm too tight. That I'm hurting him.

"Sean?"

"You're going to squeeze the cum out of me, and I'm going to embarrass myself a second time because I can't last more than a minute."

"You shouldn't have been embarrassed when I sucked you off. I *loved*—I mean really fucking loved—making you come that fast. I thought I hurt you."

"No. Just the opposite."

We move together, stopping when we need to, to keep from orgasming too soon. We want it to last. We both enjoy the denial. But he takes over when he senses my restlessness. He rolls us and stands, drawing my legs over his shoulders.

"You are going to come. And you're going to do it more than once. Do you know why?"

"Because you said so?"

"That's right. *I* decided it's time for you to get off. *I* am going to get you off. *You* are going to do as you're told."

"Yes, Sir." I smile as my eyes close. I must look ridiculous because I'm giddy at the thought of an orgasm with Sean inside me.

He thrusts over and over. I open my eyes because I don't want to miss any of this. His muscles flex, and I want to touch and lick every part of him. His body is utter perfection. He's chiseled and lean. His chest is broad but tapers into a perfect V. He has those sexy hip grooves like the ones models have when their pants hang too low. Like arrows to his dick. When I kneeled on his lap a few minutes ago, my thighs pressed against the hollows on the outside of his hips. Really his ass. I want to lower my legs, press my hands into those notches, and hold on.

"Lina, come."

I stop flexing my hips like I was, making his pubic bone rub against my clit. I barely keep myself from screaming. The last thing we need is hotel security breaking in because they think he's murdering me rather than fucking me. I claw at the bedding and grab the blankets and sheet. I refuse to get house-keeping while I stay at hotels. I don't like strangers near my stuff. I don't totally make the bed each morning like they would, but I straighten up. The nasty—and this is a five-star hotel, so it's all relative—comforter is pushed down to the foot of the bed.

I move again as the tremors subside. I want to bring him the same pleasure. I raise and drop my hips over and over, but it's only getting me closer to coming again. He seems to have found his restraint. It spurs me to try even harder to get him to come. I'm moaning and trembling. I'm so close again.

"*Cailín*, come in five... Four... Three... Two... Now, little one. Fucking come."

I've never come on demand like that before. But it's fucking hot as fuck to hear his commands. My body reacts with perfect timing.

"Sean!"

He pounds into me harder, barely letting me catch my breath from my second orgasm before he's pushing me into my third. I pull my legs back, grasping my shins. I open my knees wide, and he leans forward. He kisses me, and I feel him thrust and still. His hips rock in shorter, faster movements. I know he's coming. He's the only man who's ever done that. The only man I've ever let risk getting me pregnant. Abstinence is the only guarantee. That's obviously not happening.

He leans on his forearms as he kisses me. I lower my legs and run my hands over his chest, ribs, and back.

"Little one, that was sublime."

"I know." This time, my smile is pure bliss.

He stands up, once again holding me as I cling to him. He pulls back the covers and sits with me on his lap. He's still inside me.

"Sean—"

I don't get more than a word out before we hear someone banging on the suite door.

"Nicolina, open the damn door."

Chapter Seven

Sean

Who the fuck is that?

I watch Lina as a man continues to pound on the door. There's no fear or embarrassment or shame. It's pure annoyance. As the guy calls out to her again, it's anger.

"That's Justin. He won't go away. He's more likely to have hotel security called on him. Let me text him and see if that'll get him to stop."

She climbs off the bed, which means climbing off my dick. It's like all the warmth has leeched from my body. The cool air on my wet cock definitely doesn't feel great and ruins any chance I might have stayed hard if I'd stayed in her. Though with the load I just shot, I doubt there's anything left.

She grabs her purse from the dresser where she dropped it as we came through the door. She fishes out her phone and comes back to sit beside me. She does nothing to hide the screen or the message she sends.

LINA

Stop yelling. I'm busy. I'll text you later.

The knocking stops for a moment, then it starts again. He paused long enough to get his phone unlocked.

JUSTIN

Busy fucking an O'Rourke.

That raises my hackles.

LINA

If I were do you think screaming at me is wise? I said I'm busy.

JUSTIN

Getting busy with him. Ewan is going to lose his shit. Send him out before your brother calls.

LINA

You tattled

JUSTIN

Haydon

LINA

Short of locking me in a chastity belt and throwing away the key no one decides who I am or am not with. Go. Away.

"Nikki, open the damn door."

She must feel me tense because she types even faster.

LINA

You don't want me to do that. Leave please.

"Are you scared I'll go all Greco-Roman wrestler on him and fight with my arse to the wind?"

She looks over at me and sees my grin. I'm pissed as fuck to be interrupted, to have someone speak to Lina this way, and to have someone already narc to Ewan. Truth be told, though, I'm surprised it took this long. I didn't think we'd have this much time alone before someone interfered.

JUSTIN

Butterfly

What?

LINA

No

"We've had a code since I was a teenager. If a guy was bothering me, or I just didn't feel safe, I'd text or say butterfly to let Justin and Ewan know I needed help. He thinks you're forcing me because I said he shouldn't want me to open the door. I meant you'll beat the fuck out of him."

I would if we were alone. But I wouldn't unleash that in front of Lina unless her life depended upon it. Justin is a big guy. He wouldn't go easily, so it would take more than a love tap to take him down.

JUSTIN

This is a mistake. End this before Ewan can do anything. I didn't tell him but Haydon did. I'm worried. Please Nikki.

LINA

You could have led with that. Thank you for your concern. I'm still not opening the door. I told you I'm busy. I won't respond.

JUSTIN

Fine. Don't say I didn't warn you. This was as much about protecting you as it was keeping him alive. You're as beautiful as Helen of Troy and you're about to start a war.

I won't disagree with him about Lina's beauty. Her face could launch a thousand ships. I'll do whatever I must to protect her. But the war started well before she and I met. The war started because Rowan O'Malley stole from us and got involved with a threat to my sister-in-law's family. He left that mess to Ewan when we saved him from committing patricide. If Ewan can't remember he's indebted to us, then we'll remind him. But he stays the fuck away from Lina.

She doesn't answer, so we wait to see if another text comes in. It goes quiet. No more knocking. No more yelling. No more texts. She puts the phone on the bedside table and looks at me. The self-assurance she exuded a moment ago is gone. She looks vulnerable. I lift her onto my lap and rock her hips against me as I harden just from touching her.

This is our first true challenge. I need to feel as connected to her as I can while we figure this shit out. We knew it was coming, but I'd hoped for a few more hours. I lift her, and she slides down my cock. She's still wet from my cum. She's still tight, but not as much as the first time I entered her. I encircle my left arm around her waist as my right hand presses her head to my shoulder. I move the pillows around and shuffle to lean back. She doesn't move, and neither do I once I'm comfortable. It's several minutes of companionable silence and moral support before she speaks.

"Sean, can we stay like this?"

Forever. "Yes, little one. Let me hold you until we sort this out."

"Could I fall asleep like this tonight?"

"I'd like nothing more. I know we need to deal with this, but we came here for you to have a nap. Do you want to sleep now?" I run my hand up and down her bare back while my other hand cups her arse.

"I do. But we need to sort this out."

"It won't go away today. Sleep, little one."

"I suddenly feel so sleepy, *nounours*. I've never been so comfortable as I am right now. Feeling you inside me like this makes me want to curl up and drift off."

"You're safe with me, Lina. At least, I can promise you that in here. You can let your guard down and let me worry about this."

"No. I don't want that. I don't want you to worry about it at all, and definitely not while I sleep and leave you to deal with it."

"Thinking of different solutions is what will relax me. That and holding you. If staying like this lets you sleep, then I'll feel better."

She leans back far enough to see my face. "I could sleep for a week if we stay like this. I don't want solving this shit to be what relaxes you. I don't want there to be shit to solve."

"But there is, and we knew there would be. Please let me take care of you."

I need that more than anything. My possessiveness and protectiveness are in overdrive. I need to shield her, even if that only means having my arms around her. I need to know I can take care of her if this is going to work. It's not that I want her needy and dependent on me—though it would be kinda nice because I'm already feeling that way about her—it's that I need her to trust me. I want her to trust me.

She returns her head to my shoulder, and I start to stroke her back again. She sighs, and I feel the tension ease from her.

"Teddy bear—I like that as much in English as I do in French—if you can sleep too, will you let yourself? We're safe in here, aren't we?"

"Yes, little one. I know you saw my gun with my pants. I haven't tried to hide it. Would you feel better if I had it within reach? I don't believe I need it."

"I don't want you to need to, but I know you probably carry it most places you go. That was before you met me. I'm certain you have a knife, too. There's inherent danger with you being in a confined space on the fifteenth floor. This adds to it. I don't think Justin would break in, but someone else might. I'm not a pessimist, but we're both naked and in an intimate position. It makes us more vulnerable if someone does. I have one in my purse, Sean. There was no way I was coming to New York to spy on your family without one."

"You believed we'd shoot you?"

"I believe if you'd found me in the wrong place at the wrong time and couldn't tell I was a woman, someone in your family would shoot first and ask questions second. I met with the head of Tokyo's most powerful syndicate. If not him or someone with him, then me meeting with him might piss off someone else. A spy isn't welcome in any syndicate unless they're on that syndicate's payroll. I want to be protected in case I run into anyone else who's pissed my brother sent me."

I kiss her forehead. Everything she said is true. No one in my family would shoot an unarmed woman. We want to believe we're returning to the old homeostasis where my family doesn't target and manipulate women and get them stuck in syndicate business. But my family shattered that golden rule, and I can't guarantee the other syndicates would play nice if they found her. I definitely don't think Nishida would feel honor bound to leave her alone if he thought she were a threat.

An armed woman willing to kill us always nullified that golden rule because all of the Four Families—mine, the Kutsenkos, Mancinellis, and Diazes—have faced female mercenaries. They're fair game when they're paid to off us. An enemy combatant is an enemy combatant. But Lina should be untouchable. Maybe she is as a mob boss's granddaughter, another boss's sister, and now a general's girlfriend. Any of those could be enough to protect her; any of those could be enough to make her a target.

"*Cailín*, I'm glad you have a means to protect yourself. I hate you have to know how. This just makes me want to hold you even more while you sleep."

"I want you to hold me. I'm so comfy, I just need to close my eyes. I'll be asleep fast."

I kiss her forehead again before I rest my cheek on the top of her head. I continue to run my hand up and down her back while my other hand has a firm hold on her arse. She twitches twice but doesn't stir. Then I feel her breathing slow, and her body goes completely lax.

I reach for my phone that I tossed aside before we had sex. I never ordered the condoms. I guess that's unnecessary now.

ME

> I need to go to Boston. Can you come with me? I have to kill Ewan.

The response is immediate.

SHANE

> Do you need it to look like me?

The only way anyone outside our family can tell us apart is by a freckle on my neck. If we're wearing turtlenecks on missions or starched collars with a bow tie, it's impossible to see it. We know our mannerisms are just as identical as our appearance. We run our hands through our hair the same way. We sit with our leg crossed over our knee the same way to a millimeter —we checked as kids. We have the same stride naturally. We wear our shoes out the same way. We know because we've swapped enough times, and they always feel the same as our own. We are absolute mirrors of each other except for the freckles on our face, but we both have enough that people can't use that to tell us apart. It's the one on the left side of my throat, just a half inch from my Adam's apple that distinguishes me.

ME

I might. I don't want it to come to that. It could be a disaster if it does. But it might be unavoidable.

SHANE

Why? Who is she?

ME

His sister. She's mine.

He sends me the eye roll emoji. It bounces on my screen before just sitting there, looking at me.

I haven't told him her name, and the others suspect I met someone who's distracted me. But he just knows. He hasn't pressed me to tell him anything because I don't have to. He guessed, and it was futile to deny it to Shane. Anyone else I can skirt the issue. If I've accepted I want to be with Lina, then we both know thinking otherwise is pointless and would only hurt the other.

SHANE

You don't want it to come to that but could it if he threatens her in any way?

ME

It could if he tells Tremblay.

SHANE

Tremblay?

ME

She's his granddaughter.

SHANE

WTF you've always been go big or go home.
This is likely to get you a big bullet between
your eyes. Mine if he thinks I'm you!

ME

Don't catastrophize until there's a reason to.

That'll chap his arse. They say I'm the most patient in the family. It's really that I'm the most stubborn. I can wait out most people, so it means I don't lose my shit easily. It also meant that when I was a kid, I would simply sit down if I didn't want to do something or stand until the other person walked away. Shane isn't a hot head, but he doesn't have the patience I do. He prefers to just deal with things and get them out of the way. Between the two of us, he might be the first one in, but I'm last one out. Nobody gets around us.

SHANE

I'd like to live to see you standing at the altar.
I won't if he kills us. What's her name
anyway?

ME

Nicolina. Nikki

SHANE

But what do you call her?

Dillan calls his wife Greta, but everyone else calls her Mair, which is short for her traditional Gaelic name. Finn calls his wife Thea while everyone else shortens Althea to Ally. I guess I like tradition.

ME

Lina

SHANE

When's the wedding?

ME

Feck off

SHANE

So next week. Good thing I took my tux to the dry cleaners right after Finn's wedding. Can I come to the cake tasting?

I send him the middle finger emoji. He's not wrong per se... Lina and I should survive at least a second date before we jump into ring shopping. She might be from two mob families and already embroiled in this life, but she isn't embroiled in mine. Yet. I haven't allowed any woman to get as close as I have Lina. She's seen emotions I've either never had before or never been willing to share. If I didn't think we have a genuine future together, I wouldn't have gotten into a text conversation that's been going on for nearly a month. We definitely wouldn't be here with her sitting on my dick. I'm rocking my hips just enough to stay hard, but it won't last much longer.

ME

If the others ask don't lie but don't volunteer it either. I don't want secrets among us but it's still early. We need to see if we're as compatible as I think we are and we have to navigate our families.

SHANE

You know ours will accept her. No one picks their relatives. If we did we wouldn't be O'Rourkes that's for fecking sure.

ME

I know. But we have shite to resolve with Ewan that won't be in his favor. We have business to do with Jean-Peter. She's trapped in the middle figuratively. I don't want her there literally when this turns violent.

Neither of us will say anything more explicit than that. We

all text one another, but it isn't through the built-in app. It's not one anyone can get in an app store. I have a software designer connection. What Finn or I can't do, she can. Her dad's my dad's best friend, besides my uncles. They've known each other since preschool. Apparently, my dad liked to eat dirt.

SHANE

When should we expect Ewan?

ME

Soon. Not in person. At least not yet. But a bodyguard Lina didn't agree to saw us together. He came banging on her hotel door wanting to talk to her. She refused to even open the door. She called out to him from the bedroom and texted him. He said her brother already knows.

SHANE

Are they close?

ME

I don't think so. At least not by the Four Families' standard.

One of the Mancinelli wives coined the term, and it's gotten around. Probably at one of the twenty million weddings we've been to in the past four years. Fourteen to be exact.

SHANE

Posturing?

ME

Maybe. Probably. I think he must care for real b/c she hasn't told me otherwise. But I doubt they're hanging out and watching movies together on Fri nights.

SHANE

> Maybe not. I need to get a life now that you'll be watching movies with your fiancée. But he'll use it as the perfect excuse to make him look like his balls dropped. We might have let him take credit for fixing Rowan's fuck-up. But he's not his dad. He might want others to think he has brass balls, but he's got little more than a micro penis. That means a Napoleon complex. He'll want us to fear him.

ME

> Laughable at best

SHANE

> Doesn't mean he won't try.

ME

> And he'll sit back down in his highchair where he belongs. He's not even sitting at the kiddie table yet.

Ewan's been heading up shite for his father for years, but he's new to being the absolute leader. Rowan assumed he'd be around forever. What he couldn't do himself, he had his brother, Riley, do. He hadn't trained Ewan well enough. He's smarter than most of the lesser syndicate leaders, but he doesn't have the experience. He doesn't know all the unwritten rules.

Dillan was groomed for it. So were Maksim, Salvatore, and Enrique. Everyone in the Four Families was conditioned to step into the roles they have now. We all rose through the ranks from messenger boys to foot soldiers to enforcers to now generals. The lesser syndicates, like the Albanians, Polish, Mexicans, Puerto Ricans, and Hondurans, aren't as rigid. Too much in fighting means they're more haphazard. Ewan's somewhere between us and them. He knows shite, but he doesn't know enough to know he doesn't know shite. Basically, he's still on training wheels.

I glance down at Lina. Why the fuck am I coming up with all these children's metaphors? I never think about kids. At least, not past the most general sense or in passing about the other syndicate couples. Maksim and Laura have twins. Bogdan and Christina have a son and another on the way. Niko and Anastasia have a little girl just like Luca and Olivia. I think Sinead and Gabriele are expecting, and I suspect so are Maria and Matteo. The way my brother and cousin are, they better hope their wives' birth control is perfect, or they better plan to decorate nurseries.

SHANE

What do you need me to do immediately?

ME

Let Dillan know we're going to Boston. We leave in the morning. Find out where Ewan's going to be. If he's working from home I want him away from there. I don't want any of this shite near Lina when she gets back.

SHANE

When does she go?

ME

Tomorrow. I'll offer to fly her up with us. I don't know if she'll say yes. Line up drivers. I'll talk to Lina and see what she knows.

SHANE

You're gonna tell her you're going to Boston to probably kill her brother?

ME

Not in so many words. She wanted to tell me what's going on. She was close to doing it but her conscience got the better of her. She doesn't want to betray her family. I sense it's more about her integrity than protecting Ewan.

SHANE

Why was she down here?

ME

He sent her on an errand.

An errand. That usually means spying on someone or extorting someone. I'm certain Shane can guess which.

SHANE

God save us from nosey women

He sends the sideways laughing emoji, but there's truth in that. It's not so much nosey as intelligent and resourceful.

ME

Be sure to tell Mair and Ally that.

SHANE

Thankyounothankyou I'll get everything organized. Are you staying with her tonight or going back to your place? Should we all meet?

ME

We should but I don't think I can. I don't want to leave her alone because I don't trust her bodyguard not to drag her out of here if she's alone. I don't trust Ewan not to fly down and freak out at her. But bringing her with me is a level we're not at.

SHANE

Yet

ME

Probably

SHANE

Fine keep me posted

ME

Same

I know my brother will make all the arrangements for us to travel tomorrow. He'll come with me, and so will a few of our guys. I'd like to slide in and out of Boston with no fuss. Ideally, I'd observe Ewan for a day or two and get a read on his reaction. It could be nothing, and I'd go home. The likelihood of things playing out that way is pretty much none. Even flying commercial wouldn't hide us for long, so I'd rather have the convenience of our jet, so we can leave in a hurry. And most importantly, I could bring Lina.

The confrontation is pretty much inevitable. I want Lina far from it. But I don't trust Ewan not to put her in the middle. God save me from meddling brothers because I don't know what I'll do if Lina sees the man I really am.

Chapter Eight

Lina

I think Sean was texting while I dozed. I sorta felt his arms moving, but I was too tired to tell. I'm lying still, listening to his heart right now. The moment I came fully awake, I realized our bodies aren't joined anymore. Damn male anatomy. I've warmed cocks before by just sitting on them, but it was always a type of submission in the past. It was about them controlling when I could or couldn't get off. About them deciding when I did or didn't get their attention.

I know I had Sean's complete attention while I was awake. I sense he knows I'm awake now and that I have his attention again. I could fuck him to get myself—or, preferably, both of us —off, and he wouldn't stop me because I'm not his sub. I know he'd see it—me—as equals.

I kiss his collar bone before sitting up. "Hi."

"Hi, little one. Do you feel rested?"

"More than I did." My brow furrows. "What happened?"

His eyes widen, and I know he's letting me see his surprise.

If he didn't want me to, then I wouldn't. But I'm certain something is even more off than it was before I fell asleep.

"I'm going to Boston tomorrow."

"I figured. I don't want you to, but I'm certain I can't talk you out of it."

"Have you changed your mind?"

I shake my head. "Not at all. Me not wanting you to go has nothing to do with me ending this or wanting to hide this. I don't want Ewan trying to kill you, and I don't want you succeeding at killing him." I shrug because I feel a wave of sadness slam into me.

"Lina, I'm not going there to hurt him. I'm not going there to kill him. As long as he keeps you protected..."

He trails off, and I know he means he won't kill Ewan as long as he leaves me out of it. But my brother won't. He can't. Sean said his cousin met with Nishida a few weeks ago. I met with him today. Ewan's going to expect me to brief him on that because he's obviously found another way to try to fuck the O'Rourkes over.

"It's going to piss him off to find out I slept with you because I want you, not to get something out of you."

He squeezes my ass in response, and I jerk my hips forward. My instinct is to avoid the pain, but then I press back into his hand.

"You definitely got something out of me." He waggles his eyebrows and kisses me.

Fuck. This is perfection. The way he kisses makes me melt. The feel of his stubble under my fingers. The scent of his cologne. The sound of our mouths, and the feel of his tongue. The way he looked just before his lips met mine. He definitely deals in narcotics. The drug is him.

"The way what I just said sounded. I didn't mean I sleep with people to get things out of them."

"I didn't think you do." He brushes hair back from my face and tucks it behind my ear. It's tender and intimate. I love it.

"I can't convince you not to do this, can I?"

"No. If Ewan sent you to spy on my family, do you know why we're not getting along?"

"Not getting along? Ha." I dash my glance away before looking back at him. "Our families have never gotten along. Your family tolerates mine. And my family swallows its inferiority complex and silently fumes that once upon a time the O'Malleys and O'Rourkes were equals."

"Well, yes. But do you know why we're outwardly hostile right now?" He makes it sound so benign. We're about to discuss how his family killed my father and uncle, doing my brother a favor since he and our dad were at each other's throats.

"I know it's complicated just like it always is. My dad and Uncle Riley stole a shipment of yours. The rugs were legal, but it was what was sewn into them that wasn't. Dad supported some biker guy related to your sister-in-law when the biker went after her dad. I don't remember exactly. When your family raided the warehouse to get the rugs back, you found a bunch of other shit. Illegally kept animals. For all my brother's faults, that was the final straw between him and our dad. Ewan may dislike most people, but he loves most animals. Shockingly, they love him back."

"Did you know how strained things were between your dad and Ewan before you moved down to Boston?"

"Yes. Our dad had his moments when he genuinely wanted to put his family first. But they were only moments. It was his ambition that got him killed. It exceeded his common sense and his skills. He kept pushing Ewan to make a move on your family by setting up a deal with one of your big rivals. I don't think he cared which one Ewan chose as long as it fucked your family over. He wanted Ewan to prove himself. He wanted to brag that his son—who's younger than all of you—got one over on you. He wanted to prove our family is still relevant. And he wanted to show his men he still controlled Ewan."

"But did he?" The sarcasm drips from Sean's three words.

"No. He hadn't since that Christmas Ewan stood up to him when we overheard him talking about me. I've never respected my dad in any sense other than being a fellow human being. I didn't respect him as a father. I didn't respect him as a leader. I didn't respect him as a businessman. Those feelings started when I was too young to understand what they were. He was just a shit dad most of the time. I stopped trusting the moments when he was great and waited for the hours, days, weeks, and years that he wasn't. At least I didn't have to live with him full time like Ewan did."

"You said the animals were the last straw. Do you know what Ewan was going to do?"

I'm still sitting on Sean's lap. I lean back farther to see his face better. I lift my chin, and I know I shutter my gaze. I'm not shutting him out, and I think he knows that. I'm letting him know I'm fine with what my brother planned. I just won't say it out loud because what kind of monster does that make me?

"What did Rowan do to you to get you to this point?" He can be vague too.

"I guess you and your family came up for a wake about three and a half years ago. Maybe closer to four now. It was for a man I never met, but he was pretty high up and close to my dad. I wasn't there because if I had been, I would have met you. And I definitely wouldn't have forgotten you. He wanted me to come down for it. He wanted me to sleep with Dillan. He knew Finn hooked up with my aunt whenever he was in town. He figured getting info from Finn was good, but getting info from Dillan would be great."

"He what?!"

I press my hands against Sean's chest as he explodes.

"He's already dead. You can't resurrect him to kill him all over again." His scowl tells me he didn't like my attempt at reassurance. "He never said that to me, and he wasn't that blunt with Ewan. But he made his wishes clear to my brother, who was supposed to convey them to me. Basically, he told Ewan to get me to make friends with Dillan. To get him alone and see what I could learn. Dad knew Dillan wouldn't look to make friends with me. He wanted pillow talk."

"He tried to pimp his daughter out." Sean's hands are curled into fists, lying on the bed beside his hips. I reach for his wrists and lift his arms. I put his hands back on my ass. His grip is tight without squeezing. It's possessive, and I love it.

"Ewan and I are close sometimes and distant at others. I suppose we're like Britain and France. We generally don't care for each other but can get along. We even play nice in public. But if someone threatens either of us, we're best friends. Needless to say, Ewan did *not* try to convince me to come to the wake. He told me the truth, though. I know Ewan manipulates me sometimes since the apple didn't fall far from the tree, but he didn't do it this time. I know because I overheard Uncle Riley and Aunt Cady talking about it the next time I was in town. That was when Ewan decided it was time to prepare for a transition. The animals would have pushed him into doing whatever he'd planned."

I don't know the details of his plot to commit patricide, and I don't want to.

"You overhear a lot of things." It's an observation, not an accusation.

"Apparently, I'm easy to forget, even when I'm around."

He fists my hair and holds my head in place as he sits up. He rakes his teeth up my neck before tugging my hair, pulling me back. He lifts my left breast and sucks hard on the nipple before leaving another mark dangerously high. The wrong shirt would reveal it.

"You are the most memorable person I know, *cailín*."

His kiss is aggressive. His free hand presses my right wrist behind my back. He holds me immovable with his grip on my arm and my hair. I let him lead. Not just because he practically overwhelms me.

Because I love this. I love that he wants me, desires me this much. He can be gentle and cautious with me, so I know this is an element of him he wants me to see. It's not who he always is. He wants me to know he feels the words he just said. It makes me feel special.

When we come up for air, his hand releases my wrist, but it comes to rest heavily on my throat just above my collar bones. He doesn't tighten. It's enough to keep this dynamic going as though I'm at his mercy. That he dares me to disagree with him. That to do so will only make him prove what he says goes.

This isn't a scene or roleplaying. This isn't him being a Dom, and me being a sub. This is just us. He gets what I need. It feels pretty fucking shitty to admit your father didn't give two fucks about you past how useful you were to his ambitions. That your brother conveniently cares about you, but that's usually to get him what he wants. Sean knows I need to feel like I'm more than just a chess piece. That I matter to him.

"*Cailín*, I know this is painful for you to tell me. I know it's humiliating. You hide it well, but not well enough from me. If you want to keep telling me the past, I will always listen. But if you don't want to tell me more, or you don't want me to know more, then I won't push you. I'll hold you until I'm calm enough not to lose my shite on your brother. Will you let me?"

I lean forward and whisper to him after kissing his cheek.

"As Lina and Sean, I'll let you. As *cailín* and *nounours*, make me."

I sit back and press my hand over his that's still on my throat. I urge him to tighten his hold. It's not breath play because it remains easy to breathe. But it makes it harder to take a deep inhale. He pulls me forward until my nose nearly brushes his.

"I still have to go, Lina. For your sake, I won't lose my patience. But the moment your brother looks the wrong way at you, says the wrong thing, *thinks* the wrong fecking thing, I will make sure he and everyone else understand you're mine. We will figure out what we are to each other with time. We can define our relationship into whatever it turns out to be. Nothing about that changes the fact you're mine. Whether you're my friend or my partner, you are mine to protect and take care of. By the time I leave Boston, no one will doubt that."

I reach between us and stroke him. I move my hand tight and fast, and it doesn't take long since he was halfway hard already. I rise on my knees and sink onto his cock. He lets go of my hair and brings his hand down on my ass. He releases my throat.

"Are you in control now, little one?" His voice is an invitation to sin.

"Not at all. Knowing I'm yours is the most arousing thing ever. I want you to know how strongly I agree." And I do. Whether he's my friend, my lover, my boyfriend, my whatever, I'm his.

"Lina, it goes both ways. I'm yours. Completely."

Our gazes meet, and I know he's letting me in even further. I'm in no woman's land. I don't think he's ever opened himself up like this. It's precious, and I know that.

"Thank you."

He rolls us, so I'm on the bottom. He guides my left leg over his hip while he lifts my right. He helps hold that one up while balancing with one hand. He drives into me over and over. I'll be sore in the morning. I'll remember I'm his. Telling him about my family blew big chunks. But all of this right now—fucking hell, it's motherfucking divine.

"May I come, Sir?"

"Yes." He barks the answer.

My fingers press into his upper arms—there's too much muscle for them to sink into anything—as my cunt contracts around him. Pleasure starts as that unique sensation inside my pussy and spreads as I orgasm. My entire body tenses as I arch my neck.

"Sean!"

"Say my name."

"Sean!"

"Say it."

"Sean!"

"That's right, little girl. It's my name you're saying because I belong to you."

"Fuck, that's hot. Don't stop. Please."

"I'm not going to."

He slams into me extra hard, pushing me up the bed. If it weren't for his weight on me, I might slide out from under him. I don't know if it's even a minute later that I come again. This is so intense. It's my nails that press into his arms as my fingers turn into talons. It's so consuming I almost want to run from it, yet I want this ecstasy to last until I die. Hell, sex with him may kill me. My heart feels like it's going to beat right out of my chest.

"Lina!"

He thrusts one more time before tensing. Then he rocks his hips three more times before scooping me up and rolling us again, so he doesn't crush me. I could sleep for a week or run a marathon right now. I'm not sure which. I may not have the longest list of men I've slept with, but it's more than long enough. Sex with Sean defies reality—at least the reality I've known so far.

Yes. The way we fit together physically has a lot to do with it. But it's so much more than that. I like dirty talk. I have since I got confident enough to try it. I suppose you could categorize the things Sean said as dirty talk. It doesn't feel that way, though. Maybe it's a little over the top because it's during sex. That doesn't make it any less sincere or true.

That begs the question: How the fuck is that possible? We've texted for three and a half weeks and talked on the phone briefly right after the last thread. That was only yesterday. We went to lunch together. We did hook up the day we met, and I knew something was different even then. I was never interested in psychology before meeting Sean. At least not beyond what makes people in power tick. And that was to understand human nature in context of national security. But I'm interested now. I want to understand how every part of me is attracted to him so fast. This is more than a dopamine hit or a rush of adrenaline. I feel it every time our eyes lock.

"*Cailín?*"

"Hmm?"

"You all right?"

"Yeah." I push up onto my hand beside his shoulder.

"You didn't answer me."

"I didn't hear what you said. Sorry."

"I blew your mind that well?" He grins.

"You did. I was off in la-la land." I roll to my side and tug at his shoulder to bring him with me.

Our hands caress up and down each other's ribs and waist. We share brief pecks, closing our eyes for them, then gazing at each other in between. My eyes shut as I sigh.

"I know we can't stay like this forever, but I wish we could."

"Me too. I—"

He freezes when an alert goes off on his phone. It's not a buzz. It's an actual sound. He sits up immediately and grabs his phone. His thumb swipes up as he reads. He presses the side button and locks it as he looks at me.

"I have to go."

I knew he was going to say that the moment he reached for his phone. I've never had a man jump out of bed to pick mob shit over me, but I've seen plenty of men in my life abruptly leave after getting a call or text.

"Come here." He holds his arms out to me as he lies back down. I didn't expect that.

I scoot back to where I was a moment ago. His palm cups my jaw, and he sweeps his thumb over my cheekbone. Every way he touches me that isn't purely sexual is so calming. I want to curl up and sleep. It's not because I'm chronically tired. I don't have narcolepsy. I feel that at ease and that safe with him. He tells me he wants to protect me and take care of me. That's all good and well. He shows me he can and will. That matters more than I can put into words.

"I have to go out, and I don't know when I'll be done. It might be in time for dinner. It might be in time for brunch. Or it might not be for a couple days. I don't know yet. I need you to answer me truthfully. Is Justin going to force you to deal with your brother? Are you going to have to deal with Ewan when I leave?"

His gaze is so earnest. It's unwavering. The eyes are the windows to the soul because the way he looks at me tells me his character as though I can look straight into his mind and heart.

"Justin can't make me do anything. I just won't open the door to him. He won't bang on it again or get hotel staff involved. He knows it would make a scene. Ewan can call until he gives up. I don't have to answer. But I will have to deal with them both."

"What is Ewan going to do to you?"

I don't want to answer that because there's no good way to do it. "He'll either chew me a new one or ice me out. He'll either jump down my throat or ignore me for a week or two. I'm staying with him, so it sucks when he does it. But it also means I don't have to listen to him nag."

"Will he tell any of his men about us? Would he let any of them say shite to you about either being with me or not finishing the mission?"

"Maybe. I don't know."

He goes quiet as he stares at me. He's mulling something over, so I won't rush him.

"Do you have to go back to Boston tomorrow? Would you rather stay here? Go to Montreal?"

"However angry he might be right now, if I don't go back to Boston, it'll make everything a thousand times worse. He might ignore me while he sulks, but he expects me to be there to watch him. If I go to Montreal, he'll assume I ran to my grandfather. If I stay here with you, he'll know I choose you over him."

Choose. Not chose. Choose. As in the present tense. As in ongoing. I am, but I didn't mean to say something that sounds so—presumptuous. Like now the postcoital bliss is over, I assume everything said was real and not dirty talk. I know I said what I meant, and I believe Sean did, too. But what if he didn't, and I completely misread all of it?

"I want my cousins Seamus or Cormac with you while I'm gone. If you decide to stay in the city, then they'll rotate outside your door. I want them to go everywhere you go. That includes Boston if you decide it's there. They will fly up with you in our family's jet. If you can stay somewhere—anywhere—else, then I suggest you do. But if you have to go to Ewan's, then they will be in cars discreetly outside his house. Believe me when I say Ewan and his men won't know they're there. I know you know your brother, but I doubt you've been in this position before. I don't trust him because we're in the unknown. I trust my cousins with your protection. If the men don't share my DNA, then they aren't good enough to guard you."

"If you can send me in the jet with your cousins, does that mean you aren't going to Boston?" I know it's unlikely I'll get an answer to that. He just looks at me. I nod.

Maybe he'll fly out tonight, and the jet will be back in time to take me tomorrow. Maybe he's staying in the city. Maybe he's going to Timbuktu. I won't know unless he tells me. He won't if he believes it could jeopardize me or anyone in his family or organization. I know how it goes.

"If whatever this is, is because of me, I'm sorry."

"It isn't. Even if it were, you don't have to apologize. I hate that you already know this life, and it means I don't have to explain most things to you. I hate that I'm not the one to explain it because it means you know way more than I wish you did. I told you what I want. Are you okay with that? What do you want?"

"I want us to never leave this bed. But short of that, I'll accept your cousins being my bodyguards. I hate they're tasked with this and that this is my introduction to your family. But I know it's serious if you want it. I won't argue with you, and frankly, if you believe you can only trust your family to protect me, then I'm only going to feel safe with you or them. I have to go back to Boston, or it'll only get way worse. I flew commercial, but I accept the offer of the jet because I know that means I'm safer."

He sits up again and gets his phone. I watch him unlock it and tap a contact. Then he puts it to his ear and waits.

"Shay, I need you and Cor to meet me at The Conrad in Midtown. Plans changed."

There's silence for a moment. I wonder what his cousin's saying. Is he arguing with Sean? Will he see this as babysitting his cousin's fuck buddy? Will he think I'm sinking my hooks into Sean to use him?

My growing tension must be nearly palpable because Sean wraps his arm around my upper back and draws me up next to him. He presses my head to his chest.

"Thanks. We'll be ready when you get here. See you in a few."

He hangs up and puts the phone on the bedside table. I squeak when he scoops me up and gets off the bed. I know I'm skinny, but it still surprises me how easily he moves around with me like I weigh nothing at all. He strides toward the bathroom as he looks down and smiles.

"It's time for another kind of sex. Then I'll let you scrub behind my ears."

Chapter Nine

Sean

I lower Lina to her feet and turn on the shower. The water warms quickly, and the pressure is good. It had better be since this is one of the most expensive hotels in the city. We step under the showerhead, me moving back as soon as I'm wet. She runs her hands over me, and I can't get enough. Obviously, I'm no virgin. I've had more than one dozen partners, but less than two. I know what I like. I know what's turned me on and driven lust and infatuation.

Lina makes everything in the past seem inconsequential. It gave me the carnal knowledge I have and love using with her. But there was always something lacking. Something not wholly satisfying. It was good enough that I didn't look for more. I didn't want to. I can't imagine going back to that, though. If things don't work out with Lina, it's going to leave a gaping hole in my heart. I'd rather get shot.

"How long do we have until your cousins get here?"

"About thirty minutes."

I pour shampoo into my palm and guide her to turn away from me. She gives me a happy moan as I rub the product into her hair until it's sudsy. I massage her scalp, and she reaches back to wrap her arms around my waist. I slide my soapy hands down her shoulders to her tits. They fit in my hands as though they were made for me to enjoy. I play with her nipples until they're hard.

I shift to let her step under the showerhead. She tilts her head back to wash the shampoo out, using her hands to move her hair around. I latch onto her left nipple and suck, flicking my tongue while I'm at it. I move from side to side after I rinse my hands off. I slip two fingers into her. She's so fucking tight, even around them. I've been rough with her during sex, but I'm careful now. I'm unprepared for her to push my hand away and drop to her knees. She strokes me as she licks my balls.

Her tongue swipes up before swirling around the head of my cock, flicking the hole. I reach over her and press my hands on the wall. When she slides her mouth almost to the base, I need that wall to hold me up. I'm certain my knees are shaking. Her eyes are closed as though she relishes the task. She strokes what she isn't sucking, working her hand and mouth in tandem. Her free hand presses my arse, pushing my hips toward her. She lightens her touch as I draw my hips back. She presses again, telling me she wants me to thrust.

"Do you want me to fuck your mouth, little girl?"

"Mmhmm." She's clear even without words.

I use my left hand to cup her head, pressing against it like she is my arse. Except I keep the pressure extremely light. She isn't some cum dumpster like on a porn. The goal isn't to use her to get off. I'm not fucking her down her throat to force her into staying where she is. If she wants to stop, it ends immediately. But I am guiding her to move with me.

She opens her eyes and looks up at me for a moment.

There's something in her gaze I can't articulate. Yes, she's doing this to me and for me. Yes, she's being submissive. Yes, I'm leading even though she started this. But that's not what I'm seeing. It's as though this is the most normal thing in the world. Not that this isn't special, but that it's as though she accepts this is how it should be. She closes them again and sucks harder.

"I'm going to come, Lina. Let go if you don't want to swallow."

She lets go, but she keeps her mouth open. I get what she wants. I stroke until I can't hold back. I aim for her tits before resting my cock on her tongue. I'm blocking the water enough that my cum sits between her tits. We're looking at it before she swipes her finger through it and brings it to her tongue. She sucks her finger into her mouth, and I might come again. I help her to her feet, and I'm ready to trade places.

"Sean, no. I don't need anything in return. Yeah, I'm wet and would love to get off. But I don't need that right now. I wanted to do that. I wanted to take care of you."

I cup her jaw as I already have so many times. I love it. I think it's sensual as fuck. I take my time with the kiss. We still need to finish showering, but I refuse to rush after what she just gave me. I wrap my arm around her waist and draw her to me.

"Thank you, *cailín*. You don't have to pleasure me to take care of me. But that was incredible."

"I know I don't have to. But you're leaving in a bit, and that's what I could do for right now. Something just for you."

Is this what being in love feels like?

It's not like being a twin means I never feel special. My parents have made sure Shane and I know we're separate people since we were born. The only time we wore anything matching was for family photos, Christmas, and Easter. Then we matched Finn too. It's not like being from a large family means I never feel special. I do. We all have our own talents we bring to the table. But no one outside my family has ever made me feel special. Not like this.

I want to spend all the time I can with her. Get to know her even more. I want to share companionable silence with her as we read or work. I want to laugh with her. I want to fall asleep and wake up with her. I want far more than just sex. It's new and exciting right now because this is the first day we've been together. While I pray our mutual attraction never wears off, the novelty might. It's what comes after that. That's what I want. Hopefully, with all the normal couple stuff, our attraction—physical and emotional—will continue to grow.

"I hate that I'm leaving soon. I don't want our time together to be over. And I'm worried about you."

"Our time together isn't over, *nounours*. Just today is. If Seamus and Cormac are anything like you, then I'll be safer than all the gold relics hidden beneath the Vatican. No one will know where I am unless I want them to. I'm confident your cousins will keep me safe. If not for my sake, then for yours. I'll see what mood Ewan is in, and if he's going to be shitty, then I'll go to a hotel."

"Promise me you'll go to Montreal or come back here if it's dangerous. Dangerous by what I would deem it, not what you're willing to put up with."

She grins at me. "I'd be running away with a paper cut if I went by your standard. You can't surround me in bubble wrap. Ewan's moods aren't new to me."

"But being involved with a rival is." At least, I assume it is.

She hands me the soap and stands still, letting the water rinse her off. "No, I haven't been involved with any of my family's rivals. Not on either side."

She read my fear. It was something I purposely hid—tried to hide—from her. She could tell. It's eerie how fast that was. Only Shane can do that. My cousins take a minute or two.

We finish, and I push open the shower door, handing her a towel. She wraps it around her hair as I pass her another one. I dry off before wrapping one around my waist. I open the bathroom door and hear someone knocking. No one's yelling, so it probably isn't Justin. Lina's gaze dashes to my towel, then out toward the suite's living room. I grin as I step into the bedroom as though I plan to answer the door as I am. She reaches for me, but I sidestep. I grab my boxer briefs and put them on, then my pants. She watches as she combs her hair.

"My gun's on the bedside table. Stay in here with the door closed until I come for you."

"But you won't have a gun."

I pull a knife from each pocket. "I'll check the peephole before I open the door."

She nods as I walk out. I hurry across the sitting area, a knife in my right hand. I check to see who's there. It's Cormac and Seamus.

"*Prátaí.*" Potato.

Cormac responds. "*Cabáiste.*" Cabbage.

Anything besides those two words means it's not safe to open the door. I unlock it and step aside as I pull on the handle. My cousins are built like gladiators. We're all big in my family. Every man stands at least a couple inches over six feet. All of us are in the two-twenty to two-thirty range, except for them. Their heavy arses are nearly two-fifty. Believe me. I know. I've carried both of their dead weight. We all have single digit body fat because we work out and stay active.

Three brothers married three sisters and along came our generation. Their dad is the biggest, but my dad and Dillan's are close behind. Seamus and Cormac just came out behemoths—and Seamus was two months early.

"Lina's in the bedroom getting ready. Let me finish, then we'll explain."

"She knows you're leaving?" Cormac's looking over my shoulder toward the shut bedroom door.

"Yeah. But I didn't say where or why."

They nod. I head back to the bedroom and find Lina in a pair of jeans and cute shirt. She hands me my suit coat, shirt, and tie. I button up the shirt but stuff my tie in my pants pocket. I holster the gun at my lower back then slip on my suit coat.

"We don't have to explain your family history, but we need to let them know enough for them to protect you."

"I'm going to have to tell them at some point."

"Nothing you don't want to. Unless you want to tell the story twice, we should wait until we're with Shane, Finn, and Dillan, too."

She nods, and I'm certain nothing about that sounds appealing. She steps into a pair of flats and walks to where I'm standing beside the door. I open it and let her go past. I slide my hand into hers as we approach my cousins. Neither looks surprised. They've met women I've hooked up with in the past. There's a girl from high school we're all intimately acquainted with. But they haven't seen me hold a woman's hand since freshman year of college. The last time I had a girlfriend. The last time I thought I could have some semblance of a normal life.

I know them as well as I know myself. They aren't hiding their shock. They expected this. We've been through this with Dillan and Finn already. They know she's special to me, which means she's who I want for good. They know I wouldn't bring anyone around our family if I didn't think it was for the long haul. It's too dangerous for all of us. For the woman, if she gets caught in the middle and for us if she narcs.

"Lina, this is Seamus and Cormac." I point to each cousin. "This is Nikki."

My switching names doesn't faze them either. She glances up at me, confused. I'm not sharing a state secret, but I want my explanation to stay intimate. "The men in my family tend to pick names for their partners only they share with each other. Lina is mine."

She gazes up at me. "What's your middle name?"

"Dermot."

We both laugh. Neither of us wants to use that. Sean is too short to turn into anything else.

"Do any of them speak French?" She keeps her voice low but speaks quickly. I know she doesn't want to be rude.

"Passably, but not as well as me."

"Would they know what *it* means?"

"No."

Her smile's soft as she nods. I squeeze her hand. All four of us walk to the chairs placed around a coffee table. Lina and I take the sofa while the guys fill the armchairs.

"Lina knows I have to be away, and I don't know how long I'll be gone. She needs to go back to Boston tomorrow. She can't avoid Ewan, and she lives with him. I need you with her until I get back."

"I'm sorry you have to do this since I'm certain you had other things to do. But I appreciate it. I'm not scared of my brother. I'm nervous about some of his men. If he tells them about Sean and me, then they'll have plenty to say. He won't let any of them touch me. I'm safe that way. He'll kill anyone who tries. I'm not confident they won't try to fuck with me. I'm not confident he won't fuck with me. My relationship with my brother is tenuous. He's going to see this as the utmost betrayal. It won't go over well, so I might go to a hotel. The best I can hope for is he ignores me like he often does. Sean said you can be discreet and park on the street."

She glances at me before shifting her gaze between my cousins. It's Seamus who answers this time.

"We can. We'll have cars with tinted windows that are just short of being suspicious. We'll park at opposite ends of the block, facing each other. We'll see anyone coming from either direction, and we can get to you quickly if need be."

"I drive or take the T most of the time. I can stay home for a day or two, but then I have appointments next week I need to keep."

I wonder what those are, but I won't pry. Neither will Seamus nor Cormac.

"It would be better if we can drive you, but we can have one car in front and one behind yours. We can ride the subway with you." Cormac offers her a reassuring smile.

Most people don't believe my cousins are the shy ones of the six of us. They have the best manners because of it. We've all had chivalry ingrained in us since birth. It comes naturally to us all by now, but they're the ones who always wrote thank you cards after their birthdays and Christmas without my aunt insisting. Fecking mother's pets.

We all have no problem swearing. We swear like sailors. But the lesson drilled deepest into us was never swear in front of women and children, and never swear to or about family. We all abide by that, even in our heads. We're in our thirties and still believe our parents have telepathy. *They'd just know.* So, none of us risk it.

"I'd like to accept that offer without a second thought, but I will have an impossible time explaining why I'm getting into a vehicle with tinted windows that isn't part of my brother's fleet. Maybe I could meet you at the T station instead. We wouldn't ride, but I could get in the car there. Anything but getting into your car on my brother's block."

Seamus shoots a glance at me before answering. "If that's what you want, we can do that. But one of us will follow you from your brother's place to the station. You will not walk alone."

"I didn't think I would. I went through this the first year I moved down here for college. My grandfather insisted I have a bodyguard with me at all times. I didn't mind the first few weeks because New York can be overwhelming without worrying about which international syndicate might use you for target practice."

That hardly reassures me. She must guess because she leans a little against me before continuing.

"But it got inconvenient when I wanted to do things I didn't want reported to my grandfather. I wanted to be a normal college first year. I became an expert at slipping past them. It's no small wonder national security intrigues me." She grins. "But all of that's to say, I know the protocols and routines."

I watch my cousins as I speak. "I want you to have a burner that has my number, Seamus's, Cormac's, my brothers', and our other cousin Dillan's. Don't use it for anything but to contact Seamus and Cormac or to contact me if there's an emergency."

They nod their agreement, not that I thought they'd say anything otherwise.

"Hang on." She gets up and goes to the bedroom. She's only gone for a minute before she reappears. She's carrying four burners. What the hell?

"Do you always travel with that many?" It shocks me, but it's good to see they're still in their original packaging.

"Yes. And these don't include the one Ewan gave me. I'm not paranoid, but I am cautious since I'm traveling alone. I was coming here to spy on and hack a rival family. It's not like I wanted to leave breadcrumbs for your family to follow."

"But you texted Justin on your regular phone. Texted me on it."

"Because I didn't feel the need for anonymity. It would have made Justin suspicious if I had. He probably would have kicked the door in. I haven't with you because if this is going anywhere, then hiding texts with you is pointless. Everyone will know soon enough."

I hate the word "if." There's no if. It is going somewhere. I just pray it's not straight into the shitter. Will Lina change her mind once she's back in Boston, away from me? When her brother pressures her? When her grandfather has something—plenty—to say?

I glance at my phone to see the time. Fucking hell. I have to go. I can't linger much longer.

"It's time."

I stand and help Lina to her feet as Cormac and Seamus rise too. They say nothing as they move to inspect the suite, ignoring the bedroom where they know Lina and I were. Cormac checks the windows, peering down at the street below. Seamus is patrolling, looking out for anything that could be used as a weapon. Either for or against them. I draw Lina into my embrace. We wrap our arms around each other's waists and stare into each other's eyes.

"*Nounours*, this has been one of the strangest yet happiest days I've ever had. If you change your mind while you're gone, I understand. A lot has happened in the last four hours."

"I was going to say the same thing to you. If you realize this isn't right for you, then tell me. I only want what's best for you." *Me*.

"I know. I feel the same way. If I'm going back to Boston, and you have to come back here, I don't know when we'll see each other next."

"Me neither, but I have access to the jet. My carbon footprint is going to be as big as the Himalayas, but I can tell my conscience to shut the feck up about that."

She grins at me. "I think it's adorable that you won't swear in front of me. I think it's sexy as sin when you do during sex or dirty talk." She lowers her voice to a whisper as though we're conspiring.

"Yeah, well, my parents would rake me over the coals if they found out I swore in front of a woman or a kid. But I definitely am not sharing what we say in private with anyone else."

Her smile broadens. She goes onto her toes to give me a peck. "Be careful, Sean. Whatever this is, just be careful."

I pull her tighter and glide one hand down to her arse. She tilts her head back, and I lean in for a kiss. We linger over it, shifting from tender to passionate to tender again. She presses her cheek to my chest when we pull apart. I know what I have to do, and that man won't be the one who's holding her as though she's the most precious thing in the world. She is.

"I will, *cailín*. There's still so much of the future for us to see."

"Together." Her voice is soft as though she doesn't want me to hear the note of uncertainty. It's almost as though she's asking a question.

"I hope so. It's what I want, Lina. At the very least, I want to try. I know this is moving at warp speed for you but having a few weeks to think about you and spending a few hours with you is equivalent to months and years in my world."

"I get it. This isn't the first time someone's explained it to me that way. I like your decisiveness. I don't have to guess where you stand. It's refreshing. It means I can be myself, which is often painfully blunt. I don't have to hide behind what I want and reveal it slowly in fear of scaring you off."

"I don't know that I'll be able to call or text you while I'm gone. I may not have my phone on. If you need anything, contact Finn or my cousins. They'll know how to get in touch with me."

"I know how this works, Sean. The mob is all I've ever known. I told you. I know the protocols and routines. Trust that I'm in excellent hands with Seamus and Cormac. I know, at the very least, they would never want to disappoint you. Your bond is so strong and present that it could be the fifth person in the room."

I don't want to let go, so instead, I swoop in for one more kiss. Then I force myself to let go. I glance at her before I walk to the door. Cormac and Seamus follow me, but I watch Lina.

"*Níl a fhios agam go maithfidh sí dom. Ní féidir liom a rá léi go bhfuilim ag dul go Dún na Séad anocht chun spiaireacht a dhéanamh ar Ewan. Tá mé fós buartha faoi cad a dhéanfaidh sé nuair a thiocfaidh sí abhaile amárach. B'fhéidir go mbeinn ar ais faoin am sin, nó b'fhéidir go mbeidh mé in áit éigin eile. Ba mhaith liom go bhféadfainn a mhíniú cén fáth a bhfuil an chuid seo á cheilt agam.*" I don't know that she'll forgive me. I can't tell her I'm headed to Baltimore tonight to spy on Ewan. I'm still worried about what he'll do when she gets home tomorrow. I might be back by then, or I might end up somewhere else. I wish I could explain why I'm hiding this part.

Cormac shakes his head. "*Is é an chúis le bréag a fhágáil ar lár ná í a choinneáil slán. Ag insint di defeats go.*" The reason to lie by omission is to keep her safe. Telling her defeats that.

Seamus is a bit more sympathetic. "*Ní hionann sin is a rá go mbeidh sé níos fusa bréagadh a dhéanamh nó seans go maithfidh sí agus go ndéanfaidh sí dearmad nuair a fhaigheann sí amach.*" That doesn't mean it makes it any easier to lie or any more likely she'll forgive and forget once she finds out.

I'm looking at them when I really want to watch Lina. She

turned on the TV, probably to drown us out. A courtesy. I know her father and uncle didn't, and Ewan doesn't speak Gaelic. Jean-Peter's pretty proficient, but not enough to have taught his granddaughter to be fluent. I doubt Barnard offers Irish Gaelic in its Modern Languages department, and it wasn't one offered at Georgetown. But who knows? She could have learned it from YouTube. She's being polite.

My cousins and I continue in Irish. "Protect her. She's special."

Seamus smothers a snort that comes out sounding more like a cough. Cormac rolls his eyes. I glare at them.

"You know we will. And it's obvious how you feel about each other." Cormac shifts to glance back at Lina before returning his gaze to me. "What if we find out something about her you won't like?"

I've thought about that already, and it feels like a bear claw is reaching into my gut and pulling my stomach out through my belly button.

"I know it's a possibility. I pray there's nothing, and if there is, it's reasonable and explicable if she's given a chance. I don't want to imagine she's playing me for a fool."

Seamus shrugs. "It's more likely we'd discover something she doesn't even know. If she were truly in the thick of this shite, we would have heard about her before."

I'd like to think that's the reason.

"Okay. I gotta go." I look between them to Lina. I can't call her *cailín* in front of my cousins. They know what it means, and I'm certain they've heard Dillan and Finn call their wives that. I'm not ready to share that much. They'd recognize any other Irish terms of endearment.

"*Je reviendrai dès que possible, ma choupette.*" I'll be back as soon as I can, my sweetheart.

My cousins will understand the first part, but I doubt

they'll know what *choupette* means. It can be darling or sweetheart. I've even heard someone use it to mean baby, but not like an infant. If she knows that, then she'll know it's as close to little girl as I dare come without my cousins understanding.

"*Je serai prête, nounours.*" I'll be ready, teddy.

Chapter Ten

Sean

I hated leaving Lina behind this afternoon. Yeah, I would have loved to have sex several more times before dawn. But I wanted to talk too, and not about why Ewan sent her or the encryption I still haven't cracked. I like how she texts me questions. I like that she's curious about me. I like that she's letting me get to know her too. It would have been preferable to do that side by side or looking at each other.

Now, I'm on the family jet to Baltimore to observe Ewan. I'm certain Lina doesn't know he's outside New York. I didn't know until Finn called. A CI there called to tell him about Ewan. My brother could have gone, but no one expects him to go out of town right now.

He's a newlywed. So's Dillan. Ally felt horrible that Dillan intended to go on Finn's and her honeymoon. Not because it was someone joining them. They had five other someones joining them. She didn't want him to leave Mair behind. It was my cousin-in-law who convinced my sister-in-law that it's best to have all of us to guard the most vulnerable.

I look out the window, but there're only clouds to see. White puffy, peaceful looking clouds. I used to think heaven was just above these clouds. I didn't have an explanation for where heaven went when it wasn't cloudy. But when I was five, it made sense.

I spend this time thinking about what I know so far about Ewan's trip to Baltimore. He came down here to sell some product. You have to pass New York to get to Baltimore from Boston. He's a long way from home to sell drugs. What he's off-loading isn't going to street hustles. This is headed to Germany. They have one of the largest medical marijuana markets in the world. But this isn't the stuff meant to alleviate chronic pain or nausea during chemo. This is recreational. Now that possession is legal in Germany, that market's expanded too.

Ewan wants in. He wants to bump us out to make room for himself. He's tallying up a long list of sins he's going to have to account for. It won't be St. Peter at the gates of heaven. It's about to be St. Dillan at the gates of hell. Actually, if he doesn't get shot before we can get him to the Bronx, we'll take him to our abandoned railway station where we handle the unsavory—messy—side of this world.

If anyone told me to spy on Ewan three days ago, I would have happily put a bullet in him for convenience's sake. It's not so simple now. I didn't pull the trigger that killed Rowan. Finn didn't either. But Finn arranged for someone to carry out the hit on Lina's dad. Our hands are more dusty than dirty, but we're eyeballs deep in the shite. I don't want to be the one who puts a bullet through Ewan's skull. For being such a douche to his sister when he should protect her—value her—I should put it through his heart. Problem is, it would pass through an empty space.

The landing's smooth, so I look at Shane. The guy's out. He's practically snoring. It must have been a late night at one of his clubs. We're all silent investors in every BDSM club worth mentioning in the tri-state area. It pays to be kept off the letterhead but to have access to the member list. We know where everyone worth paying attention goes to spank or be spanked.

If we didn't hate each other, we'd probably all be friends. The other men in the syndicates aren't that different from one another. Our work is identical, and the men we become to do that work are the same. We have the exact same values, which means our family and organization come before and above everything else.

It also means we share similar proclivities. We are men who crave control because that's the key to staying alive. BDSM ensures we have it constructively. The submission offered to us isn't coerced through fear and pain—the kind that leads to death. Perhaps it's our redemption of some sort. All the things we do outside the clubs are evil. When we do some of it with consenting partners, we remind ourselves we aren't always monsters.

"Wake up, sunshine." I shake Shane's shoulder as I walk past to get my bag.

"Five more minutes, Mom." Shane grumbles as he straightens from his slumped position.

John, Luke, Nate, and Peter are with us. They're the same guys who went on the mission with Finn that clued us in to the O'Malleys' recent activities. They're among the best guys we have. Peter's the senior most of the four, and I can't stand him outside of work. But he's good at what he does, so I respect and trust him. He bitches about *everything*. The good thing about jobs like this is none of us talks much.

I sign off on the fake manifest and records before going to the hold where the other guys are gathering our weapons.

There're two SUVs waiting for us. Kelly—a man's name in Ireland for centuries—waits next to the lead vehicle. He's our CI. He'll ride with Shane and me to brief us. The other guys will follow. They're on a need to know, so they won't know anything we don't need them to.

Shane and I load our personal luggage, tactical gear, and bags of weapons in the trunk before we climb in. Kelly's driving. I take the front passenger seat, and Shane climbs into the middle seat in the second row. Both SUVs have burlap sacks with the stuff we'll use to replace the weed we steal.

"He'll be at a warehouse north of downtown, but he'll have to go to Locust Point if he wants to see the cargo off." Kelly starts the engine.

I know exactly where he's talking about. It's an industrial area that hasn't been fully gentrified yet. There's still industry there, but residential neighborhoods keep creeping closer. Baltimore's running out of good places to hide in plain sight. Locust Point has water access that Ewan can use to smuggle the shipment out to larger freight ships just past the harbor. I know all of this because I've been to both places plenty of times. He'll have to cross the city to get from the industrial park to Locust Point. Plenty of room for us to operate.

The cargo will be in a truck since there's way too much to pack into a car, SUV, or van. This is a big haul. It's like we found where our parents hid the Christmas presents. We're going to shake a few boxes, maybe open them a little. If we like what we find, we're going to play with them before slipping something back into the box. Unlike our parents, the O'Malleys will be clueless.

One year, Shane and I discovered our parents got us new bikes. They hid them in a storage room in our basement they assumed we had no reason to go in. The house we grew up in is enormous, even by most mansion standards. It's eight bedrooms in the main house with a three-bedroom pool house. Yeah, there were only three sons living there, but between two other couples, there were four more kids.

Dillan's sister, Colleen, had her own room. It's not a shrine to her, but no one in our immediate family stays in that room. My parents only use it when they have enough guests that they need it—usually Christmas and Easter. My aunts and uncles' homes are like that too. Big enough for everyone with open-door policies. They're just not open-fridge anymore.

I glance over at Kelly before going back to looking out the window. "When'd he get in?"

"This morning around ten."

Motherfucker. This is why Lina flew commercial. She might have wanted to blend in, but it was because her shitbag brother used their jet to fly down here. He made sure she was already in NYC before he touched down. I left her at the hotel today, but she won't get back until midmorning tomorrow. He'll make sure he slithers into his place with time to spare. I fucking hate him.

Shane leans forward between the front seats. "Who's he seen so far?"

"He went straight to Ellie's."

Ellie Muñez. They were together through high school and college. Her dad's around the same age as mine, so about fifteen years older than Rowan was. Rowan's mom used to babysit Scott Muñez, so he's known the family for decades. Rowan's dad, Desmond, welcomed him into the fold as a messenger boy in middle school. Scott's worked for the O'Malleys ever since. When his wife got sick, they moved closer to her family twelve years ago. It was touch and go, but she recovered. They went back to Boston, but Ellie stayed.

"Isn't she married now?" Disgust drips from Shane's words. Kelly just glances at him through the rearview mirror.

"How long was he there?" I want to get an accurate timeline.

"A little over two hours. But they just talked this time."

"About?" We've had her place bugged for years since he sees her any chance he gets.

He should have married her while he had the chance, but his ambition kept her as a side piece. She wouldn't have him, anyway. She loves him, but she doesn't want the life that comes with him.

"Ewan's sister. I guess she's living with him now. Sounds like he conned her into moving down there. Told her she would work purely behind the scenes. No one would know she was working for him. I guess she's got computer programming skills that make you and your brother look like you still have training wheels."

He isn't wrong about that. Fucking encryption situation got a shite ton more complicated now that Lina and I are— involved.

"Did that change?"

"Yeah. He told Ellie about how he sent her to New York today. He admitted he didn't tell Nikki he's here. That's her name. He plans to be back before she returns later tomorrow. His best friend's going to cover for him if he's late."

Colton Flaherty.

Douchebag.

"He said Colt could calm Nikki down if she lost her shit. I guess they were engaged."

My heart's still beating even though it feels like every ounce of blood just drained onto the floor. I don't need to look back to know Shane's watching me. It's unreasonable for me to expect Lina to have told me about her past relationships in the space of one day. We had plenty of other intense topics to cover.

"I never knew he was. Must have been a while ago." I try for nonchalant.

"Yeah. I got the impression it was probably like four or five years ago. From the way Ellie reacted, it didn't end well. I guess Colt used her because he wanted a better position, and Rowan wanted someone to keep Nikki out of his way. Ellie was talking about how lucky Nikki was that it ended since it didn't matter now that Rowan's dead. Ewan told her Colt can still get Nikki to do whatever he wants. I guess he's got a Magic Mike dick."

My hand closer to the door clenches. I don't want to know about a man she once loved. I don't want to know about a man she once slept with. I don't want to know about the man who fucked her like a stripper performing. I don't know if she'll take him up on an offer. I might puke.

I shouldn't care this much. I have no claim over her. We talked about wanting to see if this can go somewhere. She knows my goal is permanent, and she was okay with that. That makes me think she wouldn't screw someone else. But it's not like we're in an actual relationship.

Shane leans farther forward to rest his elbows on his knees. It makes it easy for his right hand to touch the inside of my left elbow, which is digging into the center console. I look out the passenger window while my brother takes up the questioning. Kelly's a good informant, but he doesn't need to know about my private life, which he'll figure out if I ask anything else about Lina.

"Did Ewan say anything about what's going on here?"

"Yeah. Schlossberg is meeting him at eight for the second installment payment and to check the merchandise. They'll meet in the morning once Schlossberg has confirmation every-thing made it aboard his ship. Ewan'll get the last installment then."

I look at my watch. Half an hour. It's going to be rushed. I shouldn't have taken so long to say goodbye to Lina. I don't regret taking my time, but it's going to inconvenience the others. It gets cramped changing into tactical gear inside an SUV. It'll be annoying enough with only three of us. There are four in the other SUV. Shane'll go in the trunk. I'll move into the third row, and Kelly'll climb into the second row. The other guys'll sort it out, but it'll be tight.

I keep looking out the window as we approach an aban-doned power generating station. It's five minutes away from an industrial complex, so it's a good place to park while we change. I still have nothing to say after finding out about Lina's former fiancé. If I don't act surprised—assuming she tells me—she'll want to know how I found out. I'll lie. This is shit I shouldn't have to keep from her. But I can't tell her a CI told me. I can't even say a friend told me because she'd want a name and how they knew.

I climb over the back of the second-row seats once Shane's in the trunk. He hands me a bag that I pass to Kelly, who followed me into the second-row. Shane cocks an eyebrow I can barely see since it's so dark in this area. We're parked where streetlights filter in, but not close enough for other people to notice. The left side of my mouth draws in. A half frown. Nothing I can do about it now.

"We're good to go." Nate's voice flows through the earpieces we now wear.

We'll talk as little as possible. The other guys' Gaelic is just good enough for us to give curt commands and answers if we can't avoid speaking. No one from the other families has both-ered to learn Irish Gaelic. We all speak fluent Spanish. We're

New Yorkers, so we'd be knowledgeable of Spanish and Yiddish, regardless. It wasn't eyebrow raising when we learned it in school.

We speak *way* more Russian and Italian than the Kutsenkos or Mancinellis realize. Anyone in my family who isn't proficient in one is proficient in the other. Seamus and I can read Cyrillic well enough to figure out most stuff. We're not the potato eating, steel pipe to the kneecaps, dock working Irish the other families think we are. We all know where we went to college and grad school. We know how many of us went to Ivy Leagues and top tiers.

Hell, Finn was in Niko Kutsenko's year at NYU. They had classes together. Matteo was at Cornell, studying architecture at the same time as me. He's three years older than me, so he was a senior when I was a freshman. Riley O'Malley was Matteo's roommate. There was a sizable age gap between Rowan and his younger siblings Riley and Cady.

"Ready here, too." I answer Nate as I pull my beanie over my ears. With our red hair, Shane and I have to cover it if we want any anonymity or element of surprise. It's a fucking beacon otherwise.

Kelly pulls out of the lot and gets back on the road. It's seven-fifty, so we're cutting it close to be in position. Both cars' lights flip off before the last turn. Kelly weaves us through the buildings until we get to the middle of the set of four warehouses. We coast to a stop after he makes a tight U-turn, so we're facing out. He shifts into park quickly to keep the taillights on as briefly as he can. That's why he let the car come to a natural stop. He didn't want the brake lights beaming for anyone to see. Peter pulls up alongside us. The man drives like he's at a monster truck rally when he has to.

We make sure the dome lights are off before anyone opens a door. In near silence, we pull our weapons out and check them. I have a pistol strapped to my right thigh and another holstered on my left hip. I'm like a fucked-up version of a cowboy gunslinger. I also have a rifle with its sling across my chest. I have knives in my pants pockets, my left boot, and on the web belt that has ammunition pouches attached to it.

We all triple check our phones to be sure they're off. We never have the GPS services on unless we absolutely need directions. We screenshot, then turn it back off. No one needs to know where we are. Those who do are already here. We just don't need anything ringing or buzzing.

While Kelly stays behind to guard the vehicles—truly the most important job in any operation—we creep forward until we arrive at a cluster of freight containers. The kind that goes on a ship, not a train. Not what should be here. Luke steps forward with the bolt cutters. We turn our backs to the doors and raise our rifles. Noise is inevitable, so we're prepared. There's a rattle, but it's not as bad as I expected. This isn't where the drugs are, but we still need to know what's at a site the O'Malleys chose. Luke swings the right door open. Empty.

Was the lock on it to keep homeless people or animals out? We shine our flashlights into it. The interior doesn't seem wide enough to match the exterior size. Filled with boxes or crates, it wouldn't be so noticeable. I step inside, flicking my wrist to move my flashlight over all the surfaces. Something catches my eye when my beam hits a black space. The rest of the container is reflecting the light from the metal siding.

I inch closer until I can point the flashlight into the nook. It's barely wider than the width of my palm, but I spotted it. I pull on the siding, making the hole larger. Interesting.

I turn toward the door and flicker my flashlight three times. Shane knows that means to approach. Luke's brother, John, comes with him. I point the light into the hole again. I reach inside and grasp the first bundle I touch. As I pull my arm out, Shane whispers what I'm wondering.

"Real or counterfeit?"

"I can't tell yet." I put the end of my flashlight—which I disinfect after every use and keep in a case—between my teeth as I thumb the stack of bills I'm holding.

There're hundred-euro bills flapping in the air. It's a full strap, so ten-thousand. I reach into the hole again and start pulling out more. I hand the euros to Shane and the yen to John. I pull out ten straps of euros, which makes a bundle. We squat, so I can stack the money as I grab it. When I lean as far in as I can to get a better look, there have to be at least five bundles worth of just euros. I gather more stacks of yen, adding pounds sterling, rupees, pesos, and rubles.

I pull a ruble loose, and Shane and John shine their lights on it from behind when I raise it between us. I shine my light from the front. I can't be certain beyond a reasonable doubt because of the shite lighting, but it looks real. I repeat the same thing, pulling a bill from the center of the strap. Fake. I do this over again with the euros, and it's the same thing. The tops and bottoms are real, but the centers are fake.

"*Am*." Time.

Peter's voice fills my ear. We have nothing to carry the bills in right now, and we'll move away from the container and vehicles. We can come back for it later. My brother and friend toss the money back in after I've dropped mine into the hole. I push the siding back to roughly where it was. We hurry but remain light on our feet, not wanting our footsteps to echo.

As I step out, I hear a car roll over a pothole. I know where it is. Luke pulls a padlock from one of his pouches. He shuts the door and fastens our lock through the holes. If we don't make it over here before someone else, they'll need bolt cutters like we did.

With our rifles slung across our backs and at least one pistol in hand—safety off, silencer on—we fan out enough to move through the shadows. The vehicle's a Mercedes G Wagon. It comes to a stop, and a man gets out of the front passenger side. We all know the type. We've all been the type. Big, dressed in black, and intimidating. I'm certain this is Schlossberg's car. A German in a German car. Both are completely reliable. I glance at my watch. It's exactly eight o'clock.

When we're within three hundred feet, we wait. It's only a couple minutes later that a Cadillac Escalade pulls up and circles around to face the Mercedes. I slide one strap of the backpack I'm wearing off my shoulder. I ease the zipper open and retrieve the parabolic microphone and headphones. I flip the switch and point it toward the conversation I'm about to fully eavesdrop on. I put the left padded side to my ear and hold the headphones like I'm some music exec in a cheesy movie.

"Mr. O'Malley." A heavy German accent flows into my ear.

"Mr. Schlossberg. Thank you for meeting me here."

"Not exactly the Michelin star restaurants where I usually conduct business. But that's because you're hiding."

"And you're right here with me." Testy. Testy.

"I'm not the one worried about being found."

"You should be, Schlossberg. The O'Rourkes might want my head on a pike, but you'll get drawn and quartered right alongside me if they find out you're part of this deal."

"Then let's skip the pleasantries."

Ewan raises his hand in the air, and a truck drives forward. I glance over at Shane, who has his NVGs on like the rest of the men. They're difficult to wear while using the headphones, so I can't see as clearly as they can. I still see plenty. While no one's talking or moving between the Boston Irish and the German delegations, Shane pulls his own backpack around to reach inside. He pulls out a camera with a high-speed telephoto lens. He silently snaps photos while Nate holds up his phone to record whatever it can see. There will be no refuting the evidence since I'm also recording the audio.

"Here you go."

Ewan unlocks the roll top door and pushes up to reveal the entire truck is filled with what looks like brand new sofas still covered in clear wrap. He hoists himself into the truck and pulls a knife. He cuts a slit in the wrapping of the sofa closest to the door. He tugs out the seat cushion, then unzips the back. Holding both edges of the fabric, he tips it upside down, allowing a cascade of marijuana bricks to land in front of Schlossberg.

It's Schlossberg's turn to pull out a knife. We're a regular ol' Boy Scout den. Always prepared. He sticks his blade into the package, wiggling it enough to get it in without ripping the cling wrap open. He pulls out the knife and uses his thumb and forefinger to pinch some of the contents. He brings it to his nose as he rubs the pads of his fingers together. He signals one of his own men to come forward.

The guy pulls out his phone and taps the screen a couple times. He steps closer, practically shoulder checking Ewan out of the way. He puts his phone on the edge of the truck bed along with a testing gadget before he takes the brick of marijuana from Schlossberg. I know what he's doing without needing my NVGs or a zoom lens. He's going to test the THC, CBD, and CBN. He draws his own sample from the open package using tweezers. He puts the flowers in the gadget and starts the analysis through the app on his phone. It's going to take three to five minutes to get the results.

This is the tedious part. It's not like you're friends with your buyer. You're not chatting about the weather or where you're spending the Fourth of July. You're not reminiscing about bygone days. You're trying to tell if they're going to screw you over more than you intend to screw them over. You're making sure none of your men get trigger-happy. That always makes for a bad night.

Our guys, Shane, and I remain still as the minutes drag. These exchanges are never as exciting as the movies make them seem. At least we have these commercial tests now. It's not like in the olden days where your tester had to smoke a joint to tell how good the stuff was.

My mic catches a soft ping, and the German quality assurance officer picks up his phone. His finger slides up and down the screen before he gives a decisive nod and hands the phone to his superior. Schlossberg appears satisfied because he waves another guy over. He accepts the envelope his guard hands him and opens it for Ewan to see.

Ewan doesn't hesitate to pull the bills out and flip through them. He does exactly the same thing I did when I examined the money I found. He doesn't go through every bill, but he goes through plenty.

For fuck's sake, hurry the fuck up. It's not like it matters at this point. You're going to be giving it back in the morning. There's no way Herr Schlossberg will let you keep a single speck of it once the pot doesn't show up. With his German efficiency, the money'll be back in his Swiss account before you can say eins, zwei, drei.

One, two, three. He'll snatch that money back from Ewan so fast it'll give the shit bird whiplash.

Ewan holds on to the envelope while his truck driver pulls the door shut and locks it. As though they're saying a lingering goodbye—no air kisses, though—neither turns their back on the other. The truck takes off, and the men fill their respective SUVs. Then they're pulling away in opposite directions. None of us makes a peep for three minutes. That's when I can no longer hear anything at all.

"We need to be fast. Nate, get the padlock undone. Luke, John, grab the gear bags from the vehicles. Peter gets the spotlights set up." I'm putting my equipment away as I speak.

We travel with solar powered, portable work site lights. We don't do everything in the dark. The guys hurry to do their tasks while Shane and I stand together. We whisper to each other. Shane looks in the direction Schlossberg's envoy drove as he speaks.

"Are you prepared to save him when Schlossberg goes after his arse in the morning? You can't let your girlfriend's brother die."

"We see how it plays out. It would have been better if this happened a month ago. Then I wouldn't have to keep his dumb arse alive. It would have been so fucking convenient."

"Do we let Schlossberg rough him up?"

"Within reason. We can't go in and save him, though. We'll have to find a way to have Schlossberg call off his *Wachhunde*." Guard dogs.

The guys have the shipping container open, and the lights set up. Peter hands me a crowbar, and I go to the spot I found the hidden stash. I pry back the metal before stepping away. Luke and John take my place and toss the various currency bundles into the bags. Finn will go through everything and decide what to do with the counterfeit—who to sell it to—and which accounts to hide the legit money in.

Shane and I search throughout the container, going in opposite directions. We find a couple more suspicious nooks and crannies, but they're all empty. We're all wearing gloves, so no need to wipe anything down. We leave the siding pulled away from the walls and the door hanging open.

It's not long before we're on the road and catching up to Ewan's truck. As we expected, it has no escort. A couple quick maneuvers, and we have it boxed in and forced onto the shoulder of the road. We all have balaclavas on now. Not that the driver or the guy riding shotgun will talk. They won't breathe. We work in silence, even with Kelly along who's never done this type of job with us. We work fast, going through every sofa, carefully extracting one cushion at a time—seats and backrests.

Nate and Peter set up a workstation with two TV tray tables while Shane and I help the other guys carry burlap sacks full of oregano to them. They get the wrapping open, then pour out the contents into empty sacks. Luke and John help them funnel the oregano into the original packaging while Shane, Kelly, and I haul the sacks to the SUV we arrived in. We aren't worried about the weight of the bricks we leave behind, so some packages look deflated.

The ones that look the worst get hidden in the far back sofas. The entire operation takes nearly four hours, but then it's done. It takes precision, which takes time. Peter's the new truck driver with Luke riding shotgun. Kelly pulls into the lead vehicle position and stays there until we're three blocks from the harbor. We hang back, trusting everything will be fine while Peter and Luke get everything offloaded.

This part feels like an eternity even though it's only another two hours. We still have our earpieces in, so we can hear what's happening. But if shite goes sideways, we can't get to them in time to save them. I breathe a sigh of relief when it's done. We meet up with Kelly's dad and brother. The three of them deal with the vehicles once they drop us off near the back entrance to our motel. Nothing flashy because we don't need anyone noticing we're in town.

"We roll out in three hours." Shane waits for my agreement.

"Don't oversleep this time."

"That was seven years ago, and I had the fecking flu which you gave me."

"But I still arrived on time at the airport." I grin at him as he flicks me off.

I head into my room and take a quick shower. It's just after five a.m. I'm about to fall asleep when my phone buzzes. What the fucking hell now?

Chapter Eleven

Lina

I brace myself as I slide my key into the front door.

Silence greets me, but I know Ewan's home because the light's on in his office. It's gray and dismal today, and it matches my mood. I didn't sleep well last night. I couldn't figure out why for a couple hours. I didn't fear for Sean because he radiates capability and a self-assuredness few people would test. It didn't scare me to come back here. There was smidge of dread, but that wasn't what woke me, then kept waking me up. I realized it was I missed Sean being in bed beside me.

We didn't even spend a night together, and we didn't exactly sleep when we shared the hotel bed. Despite that, I felt so much better in his arms than I ever have on my own or with someone else. My mom would protect me to her last breath. God help anyone who came near me while she was close. But she wouldn't be able to put up the same fight Sean could. She doesn't exude the same menace I know Sean can. I've never felt so safe or sheltered as I did in his arms.

It's not like my life is some great hardship, and it's not like I'm caught in some war zone with bullets flying. I'm a mob princess more than anything else. I fucking hate that term. I'm a mob daughter, but considering the advantages I've grown up with, I get why some would call me the former. But I've also lived with danger surrounding me since birth. Women and children are off limits, but that doesn't mean they couldn't catch us in the crossfire. It doesn't mean it hasn't been dangerous when I was close to Dad or Granddad. It definitely doesn't mean I'm safe when I'm within a hundred miles of Ewan.

I glance back over my shoulder and dip my chin as I look to my left. I know Seamus is in the car where he dropped me off. Cormac is already in position at the other end of the block. Seamus will circle around and park farther down the road but where the house is still in clear view. They'll both be within sprinting distance.

I close the door behind me with the softest click.

"Nikki!"

Fuck me.

"Hey."

"Get in here. Now."

I know his mother. I know he has manners. He generally chooses not to use them. He thinks it intimidates people. It proves he's an a-hole. The O'Rourke men have manners, and they'd scare the shit out of Satan.

I keep cutting my brother a shit ton of slack since he's still new to his role. Dad groomed him for ages, but our father wasn't in charge that long. Only as long as Dillan, so nearly five years. His father hung on by sheer tenacity. My paternal grandfather hadn't been well for several years, so Dad took over running most of the day-to-day stuff, but Grandpa—when he acknowledged me long enough to let me call him that—was still the figurehead. When he finally gave up the ghost—hallelujah —Dad became the skipper. Stupid title.

Dad's men barely finished swearing their allegiance before Ewan was plotting his mutiny. He never told me that in so many words, but I sensed it. His disgust toward Dad grew hourly. I don't know that he would have ever pulled the trigger —literally or figuratively—but Dad tempted him. I don't know what I would have done if Ewan had.

I haven't grieved my father's death. Not because I'm in denial. Not because I'm repressing my emotions. I simply don't have them. By the time the O'Rourkes killed him, he was a man I knew. Disliking him took too much energy I didn't want to spend on him. At times, I have flashes of guilt that I should feel more. That I'm no better than the real mobsters in my family if I don't bat an eye knowing he's gone. Ewan's put on a show of his rage toward the O'Rourkes for doing the dirty work for him, but that's not why he's fucking them over.

He wants to prove his dick's bigger, so he can piss farther. Not exactly the best analogy to describe a brother, but that's what it boils down to.

"Hello to you, too." I cock an eyebrow as I stand in the doorway. It doesn't thrill me to see Ewan's best friend, Colton Flaherty, chilling in Ewan's office with him. We have history.

"Hey, Nik."

"Hi." I can be gracious to Colt. Kinda.

"Fucking Sean O'Rourke."

I don't think Ewan's using that as an adjective.

I say nothing. It was a statement to which I have no response. If it were a question, then I might answer. My silence pisses Ewan off, and I kinda like it. I resent him sending me to New York in the first place. I resent being sucked into shit I was supposed to be left out of. I was anonymous behind a keyboard and the firewalls I built. For all our dad's disregard, at least it meant I wasn't in the middle of what they all like to claim is men's business. But when it suits them, they have no problem sucking in women to do the intellectual work for them. Not shocking. Just annoying.

"Did you get anything out of him?" Ewan's gaze bores into me.

Grunts. Groans. Orgasms. Cum. Yeah. I got something out of him.

"We talked." Among other things. "But not about work. It would have been suspicious if I jumped straight into grilling him about his family's wealth and their plans to dick us over now that we've dicked them over and intend to keep doing it."

"You slept with him to get nothing but your rocks off. You could have stayed home if you'd wanted to bang that badly and saved me the flight and hotel."

I fight to keep my composure and not find something to hurl at his head. He's not just speaking figuratively. He's rubbing the past in my face. I refuse to look at Colt.

"Don't send me on any more field trips, then."

"Or maybe you need a chaperone." Ewan smirks.

"Kinda like you need me to be yours, so you don't lose every motherfucking penny this family has?"

I probably shouldn't have said that.

He pushes back his chair and stands. I can see from the corner of my eye that Colt is ready to intervene if he has to. I don't need nor want his help. It comes with too high a cost.

"Just so you remember, big brother, you need me a fuck ton more than I need you."

I turn around and walk out. I hear him calling me, but I don't stop. I gather my stuff and head to the stairs.

"Colt, don't bother. Leave me alone." I don't look at him as I reach the bottom one. He slides in front of me.

"Why do you have to antagonize him?"

"Why not? It's as easy as breathing these days."

"Don't be like that, Nikki."

"Be like what? Pissed he's using me. Pissed he endangered me for nothing. Pissed this is a waste of time. Pissed he made me give up a career I loved and was good at to serve as his show pony in front of his friends and his workhorse behind closed doors. Nishida's more likely to fuck us over than actually make good on any promise. I didn't need to meet the head of Tokyo's deadliest *yakuza* in New York City of all places. Who knows how many people would love to see that man dead? While he and his men probably have Kevlar under their suits, there I was, walking around unprotected."

"You know Justin went with you."

"That wasn't a fun surprise. Even if he'd been beside me, what good would that have done against a sniper? It's not like someone's going to walk up and pop Nishida point blank."

"Ewan said you cancelled your meeting with Pablo."

"I did. I wasn't in the mood to risk my life a second time in one day. Not when the entire point of the meeting was for me to make nice and kiss the ring. Dad fucked up the deal with the Diazes and left Ewan to clean up the mess. He only made it worse. I'm not groveling to a family because my father and brother screwed us all over because they couldn't play in their own backyard. Ewan set up those meetings. If anyone was watching, seeing me with the *oyabun* before lunch and the—I don't even know how many ranks and positions Pablo has. *El secretario, el patron, el capo*. No, not that one. That's too low on the list. *El tigre*."

"How do you know all those ranks?"

"Because I know how to use the internet."

The secretary is usually the right-hand man if it's not an actual female secretary. Enrique Diaz, the *jefe de jefes*—the boss of bosses, not just in the U.S. but *everywhere*—doesn't have any kids. His oldest nephew, Pablo, is his heir. Enrique has four other nephews who make up their *corredor* or *Junta Directiva*— Board of Directors. A *capo* is a captain, but Pablo's definitely a step above his cousins. They're all *capos* now. They moved up from *lugarteniente*. Lieutenants.

Pablo's a tiger—*el tigre*—because he's a general. But not just any general. No. He deserves the title *el patron* just like his uncle and father did before they rose to the top. While Enrique oversees all of New York—all of America, really—Pablo runs NYC at its operational level. The Colombians in Colombia— Enrique's cousins—aren't as fully in agreement that he's the *jefe de jefes*, especially since he lives in the U.S.

But it doesn't take much observation to know Enrique pulls all the strings everywhere. Forget kings, and presidents, and dictators, and religious leaders. Enrique Diaz is one of *the* most powerful men in the world. Nothing comes in or out of Latin America without him knowing. One frown shuts down an entire syndicate's operations. Permanently.

Cartels are a risk to national security, so it's no small wonder I know so much about their structure. A few google searches, and I could piece together which Diaz name goes with which position. That's why I wasn't jumping for joy at the prospect of meeting Pablo, especially since I'm pretty goddamn sure they had me followed and already knew I met with Nishida. They probably found out I had lunch with Sean before I even got into the car with him. Once those two things happened, I knew I had to cancel.

"Don't be snide. It's not attractive."

"Neither is a black eye. Move." I couldn't give a flying fuck if Colt thinks I'm attractive. He obliterated that concern years ago.

He steps aside, and I head up to my room. I shut and lock my door. I don't really believe Ewan or Colt would try to come in here without my permission, but I'm not in the mood to test that theory.

ME

> I know you may not get this anytime soon and your cousins probably already told you. But I wanted you to know I got home safely.

I lock my phone and toss it onto my bed before bending over to open my bag. My phone buzzes, so I reach for it while pulling out the first piece of dirty clothes.

SEAN

> I'm glad. Thank you for texting me. Cor told me but I like seeing your name on my screen.

ME

> I didn't think you'd be able to talk.

SEAN

> Only for a bit. You caught me at a quiet moment.

I want to know where he is and what he's doing. I want to know that because I'm worried about him. But I can't ask. I can't ask because it's not my place. I can't ask because it's not my business. I can't ask, so I have nothing to tell Ewan. I can't ask because I don't want Sean to think I'm trying to get info out of him now that we're—whatever the hell we are.

ME

> What was your favorite subject when you were a kid?

Sean Recess

He didn't even have to think about that. I like how he humors me and my rounds of twenty questions.

SEAN

You?

ME

PE

SEAN

Kickball?

ME

Absolutely. Grand slam queen here.

I loved playing kickball. Basically, the rules of baseball with a ball that's not whirling through the air toward my head. I have great eye-foot coordination. I could kick hard and run fast. I was usually the last kicker because I could get a home run by kicking it far enough and running fast enough to make it around all three bases before anyone caught me. When there were people already on all the bases before I kicked, I would chase them all the way to home base. And voilà—a grand slam.

I should see if there are any adult leagues nearby.

SEAN

Least favorite subject

ME

I didn't really have one. I didn't enjoy chemistry, but that was because I was sick the week they taught nomenclature. I never fully got it so the rest of the year was fake it till you make it. That got me through finals. Barely.

SEAN

That was me with vectors in calculus. Shane and I were both out after tonsillectomies when they introduced it. Finn had to teach us. Lucky for him neither of us could talk so neither of us could complain about how boring it was. He wasn't any good at it. No patience.

Can I ask more about that? Before we discovered each other's family connections, it would have been fine. I wouldn't have thought twice about it. But now? Will he think I have an ulterior motive? Or will he understand I just want to get to know him like I did before I knew he's an O'Rourke, and he knew I'm an O'Malley *and* Tremblay? FML. This isn't the first time I've thought that.

ME

Are you the younger twin?

SEAN

Yeah. By three minutes. Three glorious, spacious, quiet minutes. Then I got bored.

I send him the sideways crying-laughing emoji.

ME

You and your brother got tonsillitis at the same time?

Sean

That was entirely coincidental. We didn't catch or develop all the same illnesses. He got swimmer's ear every summer. I had braces for six months longer than him. The braces were the only time it was easy for people outside our family to always tell us apart.

ME

Are you really that identical?

SEAN

Yes. Down to our mannerisms and voice. People say we sound exactly the same. Everyone in our family can tell us apart. My mom always knew I was the one getting in trouble despite how we'd both deny it.

ME

Was it ever strange knowing it's so rare to have a mirror image of yourself? Or is that you've just known nothing else so you don't think about it much?

SEAN

It's only strange when I think about it in the sense that most people don't have a mirror image of themselves.

ME

Was it hard for your older brother since you and Shane always had each other?

SEAN

Yeah probably sometimes. Our parents are adamant Shane and I are two separate people with two separate identities. So in some ways we're just three typical brothers. I feel as emotionally connected to Finn as I do Shane. But Shane and I are basically still molecularly connected. I can't explain it. We have our own personalities that's for sure but at the same time I am him and he's me. We just know stuff we never have to articulate.

ME

That's really cool. And it's nice to hear you're just as close to Finn. I still think it must have been hard for him at times.

SEAN

It was for sure. Cormac and Seamus are only seven months apart because Seamus was a preemie.

ME

No way. You'd never guess he was ever tiny. I guess I would have assumed they were both 10lbs babies.

SEAN

No not at all. Seamus was like a little over
4lbs. He was ginormous for a preemie at 31
weeks. But Cormac was like Dillan and Finn.
Just over 9lbs.

ME

Were you and Shane tiny too.

SEAN

God bless our mother. No. Not even remotely.
She even went to her due date. We were both
exactly 7lbs 8ozs.

That's crazy. Their size as twins but also they were exactly the same. What are the odds of that? That was fifteen pounds of baby. And that was after having a nine-something-pound baby a couple years earlier. I wonder if the woman is still exhausted. I am just thinking about it.

SEAN

Hey. I gotta go. I wish I didn't have to but I'm
glad we chatted. I still have stuff to do, but as
soon as I'm done I can come to Boston.

ME

I want to see you as soon as you're free. But
coming here isn't a good idea. Ewan didn't
accuse me of anything exactly. But he
definitely knows.

SEAN

What did he say exactly?

Can you feel rage through a text? I'm pretty sure I can.

ME

Fucking Sean O'Rourke.

SEAN

That's it?

ME

He also said that I could have stayed home if all I wanted was to bang.

SEAN

He said that about his sister?

ME

Nounours please don't get angry about this. This is just how he and I are. Sometimes we're great together and I really like him. But this isn't easy for either of us. I'm already pissed at him all the time. I don't want that spilling over to you. I know you don't like each other but I don't want you any angrier than he makes you without me in the picture.

SEAN

For your sake I'll leave him alone when it comes to how he speaks to you. But I told you before I'm only so flexible about that. Even rubber breaks when it's pulled too far.

ME

I can think of something I wouldn't mind pulling on.

That was pathetic. I don't pull on his dick.

SEAN

All the more reason for me to visit as soon as I can. It may be a few days before I can chat again. I'm glad you texted me cailín. I'll let you know as soon as I'm done.

ME

OK

SEAN

If you need anything go straight to my cousins. Promise?

ME

Promise. Be careful. Bye

SEAN

Bye

I love how easy it is to chat through texts. It's not like it wasn't easy to talk to him on the phone or in person. It's nice to have three ways—three non-physical ways—to communicate.

I kick off my shoes and lie back on my pillow. I scroll back through the conversation and reread it. I roll onto my side and put my phone next to my bottom elbow. I usually sleep pretty much in the middle of the bed since I sleep alone and can. I enjoy having the entire queen size bed to myself. It was the same way in my apartment back home. But as I look at the empty spot that a red-headed man with entrancing emerald eyes and constellations of freckles could fill, it seems huge for one person. It's enormous for someone as thin as me. Good, bad, or in between; I just don't take up that much room.

"Nikki, are you hungry? I'm ordering lunch. Do you want sushi?" It's Ewan.

He knows I love sushi. He's being conciliatory. I stand and slide my phone into my back pocket after checking the screen's locked, not just dark. I open the door and look up at him.

"That would be nice. Yes, please."

"Can I come in, Nik? Please?"

I step aside. Did he pull his head out of his own ass? Or did Colt do some tugging, too? Definitely *not* the same kind I thought about five minutes ago.

"I know I'm screwing you over. I'm not so egomaniacal that I can't tell that. Yeah, I'm doing it because it serves me. I won't pretend like it doesn't. But that's because I serve the organization. What our branch needs comes first. It needs stability after the shitshow Dad put us through for almost five years. The decline we were already in while Grandpa led. You know the danger we face every day. Think how exponentially worse it will be if I'm deposed. Another family takes over. Do you think they're going to want any reminders of the O'Malleys? Do you think going back to Montreal, or never having come here in the first place, would protect you? Being a Tremblay doesn't make people forget you're also an O'Malley. We have to stay on top just to stay alive. Knowing you not only abandoned a meeting with Pablo but then spent all afternoon in bed with Sean... I think I have a right to be pissed off as your leader. But I also have a right to be terrified as your brother. Sean will hurt you. Maybe not physically, but he will emotionally."

"You assume he's using me."

"Maybe he is. Maybe he isn't. But when it comes down to a future, do you really think you have one with a man whose brother not only put a hit on our dad but made sure it was carried out?"

I snort. "You're pissed that they did you a favor that has you indebted to them."

"Because that's the kind of people they are." He throws his hands up in the air.

"How out of touch with reality do you think I am? Like you haven't killed people to serve a greater purpose than just seeing them dead. Like you haven't ordered people killed on someone else's behalf, so they're just as indebted to you as you are to the O'Rourkes."

"Justin said you wouldn't open the door while you were in your suite with Sean yesterday. You missed your flight, but somehow you arrived home right on time. Is my concern misplaced?"

"You're concerned? About me? Oh, you mean, concerned about the mission you sent me on. You want to know if I fucked him for information. You want to know if I'm sulking and holding out on you. If I learned something, but I'm just not telling you. That's why you came to offer me sushi."

"Must you always be so antagonistic?"

"You had me build encryptions to lock the O'Rourkes out of our finances. Fine. But you had me do that, and a few weeks later, you send me to New York. The city where they all live. You scheduled meetings for *me* with not one, but two syndicate heads. You weren't willing to show your ass in New York, but you were fine sending me. You basically covered me in steaks and tossed me into a pit where three alpha lions could have torn me apart."

Sean definitely ate me. Just not in the way I'm alluding to.

"You went. It's not like I bound and gagged you, then tied you to the seat in the plane."

"Okay. If I have so much freedom, I'm not doing another thing for you. I'm done."

I walk to my closet and pull out my big suitcase. I wheel it over to the foot of the bed and lift it onto the mattress.

"'Scuse me." I walk toward my dresser, gesturing to my destination.

"What are you doing, Nikki? Stop being dramatic."

"If you're not forcing me to work for you, then I quit. If I quit, then I don't need to stay here."

"Stop already."

I'm pushing every last one of his buttons, but he's already taken a sledgehammer to mine. I pull open the drawer with my t-shirts and scoop them out. I turn back to the bed.

"I signed a lease on a condo the day before yesterday. I get the keys in two days. I'm going to stay somewhere else for now since I'm already moving out."

"When'd you find a place? I didn't even know you were seriously looking. You have a place here."

"We're adults now who don't live well together. We were fine when we were kids, and we both knew I was only visiting for a few weeks. I wanted my own space when I figured I'd be stuck here indefinitely. Now I just don't want to make yet another move, even if it means I could go home. I have no job in Montreal. I sold my house. I'd be starting over there, staying with my mom. I enjoy living alone. I'm here, so I may as well make the most of it."

That's what I figured before going to NYC and before this argument. Now I don't want to be in Boston at all. I could just abandon my security deposit plus first and last month's rent. The amount makes my eye twitch. I don't want to do that. Boston is still more affordable than NYC, and it's still closer to NYC than Montreal. For how much I'm going to pay each month, I made the property owner agree to a month-to-month. Even before this latest clusterfuck with Ewan, I knew I wanted to have an easy escape when I finally got free of him.

In no way do I believe I'm free. But I'm free from living under his roof. I know he'll make Justin and some of Justin's men watch me. They'll know if and when I see Sean. They'll know how long I'm with him. But they can't stop him from being with me. Not physically for sure. My money is all in on Sean winning any kind of fight. I know Justin can hold his own, but everything about Sean radiates he won't back down first.

I keep going back and forth to my dresser, then my closet as Ewan watches in silence. When I zip it, he finally speaks.

"Where are you going to stay? Where's the condo?"

"Just have Justin or one of his henchmen tell you. I know you're going to make them follow me."

"I can and I will. But you know Justin followed you to the city on his own. I didn't order that."

"I know."

He waits to see if I say more, but I don't.

"Nikki, all this shit aside. Are you going somewhere safe? Do you need guards?"

This is Ewan, my brother, who happens to lead the mob.

Not the mob leader who happens to be my brother, Ewan. He has moments of sincerity. I forgive a lot because of that. But I'm still not staying here, and I'm not letting him run roughshod over me anymore.

"I'll be in a good part of town. You know I have my gun."

One of the first things I did when I moved to Massachusetts was get my LTC—License to Carry. I *never* carried a gun in Montreal. I learned to shoot pistols at a range, and I used to go hunting with Granddad. But I carried nothing more dangerous than a switchblade. That was something I kept well-hidden since they're illegal in Canada. Knowing why Ewan summoned me, I made sure I got the legal right to carry a gun as fast as I could because I trust next to no one here.

"That's marginally reassuring. Would you let Colt take you wherever you're going tonight? Just to be sure you make it safely. You're right about the risk I put you in being seen with Nishida and having a meeting scheduled with Pablo."

"No. I don't need nor want a babysitter. Thank you for the offer. The best you can do right now is carry this and my roll aboard downstairs for me, please."

I get out a soft-sided carry on and start collecting the few personal touches I have in here before going into the en suite bathroom to collect my toiletries. When I hear Ewan moving down the stairs, I dash back to my purse and pull out a burner.

ME

I'm leaving tonight. I'm fine but it's time.

Now I just have to figure out what to tell Seamus and Cormac when they spot me walking out with suitcases.

Chapter Twelve

Lina

Things went smoothly with Seamus and Cormac. I know they saw Ewan load my car with my luggage. Colt stood beside my brother while I didn't bother looking back before driving away. I pulled off about a quarter of a mile from Ewan's house, into a supermarket parking lot. Cormac and Seamus walked over to the car and got in.

I told them what happened, and it took five minutes of arguing before they agreed to leave Ewan and Colt alone. They wanted to arrange for my brother and his best friend to get in a fender bender that would wind up with them beaten up when they got out of the car to exchange information. I don't need that shit added to my plate right now. I warned them that hurting Ewan would just put me in a position to help him again.

I gave them the directions to my new place, so they'd know I have an end plan. Or at least a middle plan. I wouldn't mind seeing Sean as part of the end plan. For now, I told them I'm headed to a friend's place in Belchertown, which is an hour and a half outside Boston. Nowadays, it's as much fun to say as it is to live there. I wish it were fall because the foliage is as amazing as people claim about New England.

"Hey, stay inside when I get there. I've got bodyguards with me, and I don't want to explain why I'm staying at a guy's place." I have my phone connected to my car's Bluetooth.

"I thought you left Ewan, so why do you have security?" Jesse's a guy I met while in college.

He's a semi-pro bodybuilder and gorgeous. He's also gay. I don't for a moment think Seamus or Cormac would object to that. It's the part about them seeing Jesse before I can explain I'm only into Sean. I know I could have told them while we were talking earlier, but shit's more complicated than him just being a man I'm staying with.

"It's a story better told in person. I'll use the hidden key and let myself in. They'll park on the street at opposite ends. They won't get out of the car unless they perceive I'm in danger."

"And they think I'm a threat?"

"No, because they won't see you. I'll explain what I can once I'm there. It'll be about twenty minutes."

"Fine."

"Thanks. I appreciate it."

"I know you do. That's why you have an open invitation to stay as long as you want."

"Just a couple days, but you're awesome."

"I'll see you in a bit."

"Bye."

We hang up, and I think back to when I met Jesse. I was in Boston visiting Ewan during summer break, and I still had friends I'd made during my visits as a kid. We'd hang out, so I could escape my family. They're all mob daughters, so they know my brother. They knew my dad, so they understood why

I liked to get away. Jesse worked at a male strip club, and one of my friends thought he was so hot. He is. But when she tried to get his number, he declined.

About three weeks later, the same group of friends and I went to a drag show brunch. Best brunch I've ever had. I had this niggling feeling I knew a performer. It took me the entire meal to figure it out. Jesse came by our table during a song. When I smiled and gave him a slight nod, he knew I'd recognized him. We talked after the show and hit it off. We've been friends ever since.

You'd never in a million years believe he owned a company that has three hundred vending machines throughout five counties and make him a *very* lucrative income. He's never been flashy about his wealth. He started stripping in college for the money and stays because he loves to dance. The drag shows are a creative outlet for him.

I pull into the driveway and pop the trunk. I'm certain Seamus and Cormac want to sweep the entire area before I get out. I open my door before either of them can approach me. I step out and nod as Cormac drives past. I'm pretty sure I can see his scowl. I grab my luggage from the car and wheel it to the front door. I know Jesse hides the key under some mulch, beneath a rock.

"Jesse, get out of the way!" Fuck me.

He's standing just inside the door, and I'm certain Seamus just spotted him since he drove past. He came from the opposite direction from his brother.

"Nice to see you too, sweet cheeks."

I get my suitcases through the door, and he helps roll them into the living room. I kicked the door closed behind me. I give him a hug, and it's as reassuring as it's always been. Jesse's who I turned to when my dad died. He was one of the few people I could confide in that I felt nothing about his death, but I felt guilty because I believed that made me a shitty person. My mom was the only other person. In front of everyone else, I didn't lie about my lack of feelings. I was evasive.

"I just started seeing someone new. Those guys are his cousins. They are going to wonder why it looks like I'm moving in with a guy. They're going to tell their cousin if I don't explain first."

"You could have told me that on the phone."

"And I thought you'd believe me when I said not to come out and that I'd explain it once I'm here."

"I didn't come out, and you are explaining." His grin usually makes up for everything.

But not this time. I don't want things fucked up with Sean before they have a chance to get started. I need to tell Cormac and Seamus something, but I don't want to blurt out Jesse's sexual orientation as the reason, even if it is. I pull my phone from my purse and open the group text.

"Give me a sec, please."

ME

That's my friend Jesse. I've known him since college. He knows who and what I am. I'm safe here.

I could also be safe at a hotel.

CORMAC

You could have told us first.

ME

I know. I'm sorry but I didn't want to argue about going to a hotel or coming to a friend.

SEAMUS

What was there to argue about?

He's not being obtuse. I should have trusted them to let me

decide what I want to do. They might give an opinion for my safety, but they know it's not their place to tell me what to do. They'd look out for me, regardless.

> **ME**
>
> Please let me tell Sean that I'm staying with a guy. There's NO chance at all ever that something's gone on or will go on with him besides friendship.

I include the emoji with the raised eyebrow as a hint.

> **SEAMUS**
>
> You could have told us that too. We don't give a hoot about stuff like that.

He won't swear in front of me, even in text. I noticed that about Sean, and it's the same with his cousins. It must be a family rule or something. Ewan and our dad definitely didn't have the same policy. I don't have the same policy with Ewan.

> **ME**
>
> I'm getting to know your family. He's my friend. Just being cautious.

> **CORMAC**
>
> Understood. We're here to ensure you're okay not to judge.

> **ME**
>
> Thanks

"Everything all right?"

> **SEAMUS**
>
> No problem

I look up at Jesse as I drop my phone back into my purse. "Completely."

"They aren't going to tattle?"

"What would you think if you just started dating someone, and they found out you're staying with a guy?"

He shrugs, but I see a flash of remorse. "Sorry."

"It's fine. I'm starving. What's for lunch?" I shoot him a smile as we head to the hallway with the bedrooms. I know where to go since I've stayed here plenty of times before. He brings my larger case while I have my roll aboard and hand luggage. We leave the bags there and head to the kitchen. We chat about everything but my family. I tell him what I can about Sean, and he's genuinely happy for me. He apologizes again for any problems he created.

After we eat, I head to my room to get out what I need for the next couple of days until my apartment is ready. There's an en suite, and I'm just putting my makeup bag on the counter when I hear my phone ring in the bedroom.

"Hi, *nounours*."

"Hi, *cailín*. Did everything go smoothly getting home?"

"Yeah, but Ewan and I had an argument right after you and I texted. I left and came to a friend's place."

"I know. Cormac told me."

Fuck me.

I wait to see what else he says, but he stays quiet. It's my turn to speak.

"I'm with a friend from college. Jesse's always let me stay here whenever I want, even when he's out of town. It'll be a couple days before my apartment's ready. I didn't want to stay in a hotel when I could be somewhere comfortable that I know."

"I get it. Did Ewan do anything beyond argue?"

"No. Why?"

"Lina, I'm in Boston."

Ummmmm. Okay.

"You came straight here like you said you would."

"Yes. I'd like to see you." He sounds hopeful.

"I'd like to see you, too."

"If you just got to your friend's place, I don't want to interrupt."

"Jesse and I hang out when we're both here. But we've always kept our own schedules. He really treats me like I live here rather than a guest. I come and go whenever I want. He'll get it. When can I see you?"

Did I sound too eager?

"As soon as we can be in the same place. Cormac said you're in Belchertown."

"I am. Do you know where that is?"

"Yeah. I have a friend who went to Amherst. I would fly into Hartford before visiting her. I've seen the road signs."

Ouch. Was that a dig? It hurts, even if that was like at least eight years ago. I wince because he knows I'm at a guy's place right now.

"Lina, I didn't say it to hurt you. It doesn't bother me that you're staying at a guy's house. Gay or straight. He's your friend, and you're away from Ewan. That's what matters to me."

"Thank you."

"I landed five minutes ago. Once we're cleared for takeoff, the pilot will be wheels up."

"It's forty minutes from Hartford to here after a forty-five-minute flight. You can drive in the same amount of time. I wish I'd known you'd be here so soon. I would have stayed in Boston and saved you the effort."

"Little one, there are two private airfields in Belchertown. I already looked it up."

My toes curl in my shoes. I could see Sean in less than an hour. I shouldn't be that giddy.

"Do you need me to pick you up?"

That's a stupid question. He has his cousins and probably a car service already lined up. There's a pause before he answers.

"Would you let my cousins bring you? I can arrange for a car with privacy glass. I'd like to say hello without an audience."

I'm wet. Like he soaked my panties. My pussy aches, and I close my eyes as I sit on the bed.

"Yes." It's a whisper because I think I'd croak if I spoke louder.

"Good. I'll see you soon, little one. One of the guys will let you know when to leave. I want to see the marks I left on you, and I want to taste you. Dress for it."

My belly caves. His tone was gravelly and deep when he said that. My tits remember how they felt when he sucked love bites all over them. I pull my shirt out and look down at them.

"Yes, Sir."

"I'm not your Dom, Lina."

"I know, and I wasn't being sarcastic. But I don't know what else to say when I want to let you know I'll obey."

"Sean. Just say my name. There's never a time when you can't call me that."

"Thank you, Sean. I'm excited to see you." I suddenly feel timid about admitting that.

"You can't be more excited than I am. Not possible."

"I'll be there when you land."

"I know."

Neither of us says anything. There's no more to say about him getting here. But neither of us wants to hang up. We remain quiet, but then I hear voices in the background.

"I gotta go, so I can make the arrangements. Give me an hour."

"Okay. See you soon."

"Not soon enough."

I open my eyes to hang up the call, but he already has. I really want this to work. I want there to be an us. On my flight up from NYC, I searched love at first sight to see if it's a real thing or just heightened physical attraction that makes lust seem like love.

There's no scientific proof that love at first sight exists, but the articles I read have some common denominators. Most mentioned something about the chemical reactions in the brain. A neuropsychotherapist said the amount of serotonin and dopamine is similar to someone on heroin. That hardly sounds lovely, but it certainly explains why people would think it's love. I don't know what adaptive oscillators are, but they're in the prefrontal cortex where emotions and decision-making happen. I guess when one person's oscillators connect with another's—however that happens—it's what can spur people to kiss. It was downhill from there after my first kiss with Sean.

Some articles talked about memory bias. That love at first sight is really just happy memories of meeting someone, and when they're shared, they're strengthened into a sense of love at first sight. Meeting Sean was definitely memorable. A sunny day at a funeral. Making out at the reception after the funeral.

I'm not convinced I'm in love. I'm most certainly in lust. But this feels more substantial than other times I've been in lust. There's the excitement I've experienced, but there's a calm at the same time. A rightness that has me at peace. It's fucking bizarre.

I hurry to change into a short sundress before heading out to have lunch.

✳

SEAMUS

It's time to go. You ready?

ME

Yeah. I'm coming.

"Jesse?"

"Yeah. In my office."

I walk to the other end of the house and stick my head around the door.

"Hey. I'm headed out for a bit. Sean was able to fly here. He made it to Boston sooner than we expected. I'm going to meet him. I'm not sure if my plans are going to change or what. I'll keep you posted."

"You're really into him, aren't you?"

"Yeah. How can you tell?"

"You sound comfortable when you talk about him. It's not like new giddiness when you first meet someone you like. It's like you've been together since forever. Like it's just a given you're going to see him, and you might stay with him now that he's in town. I'm happy for you. He's certainly better than shithead."

"Way better than shithead." I grin and then laugh.

I head outside, and Cormac's car is in the driveway. Seamus is in the passenger seat. I slide into the back.

"Thanks for taking me. I'm sorry about earlier."

"We get it." Seamus looks over his shoulder and offers me a smile I'm certain is genuine.

We ride the twenty minutes chatting about things to see and do in New York and Boston that aren't the usual touristy destinations. It kills the time until we're at the airfield, and we watch a private jet land. As we park, the plane's door opens and steps lower. Then he's there.

I don't run—despite the temptation—so it feels like the

longest hundred yards ever as I walk to meet him. Then I'm in his arms.

"Baby girl."

I melt against him as I tip my chin up. He cups my cheek and stares into my eyes for a moment before we're finally kissing again. It hasn't even been a day. We weren't even together a day. But this is heaven. The kiss goes on and on. I know there are people moving around us, but we don't care. We won't be rushed. His tongue curls with mine, and we swipe them within each other's mouths. I remember as a tween thinking pressing tongues together sounded stupid and gross. Now...Sean's damn good at pressing his tongue together with mine.

"*Nounours.*"

He gives me a series of pecks. Before sliding both of his hands into mine. My brow furrows as I look at his face again.

"What's wrong?" I know there's something.

"I need to talk to you in private. My cousins don't know yet, but they will. Shane will brief them, but I don't want you hearing this with an audience."

"You're scaring me."

"I'm sorry. I don't mean to, but it's serious."

Chapter Thirteen

Sean

I want to pull Lina back into my arms and pretend like nothing exists but us. I want to whisk her away to somewhere warm and sunny that only has room for two. I want to make all of this better.

"I booked a room at a hotel. We can talk there, or we can go wherever you want."

"I..." She shrugs.

I wrap my arm around her waist as we walk to my cousins. I don't let go of her as I hug Cormac then Seamus. I know they're glad to see me in one piece. They already know some of what happened. I called them during my flight up to Boston. I wanted to be certain Lina was all right. It was like I'm Atlas, and someone lifted the weight of the world off my shoulders when they told me she'd left Ewan's. I don't care who she stays with as long as she's nowhere near Ewan. I don't want her caught in the crossfire.

"Did anyone follow you?" I direct the question to my cousins.

"We thought so for the first forty minutes, but the car got off the highway. I didn't see it when I canvased the neighborhood while Ms. Tremblay was in the house." Seamus surprises Lina because I feel her stiffen.

"Ms. Tremblay?" She sounds hurt but appears thoughtful. "You've never used my first name."

She looks up at me, and she still appears sad. She doesn't get the distance Seamus put between them. I'll explain yet another thing when we're alone.

"No sign of either guy?" I know my cousins know who I'm talking about.

"No."

"Sean?"

"Let's get in the car and head to the hotel." I nudge Lina, and she walks with me to the limo. I don't want a cramped town car.

Once we're in, I lift her onto my lap before she can fasten her seat belt. She's in a dress, and I can feel the heat from her cunt pressing against my dick. I slide my hands up her thighs, enjoying the bare skin against my palms until I cup her arse.

"Feck, *cailín*. My hands have felt so empty since the last time I touched you." I've been fantasizing about her every moment that hasn't been filled with work.

"I've had a lot of time to think about the way you feel, too." She presses her pussy harder against my cock.

"Lina, we have a lot to talk about. I understand if you'd rather do that first."

"Nope."

I wrap my hands around her waist and shift until I can lay her along one of the long bench seats. This is why I wanted the limo. I unbutton the top of her dress, and she pulls down her bra. I stare at what I did the other day. I left a lot more marks than I realized, and some are going to take longer to fade than others. I have a moment of guilt.

"Sean, I love seeing them. I love that they're going to last a few more days." She lifts her head to give my lips a peck.

I scoot back and lick her left nipple over and over, swirling my tongue around it until it tightens. I move to the right one and suck. I bite, but not enough to break the skin. I keep inching back until I'm kneeling on the floor. I lift her right leg over my shoulder as I kiss the inside of her left thigh. Then I'm at the promised land.

I lave her cunt from the back to front. I press my tongue inside her, flexing it as she writhes. I move onto her clit, flicking it over and over until I suck that, too. All the while, my fingers play with her nipples, rolling them between my thumb and forefinger.

"Sean, that feels amazing... Fuck... The things you're doing. I—Fuck, I'm close... Yes. I'm—"

I suck extra hard on her clit, my fingers now in her and stroking her g spot. She lifts her hips off the seat, and I let her. She tenses as she comes. I love watching her. I love knowing I pleasure her. I don't stop. I press my pinky against her arsehole, and she sucks in a breath. I do nothing more for now, unsure what her experience is with this. An image of Colt pops into my mind, but I shove it aside. I *do not* want to know what they did together.

"I want it all." She speaks on an exhale.

The pad of my pinky goes a bit deeper.

"Have you?"

"Yes."

Again, Colt comes to mind. Fuck that motherfucker.

"I want to see you with a plug in your arse before I take it."

"You don't have to take what's given to you."

Our gazes lock before I pull my fingers from her. I move up to hover over her. She reaches for my belt. I let her unfasten my pants and push down my boxer briefs. I wrap my hand around my cock and slide it between her pussy lips, coating it. Her hand covers mine before I slip it out from beneath her. She aims the tip to her pussy, but I don't flex my hips. We're still looking at each other, so I harden my expression.

She releases me immediately. Her hands go over her head, and I thrust as hard as I dare. I'm balls deep, and I want to come just from how her cunt squeezes around me. I shift again, so my elbows bracket her head, and I bear my weight on my elbows and forearms. I cover her hands with mine, and she spreads her fingers. I entwine our fingers as I keep surging into her. I can't— yes, I could—I'll never make the excuse that there's a point of no return for men to control themselves—I don't want to stop.

I pound into her as her hips rise and roll to meet mine. I rub my pubic bone against her clit every time I sink all the way into her. I've had plenty of sex since I was sixteen and lost my virginity. I've had amazing sex, and I've had pathetically disappointing sex. Most of it's been somewhere in between. I've thought I've had earth shakingly good sex. But I know now that I was sorely mistaken. Nothing physical or emotional has felt like being with Lina.

Shane and I flew back to New York to drop off our men, then my brother and I came up here. He's still in Boston to keep an eye on Ewan. Since I was alone in the plane for nearly an hour, I did some googling. I don't want to think this is infatuation or just the strongest case of lust I've ever had. I want to think this could be more, so I looked up the neuroscience behind love at first sight. Of course, there're conflicting theories and opinions. But I found enough articles to believe there's a reasonable possibility it could be real.

"Sean, harder."

She's so much smaller than me, but she's not frail. I'm careful not to crush her, but I give her what she wants. Her moans spur me. The way she purposely squeezes my dick makes me want to come. She becomes almost impossibly tight. I let go of one of her hands to draw her right leg over my hip. I put my left foot on the floor and do as she told me.

"Fuck, Lina. You haven't gotten off yet, and I'm so close."

"Don't hold back. Even if I don't come, I want you to."

"I feel the same way. I want to pleasure you until you can't think of anything but the feel of me inside you."

"Mission accomplished. I can barely think about anything besides that."

Her free hand goes to my arse, and she presses my hips into her.

"I'm going to cuff you to a bed and have my way with you. You'll take whatever I give you. I decide, little one."

She lets go, but I press her hand back to my arse.

"What else are you going to do?"

"I'm going to slide a vibrator in you and let it run until it makes you come. You won't be able to stop yourself. You're going to suck me off while your pussy buzzes. When I'm done and know I'll last more than five minutes before I need to come again, I'm going to spank your sweet little arse with a riding crop. I'm going to take it to your swollen little pussy and make you scream. I'm going to enjoy your little pink arse while I fuck it."

"How soon?"

I grin at her enthusiasm.

"As soon as I get what I need."

She cants her head for a moment. I have a sinking feeling.

"Do you already have those things, *cailín*?"

She shakes her head. "I wondered if you did."

"I don't. Lina, I've never brought a woman back to my

194

place. I stick to my clubs. I have a studio where I've met my subs in the past. But when my last arrangement ended, I got rid of the stuff. I'd planned to just stick to scening in dungeons."

She nods, and we have nothing else to say as we fuck. I'm lasting way longer than I expected. I feel her body tense beneath mine before she cries out.

"Sean!"

"Yes, baby. I'm here. Keep going. I'm going to get you off again."

I keep working her pussy, praying she'll come soon now that I told her I was going to make it happen. I'm so close I know I'm leaking. Her nails dig into the back of my hand and into my arse as she works to meet each of my thrusts.

"I'm coming, *nounours*."

Her neck arches as her eyes squeeze shut. I don't hold back. I flood her with my cum. We're panting by the time we're done. I know she can taste herself when we kiss. I slide an arm beneath her and lift her as I shift to sit on the seat. She flops against my shoulder, her breath tickling my neck. My ribs feel like my heart's making them vibrate.

"That was incredible." She sounds awestruck.

"I agree."

She pulls her knees higher and tucks her arms between us and fists my shirt. I kiss her temple over and over as I hold her, my dick still buried in her. I stroke her back as we catch our breath. Then we enjoy the calm and silence together.

But it doesn't last long since we're at the hotel in a couple minutes. I don't want her to get up, but it's not like I can check in with her wrapped around me, my pants pushed down, and my cock still in her. We fix our clothes before I tap on the window. This is a hired car service, so I made sure to tell the driver not to open the door until I signal. No one is seeing my woman in a compromised position. Entirely possessive, I know. Protective is the intention.

She's mine.

"Welcome, Mr. and Mrs. O'Rourke. It's a pleasure to have you stay here."

The man at the reception desk beams at us. In this day and age, it seems strange to assume a couple is automatically married because they're checking into a hotel room together. I do nothing to correct him since I don't believe he needs an explanation, and it's safer if Lina's name doesn't come out. I glance down at her and find she's already looking up at me. There's mischief in her eyes, so I know she isn't upset by the title the man gave her. It suits her.

I have a duffle bag, and that's it. I carry it myself, and we get into the elevator in silence. I draw her into my arms at the same time she wraps hers around me. It feels perfectly natural. Like how a girlfriend or wife would feel. I mean, I guess since I've never been married, and I haven't had a girlfriend in nearly ten years.

We remain silent until we get to the suite. I let us in before shutting and locking the door. Our gazes sweep over the room, landing on the soaking tub that's in the middle of it. It has a view out to a park, and we're up high enough no one down there could see in. It's probably a marvelous view, but it feels out of place. I have every intention of getting her in it before morning.

I put my bag down outside the bedroom door as we walk past. When we get to the sofa, I sit first, something I would normally never do. But she understands the invitation. She sits sideways before curling into me. As it seems to be routine now, my hand slips under her dress to cup her arse. I slide my finger under her thong's thin string.

"Do not wear these anymore. When I want your pussy, I

will have it with nothing in the way. Not even this strand of floss. Do you understand?"

Her eyes droop closed as she smiles. "Yes, *nounours.*"

The word no longer means teddy or teddy bear. It's her name for me. I love it.

"If you do, I will spank you, then edge you."

"No, thank you."

I chuckle, and I feel her arse tighten. She likes the sound. It has the effect I want.

"It wasn't an offer."

"Mmm. I think it was. Maybe I want to be spanked and edged sometimes. Not right now, so I said no thank you. But another day, I might say yes, please."

I pinch her arse, and she jerks her hips upward. It gives me the space to slip my fingers between her arse cheeks.

"Are you always defiant?"

"More often than I probably should be." She sits up for a moment. "I'm not talking about how I was with Doms in the past. Sean, as long as we're together, that's part of a past that exists, but not one I want to think about or talk about."

"I wasn't hinting at that. I get the feeling you can be plenty defiant in real life."

"At times. I just want you to know I'm not comparing or pointing out my past."

This is a natural segue, but I dread it.

"I know, Lina. But it opens the door to what we need to talk about. I'm uncertain where to begin. Since I said this is a natural transition, I'll start here. While I was away, I found out about you and Colt."

She goes rigid. Anger. But is it directed at me or him? When she narrows her eyes at me, I know she means at least some of it for me.

"And just what do you know about Colt and me?" Her tone is brittle.

"I know you were engaged. I know he maneuvered you, so he could get closer to your dad for a better position."

She waits for me to say more, and it gives me a sinking feeling that's there's way, way more.

"Lina, I know nothing beyond that. I just know it was four or five years ago. I'm already well acquainted with Colt. I didn't know about you until I met you. I didn't even know Rowan had a second kid."

"It's not like I could have kept Colt a secret, but I would have liked to tell you in my own time."

"And you can. You don't have to share anything with me. I wanted to let you know I'm aware you were engaged. I found out because Ewan was in Baltimore while you were in New York. He was with Ellie."

She pushes away from me, and she would have fallen if I weren't holding her. She pushes my arm, and I let go. She gets off my lap and stares at me.

"In Baltimore? With Ellie? No."

I stand, but she backs away. I put my hands up.

"I won't touch you if you don't want me to. But it'd be rude and awkward to talk to you while you stand, and I sit. I just want to be closer to eye level. I'll stay right where I am."

Her shoulders sag. "I'm not scared of you, Sean. I don't want you to think I am. I need a moment of space. But I trust you."

I lower my hands. Not progress, but at least not a backslide.

"You went to Baltimore last night."

"Yes. I knew Ewan was there before I left. I didn't go there to meet with him, and I didn't."

"You went to spy on him."

I don't answer. She nods. She knows parts of these conversations will be one-sided. She'll ask things or say things I'll neither confirm nor deny.

"I hope it was worth it." She turns to look out the window.

She walks over to it and leans against the window frame, her forehead pressed to the glass. I inch closer, not wanting to talk to her back, not liking her out of my reach, and not enjoying being unable to comfort her.

"Can you tell me why he was there? Obviously, he used the jet. That's why he didn't argue when I said I wanted to fly commercial. I wanted to blend in. He wanted to sneak off."

"I'm in uncharted waters right now, *cailín*. You're working for your brother, so I know you're informed about a lot he does. But I don't know what you know. I don't know what I can say that's safe for you to hear. I won't lie to you while we talk. But that means I may not answer, or I may stop talking. I don't trust Ewan with your wellbeing. Not even a little. I don't want to endanger you by telling you things he'll punish you for to get to me."

"I get it. Just tell me why he was seeing Ellie. I know he's having an affair with her. Piece of shit that they both are. Her husband's a nice guy and doesn't deserve it. But she and Ewan deserve each other in spades."

"I know. I've known Ellie for years. I remember back to when they dated in high school. I saw them at events together in college. I know Ewan better than I want to. That's why it's a shock that I never heard about you. You said you spent vacations and holidays at Rowan's."

"I never went to anything where people outside the family or organization were. Dad said it was to protect me, and maybe it was. But he likely also didn't want to explain that I'm the result of him trying to get back at his dad and father-in-law. Me being in their home was enough reminder for my stepmom.

Fortunately, she never made me feel unwelcome because of my dad's shit life choices."

"I never understood them as a couple."

"It's not ours to reason why."

"Do you know Clyde Schlossberg?"

"I know of him. He's an investment banker from Munich. He's got some commercial development projects in Boston. He and Dad bought in on some of the same ones. Why?"

"Do you know what kind of relationship he and Ewan have?"

"None as far as I know."

"You encrypted your brother's financials. Do you know where the money came from?"

"Not specifically. But I know what he does. It's not exactly a state secret what our families are into."

I hate the observation that Ewan and I are even remotely similar, but we are. Far too similar. At least with work. What we do. Not how we do it.

"There are off the books deals where it's cash only. Nothing gets deposited, but it might get reported internally."

"I know. There were, but I didn't ask where the amounts came from. I just hid the information. Was he in Baltimore last night to meet Schlossberg? Is he becoming a silent investor in something down there and doesn't want anyone to know?"

I walk over to her, but not so close she feels boxed in. She looks over her shoulder at me and holds out her hand. I wrap my arms around her, and she leans her back against my chest. We look out the window together.

"Other people in his organization know. Colt knows."

"Fuck him."

Her reaction is visceral and intense.

"They had a deal, but it had nothing to do with any legit projects."

"Drugs?"

I remain silent. She nods.

"Baltimore is closer to New York than Boston. He over-stepped, so I went to deal with it. Schlossberg's in his fifties. Everything about him speaks to ruthlessness. Your brother is way in over his head. He came back to Boston as fast as he could because Schlossberg is pissed at him. Things didn't go the way Ewan planned."

"Because of you."

I remain silent. The call I got right before I went to sleep was a dock master giving me a courtesy call to say Customs and the DEA planned a bust. They raided the container ship and found the oregano. They were pissed it wasn't the weed they expected. It also meant the spies Schlossberg had at the port clued him in before Ewan left town. Fortunately for him, he was on the way to the airport when it happened. He was wheels up before Schlossberg found him.

Kelly's dad went back to the meeting spot after he helped take care of the vehicles. He watched men cut the bolt and go in the shipping container. He said they were pissed when they came out with nothing, but he wasn't close enough to tell if they were American or German. Whoever stash it was knows it's gone.

"Does Ewan know?"

"By now, probably."

"Will Schlossberg kill him?"

"I don't know. Maybe."

"Are you in danger? Like, more than usual?"

"If they figure out who interfered, probably."

I can't tell her we'll buy Schlossberg's secret—a nice way of saying we'll bribe him to stay quiet. But we'll welcome Ewan making the first move. We'll make the last.

"Did you hear about this through Ellie?"

"No."

She sighs and leans back against me.

"I'm going to tell you what I think happened, knowing my brother. You don't have to confirm or deny anything. I simply want you to know what I believe. Ewan went to Baltimore to sell marijuana to Schlossberg. I know it's a possibility. I won't say how I know for the same reason you won't tell me things. And it's not for our safety."

Because she's still loyal to her family, just like I am to mine.

"He met with the German to solidify some deal. You have the product now, or you did until you sold it in your own deal. Schlossberg'll put a hit on him if he hasn't already."

She looks over her shoulder at me for a long moment before turning back to the window.

"You won't let him kill Ewan for my sake. You'll let them rough him up, but not so badly I'll panic or feel obligated to go back to help him. I think you have a CI in Baltimore who told you where to go and probably listened to Ewan's conversation with Ellie. He probably reassured her that Colt will keep me occupied if I get nosey or pissed off. My brother made sure to get home before me—that's why he didn't object to me flying commercial—and why he wanted me to keep working for him. He didn't seem upset, so he either didn't know something happened to the shipment, or he believes he can handle it."

That about sums it up. But I can't agree. I remain quiet.

"What's the likelihood Schlossberg will find out you're involved?"

"There's always the chance."

"But are we talking five percent or ninety-five percent?"

"Fifty."

"Does Schlossberg have a history of killing people who cross him?"

"Yes."

"Will Ewan know you fucked him over?"

"He probably does by now."

She goes silent again, but her body remains relaxed against me. We just stand looking out the window. It's a miracle I see something flash near a tree. I twist Lina away and push her to the ground a second before the window shatters. Searing pain shoots through my right ribs. Fuck. I know this pain.

"Lina?" It's hard to breathe.

"I'm all right. Are you?"

"No. Call Seamus and Cormac."

I try to roll off her, but I'm lightheaded already. This isn't just the initial pain that comes from being shot or being winded from falling with her elbow in my gut.

"Sean!"

I moved enough for her to scramble out from beneath me, but it's like I'm listening to her underwater. I'm going to pass out. I watch her run to her purse and grab her phone before she tugs my suit coat off. I can't even groan from the pain as she jostles me. Things are blurring as she presses my wadded-up suit coat against my wound.

I hear her speak, but none of it makes sense.

"Seamus, it hit his lung. Get up here."

I'm either taking a nap or dead.

Chapter Fourteen

Lina

I look up when the pounding on the door registers as more than just my heart pounding. I don't want to let go of the pressure on Sean's wound, but I can't let his cousins in to help if I don't.

"I'll be right back." I know he can't hear me. There's so much fucking blood.

I race to the door, training ingrained in me to check the peephole first, then fling it open. I barely step back as Seamus and Cormac barrel forward, guns drawn. If I didn't know they'd never hurt me, I'd fear them trampling me. One of them is impressive. Both of them is fucking terrifying as they look ready to murder someone with their bare hands as their gazes scan the suite. They make a beeline to Sean, and I'm right on their heels.

"What happened?" Cormac's voice is deceptively low. It's not soft, just quiet.

"We were talking beside the window. I don't know what made him do it, but he spun me around and pushed me to the floor. Then the window shattered. He asked if I was all right, and I am. Then he said he wasn't, and I needed to get you."

Seamus is pressing Sean's suit jacket to his wound as Cormac raises his gun and looks out the window where there is nothing to see. At least nothing I notice, but perhaps he'll see more. I look back at Seamus and Sean, and Sean's face is so pale it makes me wonder if he's still alive. But the blood continues to flow from him. Corpses don't bleed.

"Did he say anything else?"

I can only shake my head at Seamus's question. I kneel beside Sean, opposite Seamus to stay out of his way. I take Sean's hand, and it's already so cold. I squeeze as hard as I dare. His fingers curl around mine and return the squeeze. It's hardly strong for a man like him, but it's something.

"I'm not dying, *cailín*. But this fecking hurts. Damn it, Seamus. Don't shove my jacket into the wound, just onto it."

"Don't whine."

I glance back and forth between the cousins, entirely bewildered by the exchange. Even in his condition, Sean won't swear in front of me. Seamus acts as though this is a paper cut even though blood covers his hands.

"You could at least take some pity on me in front of my girlfriend."

I stare down at Sean, wondering if he truly understands what he's saying. He called me little girl and his girlfriend in front of his cousins. I don't think he would normally do that if he were in the right state of mind, but I refuse to be embarrassed since I want nothing more than to be his girlfriend. I want that title. It's mine.

Cormac moves away from the window, his gun still poised and ready to fire, but he comes to stand beside his brother, glancing down at Sean in between scanning outside.

"What do we do? Can we take him to the hospital? I

thought you guys would avoid that, but do you know any doctors here? I don't know anyone."

"We will have to take him somewhere. This is too serious to avoid a hospital, and we don't have time to take him back to Boston, where we know somebody who can patch him up. If we can get him stable, then we might be able to transport him there. But right now, he's losing a lot of blood. It's not his lung like you thought, but it is very close." Seamus peels back the jacket enough to look at the wound. He reapplies the pressure.

"Should I call an ambulance? Are we wasting too much time? What do you need me to do?"

I feel like I'm peppering them with questions, but I don't know what to do in a situation like this. I've never been in a place where I've seen someone get shot. Well, I didn't see Sean get shot, but now I'm dealing with the fact that he was. That he shielded me, and there was just as much likelihood I was the target as him. He saved my life one way or another. And now I need to know what to do to save his.

It's Cormac who answers me this time. "Call the ambulance. You stay with him while we get the car. You'll ride in the ambulance with him. Pretend to be his wife."

I nod as I dial 911. My hands are shaking as I wait for the dispatcher to answer. Then I'm telling him my husband's been shot. I'm about to tell the man the hotel name and room number, but Seamus shakes his head.

"Tell them the park across the road." He mouths the words, and I barely understand him.

But I provide the information to the guy as Cormac and Seamus haul Sean onto his feet. He groans as Cormac presses his shoulder into Sean's belly and hefts him onto it. What the fuck? They can't move him like this.

They are. Seamus grabs my purse and pushes it at me

before hurrying to gather Sean's bag. Lord only knows what's in there. I expect us to get in the elevator, and I fear dropping the signal. The dispatcher isn't saying anything right now, so he must be putting out the call. When Seamus opens the door to the stairwell, I freeze. Seamus looks like he's ready to hoist me over his shoulder if I don't keep up.

Cormac still has his gun in his hand, and Sean over his opposite shoulder. Seamus is behind me, his gun at the ready. We're on the fifth floor. I don't know how they make it down the stairs without being winded, especially Cormac. But neither of them is breathing harder than normal while I fear passing out. They lead me out of a back door, and I realize it's likely how they came in. Seamus is on my heels, keeping me from slowing down as we hurry to the grassy area across the street.

"Ma'am?"

"Yes, I'm here."

"The ambulance will be there in two minutes."

"Okay. Thank you."

"I'll stay on the line till they get there. Are there any witnesses?"

My eyes widen. Cormac lays Sean on the ground in the same position as he found him when he and his brother arrived. Seamus points around. The park is empty. I can tell the truth.

"No. There's no one here. We were going for a walk."

"All right. How's he doing?"

"He's unconscious." He is. He didn't make a sound the entire way down the stairs, out the back door, across the street, or when his cousin put him down.

"The ambulance is just around the corner. I hear them. Can I hang up now, so I can concentrate?"

"Yes. They'll take care of him."

"Thank you. Bye."

I hang up without waiting for another word. I hear the siren, but I see nothing.

Seamus wraps an arm around the middle of my back, and I realize I'm trembling. What he says only mildly reassures me.

"We'll follow at a safe distance. If there's anything you don't know how to answer, and he's not conscious, pretend to be too distraught to tell them."

"What do I say when they want to know how he got shot? It's in the back, and it's clear what kind of wound it is. They'll have to fish the bullet out. How do I explain that if I was here? They'll expect me to know the answer to at least that question."

"No, they won't. Like you said, he was shot in the back. There're plenty of reasons you wouldn't see who did it if both of you were looking away."

"How do I explain why he's a target? Won't they want to know if I have any guesses at all?"

Cormac shakes his head before answering me. "The hospital staff won't be interested in that. They'll focus on getting him into surgery as soon as possible. He's O positive. He hasn't had any surgeries, and he's otherwise in perfect health. As long as you can remember that much, then you should be fine. If you can't answer questions, remember, pretend to be the distraught wife."

I'm still not convinced. "The gunshot wounds mean calling the cops. It won't take them long to get there. They're the ones who are going to want answers to these types of questions, and I won't know what to say."

"By then, we can have a reasonable explanation for showing up. We can take care of any questions you can't answer. And if they want to know why we're in town, we say business."

"It's not like Belchertown is such a booming metropolis that three New Yorkers and a woman from Montreal would gather here. We have to have some type of story to explain it." I think I'm doing a fucking great job not panicking, but I'm on the verge.

Seamus squeezes my shoulder as he pretty much keeps me from collapsing. "The only story they need to know is that we are in town for business but haven't yet held the client meeting. It is clear from your clothing, his, and ours that we're wealthy. As a wealthy businessman, it's not beyond reason he could be a target. He's a legitimate venture capitalist in New York. We stick to the truth. He owns more than one business, and there are plenty of people in the corporate world who would prefer not to see another O'Rourke make another million."

We spot the hood of the ambulance turning the corner. Seamus lets go of me, and I nearly fall over. I'm unprepared for them to back away. My fear must be clear because Cormac pats my upper arm.

"We'll follow you. But the fewer people here the better."

"And the hotel room?"

"We can take care of that."

Cleaners. I know what they are. They must have a way of getting some here. They'll come in and take care of everything in the room, so it never looked like a crime scene. I have no idea how they'll handle the window, but I don't care.

Within three minutes of the paramedics arriving, they have Sean on oxygen and on a stretcher. The bleeding slowed while his cousins and I waited. If I hadn't watched his back rise and fall while on the call, I would've believed he was dead. He's still so pale.

"Ma'am? Do you have a way to the hospital?"

"I'm riding with my husband."

"We really can't—"

I turn such a menacing glare at him—one I feel to my soul—that he snaps his mouth shut. I step up to the poor man and am so close, my forehead is nearly up his nose.

"You are not separating me from him until he goes into surgery. I'll stay out of the way, but I'm not taking some fucking Uber while he might—"

I can't say it.

"*Cailín?*"

I whip around at the sound of Sean's thready voice under the oxygen mask. I can't believe he's conscious again. What the fuck kind of pain tolerance does he have?

"Yes?" I lift the mask just enough to understand him.

"I love when you're fierce. Just hold my hand, and it'll be all right. I promise."

I stare dumbfounded. He's comforting me. I scramble into the ambulance when the exasperated paramedic gestures for me to get in. I stay out of the way as best I can, but I don't let go of Sean's hand once I have it again. I have no choice when we get to the Emergency Room. I have to let go long enough for them to get him out of the ambulance. Then I'm running alongside the stretcher until someone steps in front of me. With their hands on my shoulders, they push me back. I'm certain I could knock them out of the way. But a thread of common sense stops me because I know I can't go into the OR with them.

"Miss?"

I look up as a young man in scrubs approaches. "Yes."

"You came in with the victim."

I flinch, and he grimaces.

"Can you tell me his name?"

"Sean O'Rourke. Sean Dermot O'Rourke."

"Date of birth?"

Fuck. I stare blankly at the guy before turning back to the doors through which they wheeled him.

"Date of birth?"

"January seventeenth."

I whirl around at Cormac's voice. He and Seamus approach. Neither have a hair out of place, and neither have a speck of blood on them. I look down at my dress and hands. I'm covered in it. That is my breaking point.

I'm trembling as Cormac slips off his suit coat and wraps it around my shoulders. It's not what he was wearing earlier. How'd they have time to clean up and change? How long have I been standing here since they wheeled Sean away? I thought it was only a couple minutes. I don't even know. Numbness sets in.

"I'll answer the questions. We're Mr. O'Rourke's cousins."

The hospital staffer looks between me and Seamus. "Isn't she his girlfriend or wife?"

"Yes, and she's upset. Questions will only make it worse."

I watch them talk as Cormac leads me away. We sit, and I'm grateful for his arm around my shoulders just like Seamus's earlier. I slump against him with my eyes closed. Tears seep from them.

"Was this because of Ewan or because of me?" I speak only loud enough for Cormac to understand me.

"We don't know. Either, both, or something entirely separate. Has your brother tried to contact you since you left his place?"

I pull out my phone, surprised to see six missed calls from Justin. There're none from Ewan. I hit my voicemail as I sit up. There's only one recording to listen to.

"Nikki, you're making a huge mistake. You need to stay away from Sean. It's not safe. You're more likely to wind up dead than waking up in bed with him."

His voice is beseeching not warning. I look up at Cormac before I stand up. "I need to make this call."

I walk to where I can be reasonably alone in an Emergency Room waiting room. I listen to the message one more time before tapping the phone icon.

"Nik—"

"Did you do it?" I don't let him finish the word.

"Do what? What happened? You weren't at Jesse's when I got there. He said you went to meet Sean."

"Why did you go to Jesse's?"

"Because your brother's on the fucking rampage. I knew you wouldn't listen to me over the phone. You didn't answer my calls."

"I didn't see them come in. And you had to be here before you made the first one."

"I didn't trust you not to bolt if you knew I was on the way. What happened? Are you safe?"

"Yeah. Something happened, but I won't say over the phone. What's Ewan doing?"

"I won't say that over the phone. You need to come back to Boston. I can get you on a flight to Montreal."

"You think I need to go to Canada?"

"I don't know. I've never seen Ewan this pissed before. He believes you told the O'Rourkes about some deal. Whether you did or didn't, he thinks you leaving this morning proves you're conspiring with them. Tell me where you are. I'll come and get you. You need distance from Sean."

"That is the last thing I need right now."

Fucking hell!!!

I look at my phone screen and tap the settings icon.

Fuck. Shit. Fuck.

My location services are on. He already knows where I am. I turn it off. The moment I'm off this call, I'm turning the phone off and dumping it somewhere. I'll stick to the burners. I fucked this one up royally. I run my hand through my hair.

"Nikki, don't do this. Let me get you on the flight home, then you can sort things out once you're out of his reach."

I glance over at Cormac and Seamus, who's now sitting beside his brother. I know Sean has an identical twin, but these two could be twins, too. I was inches away from that bullet hitting me. But I don't regret being with Sean. If it was for him, he protected me. If it was for me, he protected me. Either way, he put my life before his. I'm not leaving him while he's in the hospital because that would be a shit thing to do. But I'm also not leaving him because I still feel safer with him—and, by extension his cousins—than I do anyone else.

I want to think I can still trust Justin. Sean asked if Justin had feelings for me. I don't know. I don't think so. But maybe he does. Or maybe he's trying to dupe me to get me back to Ewan. He's as loyal to my brother as Colt, and Colt would do that in a heartbeat.

"I am out of his reach. I'm going nowhere with you or anyone else connected to my brother. Goodbye."

"But—"

I hang up. I turn the phone off. This shitstorm tempts me to crush the phone or at least break it somehow, but that could be shortsighted. I go back to the brothers and relay the conversation to them. Their grim expressions leave me at a loss as to what I should think now.

"Nikki, if you don't want to go with this guy when he shows up, then you won't. If you change your mind and want to, then we'll still guard you."

"No. You are not leaving Sean here unprotected. And I am not leaving here until he's walking out, holding my hand. Justin can try, but he has never gotten me to bend to his will. It has always been the other way around."

"Would he take you?"

"Yes."

That's easy to answer. He wouldn't intentionally hurt me. But he would force me to go with him. I don't doubt he'd bind my wrists and gag me. I would go willingly if it were Sean doing that. But I'll fucking kill Justin before he takes me away from Sean.

I don't know how to account for these emotions. I'm terrified, angry, frustrated, confused. It's a fucking hurricane in my head right now. I'm so fucking frustrated. I don't know if the anger I already have toward my brother fuels my refusal to trust Justin or consider leaving Sean here. I don't know if it's fear that he's going to die, and I'll feel guilty if I leave. I know I'm confused because this might or might not be about me. I don't know if I'm terrified I'll die if I go anywhere without someone in his family with me. I don't know a lot of things right now.

The thing I do know is that I'm going nowhere without Sean. I've never felt such physical pain as I did the moment I saw the blood. It was like I was between those enormous metal blocks they push together to crush cars. For those moments when he wasn't moving or talking, when he looked like chalk, it was like being tossed in a vacuum. There was no future to guide me out of the abyss. It just felt empty when I thought he was dying. He might still die.

I'm holding myself together, but only by a thread. I don't like public displays of anger or sadness. They make me feel weak. But my hand is clutching my phone to keep from hurling it across this motherfucking room. My eyes burn from the tears that want to fall again.

I am a mob granddaughter. I am a mob daughter. I am a mob sister. And according to Sean, I am a mob girlfriend. I do not show any emotion in public that I don't want to. I control them. They do not control me.

I keep telling myself that as the minutes tick by, and Cormac and Seamus don't press for more. When I'm calm enough to control my voice, I turn to them.

"Justin is likely on his way here. He's been my bodyguard since I moved to Boston and was when I would visit. I've known him since we were kids. If he tries to take me from Sean, kill him."

Chapter Fifteen

Sean

Motherfucking son of a goddamn bitch.

Jesus, Mary, and Joseph. My Catholic grandmothers are doing cartwheels in their graves at my blasphemy. But holy fuck this hurts. This hurts more than the time Maks Kutsenko shot me for punching Bogdan after that shitwad tried to knife Dillan. This hurts more than the time Jorge Diaz shot me after I shot him. I didn't have a reason other than he pisses me the fuck off, and I didn't feel like looking at him. Mom said I got what I deserved for that one.

My throat burns as I come round, but the pain in my back and ribs threatens to make me pass out all over again.

Shite balls. Mom and Da are going to be so pissed. At least it wasn't Mom's carpet I bled on this time. She hates the smell of that carpet cleaner she insists upon using. It takes weeks to go away. If she'd just use the stuff our guys use when—

"Sean."

I didn't imagine that, did I?

"Lina?"

"Yes, *nounours*. What are you saying about carpet cleaner? I don't understand."

I said that out loud?

"Lina! Lina!"

I struggle to get my eyes open. I need to find her. I need to hold her. Did they shoot her too?

"Shh, *nounours*. I'm right here. I thought you were already awake. Shh."

My eyes finally pry open as a cool hand strokes my forehead. She's leaning over me, and I have the most glorious view down her dress.

"You have the most sensational bre—"

Her hand covers my mouth as I reach for her. I hear laughter, and I realize we're not alone. She straightens, and I see Cormac and Seamus.

"Feck off. Way to ruin the dream I was waking up to. Go away and let me say hello to my girlfriend properly."

"Sean, they—"

"They'll be the next ones shot. Go away."

Their laughter trails them to the door. When I'm certain we're alone, my left arm—the one I can lift—wraps around Lina and tugs her to me. She scrambles not to land on me, but I only tighten my grip.

"Kiss."

The fight goes out of her, and she presses her lips to mine. I probably should have brushed my teeth first.

Clearly, my thoughts aren't entirely focused coming out of the anesthesia. But nothing feels better than having her pressed against me, her mouth opening to welcome me into it. It's only when she shifts a couple times I realize the moveable bedrail must be cutting her in half. I let go and pull back, but she clutches my hospital gown and keeps me from ending the kiss. It's only a few seconds more, but it makes me feel superhuman.

"I shouldn't want to fuck a man who was unconscious five minutes ago."

I laugh, but the pain in my side shoots into my chest and down my hip. Fucking hell. What hit me? A fucking cannonball?

"I'm awake now. If you're in the mood..." I waggle my eyebrows at her.

"It's nice to see you in such good spirits. The meds must be working."

"If they are, I hate thinking what it would be like without them."

"Are you in pain?" She pulls away and looks toward the door.

"I'm uncomfortable, but I'll survive. You don't look injured. Did you get hurt?"

"No. You protected me."

"Always, little one." I've never meant three words more in my life.

She lowers the bedrail and kisses me again.

"I thought you were going to die protecting me, Sean. There was so much blood."

"But I didn't."

"Thank God. They had to remove your spleen. The bullet didn't hit your lung, so you're incredibly lucky. The doctor said she'll probably discharge you in a day or two, but it'll be a few weeks before you're back to your old self."

We'll see about that.

"I'm serious, Sean. A few weeks at least. Whatever you're thinking about can wait, or you can let someone else deal with it. You need to rest."

"Will you play doctor with me once we're home?"

Home? Do I mean New York? Boston? It seems natural to think of us being together somewhere, but I have no clue where that is.

"Only if my patient listens to me."

"I'll listen to you moan." I tug at the front of her dress and peer down it again. I groan.

Her hand brushes over my cock. She adds a little pressure, and I'm ready to maul her. But she stands up and pulls her arm away.

"Behave, and I might kiss it better."

"I'll be the best patient ever."

I hold my good arm out to her again. She perches on the edge, careful of my wires and tubes. I run my hand up her leg from calf to thigh. Then I move to her wrist and slide my hand as far as I can reach, which is just above her elbow.

"You look okay, *cailín*. Are you really all right? Did I hurt you when I landed on you?"

She hesitates, and I try to sit up. Fuck.

"Shh. Stay still. I have a couple of bruises, but I'm alive. You almost—"

She swallows, and I can tell the dam is at bursting. I grimace as I push myself over to make room for her beside me. I pat the mattress. She shakes her head. I hook my finger in the top of her dress and tug.

"Let me hold you, Lina. I need to feel for myself that you're okay. I need to make this okay."

She nods as a tear slides down her cheek. She's the perfect size to fit beside me. She rests her head on my shoulder as I kiss her forehead. She inhales and relaxes against me.

"How long was I unconscious?"

"Since yesterday."

I glance up at the clock then out the window. "Twenty-four hours?"

"About twenty-nine."

"Have you been here the entire time?"

"Of course."

She tries to sit up, sounding insulted. I hold her against me.

"Thank you for being here even if I didn't know it."

"Both of your cousins tried to convince me to let them take me back to Jesse's to sleep. They're very polite. I was not. I'm pretty certain they google translated a few of the phrases. Neither offered a second time."

I laugh, but it makes my entire body hurt again.

"Stay still, *nounours*."

"You'd never believe they're the shy ones in the family."

We lie together in companionable silence for a couple minutes.

"Sean, we don't know who did this. Your brothers are here too. Shane, Finn, Seamus, and Cormac have taken turns being our guards in here and in the hallway. Apparently, your brothers had a massive argument with your mom about her coming here. Your dad's pretty pissed too. But their brothers and sisters convinced them to let the guys here guard you. That if they came here, and this is about you, then they're just adding to the targets."

"In other words, my mom was ready to go on a holy tear, shooting first and asking questions second. And it took everything my dad could think of to keep her from coming up here to check on me, then decide how to handle this on her own. She's a little overprotective at times."

She grins. "You don't say. I don't speak Irish, so I didn't understand most of the call Seamus and Cormac made. But there was a woman with very strong opinions on the other end. She sounds fantastic."

"Only one woman?" I think I'm a little insulted.

"I heard others in the background. Why?"

"Because if my mom were coming here, her sisters would come too. Which would mean my dad and uncles."

"That's what they meant about adding to the targets. I didn't quite get how your parents coming here would make it that much worse. But it wouldn't be just them. It would be six more people."

"Exactly. My dad and uncles have lighter red hair than me. Closer to strawberry blond—at least, that's what they call it when we all know it's pale carrots. My mom and aunts have deep, russet hair. Pure fire in the sunshine. Like mythical Celtic goddesses with the tempers to match. Wicked senses of humor. Best hugs in the world. And vengeful as the day is long if you come near their sons or nephews. If this was your brother, I almost feel badly for him if my mom finds out. But he knows her reputation. That should have been deterrent enough."

"Reputation?"

"I'm an O'Rourke on both sides. My maternal and paternal families haven't been closely related in like ten generations. But every generation has had enough sons to carry on the name. The boss before my cousin Dillan was my mom's cousin. The one before that was her older brother. The one before that was her dad. She's married to a mobster. Both her sisters are married to mobsters. Three sisters married three brothers. All three of her sons are mobsters. All three of her nephews are mobsters. I know your family is the mob on both sides, but I can tell you weren't raised the same as my mom and aunts. I don't think they can remember a day in their lives that wasn't somehow touched by violence. It takes a lot of resolve to survive that. If that wasn't enough, neither her father nor brother were easy men to live with. Uncle Donovan was an arsehole by nature and by choice. He obeyed my grandfather, but he feared his sisters. My mom has always been the ring-leader. If she wanted to put a hit on someone, there's not a man in our branch who wouldn't obey. People outside New York know that."

My mom did put a hit on someone. My brothers, cousins, and I aren't supposed to know this, but we do. Uncle Donovan tried to get Shane, Seamus, Cormac, and me into something younger than our moms and dads agreed to. With three sons, my mom wasn't having it. Finn was already well into the thick of his training, and so was Dillan.

When Uncle Donovan tried to force us one day after school, my mom made sure he understood how far her reach extended. The man she picked is still alive, but he was in the ICU for three months. She called off the hit, but she made sure the guy stayed away from us because he answered to her, not Uncle Donovan. She made sure her brother understood he wasn't above his sisters' law. They were the only ones who had the power to make him back down. He hated taking on one of them. He'd come out of his office like a whipped dog when all three sisters were done with him.

"I don't know much because I know not to ask. The guys say they don't know who did this. I believe them. I think at least one of them would tell me if they knew for certain it was Ewan."

I remain quiet. I don't know what to say or ask since I assumed it was him the moment I saw the reflection off a scope. It was a moment's flash of light, but I recognized it immediately.

"Justin called several times while we were getting you here and while you were in surgery. He left one message. I spoke to him once. He wants me to go to Montreal. Whatever happened in Baltimore, Ewan knows about it. Justin feared I'd get caught in the middle when Ewan comes after you. I don't know if your family's done anything to Ewan. If they have, and this is Ewan, he's not nearly done."

"You could have gone with Justin. He could have gotten you home safely. Or do you think he would have turned you over to Ewan?"

"He would have gotten me to Montreal, though I wouldn't put it past him to give me to Ewan if my brother demanded it. But I told Cormac and Seamus to kill him if he tries to take me from you. They know I'm serious."

"Lina!"

"I am. I'm not leaving here until you're discharged. Once I'm certain you're somewhere safe, I'll go if you tell me to. But no one is taking me from you. I'll listen to your family's advice and wishes. But if the command to leave comes from anyone but them, they'll die before they succeed."

"As though you didn't have me hard as a fecking plank earlier. The things you say, little girl. You know how to turn me on."

She laughs, and I kiss her forehead.

"If I didn't think we'd be interrupted at any minute, I'd treat you with my kind of medicine."

"Tell my cousins no one's coming in here unless they want to die. Including them. Go."

I'm serious, but she thinks I'm kidding. She laughs and shakes her head against my chest. Blue balls and a splenectomy. Only one is likely to kill me. Since I don't have a spleen anymore, it's not that.

"Are you scared to go with Justin?"

"A little. But mostly, I just don't trust him. I don't trust him not to drop me off with Ewan. I don't trust him not to use me to get to you or help Ewan use me to get to you. I don't trust either of them not to hurt you to hurt me."

"You've mentioned Justin and Ewan. What about Colt?"

"What about Colt?" There's an edge there that warns me to tread carefully.

"Could he be involved in this?"

"Of course. You said you know him. If you do, then you know he's a sniper. Who do you think I believe took the shot?"

That gives me a moment's pause. It's true. Colt enlisted in the military right out of high school. He was already a sniper by eighteen. He didn't run away from home. He didn't even go in to hone his skills. He went in to make connections. Domestically and internationally. I thought that's what he did to get in better with Rowan. I never imagined he'd do something else—like offer to marry Rowan's daughter.

"If he did, why? Because Ewan ordered it? Or did he do it on his own like Justin went down to New York on his own?"

"I don't know."

"If it's him, would it be about Baltimore or you?"

Her laugh is brittle. "If it's about me, it's only because he wants to make you think his balls are bigger than yours. He doesn't give a shit about me." She glances at my groin. "He'll have to do a hell of a lot more to prove his are."

"A hell of a lot more might get you killed in the process. He can think his cock, his balls, his brains, his bank account are all bigger than mine. I don't care. I want him away from you."

She watches me as she props herself up on her elbow. It's a peek into the future and how she'll feel when I give her this look because I won't say what we both know I'm going to do. This time, it's what she wants me to do without her having to ask.

"Lina, there is no limit to protecting you. Know that because I won't get more specific."

"I'll peel the skin from his bones and make him eat it if he did this."

She lies back down beside me and nestles closer as though she didn't just go all Hannibal Lecter.

"Have you always been this bloodthirsty?"

"No. Not even remotely. I don't know why I feel the way I do. I've been trying to sort it out, and I'm still confused. I don't understand the cause, but the outcome is I'm as committed to protecting you as you are to protecting me."

"Do you hate him that much?" Please don't let that be the reason.

"I don't hate Colt or Ewan. I trust neither of them. I resent both of them. Hate is more emotion than I want to give them. At least, until today. I don't think about Colt most of the time. But I am bitter when I do. I'm bitter when I see him because he's not sorry about what he did."

I wonder if she'll tell me one day. She doesn't seem inclined to do that today. Even if she were, there's a knock on the door. She jumps off the bed like the sheets scalded her. She straightens her dress, which I realized isn't the one she wore yesterday. Someone brought her fresh clothes.

"Mr. O'Rourke?" A middle-aged woman walks around the privacy curtain wearing scrubs and her lab coat. "I'm Dr. Garland."

I extend my arm out of habit, but my IV tugs. I drop my arm, and she nods. I hold out my left hand, palm up. Lina doesn't hesitate to take it and stand by me. It's not like I'm expecting news that I'm terminal. I don't like distance between us. Physical or emotional right now. I want her to know that we're an us as far as I'm concerned.

"Hello, Doctor."

"You got very lucky yesterday. The bullet nicked your spleen and ruptured it. That's why your girlfriend and cousins saw so much blood. But the injury wasn't as severe as it could have been, or I'm certain they feared. If you're able to handle moving around tomorrow and pass some other tests, I'll discharge you. That said, it'll be at least two weeks before you should try to return to your normal activities."

Her gaze darts from me to Lina and back. She doesn't need to spell it out.

"That might be what kills me."

Lina gasps, and the doctor looks away.

"Um, just how limited should *those* activities be, Doctor?" Lina's cheeks are rosier than Santa's.

She looks at me when she answers. "Nothing strenuous that could rupture your internal stitches. Too much movement will strain the muscles around the wound in your abdomen, and you have bruising you can't see. Go slowly. See what you can tolerate or explore other types of intimacy."

Lina looks like her neck to her roots is ablaze. It makes me wonder what she's envisioning. I want the doc to go, so we can continue our conversation and add this topic to it.

"We'll remember that. So, if I can do everything you expect by tomorrow, I can go home?"

"That's the plan. You're young, and in excellent health, so there's no reason to think you won't make a full recovery. Hopefully, the police catch the men who put you in the middle of their fight. You're lucky it wasn't anything more serious."

I don't react besides nodding and smiling. Lina's fingers curl around mine a little tighter. The doctor says her goodbyes with a promise to check on me midmorning. I want out now. No one comes to a hospital to get better. How can you when they wake you every three hours to take your vitals? For fuck's sake, if the machine's alarm isn't going off, then I'm fine. I'm alive until it tells you otherwise. Let me fucking sleep. I was better off unconscious.

When I look up at Lina, I know that's not true. I'm definitely way better off seeing her and touching her.

"We've been in here alone a long time. You might have kicked Seamus and Cormac out, but at least they saw you awake. Your brothers must be ready to lose their minds."

I release a beleaguered sigh. "I give Shane five words before it's about him."

She lets go of my hand and walks to the door. I hear her murmur something, then my brothers are there. Finn casts an assessing gaze over me. Ever the big brother—when he wants to be. He's careful when he hugs me. I don't miss the sigh of relief. We speak at the same time.

"*Mo chúram.*" It means my family, but its literal translation is my responsibility.

It's something my family's said for as long as I've heard stories about the past. It's a reminder that we are family, and without family, we are nothing. It's each of our responsibility to preserve that.

Finn flicks my ear because we can't be sentimental for too long. It's not mobster manly. Shane sighs. Here it comes.

"That was my suit you ruined."

I ignore him and look at Lina. "Three."

She snickers and covers her mouth with her hand. I was generous, saying it would take my twin five words to make it about him. When he shoots me the same grin I have, I roll my eyes and flick him off.

"If you weren't on your death bed..." Shane flicks me off in return.

We never swear at, to, or about one another. But an obscene hand gesture here and there never goes amiss.

He practically chokes me when he hugs me. I use my one good arm to return his hug. He doesn't let go when I ease my hold.

"Don't fecking do that again. We arrived together. We leave together."

That's something just between us. We've been saying it since we were in middle school when kids would try to exclude one or the other of us. We said it in high school when our rivals tried to flex and draw us apart in fights. Whoever heard it usually wound up with a broken nose and broken collar bone. Those were our preferred injuries to dole out. Matching to the core.

"I'll get you a new suit. Jeez. It looked better on me, anyway."

"Be glad we have company." He smiles at Lina, and she doesn't know what the fuck to make of our family. Mair and Ally went through the same thing. Apparently, we're shockingly normal. Who knew?

I look at Lina, then Cormac and Seamus. She knows them now, and I know she trusts them. I don't want to send her away because she'll know why I'm excluding her. I don't want her where I can't see for myself that she's safe. Realizing I was out of it for twenty-nine hours makes me want to vomit because that was twenty-nine hours I wasn't aware of her safety. I know my cousins and brothers were, but I left her vulnerable. At least, that's how I feel.

I look at the clock again. "I bet the cafeteria is still open. Could you smuggle me something good? I love Jell-O, but I guarantee whatever they bring me won't be nearly substantial enough. Cormac or Seamus will go with you. Pick what you want for yourself. Their treat."

"How long do you need? Thirty minutes? An hour?" She says it without rancor.

"Let's start with thirty. I don't think I'll last longer than that."

"You've been awake a while. Do you need another dose of pain meds?"

For once, my brothers and cousins don't give me shite as the baby of the family. They step away to talk amongst themselves. She glances at them before focusing on me again.

"Lina, they know thirty minutes without knowing exactly

where you are is my limit until we settle this. They know I'll get out of this bed and look for you."

"You will not."

That stops their conversation, and they don't bother disguising their interest. Finn laughs. I flick him off.

"Be nice to your brother. He flew out here for you."

That just makes them all guffaw.

"Feck off."

"I'll give her Thea's and Mair's numbers." I glare at Finn when he makes the offer.

"Sean?"

I take her hand and smile. "You remind us of Finn's wife and our cousin Dillan's wife. I think you'll like them. I'm certain they'll like you."

"You are?"

"Yeah. You don't hesitate to tell my little brother off. His spoiled arse needs some boundaries." Finn crosses his arms.

"There can only be one favorite. Too bad it's never been you."

"Cause it's always been me." Shane butts in, and Finn and I both flick him off. He's not even remotely selfish or self-involved. We know our roles in situations like this and what helps us get through this shite. A sense of humor helps when it feels like your funny bone is the only one not broken.

"Would anyone like us to bring something back?" Lina looks around the group.

We laugh again. She's totally lost. I take pity.

"Since I said it's one of our cousins' treats, it's open season. You'll need a wagon to get it all up here. None of us are exactly skimping on meals, so it's always nice when it's someone else paying." I wink.

She nods before she leans over to kiss my cheek. Her brow furrows, and I can tell she really doesn't want to go.

"I'll be all right. Would you feel better if two of the guys go with you?"

"No. Absolutely not. I don't like taking one of your guards away, let alone two. Can't I just wait in the hall? You can see me if you open the curtain."

She's whispering to me, and once again, the guys give us space by talking amongst themselves.

"No. That leaves you too vulnerable. More vulnerable than me. I don't like the idea of you being gone more than thirty minutes. You alone somewhere—even right outside in the hallway—will make me come out of my skin. I hate sending you away, *cailín*."

"I know, and I totally get why. But you're not the only one not okay with being apart for long. I'll give you thirty minutes, but I don't think I can do more."

"Out."

The guys glance at me before they leave without a word. I open my arms—well, arm—to her. She shakes her head but sits on the edge.

"I won't fall apart. At least, not in front of you. I don't need you comforting me when you're the one injured. I know your brothers and cousins can protect you. I can't get past the feeling this happened because of me. I don't want someone finding you when they're—"

"Finish that sentence with what I know you're going to say, and I will make your sweet little arse burn so badly you won't sit for a week. Don't you dare tell me you'd rather be the target. I will lose my shite faster than anyone in my family has ever seen. I'm the patient one. But they will tell you that pushed too far, I have the worst temper of all of us."

"If they come looking for me but only find you, they will kill you. If they find me, then they'll just take me."

"We both know that isn't true. You know they wouldn't

settle for leaving me alive. And you know for fecking sure I'm not letting anyone take you."

"Then I should go."

"Go where? To Jesse's? To Montreal? You know I won't agree to that without two of the guys with you. At least two of them. That leaves all of us more vulnerable if we separate. If you want out of this, then I will negotiate with your grandfather to get you home safely."

"This—if you mean someone trying to murder you, then yes, I want out of this. I want you out of it too. If you mean us, then you're sending me away. I'm not walking away."

We stare at each other, our tempers threatening to spike. We want the same thing, and neither of us will back down. I take her hand.

"Give me thirty minutes with the guys. That's as long as either of us can manage. Come back, and I'll tell you what I can. I'll listen to your thoughts, and I'll try my best to compromise. Then we'll watch TV together until it's time to go to bed. You'll sleep next to me."

"Good thing I'm skinny."

"Good thing you're the perfect size."

We exchange a quick kiss, then she walks to the door. I hear Seamus offer to take her to the cafeteria, then the others walk in.

Chapter Sixteen

Sean

"Is Dillan with Ewan?"

"Yes." Finn's our second in command, and Dillan's best friend.

It didn't surprise me to realize Dillan wasn't with the others. It would be completely understandable if he remained in NYC to oversee our family empire. Make no two ways about it. The O'Rourkes built an empire, and we will die before we see it perish.

But I know my cousin. I know how much he despises Ewan, especially after the shite the turd got himself into when he tried to pick up where his father left off. I remind myself that piece of arse was Lina's dad too. But Rowan, then Ewan, tried to fuck Finn's in-laws over. They're all our family now. That means it's not just Finn pissed at Ewan. And the little shite knows that.

It brings us right back around to why I was in Baltimore and why Lina was in NYC before that. He keeps trying to assert himself, and we keep swiping his knees out from under him. He's either going to learn or die failing. For Lina's sake, I don't want the latter. Not just because I don't want my family responsible for another death in hers. I don't want her to lose another person. Whether she loves Ewan or loved her dad is irrelevant. It's still a loss.

"Has he found out anything?" I glance at the door even though I'm certain Lina can't hear anything.

"Not yet. He's watching him right now. You know he has questionable friends in the city. We want to see if he goes back to them or stays out of our way."

We are so New Yorkers. The city can only mean one place —Manhattan. On a nice day—since we grew up in Queens—it means all five boroughs. Though, no one means the Bronx or Staten Island.

"*Jodidos colombianos.*" Fucking Colombians.

I can say a shite ton more than that in Spanish, but that sums it up. Let those fuckers think they can do business with the Boston Irish to piss us off. The more business they do with each other, the more there is for us to steal from both of them.

"Yeah, well, Pablo's still a pain in the arse." Finn can barely get the words out without a stream of curses coming with them.

"*Que se jodan.*" Fuck them.

Pablo and I have a long history that isn't pretty. About fifteen years ago, I was dating a girl, Mei, who I really liked, but I knew it wasn't serious. At the same time, Pablo was dating Mei's cousin. She cheated on me and dumped me for Pablo. He didn't stop gloating until I started fucking Lian, his ex-girlfriend and Mei's cousin. She gave no shits about him, but I know he definitely loved her. They were together for a year.

Lian's father was the head of one of the Dragons—Chinese Triad. Mei and Lian dated each of us for the connections we brought their families. Pablo and I dated them for the exact same reason: the connections their fathers brought us. The difference is, I didn't fall in love with either of them. Pablo never forgave me.

We ended up in a fight not long after we both wound up single. He tried to stab me but missed. I cut a line from his left shoulder to nearly his right nipple. Talk about a lot of blood. He has tats that cover the scar, but we all know it's there and why. I beat his arse.

It wouldn't surprise me in the least to learn Pablo discovered my interest in Lina, and now he's doubled his support for Ewan. Lian and Lina—such similar names, but they be couldn't less alike. *Lina*—my *cailín*—is the only woman I'll give my heart to.

If Ewan's put a hit on me, Pablo's probably getting his rocks off thinking about my death. If Pablo's put a hit on me, then Ewan's probably sucking his dick to get the job. Either way, both of them have a reason to see me dead sooner rather than later.

"Where is Pablo right now?" I look at Finn since he works with me to surveil the other families.

"Margherita's back in the hospital. Pablo has questionable friends, but after what happened to his mom when she found out about his involvement with everything that happened to Thea—I don't think this is him to be honest."

Margherita's his mom and has been fighting cancer for over a year. She's been in and out of the hospital. She was home when shite went sideways for Finn and his in-laws. My brother made Pablo confess his role to his mother. It was Ally—only Finn calls her Thea—who stepped in and made Pablo stop talking. She's a doctor, and she got alarmed when Margherita's breathing became labored.

"Is she going to be all right? Did that just happen?" I've been gone two days.

Just like all the moms, Margherita knows her son's short-comings, but she's still proud of him. But that day—she looked at her son as though she didn't know him. It crushed him to see her disappointment. It really made me believe he'd think twice before involving any more women. But his memory hasn't been that great since Aleks Kutsenko gave him a concussion in eleventh grade.

His fuckwad cousins, *Tres J's*—Jorge, Joaquin, and Javier—insulted Maria Mancinelli at a party we all wound up at. Her brothers, cousin, cousin's best friend, and her now husband—who's also one of her brother's best friends—lost their ever-loving minds. The Kutsenkos and their Andreyev cousins who now lead the Ivankov bratva jumped in to defend Maria and her friend, who was also insulted. Dillan, Finn, and I started heckling the Diazes for picking on girls and the Mancinellis for needing the Russians to protect their women. We all got sucked into a melee.

By the end, we all wished we'd died because we had to face our respective leaders. Granddad went completely berserk. Uncle Donovan wasn't any calmer. We were lucky neither our grandfather nor uncle wanted to face our moms if we came home any more battered than we were. I learned Irish words I'd never heard before when they both chewed us up, then spat us out. I say we were lucky, but then again, now that I think about it, we ran back to them to escape our moms.

Shane shrugs. "We don't know. Our moms took more food over yesterday. They ran into Laura, Christina, Anastasia, Sumiko, Heather, and Katerina as they were leaving." That's all the bratva wives.

Forget the United Nations. It's the United Mothers the world should care about. Irish Catholic moms are permanent members of that Security Council. They sit at the same table as Italian Catholic moms, Colombian Catholic moms, Russian

East Orthodox moms, and I've met my share of Protestant, Muslim, and Jewish moms who sit on that committee too. Fuck. I've met mothers of all different faiths who could give PhD level seminars on how to make their children repent with one raised eyebrow. They can dole out guilt like it's their love language.

Cormac crosses his arms and rests back on his heels. "My guess is Pablo's still doing business with Ewan because he can. He won't stop Ewan, but he won't help, either. Whatever money Ewan's making from the deal with Pablo, that's as involved as the Diazes are going to get. He'll turn a blind eye, and Ewan'll pay for the hit with his profits."

"Are you certain I was the target?"

Finn, Shane, and Cormac shake their heads. I glance at the door. Shane rests his hands on the foot of the hospital bed. His knuckles are white as he speaks.

"Before I left and Dillan arrived, Ewan and Colt met some big guy who looked seriously pissed while talking to them. He was gesturing all over the place. I sent Finn his pic, and he ran facial rec on the guy. His name's Justin Monahan."

"Lina's bodyguard. The guy's in love with her."

Cormac shakes his head. "The feeling definitely isn't mutual. He left her a message, telling her to put distance between the two of you. He offered to come get her and take her to Montreal. She told Shay and me that if he comes near her and tries to take her from you, we're to kill him. She wasn't exaggerating. She was dead arse serious. They've been friends since they were kids, and she didn't bat an eye telling us what she wants. I wouldn't put it past her to do it herself if we don't."

"She told me. I saw him while they were in New York. He banged on her hotel door while we were together."

Shane picks up the story again from where he left off. "He was angry about something Ewan said. I'd just pulled up and didn't catch what it was. They were on Ewan's porch, so the mic and headphones helped. I heard him telling Ewan and Colt how pissed he was. They laughed. Colt taunted him about his feelings for Li—Nikki."

My brother catches himself before I clench my jaw. He raises his hands in surrender.

"Sorry. You keep calling her that, and I barely know her. Give me five minutes to catch up. Anyway, Justin warned them about the Tremblays getting involved if this goes much further. He left, presumably to call Nikki. Ewan and Colt went inside. I waited in the car, watching the place until Cormac called to tell me what happened. I left when Dillan got there. I think this could be as much about her as it is you. I think Ewan could have put a hit on his sister for being with you."

"Or for being uncontrollable. She won't bend to him, and she knows shite now. She's a liability in general, but now that she's with me, he won't want her talking."

We fall silent, and I know all of us are thinking about Colleen. She was Dillan's younger sister, but she may as well have been all of ours. She was the uncontested leader among us even though she was younger than Dillan and Finn. She'd get us into so much trouble, but we had a blast along the way. When Seamus and Cormac came out of it with their hands looking clean, she'd point out the dirt under their nails once we were away from our parents. We never dimed each other out. She'd mete out her own justice to make sure they got their fair share.

She was hilarious with a raunchy sense of humor, but she was also the kindest person anyone could ever meet. She was a vet and specialized in rescue animals. When Uncle Donovan died, our moms' cousin Declan seized control. It was a shitshow with the bratva that led to Uncle Donovan's death. Dillan was so pissed because our uncle didn't listen to his advice and exactly what he warned would happen did. He went out of town for a breather before he was supposed to assume the mantle. Granddad and Uncle Donovan groomed him for it.

To ensure his power grab, Declan put a hit on our moms. He died for fucking around with the bratva before he called off the hit. A woman thought she had Cormac and Seamus's mom, Auntie Saoirse, in her crosshairs. It was Colleen. Dillan was there and caught her as she fell. He called his parents. He was holding her, sitting in a pool of his baby sister's blood, when we got there. He didn't speak for a month. They were as close as Shane and me even though they weren't twins.

If it weren't for Finn, I'm certain Dillan would have drunk himself to death. Either alcohol poisoning or getting so pish drunk he wound up in a fight that would have killed him. I think that's what he wanted. Fortunately, he trusts Finn, and they survived his grief. His wife is the best thing that's ever happened to him. I didn't believe it was possible, but he trusts her and relies on her advice even more than he did Colleen's. I wasn't sure he'd ever let himself love someone so much again. But he and Mair are soulmates.

I glance at the clock again. It makes me wonder what Lina's doing. It's been twenty-five minutes. I'll give myself four more minutes before I get out of bed. Six before I go looking for them. Arse to the breeze if I have to.

"What's the plan going forward?" We only have four minutes left to decide.

"You keep your arse in bed where you belong and stop staring at the clock. We will keep you and Nikki safe. We wait for Dillan to tell us anything he learns. As soon as you're well enough to travel, we go home. Will Nikki come with you?" Finn's watching the door as he speaks.

"I hope so."

"Find out." Shane's going to say more, but someone knocks.

All of them reach behind their backs for their guns. My instinct is to do the same. One of my cousins must have grabbed my gun and belt holster before the ambulance came.

"Sean?"

"Come in, Lina."

She steps around the curtain, and Seamus follows. He has a tray that's heaping with food. She snaps the privacy curtain closed behind him, and my cousin puts the tray in front of me.

"Thanks for bringing some for us." Cormac reaches to grab a bite off the plates of fries.

"Touch them, and you'll lose a finger. You can have what Sean doesn't eat." She says it with a grin, but we all suspect she's serious.

Cormac smirks at me. If Lina weren't here, he'd probably tell me she and I are sitting in a tree, k-i-s-s-i-n-g. Fecking twat. He has the humor of a twelve-year-old.

Shane snags a fry, looking completely serious as he spews his shite. "You can't cut off my fingers. It'll give Sean phantom pains."

None of us can say more because a nurse comes in. I appreciate Shane distracting Lina while Finn sent off a text, and Cormac whispered to Seamus to bring him up to speed. Once the nurse is gone, we dive in and devour the food. Once the plates are practically licked clean, I use the remote to turn off the lights.

"Don't fall over shite on your way out."

The guys leave. I know they'll set up shifts for two of them to guard us. If Lina weren't here, two of them would crash in here.

"Come here, *cailín*. I've been lonely."

"I doubt that." She kicks off her shoes and eases onto the bed.

Once she's positioned against me, I kiss her head and stroke her hair. "Once upon a time there was a knight with red hair. He spied a fairy princess across a deep chasm. Little did he know..."

She's already asleep, and my eyes are barely open. I'm as comfortable as I'm going to get. My final thought before I fall asleep isn't the beginning of a sweet dream. It's how nightmares are made. I picture Lina bound and gagged to a chair with a needle in her arm.

I believe in premonitions. I've had plenty. Rarely are they wrong.

Chapter Seventeen

Lina

I dozed off fast, but I'm awake and listening to Sean's deep breathing. It's soothing. A nurse came in about an hour ago, and it's what woke me. I didn't get off the bed before he saw me. He shot me a terse smile but didn't object. Sean didn't wake while the guy took his vitals.

The only other sound in here is the monitor, and the volume is turned down. I didn't know it was adjustable. I thought it came with one setting: drive you batshit loud. The steady rhythm of the lines gives me something to focus on rather than looking at the tubes and cords attached to Sean.

I'm trying to think of a historical couple or movie where a relationship started this chaotically. One moment, we meet at a funeral. I pretend to be his girlfriend to get him out of an awkward conversation. Then the next, we're making out in a storeroom. A few weeks later, we're meeting for lunch that turns into afternoon delight. That's cut short when he has to run off—apparently, to fuck over my asshole brother. I go to my new home only to walk out because said brother pissed me off even before I knew Sean was on his way to meet me. Then it's a too brief reunion, and my whatever-Sean-is-to-me gets shot and is in the hospital. It's where I am now, sharing a bed with him because he had surgery to remove a damaged organ from a bullet my brother's best friend—who happens to be my ex-fiancé—likely shot. Possibly at me.

What is the world coming to?

Whether Ewan ordered this or was even a minute part of it, he hasn't called. I have my phone in my pocket, and it hasn't vibrated since I missed Justin's call. I had to give in and turn my phone back on since I needed to call Jesse yesterday because I needed fresh clothes. I couldn't stay in the blood-soaked dress. He tried to bombard me with questions, but I stonewalled.

Eventually, he gave up. He was stoic when he handed me my overnight bag. But I know it freaked him out to see me the way I was. I'd scrubbed most of the blood off my hands by then. Seamus's suit coat hid most of my dress but not all of it. I kept it pulled around me most of the time, so I didn't have to look at it.

Jesse knows just enough about my family to know not to ask. He knows I'll volunteer what I want him to know and nothing more. He suggested I go back to his place, and Cormac and Seamus offered to escort me. It got heated. That's when I got so frustrated I lapsed into Franglais—French and English. That's when all three of them had to google translate half of what I said. They learned some colorful phrases to add to their own repertoires.

I'm careful as I put my hand over Sean's heart. How does sleeping next to him feel so natural? Especially here of all places.

"Do you need another fairytale? You've been up for an hour." His hand covers mine.

"You've been awake?"

"No one is walking into this room without me knowing. I just didn't want to answer any asinine questions the machines already have. I hoped you'd fall back to sleep on your own if I didn't strike up a conversation. You've relaxed and tensed at least a dozen times. Tell me what's wrong, *cailín*."

"Besides all of this?" I'm not being sarcastic.

"Yes. You're mulling over something else."

"Do you think this is guilt and fear?" I'm positive he knows what I mean.

"If it were just guilt, I would have insisted my family get you back to Montreal. If it were just fear, my family guarding you would be enough for me. If were just guilt and fear, I wouldn't need you in my arms to sleep. This connection we have is real."

"Everything is supercharged right now. What about when things calm down? Assuming they do."

"They will, and we will figure out how to be a normal couple together. Lina, I learn more about you by the minute, and I can't stop my growing attraction. I don't want to. I already knew you were intelligent and funny. I was part of those text conversations, and I still haven't defeated your encryption. Though, I've been a little sidetracked. I knew you were independent and brave. You've moved countries three times. You're steadfast. You're loyal. You're resolved. You're—"

"A cocker spaniel." I kiss his cheek and nuzzle his neck.

"You can get on my lap anytime."

He reaches for my ass, but he can only reach my lower back. He presses it to push me closer.

"You're calm during a crisis. You're skeptical of people you don't know, and you learn from your past. You're not easily intimidated, and if you are, you've mastered your poker face. You're thoughtful. You're accepting of things you can't change but willing to push for the things you believe should. You're—"

"I get it, *nounours*. You see things about me I don't see in myself."

"And you're hot as sin."

He shifts to kiss me, so I make it easier. I push up to bring my head level with his. Our mouths meet, and there is no world around us. We recognize his limitations, so this isn't lust. This began as physical attraction the day we met. Now... It reminds me of the article with the adaptive oscillators. I still don't know what those are, but ours synced. They've intertwined.

"Did you know that everything you said about me is what I already think about you?" I whisper as my forefinger and thumb turn his head farther toward me, and I begin the next kiss.

The arm beneath me moves, and his hand fists my hair. His hold is tight, but he doesn't tug. That would pull me away from this kiss. He shifts his leg between mine, so his thigh presses against my pussy.

"Anyone could walk in on us."

"Good thing you climbed under the covers when you got into bed. Move on my leg, *cailín*. You know I would do more if I could."

"I know."

"I take care of you, Lina. Not just your safety. More than that."

"I know."

"I want to be the only man in your bed. The only man in your arms. The only man responsible for making sure you have everything you need and everything I can give you that you want."

"You are. You're all of those. I only feel safe when I'm with you. Your family keeps me from losing it. But you're the only one I trust because you've already put me first. You risked your life for me."

"And I will any time there's a threat."

"We're both into BDSM. We understand the power dynamics of those relationships. It's sexual, but it's deeper than that because it satisfies emotional and mental needs. At the same time, though, there's a distance. It's not the same as a romantic relationship. I'm in over my head, and I want to let you take control, Sean. Not just physically when you're well. I need to lean against you because everything in me tells me you're my haven. That if I let you take control—rather than me panicking when I feel out of control—we'll both feel better. I think you need that too. You can't control all of this right now, and that must be driving you nuts. You're not letting me see it, but I know it. You can control where I go and who I go with. You can control whether I'm with you or how long we're apart. You can control my physical needs. You can because I want you to. I want to let go of all of that. I want you to take it, so you don't feel adrift. It's the only way I won't feel lost."

I've stopped moving against his leg, and his hand in my hair merely cups my head. I close my eyes and sigh. I didn't know how heavy all of that was until now. The more I said, the more I felt him relax. He reaches across his chest with a wince. Then his fingers are down the front of my dress and under my bra. He tweaks my nipple. Hard. It's like a key in my ignition. My hips rock, and my pussy rubs against him.

"I am protective and possessive with you. The first isn't something new to me. The second is completely foreign. I grew up in a family with seven kids. I shared everything and never minded. I won't share you with anyone. I won't let anyone come near you that you don't want. No one tells you what to do."

"But you, *nounours*." I murmur that, not wanting to interrupt him but remind him.

"If this is what you want, then you are mine, Lina. You take

245

back control the moment you want to, and I will never argue with you about it. I will respect every limit and every boundary you have. I will never guilt you or coerce you to keep that control. But while I have it, it's absolute. Can you live with that?"

"Yes. At least until we're through all this."

"That's what I meant. When I'm convinced you're no longer in imminent danger, we reassess."

He kisses me, and it's savage. It's one to dominate me and remind me of my submission. Except he doesn't have to. I want him to lead, so I can follow. In the past, I've only agreed to this during sex and only in specific situations. I've never done this emotionally—at least, not beyond the emotional satisfaction I got from that kind of sex.

The more I transfer the crushing weight to his broader shoulders, the more aroused I become. I grind my clit against his muscular thigh. I'm so fucking close.

"Come for me, little one."

"I'm almost there."

"I know. You're going to come because I'm letting you."

I shift to rest on my right forearm as my left arm reaches across him, my hand on the mattress to brace myself. His hands finally grasp my ass as I ride his leg.

"Who do you belong to, *cailín*?"

"You." It's exhilarating to say.

"Who protects you?"

"You." Something deep in my mind is trying to break through.

"Who cares about you?"

"You."

"Who's going to look after you?"

"You."

Our gazes meet. I suck in a breath as I clench my ass. My head tilts back as I rub harder and faster.

"May I come?"

"Who am I?"

"*Nounours.*"

"Who else?"

I look back at him as my eyes open. There's an answer we both want, and I believe we're thinking the same thing. Fuck. It's so hot to think it.

"Who, *cailín?* Say it." His hand lands across my ass.

I open my mouth to, but I come. My entire body tenses as I strain to keep the bliss going. His hands grip my ass tighter. His fingers dip between my ass cheeks, pressing near a place that's even more intimate than my cunt.

"Say. It. Little. Girl."

"Daddy."

My arms give out, and I barely catch myself before I land on him. I roll to give him space, but his hand lands across my ass. It's not hard. It's playful. We watch each other as though we're not sure if what I just said was real.

"Lina, I'm still not your Dom. I'm not and never have been nor ever want to be a real Daddy Dom. That isn't the type of taking care of you I mean. I don't think that's the type of care you want to receive."

"It's not. But all the things I said earlier are the things someone would expect a guardian or caretaker to provide. I don't think that word makes me a Little. I'm not. I think it's something between us, and I don't see it as being all that different from the way Latin American women can use the word *papí.* Maybe I'm wrong about that, but that's my impression."

"If I get too controlling, tell me. I'm not inflexible about anything but your safety. I will not budge on that. Lina, my word is law for that."

"I know. We both know I'm not new to this life or safety protocols. I'm used to rules and restrictions for my wellbeing and others. You know how the mob works here in the U.S. You know what Ewan and his men are capable of. You've been dealing with them for a lot longer than I have and in ways I never have. I'll obey, Daddy."

I grin, and he purses his lips. I give him the kiss he wants as I slide my hand up his leg to his cock. I've felt how hard he's been since he became conscious. It's waned to half mast, but now he's solid titanium. I wrap my hand around him.

"Will you let me pleasure you now?"

"That's one thing you don't need permission for."

He holds the sheet up, so we can see what I'm doing. I run my fingertips over him, tempting him. Teasing him. He twitches over and over. His hand goes back to my hair, and it's another hungry and demanding kiss. Neither of us gives quarter. I wrap my hand around his dick and stroke. I feel him grow even harder as I squeeze and twist my wrist with each slide of my palm.

"You're going to make me embarrass myself. I'm so close, little one."

"I want to know you can't last with me, Daddy. That's the ultimate compliment."

"Fuck, Lina. Keep doing that... Yes... Faster. You're torturing me."

"I know."

I yelp when he pinches my nipple through my bra. He doesn't let go until I follow his command. Then I feel him pulse before the outside of my fingers are wet. I was content to watch what I was doing since I held the sheet up when he let go to touch me. When I shift my focus to his face, there's perspiration on his brow.

"Fuck, Sean. We did too much."

"I barely moved. You did all the work, and it was just right."

"You're breathing hard and sweating."

"Because I just came harder than I expected. I promise I'm all right. I wouldn't lie about this. Setting myself back means I can't fulfill my promises to you. I won't fail you."

"Sean, I never thought you would. You haven't, and you won't."

There was something in those last four words. Like he needs to prove himself to me.

I sit up as I pull my hand out from beneath the blanket. I slip off the bed to wash my hands. The water's still running when there's a single knock, and the door opens.

"It's Ewan. He's been shot."

I slam the tap off as Shane's words register with me. I grab paper towels as I walk out of the bathroom. I'm watching Sean, who's watching me. I sense Shane's gaze flickering between us. I don't know what Shane will offer while I'm here, so I remain quiet.

"When?"

"Fifteen minutes ago."

Dillan?

"Dillan?" Great minds think alike.

"No. He's the one who got to Ewan first."

"What?" I didn't mean to blurt that.

"Dillan was in the parking lot at Houlihan's. He followed your brother there. He could see Ewan was on a call in his car. When he hung up, he got out. According to Dillan, Ewan closed the door, turned around, and fell backward against the car. Dillan didn't see where the shooter hid, but he returned fire as he ran to Ewan."

"Is my brother dead?"

"No. But he's in worse condition than Sean."

"Did they take him to the hospital or David?" So much for remaining quiet.

"David's clinic."

Our third cousin's a surgeon who runs a private clinic in a wealthy part of Boston. He doesn't practice there, except for when he's patching up members of the O'Malley branch. It's a cosmetic surgery center when he isn't keeping people like Ewan from looking like Swiss cheese.

Sean's listening to Shane, but his eyes are on me. He's not sure what to make of my calmness. I'm not either. Shouldn't I feel more? It's the same way I did when I found out Dad died. Am I emotionally broken? Like I don't feel grief when I should. And I feel too much—what the hell do I feel toward Sean? Too much falling in love?

He holds out his hand like he did earlier when the doctor came in. I cross the room with purposeful strides. I accept, wrapping both of mine around his. I have nothing more to say, so Sean speaks up.

"What's the prognosis?"

I guess I should have asked that.

"Uncertain."

Mirror faces observe me. It's disconcerting. Purely by appearance, you truly cannot tell them apart except for the freckle on Sean's throat. But the expression in his eyes screams who he is. It's tender and apprehensive for me. All the while, unwavering in his reliability. This is exactly what I told him I need. He'd be like this even if I hadn't.

"Is his mom with him?"

"I don't know."

"Dillan didn't call their doctor, so who did?"

"Colt. He was already at the bar. He nearly put a bullet

through Dillan's head until he realized Dillan's hands on Ewan's chest were keeping him alive. A private ambulance showed up."

I speak up. "David's. He's a medical mogul. He's a cardio-thoracic surgeon—lucky for Ewan—who invests millions in biotech and pharmaceutical companies. He rents out the clinic space during the day and owns the ambulance service."

"He specialize in that because of your family's line of work?" Shane looks mildly amused.

"Pretty much. That, and he's a greedy fucker. The type to steal lunch money."

I couldn't stand him as a kid. He used to pick on me until Ewan would make him back off. He'd ice David out of what-ever the other kids were doing and made sure I was included. Where did that brother go? Oh, yeah. He turned sixteen and became a mobster and a douche.

My phone vibrates in my pocket. I pull it out, not surprised to see Colt. I hold it up, so Sean and Shane can see. Sean nods. I put my finger over my lips.

"Hello."

"Nik, it's me."

"I know. You're lucky I answered."

"Your brother's been—"

"Shot. I know."

"Did those motherfuckers—"

"Sean was shot yesterday. No, this wasn't retaliation. Otherwise, Dillan wouldn't have helped."

"Were you there? Did you get hurt? Where are you now?"

"Your concern is entertaining."

"Nikki, don't be like that."

"Like what? I've already seen this episode of this pathetic soap opera. I'm dealing with something else right now. If he dies, text me."

"Are you really that coldhearted? You didn't use to be like this."

"You mean before you dated me, lied about your feelings, proposed to me, let me accept your offer, then didn't have the decency to look ashamed when I walked in on that conversation. Too bad whoever this was didn't shoot you too."

"Nikki, I cared about you. I would have been a good husband, and you never should have heard what you did. It was out of context."

"Bullshit. You'd be no better than Ewan is with Ellie. Except there'd probably be fifty Ellies during our lifetime. You made your thoughts about me very clear in front of Ewan, Uncle Riley, and all your friends. Don't worry. Your conscience is clear, isn't it? You don't have to feel like a pedophile fucking a body that looks like a ten-year-old's. You can go to strip clubs purely because you love paying to see tits and asses, not because you'd miss coming home to them. Maybe I was the reason you never stayed hard enough long enough. Maybe I wasn't. But the one thing I never told you before we got together was that I belonged to two BDSM clubs. Why do you think things changed when we became exclusive? You sucked in bed, and I was stuck only fucking you. I was going to live with that because I thought I loved you. I loved the idea of being loved and accepted into the O'Malleys finally. The day we broke up, I went to the club I hadn't canceled my membership with and had a fivesome. I needed that many cocks to make up for the one you have. You couldn't fuck your way out of a whorehouse. Like I said, text me if my brother dies."

I hang up. There's nothing but stunned silence as the twins stare at me.

"The last bit was exaggerated. There weren't four." There were three.

Chapter Eighteen

Sean

"He said that to you?"

"If I didn't see both of your mouths moving, I wouldn't have believed you both spoke. That's eerie."

Plenty of people tell us that. We often say the same thing. Our voices blend to most people's ears, but our family can tell us apart. Our parents can, so I never got away with shite if I mutter things under my breath. Shane has the better sense to think his comments, not say them.

"Lina, when did Colt say all of that?"

"About five years ago. We dated for nearly a year, but most of it was long distance because of grad school. I wasn't sure I wanted to settle down and get married. I wasn't sure he was the right person, but I'd known him most of my life. It was always so comfortable being with him. I thought I knew what life would be like with him, and it felt nice. When he asked a third time and formally proposed, I said yes. He flew down to DC to do it. I came back three weeks later to surprise him. Except I'm the one who got surprised. I went to Houlihan's since we used to share our locations, and the app showed he was there. I came in through the back like I had since I was underage. There he was with a brunette on his lap, Ellie sitting on Ewan's lap next to them, Uncle Riley across the table, and most of the bar listening. I have never felt rage like that. I haven't since. I knew where the owner kept his Colt—I liked the irony for what I planned. I also knew where the Louisville Slugger was, too."

She looks down as her head tilts slightly. I see the muscles in her jaw flex as she purses her lips for a moment. She gives her head a little shake before looking at Shane and me.

"I shot the shot glass out of the bitch's hand. Fuck William Tell and the apple on his kid's head. I knew it would distract them all enough to get them on their feet. I was ready. Colt left with three fractured ribs, a broken elbow, and a busted kneecap. Denny Byrne tried to stop me. His four front teeth are implants. I rammed the end of the bat into his mouth."

Denny's name makes my fist curl, and I know Shane has the same reaction. He was Corey Byrne's son before Finn dealt with Corey, who was part of the fucked-up situation Rowan jumped into with Finn's in-laws. Denny's my dad's age. I met him the first time I came to Boston. He was a prick then. He's a prick now. Since his dad died, he's taken over leading a motorcycle club. They've stayed quiet after the reminder Finn sent them.

"I knew the woman on Colt's lap. She was my best friend in Boston. She doubled down and came after me with a broken beer bottle. The bat to her tits ruptured both implants. She got them when she was fifteen, so they were already seven years old. Shockingly easy to burst old saline ones."

"You took a bat to them?" I'm fucking stunned.

"I played softball all the way through college. I loved kickball when I was little, so it was a natural transition. I prefer kickball now that I'm older. I prefer a different kind of balls whizzing toward my face." She winks. *She fucking winks!*

Now she shrugs. Her lips turn down in a false frown.

"I was just the runt of the litter to them. None of them came to my games in high school because I lived in Montreal. None of them came to games when I was in college because I lived in New York. I don't look as sturdy as most softball players. They underestimated my strength and my speed. They lived. They learned."

"And Colt thinks he can charm you after all that?" I want to bash his face in. I *will* bash his face in.

"That's how arrogant Colton Flaherty is. He believes I'd fuck him again if he offered. He hints at it. Ewan suggests it. My brother told me I could have stayed in Boston if I wanted to get laid rather than seeing you."

I'm seeing red.

"Sean, that was a long time ago. I vented my anger that afternoon. I sold the engagement ring and put a down payment on my sports car. At least he had the decency to get me a high-quality, flashy ring. Even that wasn't about me. He wanted to impress my dad. If you deal with Colt, do it because of work. Do it because of your family. Don't do it for me because he isn't worth shit. He craves attention. The best way to fuck him over is to ignore him. It drives him nuts that he can't get me to engage anymore. Pretentious twat."

I nod, but it's because there's nothing I can do while I'm in a hospital bed. I'll ignore him for now. But Lina didn't pay attention earlier if she thinks I'm letting this rest permanently. From her resigned expression, she knows. She walks over to me and kisses my cheek.

"Don't waste the expensive bullets on him."

I glance at Shane. He's staring at us.

The women in our family are—extraordinary.

255

Truthfully, all the syndicate wives are. They have to be to survive this lifestyle, and they already are extraordinary when they enter this world. It's why we fall so hard, so fast when we meet our soulmate.

This has been a bizarre, yet informative story that confirms what I know. Lina is the person I was destined to meet and fall in love with. I'm not there yet. I'm not so drugged up I don't know that. But I'm on the way. The foundation is there. Time will build the walls. I wonder if she feels anything like that toward me.

"Lina, you were flippant with Colt. But do you want to go back to Boston? Do you want to see Ewan?"

She hesitates and closes her eyes. When she looks at me, I see conflicting emotions brewing within.

"They say there are stages of grief. It's not linear. Some-times you return to old ones. Sometimes you skip past others. Now that my anger isn't about him attacking you, my anger is that he's not the brother I had. I miss that boy. But neither of us are kids. He's made his choices about me, and I've made mine about him. It still makes me sad sometimes, and that annoys me. I can't bargain with him or God to heal our relationship. He doesn't want it, and neither do I. Not really. I didn't move to Boston because I wanted to help him specifically. I moved to help protect our community. Not everyone has been horrible to me. That's why I let him guilt me into shit. No more. If I see him, it's to say a permanent goodbye. He won't forgive me for choosing you. And I will never choose him again."

My heart hurts for her. Shane and I exchange a glance. We can sympathize that this is a shite position to be in. But we can't empathize. We'll never be able to put ourselves in her shoes to know what she feels. We can't. It's unfathomable to us ever to be at odds like Lina is with Ewan. I can't imagine it with Finn either. It's not just because Shane and I are twins. I love Finn just as much. Shane and I might be genetically identical, but Finn and I still share the same DNA. It was stamped into the very fibers of who we are before we were anything more than an embryo. It's the same with our cousins. How we feel about them, and how they feel about us.

I wait to see if Lina will say more, but she remains quiet. I turn my attention back to Shane. "What does Dillan want us to do?"

"Stay here until you're discharged. As soon as you're well enough, we go back to the city."

I nod, and Shane knows that's his cue to leave. When the door clicks closed, Lina speaks before I can.

"Can I come with you?"

"I was going to ask if you would."

"Eventually, I'll have to go back to Boston because I have stuff in storage. But for now, I have no reason to stay at Jesse's. I'd rather be near you."

"Seamus owns a moving company. Whenever you're ready, he can take care of your belongings going wherever you want." *To our place.*

She appears hesitant. I think I've guessed why.

"I didn't just mean a flight back to New York. Lina, I want you to stay with me. Partly for your safety, but mostly because I want all the time with you I can get. The doctor said I'll be convalescing for a couple weeks. I already work from home most days. I make my schedule. If you want space of your own, my place is enormous enough. If you decide you want to go somewhere else, I'll make sure everything is taken care of."

We're sorta talking about moving in together. An indefinite houseguest. This will certainly tell us if we can live compatibly.

"Thank you, Daddy." She climbs back into bed and snuggles next to me.

"I love hearing you call me that. As soon as they discharge

me tomorrow or the day after, we can go to Jesse's. You can hang out for a while or just get your stuff. When you're ready to go, we'll fly back to the city. One or two of the guys might join Dillan."

"I won't keep everyone waiting because I want to shoot the shit with Jesse. I don't want you up and around that much. Seamus or Cormac can take me to get my stuff at a reasonable hour. As soon as you're discharged, we fly to New York. Your mom is probably in agony, waiting to see you. You need to see your parents, then we can sort out everything else."

"Did you talk to your mom while I was out?"

"No. I haven't said anything to her. If my grandfather knows any of this, he hasn't told her because she hasn't called. Once we're out of Massachusetts, I'll call and tell her most of what's going on."

"All right. We have another fifteen minutes before a nurse is likely to come back. Then we should be able to catch a couple more hours of sleep. Are you comfy?"

"Way more than you are."

"I just clicked the pain med button, and you're beside me. I'm very comfy."

I close my eyes, and the comfort flees. That premonition is back.

I got a smudged bill of health—in my line of work, it's considered clean—and we're back in NYC. The doctor discharged me just before noon. I passed all the tests, but they kept me for another night. Cormac and Shane took Lina to Jesse's to get her suitcases. I asked Finn to run a background check on her friend. I admitted it before I did it. It didn't thrill Lina, but she understands. I don't know Jesse. I know nothing about him or their friendship. For anyone I'm not familiar with, to me, they're an automatic threat to Lina until they aren't. I'm not a pessimist. I'm a realist.

We stopped in Boston, and Seamus stayed with Dillan. They're watching Colt and another guy—Blake O'Malley—their accountant—because this is undoubtedly not over. It could be a coincidence we were shot hours apart. It likely isn't. They'll stay for a few more days. We all know there's a possibility the others will need to go back. I'm thirty-one, and my mom grounded me from going out to play. For her sake, my dad's, and Lina's, I didn't argue. I don't want to be more of a liability than an asset to the others.

On the flight from Boston to NYC, Lina stepped into the private cabin on the plane to call her mom. She was pensive when she came out. I didn't do more than raise my eyebrows. She told me it went okay, but she knew her mom would have plenty to say when she wasn't around my family or me. She was upfront with her mom about being in a new relationship with me and that she was staying at my place until I said it was safe enough for her to go anywhere else.

When she said that, I kept my expression as neutral as I could. I don't want her to go anywhere else. But it's far too soon to decide. At least for her. Hours in a hospital bed gave me plenty of time to think. In my world, that many hours of inactivity is rare. Having that much time to let my mind wander was a luxury I really don't remember having since I was a kid. I'm used to deciding in seconds and minutes not hours and days. I'm used to decisions that can't be undone once made. I worked through things slowly. I still came to the same conclusion, but it doesn't feel impetuous.

"Sean?"

"I'm in the kitchen."

We went straight to my parents when we landed. We had

dinner there, and I was certain I was stuffed. Apparently, I'm not. Or I'm a Hobbit. I need second dinner.

"Would you like something?" I hold up half of my sandwich as she joins me.

Her hair's wet from a shower I wish we'd taken together. But I had some work emails to sort through instead. Fucking adulting's getting in the way of my sex life.

She's careful when she wraps her arms around me not to touch my incision while she rests her chin against my back. I haven't admitted it, but the hospital grade pain meds kept me from feeling much. I could even put pressure on it when I was in bed. Now, I feel every breath shoot through me like a searing fireplace poker. I glance at the microwave clock. Thank God. I can take another dose.

"I'm fine. Your mom must have given me five pounds of food, and I ate all of it."

"Good. You're going to need all that energy." I turn in her arms, spinning her until she's backed against the counter.

"Is that so, Daddy?"

The mirth in her voice makes me even harder. I'll show her. I press more, trapping her in place. She can feel my cock, and she tries to flex her hips. She doesn't have the room to do it, but I can. I rub against her as I take her hands and cross her wrists behind her. I start to stretch to grab the dish towel, but pain shoots through me, threatening to make me sick. I have to step away to get it, but once I have it, I twirl it until it's coiled, then I wrap her wrists in it. It only takes seconds before she's restrained.

I push her yoga pants down but leave her panties up. I grab the front of them and bunch them in my hand, tugging on them. The material rubs her clit, and she moans. I grab the back of them and saw them back and forth through her pussy lips.

When she tries to kiss me, I let go of the back and wrap my hand around her throat.

"Are you into breath play?"

"I haven't been in the past. I haven't trusted enough for it. I want to now."

"I've done it, but not often. Can you still snap?"

She tries, and I hear both sets of fingers. I incrementally increase the pressure. I use the space between my forefinger and thumb to tighten my hold. I don't want to leave bruises if I use my fingers. I don't want anyone to recognize them as finger-prints, nor do I want anyone to think she's trashy with hickies mottling her neck. Those are only for her tits.

If and when we go on vacation alone—plus the inevitable family contingency of bodyguards—I will mark her any and every-where. The guys won't pay attention, and they have the sense not to pass judgement on her. We won't go anywhere for others to see. But it's the knowledge that I've marked her, and someone else would know I've claimed her that arouses the fuck out of me.

I flick her earlobe before tugging on it. I kiss just behind her ear before bringing my lips beside it.

"Wear panties again, and I will edge you for keeping me away from what's mine. If I want my fingers in you, my tongue in you, my cock in you, there better not be anything in the way. Do you understand, *cailín*?"

I let go long enough for her to answer. "Yes, Daddy."

"I will shred them and make you walk around here without a fucking thing to cover *my* pussy."

Her pupils dilate, and it's not from the weight on her throat. It's arousal. I push the offensive thing down, and she shifts her weight to kick off her pants and panties.

"Open your legs."

She obeys immediately. I slip my finger into her. She's still impossibly tight, even for my finger. Her narrow hips made me question whether she could take me. I'm not just tall and broad. I'm proportionate. But I remember the feel of sliding into her cunt for the first time. She could take all of it, but it was like a vise. A tortuous, erotic, euphoric vise.

I add a second finger, rubbing her g spot. She trembles and tries to ride them. I slip a third one in and thrust over and over. I keep my thumb away from her clit on purpose. My lips snag hers, and my kiss threatens to swallow her whole. I release all the weight from her throat as I pull back. My hand just rests on her throat.

"Are you still all right?"

"Don't stop." She lifts her chin, inviting my hand back.

I watch her expression as she struggles to come, but without me rubbing her g spot or her clit, she can't get there. I feel her tugging at the towel, trying to get it loose. I've tied too many people up. She'll only get free of my restraints if I want her to. Right now, I don't.

I squeeze, making it harder for her to breathe as she tenses again, trying to orgasm. I pull my fingers out. She opens her mouth to protest, but no sound comes out. I observe her as I tease her, finger fucking then stopping over and over as I progressively block her from breathing. I haven't done much breath play during sex, but I'm an expert at this.

The moment her eyes widen, then look like they'll droop, I let go. I thrust into her, rubbing her clit. Her head falls to my shoulder as she cries out.

"I'm coming, Daddy."

My now free arm wraps around her as she leans her weight against me. My touch gentles as I run my fingertips over her pussy. I step back, making sure she has enough room to inhale deeply. It gives our bodies enough space for her to drop to her knees. I step back again, cupping her jaw.

"Do you want to suck me off?"

"Yes."

"Why?"

"Because I want to pleasure you. Because I want to give you what you gave me."

"I did that for you not to get something in return. You never have to do that. It isn't tit for tat. When I make you come, it's never a prelude or a dupe to make you do the same."

"I want to, Sean. I know I'm not obligated or expected to. That's not how things are between us. I'm offering because it would make me happy."

"Thank you, little one. The floor is hard. Would you rather do it somewhere else?"

"Is there anywhere that won't press against your back?"

The bullet hole allowed the doctors to pass the laparoscope in. Not their ideal method, but it prevented another wound site. That still has to heal as much as my inner abdomen now that there's an organ missing. Pleasuring Lina is a serotonin and dopamine hit. It helped relieve the pain. But she's right. Anything that presses against my back will hurt. I have to sleep on my side now.

I look around my place and spot my dining room chairs. I cup her elbow and guide her there, since she's still restrained. I'll do that properly in a just a few minutes. I grab a chair and turn toward our bedroom. She didn't ask for a separate room and took her bag in there when we arrived. I know she was nervous assuming she could do that, but I love her bravery to do it, anyway.

"Go in our room and stand facing the side of the bed farther from the door."

In my compromised condition, I can't move as fast. I want to face the door just in case. It puts her closer to it because she'll be standing in front of me, but that'll only be for a couple minutes. I'll remain the easy target.

I put the chair down and go to the dresser. I hurried through my emails while she showered so I could put away the things I got. As I pull out the drawer, I explain, so she doesn't think I reduce, reuse, recycle.

"While I was on the first flight to Boston, I had time to do some shopping. I picked some things out for us. If you don't like anything, say so. It's not just about limits and safe words. Your preference matters. You can always tell me what you're in the mood for. I may or may not oblige. But if you tell me there's something you don't want—besides when it might be a punishment—I will listen to you."

"Punishment? I'm not a Little, Sean."

"I haven't started thinking you are. Nor do I want domestic discipline. But if you endanger your safety or the men tasked with protecting you, I will punish you. If it's on purpose, you know better. If it's on accident, then you should have thought better about your choices. If something happens that makes you feel unsafe or scared, and you don't tell me, I will punish you. Your thoughts are your own, but I will demand to know what scares you. You will tell me. You are not someone easily spooked. If it's bad enough to scare you, then I consider it a full-blown threat. If anyone threatens you, coerces you, guilts you, manipulates you, you will tell me. If you don't, I will punish you. I consider those threats, too."

I go back to stand in front of her and wrap my arm around her to grab her arse.

"You know what kind of man I am, Lina. You know I can be violent. I will never tell you how violent, and I pray you never find out. But there won't be a shred of humanity left in me if someone hurts you."

She swallows and nods. "Sean, I believe you. I need you to

understand that is not one-sided. You won't agree to that. I already know that, so you don't have to tell me. But you will never change my mind. I told you I shot a shot glass out of someone's hand. It wasn't one of the short, stout kind. It was the narrow tube. There was less than an inch visible below her hand. I don't regularly carry a gun, and I don't want to even though I'm licensed to in Massachusetts. I've hunted with my grandfather. I'm a good shot because I've always wanted to be humane to the animals we'll eat. But that humanity ends the moment I need to defend you and our future together."

Her tone and the hard set of her jaw, along with the determination in her eyes, tell me I can argue until I'm blue in the face. I won't change her mind.

"Thank you. You do not go looking for trouble. You do not instigate trouble. But I feel relieved you can shoot. And I won't lie. It feels special to hear your conviction to protect me."

"I know how I feel when you promise to keep me safe. It's not a one-way street."

Our kiss is gentle and quick before I let go. I return to the dresser and pull out what I want. I bring them back to the bed and spread them out on the comforter, so she can see what I plan to use. She looks up at me and nods, then turns to face the bed like I originally commanded.

I take the leather wrist cuffs and replace the towel with them, making sure they're snug, but I can still get a finger between her and the restraint. I press her forward onto the bed.

"Turn toward me on your stomach." She does it. "Bend your legs."

I slide a leather garter beneath each thigh. Both have chains and hooks that fasten to the ankle cuffs I buckle. I snap a chain that connects the links between her wrist cuffs to the metal loop on her right garter. Once I see the position this puts her in,

I grab two pillows to tuck under her shoulders and neck, so she doesn't have to strain to hold her head up.

Then I strip. She only has a tank top on. I'll take it off later. I move the chair, so it's sideways. The back is toward the footboard. I rest my right knee on it, and it takes weight off my legs. I can stand like this for a while.

"Open for me."

I fist my cock and point it toward her. I outline her lips with the tip before I tap her tongue.

"Lick."

She does. The top, flicking the slit. Then the entire length. She does it over and over until my entire dick is wet.

"Suck."

She only takes the tip at first, her cheeks caving. She inches toward the base, driving me to the brink of grabbing her head and shoving my entire cock down her throat. I let her have control since she offered this. I grip the chair back as my cock swipes the back of her throat. She gags, and I'm ready to pull back. She sucks harder. She's still for a moment, and I don't rush her. I feel her throat relax before she works me some more. I need the chair's support to keep me upright. I drop my head back with my eyes closed.

Fuck. This is amazing. Hands down the best blow job I've ever gotten. Yeah, she knows what she's doing. There's no doubting that, but it's Lina. It's because it's her. My subs had experience, even talent. But this transcends anything I've known. I have to tilt my head forward because I'm growing lightheaded. For a moment, I worry I'm overdoing it. But my mind clears. It's Lina. It's all Lina. It'll always be Lina.

I keep telling myself that. It's true. There're emotions here I don't recognize. They're foreign to me. They're both unsettling and reassuring in equal measure. I cup her jaw, and a wave of tenderness I haven't experienced while a woman goes down on me crashes over me. Her eyes are closed as she concentrates. But she looks up when she feels my hand. She's enjoying this, too.

"*Mo stór.*" My treasure.

The term of endearment rolls off my tongue. I brush my thumb over her cheekbone, and she redoubles her efforts.

"Fuck, little one. I won't last long."

She hums. The vibration sets me off. My fingers tunnel into her hair, something I love doing. It's like yards of silk threads. I don't hold myself down her throat. There's no pressure.

"If you don't want to swallow, let go."

She sucks harder. Fucking vacuum cleaner attached to my dick.

"Lina!"

My head falls back again as I bellow her name, then groan. I feel her tongue swirl around my cock before she draws back. I take a moment to gather my thoughts. I also need to catch my breath before I get woozy. Coming that hard standing up wasn't the smartest choice, but it was the best feeling choice I've ever made.

"Are your shoulders okay? Knees?"

"I'm all right, Daddy."

My cock twitches. We both look at it and laugh. Then I have my hands on her waist as I pick her up and turn her around, quickly putting the pillows beneath her again.

"Sean! You're going to hurt yourself. Stop being foolish."

My hand lands across her arse three times.

"I got shot. I'm not dead."

Even if I thought I was going to be.

I draw her knees to the edge of the bed and push them wide before I kneel on the floor. It's my turn to feast. Fuck the sandwich I forgot about until now. I grab her arse, lifting, spreading, squeezing as my tongue runs the length of her cunt and to her arsehole. I watch her hands clench, then relax when I move away from there.

"Is that a no?"

"It's a I'm unused to it but not opposed to it. I've always thought that was—um—it didn't appeal to me. But you've done it twice, and I like it. If you're okay with it."

"More than okay. All of you is mine, and I will have it before you fall asleep tonight."

I reach for the butt plug and lube I'd put on the bed. I squeeze some onto her arse, enjoying watching it glide along a place I'll fill as soon as she's ready. A place other's might have been before, but no one but me will ever go again. Her cunt is the same. A given. But there's something even more intimate about this.

I cover the plug with lube and press it into her. She remains relaxed, taking it without hesitation.

"It's because it's you."

I pause and look around her bent leg. She's turned her head toward me.

"I've had anal before. I've worn plugs before. It's not my most favorite when it's the only thing going on. But I've never been this at ease before. I trust you."

She's told me that several times. It doesn't grow old hearing. My men trust me because they know I'm committed to our branch. They know my honor demands I do my best for them. My family trust me because we're family. But Lina doesn't have a reason to. She hasn't since we met, but she does. Her trust means more to me than everyone else's combined.

The other part of what she says registers with me.

"Only thing?"

She sighs. Am I going to want to hear this confession?

"If it's anal just for the sake of anal, it's okay. If there's a vibrator, a dildo, or someone else, then I like it."

Someone else!

"Sean, we can discuss our pasts if you want to. I won't hide what I've done, but I don't want to know about yours. It'll hurt and make me jealous. I don't even like knowing you have long-term subs and a place you own just to meet them."

"I bought the place as a rental property originally. Had not have. Owned not own. Met not meet. And I'd rather not talk about our pasts either."

"I only said what I said, so you'd know what I meant. I trust you, and I want you to trust me. I want to be truthful, but not out of spite or thoughtlessness."

"I know." I kiss her arse cheek.

"I want to be sure I'm clear, though. The vibrator and dildo I'd like to keep doing. I will *never* ask for someone to join us."

I hear what's unsaid. I stand up and do my best to lean onto the bed, so we're face to face.

"I won't either. I don't want another woman looking at or touching me. I sure as feck don't want to touch another woman. I don't want another man looking at or touching you. I sure as feck don't want you touching another man." I take a long blink. "If you change your mind and want another man, I can try to come to terms with it, if that's what would make you happy. I won't agree to another woman. I can't."

She twists to rest on her left shoulder and hip as best she can.

"You'd let another man join us, but you won't allow another woman. I would have thought it would be the other way around."

"If another man is what you fantasize about, and you really need it, then I can deal with my feelings. But I can't touch another woman. The thought is worse than you with another man."

"Because you don't want to betray me. Sean, I do *not* want

another man touching me. I would feel I'm betraying you, even with your consent and participation. I wouldn't be okay with you suggesting you share me. As for another woman, she wouldn't survive the first step through the door. You might not either if you suggest it. I've done things in the past that were fun, but repeating them with you would hurt and likely leave you having to dispose of a body to keep me out of prison. If I kill you, then who's going to help me?"

She grins as she strains to give me a kiss before shifting back onto her stomach.

I feel about a thousand times lighter than I did a second ago. I move back to where I was. I toy with her clit for at least five minutes. To where I'll make it painful if I keep going. I stroke her g spot, petting it like you would a pussycat. Lame pun intended.

I could fist my cock to get hard again, but I don't need to. The way her breath hitches and her moans—I'm aching to be inside her again. When she shifts restlessly, I stand. Keeping her legs apart, holding her ankles, I inch into her. She whimpers, needing more. I'm testing both of us. She pushes her hips up, and I let them stay that way as I slide in until my balls touch her. I don't move.

"Aside from orgasms, I don't think there's a more enjoyable feeling than you entering me."

Her voice is breathy as she says what I already know. My hands shift to her hips as I pull them back toward me. I rock my hips back and forth, not pulling out at all.

"If I stay like this, I'll come." I kiss the inside of her ankle because it's what I can reach.

"If you move, you'll come." I hear the teasing.

I land my hand on her arse before reaching for the crop I brought over to use. I tap her arse, but it's not a spank. I reach around her with my other hand and rub her clit—careful after playing with it a few minutes ago.

"May I come, Sean?"

"Yes."

I don't care what she calls me as long as she's asking *me*. I don't need deference or obedience right now. But I'll take acknowledgement she's with me and only me.

Her body tenses as she pushes back, raising her hips even more. Her moan lingers until she sucks in a hard breath. I pull out of her cunt as I pull the plug out. I coat my dick in the lube.

"Are you ready for this?"

"Yes."

I step away, and she twists to see what I'm doing. I go to the magic drawer and grab a vibrator. I'm ripping the packaging off as I walk over. The boxes for the other stuff are on the dresser where I practically shredded them to unwrap the other toys earlier.

"I have one, and that looks nice. But now that I've fucked you, I'm going to need something way bigger than either of them. That's just going to be disappointing." She grins.

I take my place again behind her. I make sure the lube hasn't evaporated too much on me. Then I ease into her, not forcing past the ring of resistance.

"Lina?"

"I'm okay. Keep going. I know we're getting used to each other, but you don't have to check on me so much, and you don't have to keep getting consent for everything. I consent for it all, and I'll tell you if something's wrong."

"If it's more than just hurting—if it's painful—and I harm you, I—"

"Daddy, I want you to believe me. And I definitely don't want to ruin this. I would never put you in that position. That's not what I want. I want to share this intimacy with only you."

"All right."

"Though I doubt this was the type of intimacy the doctor meant when she suggested alternatives."

"I know. I can't be as rambunctious as I'd normally be."

I turn on the vibrator and reach beneath my cock to slide it into her. The little extension isn't pressing against her clit. It's against the thin strip between her pussy and arsehole. I have it on high. I only rock my hips as I pick up the crop. I bring it down medium hard. She clenches her arse. I groan. I do it over and over, alternating sides until her arse is bright pink. I twist the vibrator around, and immediately, she's coming. Her arse clenches so tightly, it's painful. But it sets me off. I toss aside the crop and use both hands to hold her arse to my pelvis.

"Fuuuuck." I growl. I don't know if I've ever made that exact sound before. Totally primal.

Neither of us moves as we pant. Then it hits me. I clench my jaw, refusing to let on that the surge of pain makes me want to vomit. I squeeze my eyes shut as I pull out and bring the vibrator with me. I'm sucking air in through my nose. I work to unfasten everything as I half kneel on the chair again. I feel the sweat on my forehead. It's clammy now. She's going to flip, and it's going to ruin everything. I swallow the bile burning up my chest.

"Move around, little one. Are you in pain?"

She flips over. Immediately, her eyes widen. I thought I sounded normal.

"Fucking hell, Sean. Sit down. You're nearly as pale as you were when you got shot."

She's gentle but firm as she pushes me onto the chair. She sweeps the back of her hand over my cheek before pressing it to my forehead.

"I'm fine. Really."

"Bullshit. Stay here."

She bolts across the room. I twist to see her sprint to the kitchen. She yanks open the fridge door and scans the contents. I know she's looking for juice. She'll have to move some leftovers out of the way. My fridge is full since I cooked a few days ago. I meal prep for the week. A regular Martha Stewart.

The door slams shut, and she's running back to me. She didn't even bother to search for a glass. She shoves the apple juice toward me after taking off the lid.

"All of it Sean. It doesn't have the sugar orange juice does."

I happily oblige because I'm parched. I guzzle it down and feel marginally better. While I do, she's watching me, but she takes the vibrator and plug into the bathroom. I watch her set them on a stack of tissues she lays out next to the sink. She comes back to me and looks mildly relieved that I haven't keeled over. She pulls back the sheet and comforter.

"Get in, Daddy. Do you want your sandwich? Would eating help?"

"Later. I'm fine, Lina. I promise."

"Get in." She's not backing down.

"I like you fierce."

"We'll see." She arranges pillows around me.

She didn't bother trying to convince me I should sleep on the other side of the bed to keep weight off my right side. She knows I'll always sleep closer to the door. She props my back up with the pillows and gets in beside me. She cradles my head on her shoulder like I did hers the last two nights in the hospital.

"Let me take care of you for a bit."

My eyes drift closed. For the third time, I have that vision of her tied to a chair. This time, there's no needle. She's already dead.

Chapter Nineteen

Lina

The past month has been anticlimactic bliss. We've all been waiting for someone to make another move, but it's been silent. I know Sean's impatient to resolve this, but as far as I know, he and his family don't know more than they did when we flew here from Boston. It's been bliss because nothing's taken Sean away. He spent the first week as a good patient.

Our sex life exists, but it was tame for the week after the first evening. The second week, we started getting rougher. A lot rougher. Sean still has limits to his endurance, but if this is him recuperating, I don't know that I'll survive him at full strength. He's insatiable. But then again, so am I.

When he's working on things that are safe for me to see, I often sit on his lap. I warm his cock, and I love knowing he's not paying attention to me when all I want is to get off. At least, he pretends not to pay attention to me. When I shift to stay comfortable enough to remain on him, he groans. It makes him twitch inside me. I've given him blow jobs while he works at his desk or on the sofa.

Yesterday comes to mind, and I can't help but sigh.

Cailin, I have some inventory lists to go through for the clubs. It shouldn't take me long.

I glance up as I finish putting away the butter and jam from the toast I had at breakfast. I nod, considering what I might do to fill the time since I have no work of my own. I know what I want to do.

When Sean reaches out his hand, I grin. I know what he wants, and it's exactly what I want. We walk together to his office, and he pulls back his chair. I slip beneath it and rest on my knees and shins. He takes his seat and is careful as he rolls forward. He unfastens his pants and pulls down his boxer briefs. I eye it like a kid does one of those giant pinwheel lollipops. I scoot forward and lick him as I hear him shuffling papers on his desk. Then I see him pull his cell phone from his pocket. I love this part. I love when he's on the phone, trying to concentrate on his call while I lick, suck, and fondle him.

I don't know who he's calling, and I couldn't give a shit. I wait until I hear the first sound of him saying hello, then I pounce. I slide my mouth down the entire length of his cock and suck hard. He clears his throat. I focus to keep from laughing. He senses my amusement and fists my hair. I look up to find his warning glare. I shrug as I slide my mouth up and down him.

"Shane can meet the distributor at 4Play to go over the display for the promotion."

I can't hear what the other person says. But it's not long before Sean speaks again.

"I'm feeling much better, but Shane can handle all of that. I'll check on the mini mall project. Finn's going to that doctor's appointment with Ally. I can check the inventory and report the numbers to him. I can count screws as well as he can."

There's a pause.

"Yes, I will make sure I don't miss any. I know how he is about his numbers being precise. Remember, I'm the one who had to account for even a single missing Lego. Hell, half the time he was the one who accidentally pushed them under his bed. Goodbye, Dillan."

I hear the playful exasperation in his voice as he cups my jaw and strokes his thumb over my cheek. It's affectionate and erotic.

"Come here, little one."

He slides his chair back and makes room for me to stand. He pulls a bowtie from his top desk drawer where he now keeps it. He binds my wrists behind me and slides on the sleep mask I wear when he wants me near him, but it's not safe for me to see what he's working on.

I'm naked, so there's nothing in the way as I slide down his cock, facing away from him. I sense he moves his laptop to the left, so he can see around me. I remain quiet, doing Kegels every so often. His hands trail over my legs, belly, and tits absentmind-edly. I feel him twitch inside me periodically as he lingers some-where. It's pure torment when he fondles my tits and plays with my nipples. I can do little with my hands behind my back, but I can feel his abs through his shirt. It's the only concession I get to my unspent lust.

I nearly ran from the room screaming the first time he had a conference call on his computer. He slid the mask up, so I could see his camera was off. Now I don't panic when I know a meet-ing's starting. It's boring since it's about employee retirement options. He pulls my right leg wider over his thigh. He plays with my clit, rubbing slow circles until I fist my hands between us. I shift restlessly, and he pulls away. I swallow my moan. His camera is off, but his mic isn't. When I still, he presses his thumb against my asshole. I clutch his shirt. He strokes my pussy with his other hand while kissing my shoulder. But the moment I get close, he pulls away again.

The way he moves, I can tell he's reaching around me to type something. I warm his cock as though it's only my pussy that's here. He hasn't forgotten me, but he ignores me. He knows what it does to me. I love that he wants to be inside me. That he gets pleasure from him denying me. That his denial is my own sort of pleasure. When the meeting ends, he grips my hips and moves me until he comes. He taps my ass as I get up and leave his office.

It's not all give and no take. He reciprocates and...holy hell. The man can do things with his tongue I didn't know were possible. He's a glossal contortionist. Not to be confused with him being a colossus. He doesn't have poor posture by any stretch. But there have been two times when we've left his place, and we've run into people he wished we hadn't. When he stands with his shoulders pushed back, you realize just how big he is. He's not as thick as Cormac and Seamus, but they could swap clothes, and no one would think they weren't his.

Both times were last week. The first person was Pablo Diaz. I cringed because the Colombian Cartel member got involved with my dad, then Ewan. I cancelled my meeting with him to be with Sean that first afternoon. I was waiting for him to say something because he spotted me first. Finn was with us, and I thought Pablo was going to die on sight. The rage that rolled off Finn reminded me of what I felt when I caught Colt not only cheating on me but insulting me.

The second person was a *Cosa Nostra* member, Marco Mancinelli. He was with his wife, Elizabeth. They've only been married a few months. Their wedding was right before Finn and Ally's. Here's something I learned: they go to each other's wedding receptions. Not the ceremonies, but appar-

ently, the hoity-toity of NYC get together for these mafia—
sorry, syndicate—soirées.

Sean was adamant I know the Mancinellis insist they are
the only Mafia in NYC. Mafia with a capital M. He said the
Cosa Nostra—"our thing"—are whiny bitches if they get
confused for anyone they believe is inferior. So pretty much
everyone else. They don't want riff-raff associated with them
either. According to Sean, his family falls into that category
since they're *only* the mob—with a lowercase m.

Between Pablo and Marco, it threatened to turn the
weekend sour, but Sean didn't let it. He took me to brunch on
Saturday at La Petite Fleur, the restaurant Finn owns. We went
for a walk through Central Park, and we pointed out places we
like to run and bike. I hadn't been there since college. I showed
him around the Barnard campus. My old dorms, some of my
classroom buildings, the bars where I drank underage. We went
to McGinty's that night for a live Irish band. Finn owns it too.

Last Sunday, we slept in. And by sleep, I mean woke up
before dawn and didn't stop touching until nine. It was such a
typical couple's day at home. We cleaned—I learned his
parents' generation forbade his generation from hiring house-
keepers—and did laundry. I pressed on the maid thing because
I was curious. His parents and aunts and uncles remind their
children they'll never be too good or too rich to scrub a toilet.
And if they can make a mess, they can clean the mess. I love it.

We're headed into another weekend, and we have plans to
go on a triple date with Dillan and Mair, and Finn and Ally. I
met the women at three Sunday dinners I attended. Those
were experiences of their own. Boisterous. Hilarious. Delicious.
So fucking normal. According to Mair and Ally, it completely
threw them to see the O'Rourkes in their natural habitat. I felt a
little less rude for staring.

Mair—short for Márgrég—her Irish version of Margaret—
and Ally—short for Althea—have invited me to hang out, but it
didn't insult them when I hesitated. Between not wanting to be
away from Sean and the unexplained shooting, it made me
uncomfortable to go somewhere without him. I didn't feel right
inviting them to Sean's, even though I know I could have.

"Lina?"

"Yeah. I'm almost ready." I step out of our bedroom as Sean
comes out of his office.

I'm carrying my shoes since I discovered he and I are alike
and prefer shoes remain at the door. Since I haven't unpacked
all my things from the boxes Seamus sent a crew to get, I still
have some of mine tucked away. He slips his arm around my
waist, and I happily accept a hug. We've been apart for a whole
fifteen minutes. I nuzzle his neck as his hand cups my ass.

"We can still have dinner with the others, but I have to go
out tonight."

I freeze. We haven't done this before. He hasn't left me
behind. I don't know if it means he's really going "out," and
there's a chance he'll get shot again. Or if "out" means wherever
their place is. All syndicates have an abandoned place local law
enforcement isn't dumb enough to raid, and the feds can't get
permits to search something that doesn't exist in city, county, or
state records.

These warehouses and garages and whatever else they pick
are where the families take people who pretty much breathed
their last the moment they looked sideways at a syndicate
member. I don't know the specifics because I've never asked
and never want to know, but they control the place. They can
take their time, which means being away a few days at a time in
some cases.

"Okay." I kiss his cheek and pull away.

Sean shakes his head. "It's not what you think. I can tell you know what that usually means. I have to go somewhere I don't want to, but it's unavoidable. I'm sorry."

That makes me stare at him, my stomach sinking. What the fuck does that mean?

"I have a meeting at one of our strip clubs. The people who'll be there do not want the finer parts of society seeing them with my family. They want the dim lighting and the distracted clientele for anonymity that doesn't exist."

"One of your strip clubs?"

"Yes. Among my brothers, cousins, and me, we own ten. We have nightclubs and casinos too. Finn and Cormac both own some restaurants. You've seen Fleur and McGinty's. They're totally reputable."

"Do you spend a lot of nights at them?"

"No. None of us like going to them. It hasn't been our thing since we were in college. It got old fast. Short of holding this meeting under a bridge somewhere a drone or telephoto lens could catch us, there aren't too many more obscure places to go than a club. I'm sorry."

"Why are you apologizing? Are you planning to do something you already feel guilty about?"

"No. But it wouldn't thrill me to have you surrounded by swinging dicks."

I stifle a giggle. "Daddy, you looked like you were going to cry or puke when we discussed threesomes. I'm not worried about you being around other naked women. I don't love it, but I'm not scared of it. As for swinging dicks, there's only one I'd want to see in a banana hammock." I cup his dick.

"I still don't like putting you in this position."

"Do the women come on to you? Do you have pasts with many of them?"

"No. I've known some of them since we were kids. I've

been with a few of them, but that was in high school and college. Nothing recently. It just feels dirty to go to a place with tits and arses hanging out all over the place when I'm in a monogamous relationship."

"Work is work." I shrug because what else can I do? Then something hits me. My gaze hardens as I watch my boyfriend— we defined the relationship the third day we were here.

"This is what I'm worried you'll think. I've told you there're no limits to what I'll do to protect you. You know the man I am, so you know there aren't many limits period. But I will never have sex or the suggestion of sex to get what I want. I will not cheat on you, Lina. Never. If it's that or go without what I need from that person, I'll find another way. I don't want you to think I see an out or a loophole."

"Sean, I told you. You looked sick when we talked about bringing other people into our sex life. You were willing to make concessions for me, but you made it clear with your body language how opposed you are to being with another woman. I know you won't cheat. Besides, if I didn't castrate you, you have a massive family who probably own every type of pliers ever made. Someone would do it for me. Come on. We'll be late."

I didn't lie. I know he won't cheat. He just wouldn't. Regardless of his feelings for me, he wouldn't disgrace himself that way. But I don't love naked women fawning over him, offering lap dances and delivering drinks with their tits in his face. I've accepted how I'm built, and Sean obviously likes it. I have love bites all over my boobs, ass, inner thighs, and belly. He touches me every chance he has. But it doesn't feel great knowing beautiful women will surround him.

"Lina, wait."

"Sean, you're making a bigger deal out of this than you need to. I'm okay with it. I swear."

"I'm still sorry that it means cutting our night short with the others. And it means I probably won't be home until two or three."

"I already figured that. Come on, Daddy. All that worrying is giving you wrinkles."

I lace my fingers through his and tug. We head out, and in twenty minutes, we're sitting down to dinner with the two other couples. It's fun watching Sean's brother and cousin with their wives. They're so much like Sean. They pull out their wives' chairs. They stand whenever one of us gets up. They don't take the first bite until the three women have. It's little chivalrous things probably drilled into them since the womb. But at the end of the night, the other couples are going to their respective homes together. Shane meets us outside the restaurant and takes me back to Sean's place.

"I'll be in the guest bedroom if you need anything, Nikki. Goodnight."

"Night."

It didn't surprise me when Sean explained Shane would stay over until he gets home. Sean has security outside his building and in the lobby. No one who isn't a resident gets past the building's front door without showing ID and being checked. All packages that arrive for him get x-rayed and opened. I didn't love learning that, but I feel safer knowing it.

I climb into bed as my phone buzzes.

SEAN

I'm here. I wish I weren't. I'll be home as soon as I can.

ME

I'm just getting into bed. I'll be here when you get home, honey.

I send him the smooches emoji and a crying laughing one.

SEAN

Ok sweetheart. Nite cailín.

He sends me three snoring emojis.

ME

Nite Daddy.

"Nikki! Nikki!" Bang, bang, bang. "Nikki!"

"Shane?"

I wake to the sound of pounding on the bedroom door. I glance at the clock on Sean's side of the bed. It's already four a.m. Sean definitely hasn't been here. There isn't a wrinkle on his side of the sheets. And since we started sharing a bed, I haven't woken yet to him not touching some part of me.

"Can I come in?"

"Yeah."

It's also the first night I've worn pajamas. Sean threatened to throw them away just like he already has three pairs of panties I dared wear. Shane eases the door open, and I sit up. I reach for the bedside lamp and flick it on.

"What happened to Sean?"

"We don't know. He texted me to say he was leaving the club and on the way home. That was an hour-and-a-half ago. When he didn't show up within forty-five minutes, I tried calling and texting him. He didn't answer. He didn't set off his alert, but I can't pull him up on our app."

"His alert?"

"Do you not wear one? Our watches are trackers. The larger dial sets off a distress signal if it's pressed. The alert goes to all of us and our dads. No one's heard from him."

I throw back the covers and get out of bed. "Who was the last person to see him?"

He hesitates.

"Shane, who was it?"

"Lucy. She's one of the dancers. She said they were in the office for a while, then he left."

I refuse to assume the worst about this part. "And you trust her?"

"Yeah. They used to—"

"Were involved?"

He looks toward the window before meeting my gaze. "She was his sub until six months ago."

He said he hadn't been involved with any of them recently. That it hadn't been since high school and college. He lied to me. I expect him to lie about people he'll see, places he'll go, and things he'll do. I get that. I learned that when I was a kid. But he swore up and down, left and right that he wouldn't cheat.

"Did you speak to her? Did they leave together?"

"Dillan did. It surprised him that she called. She doesn't work at that club often. I didn't know she was on the schedule for tonight, and I'm the one who made it. She traded with someone."

"To work there tonight? Or someone asked her to cover for them?"

"I don't know."

"Well, there's a fuck ton difference between the two considering she was the last person to see my boyfriend, and they were tucked away in an office together." I inhale. "Shane, I trust Sean. But I don't know this woman, and they had one of the most intimate kinds of relationship. I don't know how things ended. I don't trust her. Is she affiliated?"

In other words, is her family mob?

"They are. It's why their arrangement worked for so long."

"Long?"

He looks like he'd like to swallow his tongue.

"Shane, how long were they together?"

"They weren't 'together' like you are with Sean. They had an arrangement for about fourteen months."

And I've barely had one for four weeks.

"You said you trust her. You're telling me he isn't cheating. Fine. I'll believe you about trusting her, even if I don't. But I know he isn't with her or any other woman. Something else is very wrong. What're Dillan and the others doing?"

Shane looks at me blankly. I march over to him and get in his face. I'm not as tall as him, but I'm tall for a woman. I look him straight in the eyes.

"Unless they are doing something that could put them on death row, tell me, Shane."

"I can't."

"You won't."

"Same difference."

"Hardly, and you know it. You woke me, pounding on my door to tell me he's missing. If you didn't want me asking questions about what's happening, why'd you even bother waking me?"

"Because we need to leave."

"And go where?"

"Dillan's."

I glance at the closet and nod. He backs out of the room and shuts the door. I dash to my cell phone and unlock it. I pull up the app that has Ewan's, Justin's, and Colt's phones entered. I go through each. Their phones say they're all in Boston. I look toward the door. My laptop is in Sean's office. We were both in there earlier. He was working, and I was doing some online shopping for more toys. We agreed to get a swing because it's something we both like.

I pull clothes from the closet and get dressed before snapping open the gun case that's on the floor behind my empty roll aboard. Sean knows I have a gun and a Massachusetts permit. I'm certain he's seen the box, but he hasn't asked me about it. It's got a biometric lock, and I haven't added him as someone with access.

Shane knocks again.

"Give me one more minute. I'm almost done."

I lift the gun out of the case, checking that it's loaded. I know it is, but my grandfather drilled it into me to never touch a gun without checking to see if it's loaded with the safety on. I stand and stretch onto my toes for a storage tub of purses, belts, and my thigh holster. I'm wearing a long, loose dress that won't easily show the gun's outline. There isn't a chance in fuck I'm leaving without it. I'd rather have it and not need it than need it and not have it. Once I've cinched the holster around my thigh, and the gun's safely stowed in it, I head out to the living room.

I grab my purse and coat from near the front door and follow Shane out in silence. We ride down to the underground parking garage and step out to find a massive SUV waiting outside the elevators. The thing's a fucking tank.

Seamus, Cormac, and Finn are standing outside it. Finn's by the driver's door, and Cormac's at the front passenger's. Seamus is next to the trunk. I glance up at Shane. He's looking at Cormac. As we walk over, Cormac opens the rear passenger door. Seamus is going around to the other side. I'm soon sandwiched between Seamus and Shane.

Seamus, Shane, Sean. Sounds like the beginning of a tongue twister or nursery rhyme. I say nothing as I put my belt on. The engine revs as Finn puts it in gear and accelerates. I look out the window beside Seamus. The glass is thicker than normal. I also noticed it sits higher than most, even with the hydraulic step.

This is a tank. The glass is bullet proof. The raised chassis probably means there are metal plates covering it to protect it against IEDs—improvised explosive devices—and spike strips. My guess is the tires are the kind that will still roll even if punctured. Short of shredded, they'll still work. The doors and frame are probably impact resistant, and the bumpers are battering rams.

"If I ever need to find an O'Rourke SUV in a mix, what do I look for?"

Finn glances back at me in the rearview mirror. Seamus peers down at me, and I can tell Cormac and Shane don't want to answer.

"I haven't been at a shootout, but I have been at events where things have gotten uncomfortable fast. The SUVs all look the same. There has to be something you customize that tells them apart. Otherwise, you'd all be getting into each other's vehicles unless you memorize the license plates. Those aren't always easy to see. Is it the front grill? That's what the families do in Montreal."

"Hub caps. I'll point them out." Shane sounds less than thrilled, but whatever.

"I may have grown up in Montreal, but the mob there isn't that different from here. Just because we're Canadian and polite doesn't mean we're weak. Don't underestimate what I grew up with and what I've seen. I'm not ignorant of what goes on, so there's no dark to keep me in. Tell me the stuff I need to know to stay alive if I get separated from you. If this could happen—if Sean is—then it could be any of us. I deserve to be prepared."

They're silent. I look at all of them. They—Fucking A. For fuck's sake.

I open my purse and dump out the meager contents. I unlock my real phone and hand it to Shane. I unlock the two burners and hand one to Cormac and one to Seamus.

"Keep them."

I snap at them because they don't trust me. They think I might call my brother or someone in Boston. Or that I'll squeal to my grandfather. I close my eyes and sit back against my seat, squashed between the giants. I've never felt smaller despite my height. I wish I were small enough to disappear. I know we're all tense because we don't know where Sean is. The unknown only amplifies it for me. Not knowing or trusting me amplifies it for the guys. I keep reminding myself we all want the same thing. Sean's safe return.

We ride in silence until we reach Dillan and Mair's home. It isn't far from the neighborhood where all the other married syndicate couples live. I don't just mean the O'Rourkes. I mean *all* the syndicates. The Four Families is what they're called now. I guess one of the Mancinelli wives coined it. Whichever woman it was is right.

The O'Rourkes are *the* Irish, *the* mob. *The* Diazes are *the* Colombians, *the* Cartel. *The* Kutsenkos are *the* Russians, *the* bratva. *The* Mancinellis are *the* Italians, *the* Mafia.

Sean's generation and his parents' basically commandeered two neighboring communities and have taken over in the past thirty years. Really, within the last five because that's when Sean's generation started moving in. Five bratva couples, six Mafia couples, and now two mob couples. I thought we might be the third. That makes my heart ache as I wonder where Sean is and what's happening to him.

We drove past several of these homes the night Dillan and Mair hosted Sunday dinner, and we're doing it again. I can tell the guys are even more vigilant than Sean and Shane were when we rode together that night. Cormac and Seamus's parents hosted the second Sunday dinner, and the twins weren't any more at ease while driving through the other neighborhood. If they hadn't taken me this way before, their hyper awareness would only add to my anxiety. Knowing they're scanning every inch of our surroundings makes me feel mildly safer.

We pull into one of the five garages at Dillan and Mair's mansion. I know the rules, so I don't even unfasten my seatbelt until the garage door closes and Finn turns off the engine. I slide out on Seamus's side and follow the men inside. Sean's parents, Breda and Ronan, rush to me. They engulf me in a hug that threatens to break me—physically and emotionally. They nearly suffocate me, but the comfort I feel—that I need—is reassuring me. Breda reminds me of my mom, and the familiarity is welcome. But it's Ronan's hug that I want to turn into. Irony is a bitch. He has the same name as my father, but he couldn't possibly be more different. Be more of a dad.

I may call Sean Daddy as a term of endearment, but he's not even remotely a father figure to me. I don't see him that way. But Ronan is the dad I wish I had. I saw how he was with his three sons and three nephews. I know he treated me kindly and spent time getting to know me at the family meals. My dad never did that. Hugs from him were to be endured and blessedly brief. He never took an interest in me unless I could do something for him. And my dad was incapable of being kind to anyone other than my stepmom.

I don't want to be inappropriate or make anyone uncomfortable, so I pull away. Breda and Ronan keep their arms around me as they guide me to the living room. Everyone is there. But it's so quiet while we look at each other. The men drift toward Dillan's office, and that leaves me with Breda and her sisters Saoirse and Siobhan. Mair and Ally are beside me on the sofa with Ally in the middle.

Saoirse, Siobhan, Mair, and Ally chat, but Breda and I stare off into space. I can't imagine what she's going through. A month ago, her son got shot in a town a hundred-and-fifty miles away. Now, he's disappeared. She appears calm, but I know how I feel about Sean being gone. I want to climb out of my skin because I think I'm in love. But if it were my child—my youngest child—I wouldn't have my shit together. It would be splattered all over the walls. If Sean and I make it—not because he lives, but because we're compatible—I'll have to become a mom like her. Am I strong enough for that?

A phone ringing interrupts the low murmur of voices. I look at the purse by my feet. The guys gave me the phones back. Turning them over unlocked placated them. They didn't want them, so they handed them to me as we pulled into the garage. It's a burner. I recognize the number. Do I answer here, so they can report everything to the guys? Or do I take it in private in case it has nothing to do with Sean?

"Excuse me." I stand and walk to the foyer. Everyone can still see me from the living room. I inhale and tap the screen. "Hello."

"Nikki, where are you?"

"Safe. Is Ewan dead?"

Justin hesitates before he answers. "No. The doctors plan to release him tomorrow. It was touch-and-go the first few days. He's been improving. He's been asking for you, Nik."

"That's nice."

"Nikki!"

"What? It's nice that he's improving and that he's well enough to ask for anyone."

"He's only been asking for you." I know what he isn't saying. My brother hasn't even asked for Ellie.

"Justin, I don't want to talk to him. I can't right now. I have other stuff going on."

"You mean Sean being missing?"

I freeze. Only my eyes move, and that's to dart a glance at the women in the living room.

"What do you mean?"

"Nikki, we know someone took Sean."

"Because Ewan ordered it."

"No."

"Colt?"

"It wasn't us."

"Sure." Maybe it was and maybe it wasn't. I won't believe anything Justin tells me until one of the O'Rourkes confirms it.

"When are you going to understand you're in more danger with them than you've ever been?"

"Funny how that is. I date an O'Rourke while my brother and his men are deeper in the shit than they've ever been with the O'Rourkes. Now I'm suddenly a target when I haven't been one before, despite my connections to two other mob families."

"It's the O'Rourkes. They are the reason you're in danger. It isn't us. Ewan's a lot of things, but he isn't into sororicide."

"Of course not. He didn't have to commit patricide because the O'Rourkes took care of that for him. He doesn't shoot well enough to have come close to the mark when Sean was hit. But Colt does. He could have ordered Colt to do it. He's biting the hand that feeds him."

I ease down the hall toward men's voices. I hit mute as I knock.

Finn opens the door, and he's pissed to see me. I hold out the screen, so he can see the call's muted. He can hear Justin's voice, but it's hard to tell what he's saying. I put my finger over my lips.

"It's Justin."

I unmute the call and put it on speaker.

"...You end up dead if you stay there."

"If Ewan isn't doing this to Sean, and Sean isn't doing this to Ewan, then whoever this is will keep me caught in the middle. I'm safer with the O'Rourkes than anyone else."

"You didn't use to think that. You used to trust me. You even trusted Ewan to keep you safe."

"He shouldn't have sent me into the lion's den to meet with Nishida and Pablo."

I hadn't a clue about Sean and Pablo's history until Sean told me. I hadn't met Pablo before Sean and I ran into him. I wouldn't have known who he was at the meeting that never happened unless Sean introduced him. I only knew of him. When I think back to the meeting I canceled to spend time with Sean instead, I realize how lucky I was. I at least knew Nishida in passing. I had an idea of what to expect. Sean would never put me in that position.

"You were fine with them. You're in the shit now. Come back to Boston or let me come and get you. I'll take you back to Montreal."

"That isn't happening. I'm going nowhere with you or anyone else connected to the O'Malleys."

"I'll tell your grandfather."

"By all means, run to him like a little bitch. He already thinks you are one."

"I'm trying to be nice, Nik. Don't be like this."

"Don't get my grandfather involved. This is messy enough."

I watch the guys as they watch me. I need to get this conversation moving or end it.

"If you won't come to us, then you should go home. That's where you'll be the safest."

"Why? Because it's Canada? Or do you know something?"

"You mean, is this your grandfather? I don't know. If it is, then going to him will keep you away from all this."

"Or it'll clear your consciences, so you can go after the O'Rourkes without me being a casualty of war."

"For fuck's sake, Nikki! We aren't doing anything!"

I laugh. "You are not that high up to know what my brother is or isn't doing."

"I am for you. Nikki, please. All I've ever done is try to protect you. I tried to warn you about Colt. I warned you about Sean. I'm not clairvoyant. I have fucking common sense."

"You've been a good friend, but I'm not changing my mind. In the end, you will always be loyal to Ewan. That means you are inherently untrustworthy now."

"Loyal to Ewan? Because I love you. That's the only reason I can tolerate him. He's going to get you killed if Sean doesn't first."

I stare at the phone.

"Nik, did you hear me? Did you hear what I just said? You have to know."

"I did not."

"How could you not? I've been in love with you since we were teenagers. Your dad never assigned me as your guard. Ewan never did. They didn't have to. I volunteered. I get you don't want me. I've learned to live with that. But I have put you ahead of Ewan over and over since we were kids. I will do it again now. I will take you wherever you want as long as it's away from the O'Rourkes. It doesn't have to be here or Montreal. Just somewhere where Sean can't get you killed."

"This might have nothing to do with the O'Rourkes. It could just be Ewan and me. Maybe the sniper missed. Maybe they aimed at me, but Sean saw them in time."

"Then who took him?"

"How do you know about that?" I cock an eyebrow. This is what I want to know. What I wanted to get out of him.

"Lucy Leonard has been reporting to Ewan for two years. Do you know who she is?"

"Yes. I know Sean's past with her."

"She's been telling Ewan everything from the type of underwear Sean wears to his schedule seeing her. She recorded their conversations."

"You want me to believe Sean was into pillow talk with his sub? Bullshit. Sub or not, Sean isn't sharing state secrets with anyone who isn't a man in his family."

"She works at his strip clubs. She sees who he meets. She's been telling Ewan that, too. It's how your dad knew about—"

He stops himself.

"Knew what?"

"Knew about the deal he butted into that pissed off the O'Rourkes enough to kill him."

I don't know what he's talking about, but the guys seem to.

"Where is Lucy now? She was the last person to see Sean. Did she arrange this?"

"What do you mean? She wasn't the last person to see him. She left the club an hour before closing. She said he was still there."

"Then how do you know from her he's missing?"

"Because she arranged for him to be taken. I just don't know by who."

"Where is she, Justin?"

He hesitates.

"Justin, tell me. You've been a good friend to me, and apparently, I've been a shit one to you because I never realized your feelings. But I choose Sean. I have, and I'm going to keep choosing him. You know me better than most people. I'm telling you right now, tell me where she is."

"Nikki, don't get involved."

I snort. "I'm already involved. That's why we're having this conversation. I'm serious, Justin. You know me. You know what that means. Tell me the truth. If you don't, you know I'll put a bullet between your eyes from five hundred yards. You've been hunting with me, and you've been to the range with me."

"You wouldn't—"

"Come down here and try to take me from Sean. I already told his cousins to kill you if you try. I'll do it my own fucking self. Where the fuck is Lucy?"

Chapter Twenty

Sean

I'm going to hurl.

I'm going to kill her.

I'm going to—

I don't even fucking know at this point. All I can do is keep swallowing down this bile. I'm awake, so why won't my eyes open? What the fuck happened to me?

Fucking hell. That stings.

My eyes are finally open, and I see the needle in my arm. It's attached to nothing, but it has the same clear tape cover that was on the back of my hand while I had an IV in the hospital. I'm bound to this fucking chair.

My premonition. Thank God it's me and not Lina.

Lina?

I'm frantic as I look around in the dim light. I can't tell where I am, but I can see enough to know I'm alone. Lina's not here. At least, she's not where I can see her. Did they go to our place? Did they hurt or take Shane when they went for her?

I've never hurt a woman before, but I'm going to kill Lucy. Fucking cunt. And not the type I like—not Lina's. This is her fault. It's all coming back to me. Why I ended things with her and what she did.

I knew something was off when she was at the club. Ever since we ended things, she's avoided me. She never worked at 4Play, but she was there tonight. Normally, she hides in the dressing room if I'm at either of the other two places she dances. She only makes an appearance when it's her turn on stage.

We met at one of the BDSM clubs I'm a part owner of. No one outside my family knows we all own various clubs where we're silent investors. Comes in handy for work and for pleasure. She and I were masked, so we didn't recognize each other. When I scened with women, my voice was always deeper and rougher than it usually is. It wasn't until four months later, after meeting each other three times a week, that I spotted a birthmark on her left hip while she was performing.

I confronted her, and we created a new arrangement. We still met at the club when we wanted that environment. I had a studio I'd used with previous subs and was between renters at the time, so I made it a place where we could go when we wanted more privacy or just something different. She never came to my home. I never went to hers. We never went on dates. We didn't talk or text beyond confirming our rendezvous.

But she started hinting at more. She wanted a more permanent arrangement. One that involved us seeing each other more than two- or three-times week. It was when it started falling down to only twice a week that she hinted we should see each other outside the club and studio to be sure we had time. She didn't hint at a romantic relationship, but it became clear she wanted a 24/7 dynamic. One where we would go to each other's places and go out on what would appear like dates to most people, but they would be scenes.

It didn't interest me. I didn't want a commitment to her of any kind. Letting her come to any place I owned was as close to her coming to my home as I would allow. I didn't want to go to her place. I wanted to fuck. I wanted to bang. I wanted to tie her up, edge her, spank her, toy with her, and make her come. I enjoyed that, and she was good at being a sub. But that was purely in the sexual sense.

I ended it when she pushed too hard and told me—*told her Dom*—that we would go to the movies together, so I could edge her then make her come in public. I punished her for it. That didn't deter her. That same week, she showed up at 4Play when I was running payroll. No one thought it unusual for her to go to the office. She told the bouncers she needed to see me about a problem with her paycheck. She slipped into the office, locked the door, and stripped. I watched her.

When she was naked, I stood up from where I sat behind my desk. I walked over, reached past her, and opened the door. I told her she could get her arse on stage, or she could leave and never come back to any O'Rourke establishment. That if she tried that shite again—taking control and backing me into a corner—I would make sure no club or bar would hire her.

She had a key to the studio, so I changed the locks. I made sure the desk staff knew she was no longer allowed anywhere past the building's front door. Inevitably, she pitched a fit. But she never pushed the issue again and accepted we were through. We enjoyed our arrangement for more than a year. It was good while it lasted. But it would have ended the moment I met Lina if it hadn't already been done.

"You're awake." I don't know the voice.

It's piped in from speakers in the ceiling. I sweep my gaze

around the space again, and I realize I'm in a gymnasium. It's not a vacant school; it's obvious students have been here recently. Why the fuck would this person bring me here? Because it's so unlikely?

"Thanks for the nap. I needed the sleep."

"Because you've been so busy fucking your new subby that you haven't gotten any rest. You even moved her into your place."

How does this stranger know that? I didn't get the sense Lucy believed I'd replaced her. Just the opposite. She spoke as though we'd pick things up where we left off because I'd had time to miss her. She'd been fine with the distance because I've been traveling a lot during the past six months.

"What do you want?"

"To have a little fun. I won't kill you. But I am going to make your family search. I am going to make them frantic. I am going to make the skinny bitch believe it's her fault you're missing. It'll be a few days, but once I've tormented them and you enough, I'll knock you out again. Then I'll dump you in the Bronx. Mott Haven most likely. We'll see how long a white guy with red hair lasts."

Mott Haven isn't a good area. None of the Bronx boasts the best of New York City. But Mott Haven has been among the poorest neighborhoods in the poorest borough for decades. He's not wrong that I probably wouldn't last long if I'm drugged or hung over from them.

I glance at my arms again. Nothing makes me think he gave me heroin or meth. It was some type of anesthesia or heavy sedative. It's wearing off faster as I continue to speak. I need to keep the conversation going, not just to learn where I am and why but to recover sooner.

"You're a friend of Lucy's."

"Hardly. That bitch is the last person I'd trust enough to call a friend. I know you two used to fuck, and she's pissed you aren't anymore. She was happy to help dick you over. Don't you remember?" There's a pause, then a laugh. "She let me in through the back door. She kept you occupied, arguing with you while I checked out the best way to get to you and get you out of the place without any questions. She left an hour before we did, so people won't guess she was part of this."

"My ex-sub comes to see me, and we argue. You think no one noticed. I remember that part. She confronted me near the bar. I didn't take her to the office but down the hall toward it. We were in front of cameras the entire time. My family has already reviewed the footage and will know Lucy was part of it. Why take an interest in me?"

"Why not? You were the easiest person to get to this week. Your injuries meant you were more susceptible to the sedative hitting you harder. You aren't moving as fast as you usually are. You tire more easily. I picked off the runt in the pack of antelope."

"What do you want with my family?"

Silence.

I didn't expect an answer since that would clue me in on who this is. But I hoped it might be someone naïve enough or prideful enough that they told me something that could help me figure this shite out.

I wait, but this person says nothing more. Instead, I hear a door slam in the distance. It surprises me when no one appears. If I'm in a school gym, then those loud doors likely led outside. I strain to hear anything, but it's silent again. I suspect what woke me was the door slamming when whoever this fucker is came into the building. The dose is wearing off, but not completely. Something had to disturb me.

I spot the doors that appear to lead into another part of the school and the ones that lead outside. I move my ankles and wrists to see how my circulation is and to figure out what's keeping me tied to the chair. Zip ties have my wrists restrained behind my back. My arms pulled tight is why the needle in my elbow stings. Duct tape is around my ankles and the chair legs.

I test whether I can stand. It's fucking awkward, but not impossible. I shuffle my feet a few steps forward. This will take forever, but I can cross the gym. I may have to rest because the shitbag is right. I'm not at full capacity yet. But I'm stronger that he realizes. Strength of mind and strength of body.

I need to find Lina.

Nothing matters more than getting free right now because making sure Lina is safe is my only priority. I can reflect on what I heard later. I can consider whether this is connected to the shooting and whether this is connected to Ewan's attack. I can plan revenge once I've touched Lina and am convinced she's okay.

I don't know how long it takes me, but I'm drenched in sweat. My incision prickles. I want to throw up. But I'm at the doors that lead outside. There's a vertical rectangular window in each door, so I look both ways. The parking lot is empty. Good. I press the metal bar that opens the door but don't push. No alarm sounds. I open it a crack. The brick exterior has rough edges. I'm likely to rub off seven layers of skin, but I can twist enough to work the plastic zip ties until I cut through them.

The moment my arms are loose, I move back inside. I keep a chair leg propping the door open. I peel the clear tape off my arm, taking half the hairs on my arm with it, then ease the needle out of me. I'd love to toss the needle aside despite the biohazard that would leave for someone else to clean up, but it's biohazard. It has my markers on it. I use my teeth to hold on to it while I lean forward to get the Duct tape off my ankles. Once I'm free, I pick up the plastic chair. Not ideal, but it'll work. I carry it with the legs out in front of me. It might protect me from a bullet, but it's a battering ram or sword if I need it. I'd just need to buy myself time to run.

I sweep my gaze over my surroundings. I look up at the building. I'm already in Mott Haven. But it's daylight. Probably around seven or eight. My family doesn't panic, but they'll be in full-blown war mode by now. I've been missing for four or five hours. I need to get in touch with them somehow. I head toward the street and keep watching my surroundings. I don't have a phone, so I can't order an Uber or Lyft. I don't have my wallet to pay for a cab.

When I get to the edge of campus, I put the chair down. Now's the time to blend in and not look—questionable—with a plastic chair that clearly comes from a school. There's only one place you find this specific shaped and uncomfortable chair. I know where I am. It'll be a walk, but I can get to our place.

The abandoned train station hasn't been in use for over a decade. The city's done nothing with it except send an inspector around occasionally. We've made the entrance to our hideout practically invisible. If you don't know where to look, you won't find the door we cut out. We have a satellite phone that we only use for absolute emergencies. I think this counts.

I already noticed I don't have my watch. I can't send an alert. I also don't have my belt. Whoever this is must know those are two things syndicate men almost always wear no matter where they go. It's where we hide our trackers. The Diazes and my family favor the watches. The Kutsenkos and Andreyevs along with the Mancinellis favor the belts.

My suit coat is gone. I still have my tie on—surprised they didn't use it as a noose—so I pull it off, wrap the syringe in it, and shove it in my pocket. I unfasten the top three buttons, including the collar, and untuck my shirt. I roll the right sleeve up to match the left where the fucker injected me. Probably more than once since they left the needle in. I don't blend in, but I don't look as suspiciously out of place.

Fuck. I spot a liquor store we do business with—extort. I could use their phone, but then they'd know something happened to me. Why else would I need to use it? Who doesn't have their cell with them every day all day?

It's worth the gossip. I duck inside and look around.

"Hey, Manny."

"Sean?"

He gets uncomfortable real fast. His gaze darts around. Is he hiding something? Or is he afraid I'm here to do a random collection?

"Yeah. My phone died, and I need to make a call. Can I use yours?"

I could say please. I should say please. But manners aren't what I'm known for here. At least I asked.

"Sure."

I know where it is since I've seen the clerks on it enough times. I definitely am not using his personal cell phone. I walk around the corner and pick it up. I prop it against my shoulder and use my knuckle to dial.

"Sean!" Dillan's so loud I nearly pull the phone from my ear after I greet him.

"Yeah. Aguardiente."

"Ten minutes."

That means he's at the station. There's no way it would be that fast if he wasn't in the Bronx already. Aguardiente is a distilled spirit that, ironically, the Colombians favor. The name's what got our attention when Finn and I were checking out the area to see who needed "protection." Mott Haven is heavily Dominican, Puerto Rican, and Mexican. Not a Colombian hang out. If only. That would have pissed the fuck out of Enrique.

I hang up and roll down my sleeve enough to wipe it over the receiver and keypad. I step around the counter and glance up at the security camera. No erasing I'm here. I listen for Manny and whoever else is here. Someone's talking in the stockroom. I get closer.

"Yeah. He's here. I thought you had him knocked out. You said I wouldn't have to be involved beyond getting you into the school. If my dad finds out I swiped his keys to let you in, he'll kill me."

Interesting. Manny's dad is a custodian at the school. That solves one mystery.

"How'd he get out?" I don't recognize the voice.

"I don't know how he escaped. That's not my problem."

"It is now that you let him use your phone."

"What else was I supposed to do? Say no? Not likely."

I slip back behind the counter. I know where Manny keeps his gun. Definitely not in a gun case or the safe. I grab it, check that it's loaded—full clip—and take off the safety. No silencer. Inconvenient.

I creep closer to the door that's ajar. I listen for a little longer.

"Look. You made me help you. You said you'd let Josue go if I did."

Josue is his nephew. The kid's like ten. Who the fuck held him hostage?

I shift to see a different angle as I stand outside the door. I spot Manny. I can't tell who the other person is. It's unlikely Manny'll notice if I open the door wider. I use my shoulder, easing it open a few millimeters at a time, waiting for someone to sound the alarm. Nothing happens, and I can slide through the doorway.

It's not like this is a warehouse. There aren't stacks of crates to hide behind, but there are some boxes piled up that I crouch near. It puts me in the right place to see who Manny's chatting with.

Surprising, but not entirely shocking. How'd I not know his voice?

Mikhail Agopov. He's one of the Kutsenko brothers' most trusted men. He's usually one of their wives' bodyguards. I don't know why he's in charge of this operation, but there he is.

It's a shame because I like Manny.

I put a bullet through his left temple. Mikhail swings around, but I fire off four rounds. One in each shoulder and one in each kneecap. I don't want him dead yet. Just disabled.

I prowl closer, making sure he sees I'm taunting him by taking my time. He's on the ground, trying to stretch for his gun, but neither shoulder allows him to raise his arms high enough to reach where it fell. I kick it out of the way and kick him in the gut. While he's gagging, I check him for his other weapons. He's Russian, so I know he has at least three. Their training is still Soviet era paramilitary. I find a knife in each side pocket, a small can of mace in his left pocket, and brass knuckles in his back right one. The image would be complete if he carried cyanide tablets.

"Which one sent you?"

He clams up.

"I was the easy one to get. Who did they really want?"

Still quiet.

I assess him. The Russians are the hardest to break because of their training. Especially the ones the Kutsenkos' age. A psychopath who got his rocks off torturing people trained them and their Andreyev cousins. He was KGB and bratva back in Russia. Once again, my family knows shite no one else knows we know. We witnessed some of their training—the kind that emotionally scarred them enough that those eight men show no emotion to pain. It's how they survived.

No one knew Dillan, Seamus, Cormac, Finn, Shane, and I used to spy on them. We found a way into the place Vlad used. It wasn't the same warehouse they use as their torture palace now. They still use the abandoned grocery store where the meat department used to butcher their fresh meat but for other stuff. If Upton Sinclair hadn't died in the sixties, he could have written *The Jungle* about the unsanitary conditions in that meat processing place. The grocery store wasn't abandoned when they first started using it. Vlad forced the owners out.

Thorough as they were securing the place from the outside, they didn't think about the tunnel that led out near the Flushing River. It was how the blood drained. I dared Shane to go in there. The thing about anything I dared Shane was it meant I had to be willing to do it too. We did nothing like that shite alone.

We all saw shite we never should have. We pitied the now bratva leaders back then. But it didn't stop us from giving as good as we got, even when we were teenagers. It just meant we prepared for how they fought. It's going to come in handy now.

I put my foot on his chest and slowly transfer my weight to it. My heel is over his sternum, and I'm certain it feels like it's about to snap. I'm slow to increase the pressure, not wanting to snap his xiphoid process, the bit of cartilage that could break off and lacerate his diaphragm or even puncture his liver. That would—hopefully—lead to him bleeding to death internally. That's what I'll aim for at the end. I've already left a mess that'll need cleaning.

"Who sent you?"

I lean forward and put the muzzle of the gun to the bullet hole in his right shoulder and press there, digging it into his wound. He groans, unable to remain entirely silent.

"Your funeral."

I twist and put a bullet in his groin. Not quite his junk, but so damn near it, he can't help but try to coil to protect himself. I press harder on his chest. Rolling into a ball just makes it easier for me to put a bullet in his arse. I pull my foot back. If I do too much more right now, he'll pass out. That's not what I need. He just needs to understand I'll torture him. I might have finished Manny quickly, but that's because he was useless. Mikhail might wind up at the house we have on Staten Island where we hold people until we're ready for them at the station. It would give us time to round up some more of his associates.

I pull his wallet out and thumb through it. I don't expect to find photos of his family. I don't need to. I already know he has a seven-year-old daughter and four-year-old son. He's been married for nine years, and his wife works at one of the bratva's casinos. I find what I want.

I pull out the tiny disc and turn it over in my hand, rubbing it against my palm.

"Was that loud, Sergei? I hope it didn't hurt your ears."

I lean over and put the bug in front of Mikhail's mouth, so his labored breathing surely comes close to blowing their eardrums if they're wearing headphones.

"Too bad you can't see with this thing. Your man's on the way to looking like Swiss cheese. How many bullets have I put in him? I'm certain you're keeping count since you can hear me. But it's time for a private conversation, so I'll bid you adieu."

I stomp on the listening device, crushing it. It's in tiny pieces, but that's not enough for me to believe it's broken. It just reveals the inner workings. I grab a bottle of vodka—intentionally, so it's not really ironic—and unscrew the lid. I drop the device in there and close it. I put the bottle in front of Mikhail, who's still curled into a ball. The toe of my shoe nudges his left shoulder where the bullet wound is. I push him onto his back.

"They can't hear you anymore. You're going to die. You know I'll have a team in here to clean up so well no one will know you've ever been here. Not today. Not ever. I can keep putting bullets into you until you bleed to death. I can use your knives to fillet you until you bleed to death. I can peel skin off you and pour this cheap arse vodka all over you. Or you can tell me what I want to know, and I put a bullet through your brain. Which sounds most appealing on the menu?"

He stares at me mutinously. That's fine. I flip open the knife from his right pocket. The blade's longer than either of the ones I carry. I cut the hem of his shirt along his right ribs. I tear the material apart, leaving his arm in the sleeve. It's not in the way. I start the incision in his arm pit and draw the blade downward.

"This is sharp, but not as sharp as I expected. It's your shite knife, not my unsteady hand that's making my handiwork so jagged. Such a shame. I pride myself on my work."

He can't help the tears that stream down his face. I'm standing behind him because I've done this enough times to know. He pisses himself.

"I will keep going. You know that. I will crack your ribs and pull them apart using the crowbar I know Manny has. Then I will slice along your lungs and kidneys to butterfly them. Then I will cut that fillet like I said and send it to your wife with a nice bottle of wine. Hell, I'll cut and section you, then send you one piece at a time, once a month, like those steak subscriptions. I'll be sure to pick a different date, so it's stays a surprise. What would she do? Run to Maks? Let him come. You'll already be dead, and not even he can stop the U.S. Postal Service. Rain or shine, snow and sleet. However that goes."

I'm working as I speak. I grabbed the crowbar from near the back door. I'm not worried about Mikhail getting to his gun.

When I line up the crowbar with the wide cut I've made, he sobs. He knows I'm serious.

"All right. Don't do that shit to my wife. She doesn't deserve it."

"She knows exactly who you are. If she didn't deserve it, she wouldn't have married into the bratva. She knew the man she was getting. I've known both of you since we were in second grade. She used to pick on Colleen."

It was a good thing my cousin could defend herself. There was nothing any of us could do against Mikhail's wife when we were kids. Hurting a girl would have been indefensible, no matter who she picked on. I'll fuck with her mind now.

"That was twenty years ago."

"And the Soviet Union fell more than thirty years ago. It doesn't stop the bratva from using their old tricks. Who do you think I learned this from? Vlad the Impaler didn't just teach the Elite Group. I learned plenty from watching. Your security was shite back then, and it's shite now. I'll send whatever the fuck I want to your wife, and no one will know how to stop me. Speak."

There are things we learned from watching Vlad train Maks and his family. They were fucked-up and gruesome. But that wasn't our only training. Dillan and Finn refuse to speak about the training our family gave us. They may use the skills, but they categorically will not say aloud what we were forced to do. Speaking of it makes it too real, even if we do exactly as our grandfather and uncle taught.

Declan was as fucked in the head as Vlad. My mother's and aunts' iron wills are unbendable. There were things they could control because they could control Donovan when it came to their children's early training. But they didn't know—don't know—the shit Declan put us through. Our grandfather sanctioned it. My brothers, cousins, and I swore we would never let our parents know.

It would make them feel useless and like failures because they couldn't protect us from it. Our dads know now because they've seen us. Our moms might have a clue, but they will never know the extent of our depravity. Or at least the extent we're capable of.

"It was Bogdan. He ordered this. He wanted you drugged then left out there tonight. He wanted you to get jumped."

I'm only half listening to Mikhail as I think back to our own training. Dillan turned some of that training on Declan when he leered at Colleen one too many times when we were teenagers. Declan got off on mistreating women. He wasn't like my generation. We enjoy BDSM and the things we can do in a controlled environment with consenting partners. Declan wasn't like that. The less consenting a woman was, the more he enjoyed it.

Colleen told Dillan how uncomfortable Declan made her when she was fifteen. He was livid. The rage we saw terrified all of us. No one threatened his baby sister. I believe there can be platonic and sibling soulmates, not just romantic ones. Colleen and Dillan were the former. They may as well have been identical twins, like Shane and me. Dillan's not an empath. That would be laughable to suggest he was. Except for where Colleen—and now Mair—was concerned.

He felt her fear, and he made Declan pay. He got our moms' cousin drunk off his arse at McGinty's until he blacked out. He dragged him into the alley behind the bar and stripped him. Dillan didn't fully castrate Declan, but he cut out one of his balls. He took his time and stitched it up. Not neat and tidy like our doc does. He made sure it never healed right. Declan could still get it up, but he never came again.

He carved a D and an O on the inside of Declan's arse crack. Not for Declan, but for Dillan. He wanted Declan to know he was Dillan's little bitch.

"What does Bogdan have against me right now? What's worse than usual?"

I pay attention to this answer. "He knows you're with Ewan's sister. Ewan's still useful to them, but they want him to understand that if they can manipulate your family into blaming him, then they can make Ewan do anything they want."

"And if we retaliated and killed Ewan?"

"You won't because of his sister."

Ewan isn't Dillan. He doesn't love Lina the way Dillan and the rest of us loved Colleen. Dillan's warning to Declan worked until Donovan got himself killed. Dillan was so pissed that Donovan didn't listen and stay away from Laura Kutsenko, he took the only vacation of his life that our parents didn't organize. He came back to discover Declan seized power and put hits on our moms. Our dads made sure he was at the warehouse when the bratva struck back.

But not before we had a go at him. He went to our Staten Island house. He's the only one ever to leave alive and not go directly to the station. Hours before Declan died, I slashed two vertical slits down his eye lids. Shane cut deep grooves from each side of his mouth to his chin. Cormac connected his collarbones with his own slice. Seamus cut from hipbone to hipbone as close to his junk as he could get on the fucker's manscaped groin. Finn cut from ear to ear along his hairline and would have scalped him if there'd been time.

"Does Bogdan believe we won't retaliate against him and his family? He has to know we'd find out it was them one way or another."

"By then, you and Ewan might have killed each other. Or Ewan would be so indebted to Bogdan for the bratva keeping his ass alive, that Bogdan could make Ewan take the fall for something else. Whatever it was, it would keep the peace with you. Then you'd owe them."

One of the things our grandfather taught us while he was the boss was *lingchi*, or death by a thousand cuts. That was the plan for Declan, and we started it. But we planned a twist. None of the cuts were deep enough to kill him. After each one, Dillan got out his needle and thread. He sewed up the other wounds as well as he did the time he semi-castrated the fucker.

But we had to cut our torture short—that pun intended—when we found out the bratva was going for our dockside warehouses again. It wasn't hard to guess and put extra guys there to watch. When they went after the warehouses the first time, we moved what we could out of them and stopped storing shite there. That's when we used a storage unit. It's not our place like the other syndicates think. But we keep contraband there.

Declan could barely move on his own. He could barely stand. Our dads took him down there. They tied him up in Shane's office since it was his shipping company they hit. When the warning went up that the bratva was a mile away, we sent out cars to slow them down. We knew it wouldn't stop them. It just gave us time to get our arses out of there and leave Declan and his most loyal men behind. One of them freed him.

When the bratva rolled up, they thought they were such hot shit for killing Declan. Shot him from behind a couple times. More than one shooter. Bully for them. He couldn't get away because he was barely conscious. No one in our family had to live with the guilt of killing a family member, and it wasn't technically a mutiny since we didn't kill him. Dillan assumed the throne.

Death by a thousand cuts isn't fast enough for Mikhail. I figure I have about six or seven more before he's done.

"What does Bogdan want from me? What does the bratva want from my family?"

"They don't want your alliance with the Tremblays to be anything more than a pleasant business relationship. If you're with the Tremblay boss's granddaughter, then it's more than an agreement. It's family."

And nothing means more to the bratva's upper echelon than family. I get that. We're all like that. I won't get Bogdan without getting everyone who comes with him, and he knows he can't get me without everyone who comes with me. They're willing to go to war.

"Sean!"

"In the back."

Shane barrels through the door, slamming it wide open. He takes in the scene. I have the crowbar under Mikhail's ribs, but I have done nothing with it yet. I'm standing in the pool of blood he made. I have some splattered on me, which was inevitable.

Finn's right behind our brother. He assesses the situation the same way Shane does. "I'll get your clothes and the bag."

The bag. It's our go bag, and in it we keep all the essentials. Fresh clothes, fake passports, a few thousand dollars' worth of foreign currency, three extra handguns, four knives, camo paint, a balaclava, a beanie, NVGs, and preoperative wipes that have a few extra chemicals in them to remove blood, brain, and whatever other bodily "stuff" that winds up on us.

"Lina? Where is she?" Finn spoke before I could, but she's the only person I'm thinking about. I don't even look at Mikhail as I step away. I haven't decided if I'm done with him yet, but he's easily forgotten.

"She's at Mom and Da's. Mair and Ally are there, too. She's all right."

"Does she know I was missing?"

"She guessed as soon as I woke her. I didn't lie."

"Good."

"She knows about Lucy."

I stare at my twin. Our expressions are not identical.

"What the feck did you tell her about that bitch?"

"That you had an arrangement with her that lasted a while, but it was nothing like what you have with Nikki. That you have a relationship with Nikki."

"Wonder-fecking-ful. All I want is to see Lina, and she's probably halfway to Montreal. Are you sure she's still with Mom and Da?"

"Yes. She'll have questions, but she accepted my explanation."

"You truly couldn't maneuver around that part of the truth?"

He's contrite because he knows he could have. There were plenty of ways he could have avoided mentioning my last sub. One who I was with longer than any other.

"I need to get clean and get to Lina. Bogdan did this. He wants Ewan to know he has no shot against the bratva. That he can manipulate us into thinking Ewan's at fault for this. They don't want us getting closer to the Tremblays."

"A bit late to keep them out of bed with us."

I step closer to my twin, and he realizes he's about one word away from his easy-going baby brother exploding. He puts his hands up and shakes his head. He steps back.

"I was just trying to lighten the mood. Believe it or not, but I'm about two seconds from losing my shite too. *They took you.* Until you're checked out—I see that puncture wound in your elbow—I don't want you more worked up."

"Then you shouldn't have told me that Lina knows about Lucy. But there was no way around that. You're really certain Lina's all right? Not just safe from this shite storm, but with finding out about Lucy."

"Yeah. She wasn't pleased, but she accepted it."

Finn comes in with my bag, and it doesn't take long before I'm clean enough to be presentable. A shower wouldn't be remiss, but I can see Lina now. I have fresh clothes and shoes. Finn's taking care of getting Mikhail to the station for more questioning, and Shane's driving me to our parents.

I don't like seeing them rush out of the front door to greet us. The look on my mom's face isn't relief.

"Nikki's gone."

Chapter Twenty-One

Lina

"Nikki, what the hell are you doing? Go back."

Ewan's been pissing vinegar since he called me the first time. He relented and called to check on me, even though he was the one who got shot. I guess being near death makes him want to make amends. Is there a twelve-step program for recovering douchebags?

I shouldn't think that about my brother. There are more days than not when he doesn't feel like a sibling. He's more like a stranger or someone I don't have more than a passing relationship with. Other days, he's someone I barely stop short of loathing. When I answered the phone, that's where I was at. This is one of the rare moments when he's being my brother and not a manipulative fuck.

"You shouldn't have told me where she is if you didn't want me to do something about it."

"I wanted you to tell the O'Rourkes."

"Unless it's Sean's mom or aunts, no one will make her talk

because none of them will lay a hand on her. They won't torture her, but I will."

It was no easy feat to slip off Breda and Ronan's property. They have armed guards patrolling it the same way all the O'Rourkes do. There's a wall that runs around the perimeter that's ten feet tall. It's not concertina or chicken wire at the top, but it may as well be. There are spikes that are barely more than two inches apart. They stand at least six inches tall. No one is coming over that easily. They could make it, but not before guards spotted them.

I came outside to take this second call from Ewan because I didn't want anyone around me if I lost my temper. I was sorely tempted the first time he called. He wanted me to go back to Montreal. He was prepared to send his jet for me. He wanted to tell my grandfather what's happening and convince him to make me leave. For once, it wasn't to coerce me into doing something else he wanted. He genuinely wants me safe. He told me he thinks it's the bratva that targeted him and Sean, and if that's the case, they're the most likely to make me collateral damage.

I ended that call because Breda came to check on me. She had a cup of tea for each of us. We sat together on Sean's old bed. She said nothing. She was just companionable silence. No platitudes. No explaining things I already know. No encouraging me to talk about my feelings. Eventually, I leaned against her, and she wrapped her arm around me. I felt badly for a moment, putting the weight of how I feel on her shoulders when she's scared for her son. But when I reached across her lap and took her hand, she gave it a squeeze and held on to it tightly. It was a moment of shared fear and sense of uselessness.

When Ewan called again an hour-and-a-half later, I was downstairs with everyone else. We've been on the phone now for twenty minutes. I wandered the front garden for a while, not really paying attention to what Ewan was saying, since he was repeating himself from our first call. When Siobhan and Tate arrived, I heard the Elton John version of that oldies tune, "Lucy in the Sky with Diamonds."

My rage flooded me. It was a sign. I needed out, and I needed to go immediately while I had the chance. I crept around the back of the guard shack right by the gate. I kept to the shadows and slipped out while the guard spoke to Tate. It was like good fortune shone upon me. I'm still on foot, but I'm about to hail a cab and head back to Sean's for my car.

"Ewan, enough. Either give me her address or don't, but I know you have it."

"No. I'm not helping you with this. I'm going to call Dillan."

"Do that, and the first thing out of my mouth when Sean gets home is the key to my encryption."

I refuse to imagine anything besides Sean coming home. Finding Lucy isn't about finding Sean. I pray it helps, but I trust his family to find him. This is answers. This is retribution.

"Really? You're going to be spiteful right now?"

"I'm going to do whatever the hell it takes to find out what else these pieces of shit planned for Sean. And might I remind you that the bratva is pitting you against each other. If I find out what they're going to do to Sean, I'll probably find out what they're going to do to you. I'd tell you that."

"She won't know anything. They probably paid her or threatened her, and she played her part."

I know that. I don't expect Lucy to know shit. But I'm not confessing to Ewan before I commit the crime. Lucy isn't going to live.

"If she's not a threat, then why shouldn't I talk to her? The O'Rourkes won't interrogate her like I can."

Ewan and I both know that's bullshit. They can interrogate

even better than me. But they won't hurt her for the information. I will. And that brings us right back around to what I was thinking about earlier.

"Ewan, get me the info or get off the phone, so I can find it."

"Fine. Hang on."

I raise my arm and get a cab driver's attention.

"I got a cab. I need to know where I'm going." I changed my mind about getting my car. This is faster.

He rattles off an address, and I know where it is. It's not too far from my college campus. Higher rent area than I expected a stripper to afford. Shane filled me in a little more about Lucy, but barely anything at all. Just that she was a dancer at a couple of their clubs, and she always stayed out of Sean's way—and Shane's since she usually couldn't tell them apart at a distance —whenever one of them was there. She fucked Sean for more than a year and couldn't tell him apart from Shane. I already can, and I haven't known either of them that long. It's more than the freckle.

I know how Sean stands. It's not the same as Shane. It's subtle, but Shane rests his weight forward on his feet, like he's ready to pounce. Sean rests his weight evenly, like he's going to take a stand. Sean tends to put both hands in his pockets, whereas Shane only puts his right hand in his. Shane is content to only feel one of his knives when he thinks he might need them. Sean likes to have both in his hand, ready to draw.

When Sean laughs, his right eye narrows slightly more than the left. It's the reverse on Shane. They are mirrors of each other, so that makes sense to me. Shane's quicker to smile, but Sean will smile longer. I think these are traits their family recognizes whether they've considered them or not. They stand out to me because I'm still getting to know them. But once I realized these few things, it made it impossible to confuse one for the other.

"Thank you." I pay the driver and slip out. I didn't want this ride recorded in my app.

"This is a mistake, Nik."

Ewan's been prattling off and on the entire ride from Queens to Manhattan. We haven't argued because he doesn't want the driver to hear us any more than I do. But he repeats himself about getting my grandfather involved. He's even threatened to get my mom involved. That got him a response in French he learned when we were kids. I knew a few swear words he didn't.

"Ewan, you can stay on the phone with me if you want. I'm putting my phone in my pocket, though."

"You better not fucking hang up, Nicolina. I will call Sean's entire family if I hear you make one sound of distress."

"I know. Now shut up. I just got into her building."

I notice the cameras in the lobby, so I keep my face turned away from them. There's a guy at the desk, so I scan the names on the mailboxes across from him. Then I hold up my keys.

"Hi. Tara Millingham sent me over to grab some documents she left in her place this morning. She told me where they'll be, so I'm just going to pop up and down. If I don't hurry to get back to the office, I'm screwed."

I'm assuming Tara works in an office. There's a flyer sticking out of the box that has T. & L. Millingham written on it. The flyer's addressed to her. It's for a corporate retreat. I don't slow as I go past the desk, making a beeline for the elevators like I belong there. I spotted their names because it was right next to L. Leonard. Lucy.

I get on the elevator with no problems. I slide my phone out halfway and wake the screen. The call is still active. I scan the hallway as I get off and notice there are no security cameras. I hike my dress up enough to pull my gun from the holster. I considered taking it off at Breda and Ronan's. I'm glad I kept it strapped to me. I find her door and knock. It's not loud and demanding. I'm not pounding on it. But it is purposeful.

I take the safety off, keeping the gun next to my right thigh as I angle myself more to the left side of the doorway. It'll be harder for a bullet to hit me, but it'll also put Lucy right in front of me and indefensible if I shoot. I have my head turned just enough, so she can see my profile but not my full face if she looks through the spyhole. I hear the latch move and the bolt turn. When the door opens, I tilt my head enough to see the woman who answered clearly. It's her.

My left hand goes for her throat as I raise the gun. I shoulder the door open wider as I push her backwards into the apartment. I kick the door shut. I move the gun to her forehead as I release her throat and reach back to lock the door. I shouldn't without knowing we're alone. But I'm not giving her an opportunity to escape. My hand wraps back around her throat and squeezes as hard as I can. She tries to pry my hand loose. She kicks and flails. She can't headbutt me because the pistol is still pressed to her forehead.

I let go and shove her backwards. "I can squeeze the life out of you if I want to make it agonizingly slow. Or I can put a bullet through your pretty face. Either way, I won't hesitate to kill you if I don't get what I want. You know who I am. You're scared, but you're not confused."

"You're Sean's new sub."

"I am not. I'm Sean's girlfriend."

"He doesn't date."

"We aren't dating. We don't need to go out on agreed upon days at agreed upon times. We're together too much to need that. We go to breakfast because we wake up together. We have dinner together because we go to bed together. We hang out with his family because he's made me one of them."

We'll see if that's true if I survive this.

"He commanded you. He fucked you. He walked away from you. For once, two out of three ain't bad. He's coming home to me."

"He's already dead."

"Nope. Try again." I pray she isn't right.

"He will be soon enough."

"Nope. His family's on their way." To hell? Maybe one day. But not on their way to Sean yet.

"Bullshit."

"If it is, it doesn't matter either way. I have a gun to your forehead. You're going to answer my questions."

"You won't shoot me."

"Won't I?"

I pull the gun from her forehead, shoot her right foot, and put it back to her forehead before she probably even felt me move it the first time. My grandfather gave me this before I moved to New York for college. He insisted the silencer remain on it anytime it wasn't in the case. It's an awkward size, but if I'm in a situation where I need the silencer, I'm probably in a situation where there won't be time to put one on. In this case, I'm glad I came prepared.

She falls backwards onto the sofa and opens her mouth. I squeeze her throat as I rest my weight on one knee beside her.

"Scream, and I'll put this down your throat and blow the back of your head off whether or not you give me information."

"Fuck you."

"I'd rather not. Sean refuses to share me."

"He and I were monogamous, too."

"Yeah. And you fucked for fourteen months. He let you go to his studio. He met you at his BDSM club, then shared a fuck pad with you when he let you come over. But you've never been to any of his homes. You've never been in any of his beds. I live with him already. Why? Because he wants me

322

all day and all night. There's no turning off his desire for me."

I'm baiting her. I know my brother can hear this, and I don't give a shit if he gets insights into my sex life. Maybe he'll let Colt know I wasn't a prude. He just couldn't get me off.

"What do you want?"

"Answers."

She's not cooperating, but neither does she want to keep hearing me throw Sean's feelings for me in her face. She must know I'm telling the truth. That begs the question how does she know about us?

"Who told you about us?"

"No one. I saw you together."

"Stalking Sean?"

"No. I was on a run, and I saw the two of you having breakfast in a restaurant I pass. I happened to look in and saw him kiss you."

"And that pissed you off."

"I couldn't give a shit about you with him. You won't last. Look at you and look at me. He saw me three times a week for more than a year."

"That's four days a week he didn't see you. There was never a week where he saw you every day. We've been inseparable. Hard for him to go back to you when he refuses to let go of me. He adamantly refuses to consider bringing another woman into our sex life. I'm not worried that I'm not permanent. Why'd you get involved with someone kidnapping him?"

"Because they asked me to."

"Asked or told."

"Asked, and I said yes."

"If you're so confident he'd come back to you on his own, why would you endanger him? Why would you help someone hurt him? Why would you make him hate you? There's no way he's going to want to be anywhere near you, let alone screw you."

"He doesn't know I had anything to do with it."

"It was a good thing you were pretty if you were really that stupid." Past tense because she's not coming out of this alive with that attitude. "Why?"

"Because he shouldn't have ended things. I was going to be there to help him recover from this."

"But you already knew about me. Am I next?"

"You should be. But he'll pick me over you, so I'm not worried."

She doesn't get it. She's lost in some warped sense of her relationship with Sean. He's had time to go back to her. Shane said it's been over for months. Sean hasn't been with her since he ended it. At least, that's what he's led Shane to believe. I don't think he'd lie to his twin about this. I don't think he'd lie to Finn either.

"Who asked you?"

"Wouldn't you like to know?"

"I would. That's why I asked. You're making me impatient."

I lower the gun long enough to shoot her foot again.

"Wait!" She wails as tears stream down her face from the pain. It must hurt an awful lot. All the sarcasm in the world intended.

"Who asked you?"

"This guy."

"If you aren't going to be useful." I put the gun to her forehead and push.

She whimpers. Maybe now she understands I'm serious. Apparently, two bullets in the foot didn't convince her.

"This guy came into a club while I was working." She's panting every few words. She better not fucking pass out. "He knew I'd been working for the O'Rourkes for a while. Said he'd seen me at a couple of their strip clubs. He got me chatting, and before I realized what I was saying, I admitted I'd been Sean's sub."

The defiance has evaporated. Now there's fear, and it's not directed toward me.

"What did he look like?"

"Big. Just like all the other guys."

"Accent?"

"Yeah."

"New York?"

"No." So not *Cosa Nostra*.

"Boston?"

"No." Thank God for small mercies.

"Spanish?"

"No." So not Cartel.

"Russian?"

"No. I know the bratva men. I've worked for them too. It wasn't one of them."

"French?"

"Maybe. But not like I've heard in movies."

They say that Québécois is more sing-songy than other French dialects or accents. I don't know about that. But I infuse it into my accent as I continue in English.

"Did the person sound like this?"

"Yes."

I want to close my eyes and scream. This cannot be true.

"Did you hear the person speak French?"

"No. They called someone right after I agreed to help, but they spoke English."

My phone presses against my leg as I kneel on my dress.

"Did the guy you met sound even more like this?" I exaggerate the accent I have when I speak French.

"Yes! How'd you know?"

Motherfucker. I tried to teach Ewan and Colt French when we were kids. They learned a little, but they never cared that much. They used to tease me about how Canadian French didn't sound like what they heard in movies. No shit. Not the same French. Ewan and Colt would mimic me, then try to sound like Parisians. They got pretty good at it.

"Did you meet this someone they called?"

"Yeah. Once."

"Man or woman? Could you hear any of their conversation? Did they have an accent?"

"Yeah. A man. Definitely had an accent."

"What kind?"

"English from like England."

Who the fuck is that? Who does Ewan know that would get involved in this?

"What'd they say?"

"The first guy I met confirmed I would lead the second guy through the back alley and into the strip club. That's all I had to do. I had to distract Sean long enough for the English sounding guy to get in and look around. Then I had to leave fast once he gave me the signal he was in place. I don't know anything that happened after that."

"What did the English sounding one say?"

"Not much. He just agreed."

"How'd the call end?"

"The man I met said he wanted it done soon, or it would get messy if he had to do it himself."

"How much'd you get paid?"

I try not to speak through my teeth, but my jaw wants to clench.

"Ten grand."

"You got the money already?"

"Yeah. Five upfront. Five was waiting for me here."

"In your place?" I sound skeptical.

"Yes."

I grin. "You gave them a way into your place?"

"No. It was just waiting here."

"And that didn't freak you out?"

"Of course it did. Why do you think I'm packing?"

She jerks her hand in the bedroom's direction. I'm not taking my eyes off her long enough to check. Her phone rings in her pocket.

"Pull it out."

She eases it, not trusting me. Smart. I wouldn't trust me either.

"Answer it."

The area code is Boston.

"Hello."

"Allô." Fucking shit French accent.

"What do you want?"

"Did you get your money?" It's supposed to be just enough to flavor his English like my French accent sometimes slips into my English one. Rarely is it the other way around. I grew up speaking both from the moment I could talk. I would interchange them.

"Yeah. Do you want anything else?"

"I hear you like it rough."

"You want to fuck?"

"If you have time." I know that smug laugh. He's only half teasing.

"He—"

I stick the barrel between her lips. It was obvious she was about to say help. I shake my head. I'd already let go of her throat because the angle was awkward, but I wrap my hand around it again.

"Lucy?"

The accent slips a little. I pull the gun from her mouth, my glare warning her.

"Yeah."

"What was that? Who are you with?"

I put the gun to her throat. I keep picking different spots, so she doesn't know for sure whether I will or won't. If I keep it in one place too long, she'll figure if I was going to shoot her, I would have already. She'd be wrong. But it would give her a false sense of security, then she might do something that fucks up me learning what the fuck is going on.

"No one. I almost dropped the phone. I'm putting away dishes."

She lies with ease. Not a surprise. If she hadn't gotten this call, I wouldn't have entirely believed her about the accent. I would have had to check. Now I don't have to.

"Is Sean all right?" She watches me.

"Maybe for another hour or two. My guy's going to be sure he winds up where he belongs."

I knew he wasn't working alone. Fuck nut can't even do this without needing someone to hold his hand.

"You got someone else involved?" Lucy's fear just amped up. Who does she think it was?

"Just the guy you recommended. He was happy to do it. If he's caught, he knows I'll kill his family if he tells the truth. He'll pin all of this on the—"

"Good for you. I can't believe you convinced him." Lucy cuts him off.

Who's she protecting? She's the one who brought the guy with the English accent into this. Not the other way around. Or is there a third person?

I shake my head. She knows that wasn't a good idea.

There's noise at the door. She shifts to look past me, but I don't turn. I grab the phone and put it to my ear.

"This shit isn't over." I hang up before the piece of shit says anything else.

Lucy tries to push me and bolt for the door as it crashes open. I know who it is. At least, I'm pretty fucking certain. I shift, so Lucy can't get past me. She opens her mouth to scream again, and the gun slips past her teeth.

"Sean, I will kill her. Back off until I'm done."

"*Cailín—*"

"Not yet."

I want to turn and run into his arms, but this isn't done yet. I pull my phone from my pocket and tap the screen. The call's still connected. I unlock it with my thumb and hold it up to my ear.

"Did you motherfucking know?"

"No, Nik. I swear. I'll kill him myself. This is shit only you can fix."

"You think I want to. I don't. You're on your own, big brother, and so is he."

I hang up and pull the gun from Lucy's mouth.

"Who was he going to say before you cut him off?" I'm not ready to name names yet in front of Sean and his family.

"Sean, she's crazy. She broke in here and is holding me hostage. Help me."

I hear Sean approach, and for a moment, I think he's going to stop me. He's going to choose her.

"Help yourself." I speak before Sean can. "Who was his guy? Who'd he get to help him?"

"Mikhail someone or other."

"Bratva? With an English accent?" I don't dare glance at Sean, but I want to.

"Yeah. I guess. But this guy's been an independent contractor kinda deal."

"There's no 'I guess'. There's no someone or other. You tripped up with your lies. You'd met him more than once. You definitely heard him speak more than once. You recommended him. What's his name?"

She hesitates. I point the gun down and shoot her other foot. She howls.

"You were never going to walk out of here. Who took Sean?"

"Lina, I already know."

I ignore Sean. "Answer me, Lucy. Look at me, not Sean. Answer me. I will make this quick if you do. If you don't, you'll wish you were a man, and an O'Rourke got to you first."

"Mikhail Apagov."

"Was this the bratva? Did a Kutsenko order this?"

"No. Mikhail and I—we have a history. I get him odd jobs sometimes. This was one of them."

"You just lied about a man with an English accent, didn't you? It was Russian."

"Yeah."

I cock an eyebrow before my gaze really sweeps the place. I spot a couple of things that confirm what I suspect.

"He pays for this place, doesn't he?"

She darts a glance at Sean. And the guilt... Oh, the mother-fucking guilt.

"You were fucking Mikhail while you were with Sean. It was supposed to be monogamous. You betrayed him even back then. You aren't loyal to Mikhail because you just gave up his name. You weren't loyal to Sean when I'm certain you swore you weren't taking anyone else up your ass. What about our little friend on the phone? What's your connection to him?"

"I told you. He came into the club and approached me. We talked, and I let it slip about being with Sean."

"When was this?"

"A few weeks ago. He was in town for a few days."

"Why'd you agree?"

Sean hasn't stopped me interrogating her, so this is information he either doesn't know yet, or he wants confirming. He hasn't made me lower the gun, which I really thought he would. Not just for Lucy's sake, but to keep me from putting someone's death on my conscience. I will sleep just fine tonight.

"Because I knew he was with you!"

The venom in her voice would be shocking if I didn't already know the answer.

"Anything you want to know from her, Sean?"

"No."

"Anyone else?" I speak to the guys behind me. My guess is they're all here, but I don't know."

"No." There are a couple voices behind me, but I don't know who's who.

I step closer, and Sean tries to intervene now. I wrap my hand around Lucy's throat. I know Sean already saw the bruises there. You can't miss them. I squeeze as tightly as I can, and her mouth opens in panic. Once more, I stick the gun in there, but I angle it up this time. I ease the hold on her neck.

"Look at him."

She turns pleading eyes on Sean. He does nothing.

"Look at me."

She whimpers as her gaze meets mine.

"He chose me."

I squeeze the trigger.

Chapter Twenty-Two

Sean

I do choose Lina, and I will over and over.

After I spank her until my hand hurts, then spank her for making it hurt.

We watch Lucy crumple to the floor as Lina lets go. If I hadn't seen the result of this kind of gunshot wound to the head, it would make me puke. It did the first few times. I watch Lina. She appears completely unaffected. She turns to me.

"I'm not a sociopath, Sean. Don't look at me like that. It's not that I'm unmoved by killing someone. She just isn't the first person I have. She isn't the first person I've seen die that way, either."

I put the safety back on the gun after I take it from Lina and drop it onto the sofa. Then she's in my arms. We collide, then cling to one another. I hear my brothers, but I'm not paying attention to them or my cousins. I have my *cailín* back in my arms where she belongs. We turn our heads to face each other, and our lips meet. I can't get enough of her. The way her plump lips feel against mine. The satin insides of her cheeks. The smoothness of her tongue as it tangles with mine. I lift her, and she wraps her legs around my waist.

I break the kiss long enough to look toward the hallway where two bedrooms must be. We say nothing as we walk past my family, who ignore us. I know they're getting people over here to deal with the mess. I'm certain they're making calls to find out Ewan's role in this. I'll ask Lina, but I'm sure she doesn't know more than a sliver.

I kick the door shut and turn us until her back is against the wall. When I wrap my hand around her throat, it isn't in a punishing grip like Lina had on Lucy. I just realized both names start with L. Start with the same sound. Yet they couldn't be more different. Besides the kinky sex, they are nothing alike. They don't look similar. They don't sound similar. Taste, touch, scent. Not the same.

But it's so much more than that. I never trusted Lucy completely. I've trusted Lina since the beginning. Moments of doubt have cropped up—like finding out she'd run from my parents' home. But her loyalty to me is everything. She did this to protect me.

She came to learn things she knew none of us would get from Lucy because our means to coerce her weren't the same. She knew none of us would inflict pain on Lucy, but she also knew Lucy had a threshold for pain that wouldn't make her easy to persuade. The gun surely helped, but Lina's intelligence made Lucy talk.

"Little one, my heart stopped when I found out you were gone."

"Like mine did when I found out someone took you."

"I couldn't get to you fast enough."

"And I couldn't find out how to end this fast enough. I didn't run from you. You know that, right?"

"I do. You couldn't have known I got free before you left my parents'."

"I didn't. If I'd known you were on the way, I would have stayed. But I don't regret coming here."

"I know. But fecking hell. I'm glad to hold you."

"Daddy, I knew everything was going to be all right when you arrived. I don't know how, but the moment I heard a hand on the doorknob, I knew it was you. Your cologne isn't that strong, but I recognized it when the door opened. I knew I had more I needed to get out of her, but knowing you were safe and here—I wanted to shoot her and fling myself at you."

"Fling?"

"Yes, Daddy."

"My arms will always be open and ready for that, *cailín.*"

I slide my arm beneath her arse, so my free hand can touch every part of her I can reach. She watches me as her hands run over my face, hair, shoulders, chest, arms, and upper back. These aren't quite loving caresses even though she's gentle.

"I'm not hurt, little one."

"I'd see bandages if it was bad enough. But did they do anything else?"

"No. I woke up in a school gym in the Bronx. I had a needle in my arm, but I'm pretty certain it was just sedatives to knock me out. I think they dosed me more than once and expected to do it again."

"How'd you get free?"

"Slowly. I hobbled my way to the door with the plastic chair bound to my legs. Scraped the zip ties on the bricks until they snapped, then got rid of the Duct tape at my ankles. I recognized where I was, so I headed to a liquor store I know."

"You don't have your watch or your belt."

"I know. The guy who took me knew to get rid of them. I don't know if he took both because he wasn't sure if my tracker was in my belt or watch, or he knew about the watch and didn't want to leave the belt as a weapon."

"Was it this Mikhail guy? Did your family find him?"

"I did. He was at the liquor store. Turns out the owner helped him get into the school after Lucy helped him get into the club."

"He's dead."

It's not a question, so I don't need to answer.

She rests her head on my shoulder as she kisses my neck. I tighten my arms around her. Our need resurfaces, and we're back to kissing. God, how I want to be inside her. How I want to hear her moan my name as I make her come. It's almost like that's the only way I'll truly believe she's all right. When I can feel my body inside hers. When I'm part of her.

"Are they going to assume we're having sex?"

"Maybe?"

"Then can we? I need you closer. I need to know you're truly okay. I need to give you control over me while everything else feels completely out of control."

"I want to take care of you, Lina. Always. Whatever you need. And you understand me. What's going on outside this room isn't under my control yet, and it's silently driving me crazy. You get that. I can breathe for a moment if I can be in charge."

"I need you inside me, Sean. And I need you to decide how."

I lower her to her feet. I pull my phone out of my pocket and pull up a group text. Lina can see what I'm doing. She reaches for my phone, frantic.

ME

I need time to talk to Lina. Do not interrupt. If you need me, figure it out on your own.

Her eyes are so wide, I think I can see every millimeter of white. She shakes her head as she looks past me. Her voice hisses.

"They'll know."

"Then you'll have to be quiet."

I take her hand and lead her to the bed in the corner. It's as far from the door as we can get. I sit, and she tries to move beside me.

"No, *cailín*. I'm proud of you for getting the information we needed. I'm proud of you for being brave enough to follow this through. I'm proud of you for your resourcefulness. It pissed me off you left without protection. I'm not angry anymore. I will never punish you while angry. I never want to risk my temper making me careless. But your arse is going to be sore for a week. You could have died. That wouldn't even be the worst that could have happened. You didn't know who was here. You didn't know if someone might come over. You didn't know you were safe just getting here. I know you had freedom in Boston, but I doubt your grandfather allowed you to do things this reckless in Montreal."

"I've never been in this situation before. I'm sorry for scaring you and your family. I'm sorry for being deceptive. I'm sorry for dragging your family away from whatever else they should be doing. But I am *not* sorry for finding out who did this to you. I am *not* sorry for killing one of the people involved. I am *not* sorry that I will kill anyone else involved. I will repent for the first part, but I will sin with a clear conscience for the second part."

"I'm not upset about the second part. I'm unhappy about the first part. I get why you did it. You didn't think anyone would bring you here. And they probably wouldn't. But this information—this vengeance—none of it is as valuable as your life, your wellbeing, your safety. There were other ways.

Maybe not as efficient, but effective. I need to know that you won't do something like this again, Lina. I thought I'd been terrified in the past. But nothing prepared me for my mom telling me you were gone. That is a degree of fear I pray I never feel again. If finding you weren't so urgent, it would have paralyzed me."

"Then you know how I felt. The longer I sat with your mom in your room, the calmer I felt. But that was physically. My heart didn't race. I didn't feel like I was going to vomit. I didn't think I would sob until I couldn't breathe. It did nothing to cease the terror I felt because I would never see you again. I will obey your rules, Sean. But only to a point. I will not promise I won't do something like this again. I don't plan to. I don't want to. But if it's your life or our children's, then you will never be able to stop me. I promise you that. I will find a way."

"Children?" I love the sound of that.

"Yes. Children. If we can have them, then we will. Do you not want kids?"

"I only want kids with you. But that's binding our lives together forever. Are you ready to think about something like that?"

"Yes. Or rather, I'm ready to talk about what that would look like. What we want. How we could make what we both want work. If we agree our future is together, then I stand by what I just said. I will obey your rules. I will take the precautions to protect myself and our family. I won't disregard your men's welfare. But I have a limit to that. You will never convince me not to do any and everything I can to protect you and our family. You are not the only one able and allowed to make that pledge."

I stare at Lina as she speaks. I never imagined someone outside my family would speak this way about me. My men are loyal because it's their duty. My family is loyal because we're blood. Lina is loyal because she chooses to be.

"I get to decide when the situation warrants you breaking my rules." I grin.

"I believe you want to spank me. I want my spanking. Should I strip?"

I hesitate. "No. Just pull your dress up."

I know she's confused. I can't blame her. I never suggest she stay clothed. Just the opposite.

"Lina, if you're naked, I will get distracted. This isn't to arouse you. It isn't to edge you. That's not part of this. This is a real and true consequence for you risking your life."

"Do you think we can find a belt?"

"What? No. Absolutely not. No."

I have a visceral reaction to that idea. I don't mind the idea of a belt or something else when we're doing this for pleasure. I don't like the idea of taking anything to her but my hand as part of a punishment. It's already going to test my fortitude to trust I won't hurt her. I don't think I will. I don't believe I'll lose control. I won't be in the headspace I am when I'm at the station. But it is a different mindset from kink, and I fear I'll inadvertently hurt her.

"Daddy, tell me what you're thinking. Or let me say what I think it is."

"I don't like the idea of using something on your for a punishment that we could also use for pleasure. I don't want to associate the two. I also fear being too rough with you if I use anything but my hand when I punish you. I won't confuse being with my girlfriend with being with—I just don't want to make a mistake."

She cups my jaw. "You are the sweetest man I've ever met, *nounours*. I wouldn't consent if I didn't know you'll always do your best for me. My trust is unconditional just like the rest of my feelings."

She gathers her dress and lays across my lap. She's not wearing panties and hasn't for days. I palm her arse and squeeze until she squirms. I do that to both sides. Then I bring my hand down heavily. The sound of flesh on flesh fills the room.

"Lina?"

"That fucking hurts, *nounours*. Keep going."

I land a second.

"Ten, *cailín*. Can you do that?"

"That's all?"

"I will never just spank you over and over until I get too tired or get bored or fear more will harm you. Ten, little one. You've already had two."

"Yes, Daddy."

My hand crashes down again.

"Three. Thank you, Daddy."

Smack.

"Four. Thank you, Daddy."

Smack.

"You don't have to thank me, Lina. I didn't demand you ask for a punishment. I doubt you're feeling grateful for the way your arse already feels and what you guess it will feel like. I won't make you promise false gratitude."

"I'm thankful you care enough to punish me."

I land the sixth, and she kicks her feet. She says nothing, and I hear her labored breathing.

Seven and eight are in quick succession. She clings to my ankle to keep from reaching back. I aim number nine at her horizontal crack. She howls. I glance at the door. She turns her head to do the same before looking up sheepishly at me.

My guess is they've figured out I'm spanking her not

fucking her. I'm ninety-nine-point-nine-recurring sure Dillan and Finn would do this to their wives.

"Ten."

The last one covers the top of her thighs and horizontal crack. She lays limply across my lap. I help her stand, and her knees are shaky. I ease the dress over her head, then guide her to straddle my legs while standing. I unfasten my pants and pull down my boxer briefs. This isn't about pleasure.

She slides down my cock and clings to me. She bursts into tears. I hold her as she sobs. This isn't the burning skin from her spanking. This is her fear finally finding an outlet. She's tucked her head against my chest, and I'm looking across the room. I'm fighting not to cry, too. My fear hasn't dissipated completely.

"Daddy, your heart is racing, and it wasn't a moment ago. You're breathing heavier, too. What's wrong?"

She sits back. Her face crumples when she sees mine. Her anguish mirrors mine.

"I thought you were dead, Lina. I thought someone took you. Or that you'd run, and someone got you. I came here to beat the truth out of Lucy if I had to. I've never killed a woman before, but I would have if it meant I found you. I was calm when I spotted you for the sake of you finishing what you started. I didn't want the risk to be for nothing. But fecking hell, Lina. I thought you were dead."

I did. I didn't admit it to anyone, though I think the guys knew how I felt. I think they might have believed the same thing. My fear is why I need to be inside her. It's not just to comfort her right now, to show her we've reconciled everything between us. It's for me to know she's truly alive and well.

"Daddy, I'm so sorry I made you that scared. I feel like I'm feeling your fear now, and it's greater than I imagined. But it's the same as mine."

"I know, little one. Let me hold you."

"Always."

We sit together for a long time. Until it grows quiet in the living room. We could hear the cleaners moving around. I'm certain they want to get in here and make sure we've left no evidence behind.

"We need to go, don't we?"

"Yeah."

"I know my punishment doesn't come with pleasure. But that doesn't mean you shouldn't enjoy it. Let me—"

"No, Lina. Forgiveness is given with no expectation of something in return. My feelings are unconditional."

"I don't offer as penance. I offer it because I want to comfort you."

"Later. Right now, just don't get beyond my reach. I will panic."

She nods slowly before she presses a kiss to my forehead. We stand and fix our clothes. I lead her out to the living room. It's only the cleaners.

"They're in the SUV."

I nod to the guy who lets me know where my family went. I figured as much. One man walks over with Lina's gun. He's about to hand it to me when I tilt my head toward her. Once we're in the hallway, I watch her pull up her dress and slide it into the thigh holster I saw but didn't comment about.

We go out to the vehicle in silence. It's not until we're two blocks from Lucy's apartment that any of us speak.

"Justin did this."

I suspected that was a possibility, but I didn't expect it. I suspected he'd find a way to fuck me over because he loves her. But I didn't expect him to take it this far. There has to be another reason than just a tantrum over not getting the toy he wanted.

I watched Lina as she said those three words. I wonder if

there's a twinge of sadness that her friend put her in the middle, and now that friendship is over.

There's not.

It's calm anger.

As in, she won't explode. But after what I saw with Lucy, Justin's fate is sealed. She will do something far worse, given the chance. I don't want her anywhere near that. I know she said she's killed before, and that's something I need to hear about. But I don't want her to have a childhood friend's death on her conscience. When she reflects on this with time, I don't want that to be a memory.

She turns to look at me. We read each other's minds at times, and this is one of them when I wish she couldn't.

"You will not convince me to go home and wait for you. You don't know Justin like I do. You don't know how he'll act when cornered. He won't lash out, but neither will he give up. He threatened your life, but he betrayed me."

Loyalty is as important to her as it is to me and the rest of my family. That is the bedrock of a syndicate's survival. Loyalty to the organization above all else. Loyalty within my family before anyone else keeps our syndicate strong. Betraying Lina was the worst crime Justin could commit in her eyes. It's a betrayal of Rowan and Ewan. She might not care about either of them as a father and a brother, but she cares that Justin betrayed their family, their branch's bosses.

"Ewan was on the phone with me since I left your parents' house. He heard all of it. He will send men for Justin. If Ewan gets to Justin first, he won't turn him over to you. But he knows me well enough to understand if he kills Justin on my behalf— or claims it's on my behalf—things will be irrevocably severed. Justin's betrayal of me is one of several to Ewan and my dad as his bosses. But they trusted him with my life. *I* trusted him with my life. Ewan knows Justin is mine. Sean, you have no more chance of convincing me otherwise than Ewan. He did this, at least partly because of me."

I lean to whisper in her ear even though this isn't something so private the rest of my family won't hear me say at least once more.

"I don't want this for you, *cailín*. I don't want you to have another death on your hands. In your memory. I need you to trust that I'll handle this. You've already been sucked in too far. You were born into this world, but this is a part of it you were never meant to join. Let us take him to our place. Let me get justice. I will never let you see what I'm capable of. But he deserves all of it."

"That's all true. But physical pain won't break him. Justin was diagnosed with Borderline Personality Disorder several years ago and has been under medical care for it ever since. It's well managed and not as severe as for some people, but one characteristic of BPD is a high tolerance for pain. I think it stems from the disassociation that can be part of the condition. It's not that he has no threshold for pain. He does. But he's been a thrill-seeker since we were kids. He injured himself all the time, but it didn't deter him. He got used to being in pain and has a high tolerance. When things came to a head, and he sought treatment, it was because he'd started harming himself. In some ways, he believes he deserves the pain. I'm telling you, stringing him up and beating him won't get him to talk. I know what will."

"Tell me what to say to him."

We're not whispering, but we're speaking quietly. I know the others can hear. It saves me having to repeat it, but it gives a sense of privacy at the same time.

"It's not that simple. There are things only a handful of us would know, and it would only affect him hearing it from us. Ewan, Colt, and I are among the people who've known Justin the longest. Ewan and Colt know him better than I do, but Justin has guarded me since we were in high school. If you want Justin before Ewan gets to him, then it'll only be worth it if I'm there, too."

Could Lina be spinning me a tale just so she can have her pound of flesh? Is revenge that important to her? I think it is important, but I don't think she'd lie. It makes me wonder what the fuck she has on him. What could be so traumatic or triggering that only a handful of people could talk about it, and only that would make him crack? Would it bother him if other people found out, or would he still stay silent? Would my knowing whatever this is do nothing at all?

I've worked over plenty of people able to disassociate themselves from the situation without having any mental health challenges. Hell, every bratva member fits that description. What is it about Justin that makes his disassociation so different? From what I know about BPD, people who have it often fear abandonment. Is that part of what Lina knows from Justin's past? Is this what spurred Justin into attacking me? He fears Lina abandoning him?

"Where's he likely to be if he's in New York?"

"I don't know. As far as I know, he doesn't have that many connections down here. He followed me here the last time, and he's traveled with my family and me when I came here with Dad and Ewan. But I never asked or was told if he came to the city on his own."

"Would he answer if you called?"

"He knows I know, so probably not."

"Texts?"

"Maybe. I can try."

Lina pulls out her phone and taps her contacts, scrolling until she gets to his name. She taps the screen again and pauses as she considers what to say.

LINA

I could have been hurt if I'd been at the club with Sean. I've been there before.

She looks up at me. She's holding her phone so I can easily see the screen. We wait. We're entering my parents' neighborhood when a response comes in.

JUSTIN

No you haven't. That's why it had to be there. Somewhere you couldn't get involved.

LINA

Involved. Not hurt.

Her face shows her disgust. I can practically hear her saying fuck you.

JUSTIN

Obviously you can defend yourself better than the little bitch you think you're with.

LINA

Think?

JUSTIN

You can't fuck someone when they're dead. At least that's not what you've been into.

LINA

Gross. I am with Sean.

JUSTIN

For now. You can't be everywhere. You won't find everyone. Lucy was too obvious. I'll do better next time.

LINA

And if I really am with Sean next time? You'd let me be a casualty?

345

JUSTIN

You'll be home the next time.

LINA

All the more reason I'd be with him if we're home.

JUSTIN

Don't be stupid. Boston

LINA

Boston isn't home and never will be. Sean's home. Montreal's home.

My hand's been resting on her thigh. I squeeze it when I read she considers me home. Not the city. Not my place. Not even a place we share. Me. Like being with me—being in my arms—me inside her—that's what feels like home. I get that with a soul deep understanding I never imagined I'd experience. I knew it was possible from the other couples in my family. I just didn't think I'd have that too.

JUSTIN

Whatever. Stay away Nikki. This is happening.

LINA

Why?

She looks up at me. I wanted her to get to the point sooner, but now I realize she purposely strung this out. She wanted to get him chatting and slide in the question.

JUSTIN

I told you how I feel. Not only isn't he good enough he's likely to get you arrested or killed. Ask him what happened to Dillan's wife. Go on. He's sitting right there.

Is he assuming? I glance out the windows in front and

beside me. I don't want to look over my shoulder in case he really can see us. I don't want him to know that unnerves me.

LINA

You know what happens when you assume

JUSTIN

Where else would he be? You're probably sitting on his lap with his dick in you.

Lina turns a horrified face to me. How the hell does he know what we do in our place? No one comes into my place besides my family. I don't have a housekeeper because my mother would never let that "laziness and entitlement" fly. Deliveries are dropped off at the desk and searched, then x-rayed for bugs and any other threat.

JUSTIN

You should keep the curtains closed even if you aren't on the ground floor. You know flying things fascinate me.

Drones.

LINA

You've watched me before but you asked. Do you think invading my privacy is winning me over?

What the ever-loving fuck?!

JUSTIN

I don't have to win you over.

LINA

Punishing me?

JUSTIN

Punishing him. He endangers you. He doesn't even know you. I do

LINA

Punishing Sean and wanting me away from him isn't enough for you to do all this. Did Ewan put you up to this?

JUSTIN

Don't think I came up with this all on my own?

LINA

You couldn't

I nudge her shoulder. If she pushes too hard... The answer is immediate.

JUSTIN

Someone approached me. I decided how it would go.

LINA

Why couldn't you just talk to me?

JUSTIN

You wouldn't have listened.

LINA

You WERE one of my oldest friends. Sean or any other guy-- doesn't matter. You say you didn't do this to punish me. You did it to hurt me. Same difference

I want this conversation to move along. It seems like we're going around in circles. She senses my impatience because she puts her hand on my thigh.

JUSTIN

Come back to Boston.

348

LINA

No

JUSTIN

Leave him and come here. This ends when you aren't there.

LINA

Because you kill him. That's what you think is going to happen. FFS you cannot believe that will happen. You aren't the first person to try. He's still alive. I promise you those people aren't. Lucy's not.

JUSTIN

Fuck Lucy. I don't give a shit about her. She did what I needed her to do. I would have killed her anyway.

That makes Lina tense. She glances up at me. She didn't expect that.

LINA

If you'd kill a woman how am I supposed to believe you wouldn't hurt me?

JUSTIN

Because you're you.

LINA

You really care that much?

JUSTIN

I love you

LINA

Will you kill me if I stay here? What are you going to do to me if I go to Boston?

JUSTIN

You keep saying I'll hurt you. You know I would never lay a hand on you. You know you're not that serious about Sean. You've known him a minute. You can be with someone who loves you. You love me. You've said as much.

Lina's eyes close for a moment.

LINA

As the brother I should have had. I've told you that for years. That I love you as a close friend and that you're the brother I wish I had. You know that's not the same. You know it'll never grow into something different. You don't want someone else to have what you want. If you can't have me no one can.

JUSTIN

High opinion of yourself. No. Sean is a threat to you. Find someone who won't put your life in danger. Even if it isn't me.

LINA

This is getting too hard to text. We're going to go around in circles. Meet me. Talk to me Justin. Don't terrify me. Don't manipulate me. Talk to me

JUSTIN

So you can manipulate me?

LINA

I don't manipulate you. I tell you flat out what I do or don't want you to do. If it doesn't match what I want then oh well. I don't trick you. That's the shit everyone does to me. Fuck you if you think you can manipulate me. That's what you're trying to do. Don't turn this shit on me. Either you talk to me in person like a grown ass man or don't talk to me ever again. I won't care what the fuck happens to you. You can fuck all the way off.

It's my turn to tense.

She raises her right hand and pats the air, telling me to hold on.

JUSTIN

Come alone

LINA

You know there isn't a snowball's chance in hell that's happening. I don't trust you and Sean will go fucking ape shit. We meet somewhere neutral. You can have your knife, and I'll have mine. No guns for either of us. My guard stays where he can see me and get to me but neither of you have a clear shot. Our backs to walls facing the doors and windows.

JUSTIN

Fine where?

LINA

The restaurant at the hotel I stayed at. Crowded but won't make my guard twitch.

JUSTIN

When?

She glances at her watch.

LINA

An hour

JUSTIN

Fine. Cross me Nik and he'll still pay. I don't work alone.

LINA

I know. You better tell me enough that if this shit really goes sideways and I need to get out I know who not to run to.

JUSTIN

Run to me.

LINA

One hour be there. I have no patience left.

JUSTIN

I know what that means. See you there

She sighs before she looks up at me. Then she closes her eyes and sags against my shoulder.

"I know that went back and forth way longer than you wanted. But the first step to breaking Justin is to whip up his fear of abandonment. He knows what I'm like when my patience is gone. He's seen it with Ewan and Colt. He saw it when we were teenagers. I directed it at a few guys who worked for my father. He'll change course to placate me. He'll be more conciliatory because he thinks he has to win me back over to his side."

"The abandonment—is that the BPD?"

"Yes. There are things from his past, like I said, only Ewan, Colt, and I, along with a few other people know. That's what I need to use in person. I know you don't want me to see him. You're practically vibrating with anger that I suggested it. Trust me on this, Sean. I can't be absolute about anything someone else will do. But I know Justin, and I know how he's predictable. He said he wants me back in Boston, but he only disagreed with New York being my home because of you. He didn't disagree that Montreal is home. He said nothing about my grandfather, which makes me think he believes Montreal is safe for him. He knows Boston won't be because of Ewan. Unless he put a hit on Ewan too, he can't stay."

"How do you know he's here?"

"The drones. If he got photos of us somehow, it had to be that way. He has the kind that can take photos, and he's an expert at using them. He does surveillance for Colt."

That reminds me of something. I clench my jaw. She kisses it where the muscle sticks out and puts her lips to my ear.

"I will explain what happened when he watched me once you and I are somewhere we can really talk. We need to head back to Manhattan."

We've been sitting in my parents' garage, alone in the car since the others already went inside. She slides her phone back into her pocket and climbs out on her own since the garage door is shut.

No one's said anything about what happens next, so I have to fill them in. Her arrangement to meet Justin won't go over well. If anyone is going to stop her, it'll be my mom.

Chapter Twenty-Three

Lina

I'm exhausted. More from that text conversation with Justin than everything that happened with Lucy. That took mental and physical strength. Texting Justin took emotional strength. Sixty minutes is going to cut it tight to get back into Manhattan. I feel badly that I wasted the drive into Queens.

Sean's explaining to the others the change in whatever their plans were. I'm upstairs getting cleaned up as best I can without spare clothes here. The way I killed Lucy ensured the blood splatter went away from me. I'm not at my best, but I'm also not covered in anything gory. I don't expect a knock.

"Come in."

"Nikki?"

"In the bathroom."

I step out to see Ally with some clothes over her arm. She holds them up.

"I know we're not the same size, but we're close in height. Maybe something will work. When Finn told me Mair and I needed to come here, I knew it could be an hour or a few days. I brought stuff with me. You're too tall for Mair's clothes."

"Thank you. That's kind of you."

She lays them out on the bed, and I find a pair of pants with a drawstring waist I think I can cinch tight enough. There's a top that should work well enough. I just won't be able to lean too far forward.

"I'm going to take a quick shower now that I don't have to put this back on. Can you tell Sean I'll be down in five minutes, please?"

"Sure."

I'm walking into the bathroom as Ally leaves. The water's frigid since I don't wait for it to warm, but I scrub myself from neck to toes. I'm in and out in a couple minutes. Then I'm pulling down the shirt and grabbing my shoes as I walk to the door. Sean's waiting for me at the bottom of the steps.

"You and I will take a town car. Shane, Seamus, and Cormac already took off to scout the place and get in position. We've all eaten there before, so they know where to hide. They just have to make sure they can. Tommy's going to drive, and Ted's your guard. He knows the restaurant too. He's already picked out a spot where he can see you and get to you, but it'll look like he doesn't have a clear shot. Four steps to the left, and he will."

"There're going to be too many people there to start a shootout. Justin knows that. I have to meet him outside and go in with him. I need to call the restaurant and make a reservation to get the table I want."

"I already did. I want you in there and seated before him."

"That won't work. If he's already in Manhattan, he'll get there first. Plus, I have to meet him outside. He won't go in without seeing I don't have a gun. He knows there's not a chance in hell I'll go in without him showing me he doesn't have one either."

I noticed someone picked up my purse from where I dropped it in Lucy's place. I snap it open and show Sean the hunting knife I carry when I can't carry my gun. When I know I need protection, but don't want to carry my gun.

"Nikki?"

I turn to see Sean's mom approaching. Sean has his arm around my waist, his fingers pressing into my waist. Breda looks at her son and tilts her head. When Sean doesn't let go, she shoots him a look that makes him release me. He looks down at me as I look up. I nod, but he's still reluctant.

"Nikki, Sean told me what's going on. I believe he hopes I'll stop you. My son's not naïve, but sometimes I think he forgets who I am. I'm not just his mom. I am you, but thirty years older. My dad was the boss. My brother was the boss. I married a mobster. I understand you better than anyone but Saoirse and Siobhan. My sisters and I are the same. Who's loyal to you among your brother's men? Someone who would follow your orders?"

"I don't think there is anyone."

"There has to be. Someone who may not like you but hates your brother more. Someone who thinks they're important enough to weather any storm. Someone already taking bribes. Who is that?"

"I don't know. I know my grandfather's men who would help me if I asked. But I don't know about Ewan's."

"You do *not* want your grandfather involved in this. He's more like my father than any of these guys realize. We've never done enough business up there for my sons and nephews to know your grandfather well, but I do."

She cocks an eyebrow at me, and I nod.

"It has to be someone from Boston if for no other reason

than they can get to Justin faster than someone in Montreal, and they know him. Before you get to that meeting, you need to put a hit on him. If you can't get to the money easily, I can. I have more than enough to kill off most of the men on the Eastern Seaboard. Call it a rainy day fund my sisters and I started before we even met our husbands. They know, and they've contributed. If you truly can't think of anyone, I know a guy."

She winks. I stand there like an owl staring at her. *I know a guy.*

"Nikki, think. Do you have someone you can call or text before you get to that restaurant? If you don't, I need to make that call now. You cannot go into that meeting without having this arranged. If Sean and the others can't get to him for some reason, there has to be someone waiting for him. It needs to be one of your brother's men. Ewan needs to know you can turn his men. His men need to know you're a threat. Being with Sean makes you untouchable to most. But things in New York aren't the way they once were. A mob family is as much a curse as it is a blessing. Do this, and you make yourself untouchable. That scares the shit out of men way more than anything they can do to each other."

"Hell hath no fury like a woman scorned. That has nothing to do with romance."

"Exactly."

She waits for me as I consider my options. My mind bounces from one person to another in my brother's organization. Finally, a name comes to me.

"Colton Flaherty, Senior. He's my ex-fiancé's father. He did three tours in Iraq and was a sniper. He taught my ex-fiancé. He was loyal to my grandfather, but he couldn't stand my dad. He liked Ewan before he became boss because Ewan and Colt have been best friends since preschool. But he doesn't agree with Ewan now. I can barely be in the same room as Colt without antagonizing him on purpose. But I'm still close to Colt's mom and dad. If Colton Senior knows Justin threatened me—and honestly, even worse, threatened an O'Rourke—he'll kill Justin without a second thought."

"Make the call. On a burner."

"I will. If he agrees, it'll be pro bono."

"What's the chance he'll turn on you?"

"None. And if he does this, no one will know it was him. He's a ghost. Ewan doesn't know half the jobs Colton Senior did for my grandfather. I had access to records no one but my employer knew I had. I know Colton's kill record from his deployments. There's no way he's told anyone that number."

She hugs me, and I lean into it. I miss my mom. I'm used to not seeing her for months at a time, but today's been a lot. Breda's hug is what I need. It nurses a part of me that Sean can't, and it's the closest I have to my mom.

"Thank you."

"I'm a boy mom through and through. I didn't realize how nice it would be to have a daughter. If one is good, two is better."

She offers me a smile that could make any boo-boo better. But this is a lot bigger than a scraped knee. She squeezes my hands as her gaze hardens. She gave me reassurance. Now she's giving me strength.

"Lina, we have to go."

The guys say goodbye to their parents, and Finn and Dillan say goodbye to their wives. This is a mission of sorts, so we all know things could go wrong. I can tell the O'Rourkes never miss an opportunity to show their love. It's refreshing and foreign at the same time. I like it.

Sean and I get in a town car, and I expect him to ask me what I meant earlier. I'm ready to explain, but he says nothing. When I dart my gaze up to him, I know this isn't the time. He's focused, and I sense he's running through his plan again.

"I need to make a call, Sean. It's your mom's advice, and I agree with it. It's not a reflection of you or the men in your family. I don't doubt anyone's capability. It just needs to be someone from Boston."

His eyes widen before they narrow. He doesn't like it, but he nods. He knows what I'm going to do. He watches me enter a number into my burner and wait while it rings.

"Hi, Colton. It's Nikki... It's nice to hear your voice too. It's been a long time."

Sean's hand goes around my wrist like a manacle. He's not hurting me, but he wants the phone away from my ear. I change sides and shake my head. He reaches again.

"No, I haven't spoken to Colt in a few days. Not since I left Boston."

Sean's brow furrows as his hands drop. I put a finger to my lips and put the call on speaker as Colton continues the conversation.

"He asked if you called."

"Did he say why he thought I would?"

"No. But he told me you're involved with an O'Rourke. He wanted to know if I'd heard. I had."

"Still watching out for me?"

"Always. My son might have screwed up the best thing that ever happened to him, but I don't blame you for his shortcomings. I blame your brother and father, but not you."

"We're still more alike than either of us is to Colt. I want to chat and catch up, but I'm calling for a reason. I need something."

"Anything."

"Hear me out first before you make any blind promises."

"Nik, tell me what you need, and it's done. I won't ask why."

"Justin."

There's a long pause, and I'm certain Colton's wishing he hadn't just said he wouldn't need the reason.

"Justin is working with someone. It's not Ewan or Colt. He hired a guy to take Sean. He used a woman from Sean's past to get this man into one of the O'Rourke clubs. Justin had his guy drug Sean, but they underestimated him. Neither the woman nor the man involved survived. But Justin wants me to leave him and either go to Boston or Montreal. He's still threatening him."

"Do you want it done here or there?"

"I'm going to meet him right now. It'll be a public place, so he won't take me. But if something happens, and the O'Rourkes can't scoop him up as we leave, then I need you when he goes back to Boston."

"Does Sean know all of this?"

I'm watching him, and I can tell he's more pissed than he's ever been with me. More than about me leaving his parents'.

"I'll fill him in."

"It's gonna piss him off that you're involved, and it's gonna piss him off that you think he can't handle this."

"It has absolutely nothing to do with the second part. Sean alone can deal with Justin. With his entire family, any trace Justin ever lived will disappear. That's not why I need you. Anyone who knows I'm involved with Sean knows I'm untouchable. But there will always be people like Justin and Ewan who believe that doesn't apply to them. If I can get one of Ewan's men to carry out a hit for me, then I make myself untouchable."

"You've been talking to Breda."

"How'd you know?"

"She's Sean's mom. Dillan's already married, but if you were with him, Siobhan would tell you the same thing. If you were with Cormac or Seamus, Saoirse would tell you what Breda did. I doubt Breda knows the lads discovered she ordered a hit on a guy who worked for Donovan, but it's been a poorly kept secret for the past decade. You sound like her. Count your blessings she's your mother-in-law."

"She's not—"

"Nicolina, you've met Breda. You're as good as married to Sean. The O'Rourkes don't bring people home to their family unless it's permanent."

I'm watching Sean. His expression closed off as soon as he realized I'm talking to Colton Senior. I can't read his feelings. This distance scares me more than anything until now. I fidget. I'm uncomfortable hearing Colton make these assumptions while Sean can hear.

I'm unprepared for Sean to reach across me and unfasten my belt. He sees the flash of worry in my eyes. He kisses my temple before lifting me onto his lap. I lean my head against his chest, listening to his heartbeat for a moment before responding.

"Breda spoke to me before I left her house for this meeting. She explained it to me, and I believe she's right. Will you do this for me?"

"I've known Justin his entire life. He's had his struggles, but he's been a good guy. He's also been in love with you since you were fourteen, and he was fifteen. Puppy love back then. It's more now. He hated you being with Colt, and it devastated him when you accepted Colt's proposal. But he stayed silent. I'm certain it relieved him when you left Colt. I'm certain he was ecstatic when you moved down here. He believed you'd always turn to him whether you were with Colt or alone. The moment you chose Sean O'Rourke, Justin knew he had no place left in your life. You know he can't accept that."

"I do. If he'd only threatened me, I wouldn't be on my way to use that against him. But he went after Sean. I'm not interested in forgiving, and I'll definitely never forget. He's a threat to Sean. Whoever he's working for—whoever's feeding him false encouragement—is a threat to the O'Rourkes. Whoever this is won't let Justin live once he's no longer useful. Justin will die. That's inevitable and unfortunate. I won't let whoever this silent partner is have the satisfaction of tying up that loose end. If Sean doesn't do it to remove Justin as a threat and to prove to this unknown person that the O'Rourkes aren't to be effed with, then I need you to do it for me."

"And if I can't?"

"At least you didn't say you won't."

"Nikki."

"The only way you can't is if something logistical messes it up. Your skill is unquestionable."

"You haven't answered my question."

"Because you know the answer. Sean doesn't want that for me. I killed someone today, Colton. He doesn't want me forced to do that again, especially not to a childhood friend."

"For your sake and your sake alone, I will do this. But Sean needs to know you're capable."

I watch Sean as he listens, his eyes on my phone. I'm not sure what to make of his shift in focus.

"He saw what I did today."

"But does he know I taught you?"

Sean's gaze jumps to me. I offer him an apologetic expression, but I'm not sure why. Maybe because I hadn't already told him. But there's still so much we don't know about each other. Maybe because I have the skills a sniper taught me.

"Not the details."

"I don't want you having to do this. I know you'll put Sean first, but you've still known Justin for most of your life. Contact me when you know if I need to make a move."

"I will. Thank you, Colton. Outside of Sean's family, you're the only one I trust."

"We love you, pipsqueak."

"Love to you and Daisy."

I hang up the call and lean away to see Sean's face clearly.

"Explain, Lina."

There's no bite to his tone. It's the opposite. His voice is soft as though it's full of regret.

"I will, but Sean, I didn't ask Colton to do this because I don't have faith in you."

"I know. I know my mom, and I get what you told me and him. I'm sad that it's coming to this. I can tell Colton doesn't want this for you, and neither do I. Why'd he train you? And what did he mean 'capable of'?"

I sigh and look out the window.

"My maternal grandfather used to take me hunting once I turned twelve. We only killed what we could store and eat. It was never for antlers or trophies. I took to it easily and got good at it. Eventually, Granddad taught me to fire a handgun. I had a permit to carry in Quebec only because of who my grandfather is and got one in Massachusetts. When I visited my dad in Boston, one of the few things he'd do with me was go to the range. I met Colt's dad, Colton Senior, there the year I learned to shoot a 9mm. I was fourteen. Ewan, Colt, and Justin were fifteen. Justin was around, but he had other friends."

Justin said that's when he fell in love with me. Colton confirmed it. I never realized. I was completely oblivious all these years.

"Ewan and Colt teased me because they'd never gone hunting with me. It took one round for them to realize I knew what I was doing. They stopped teasing. They also found some-thing else to do because they hated I scored better than them. Colton noticed I was standing alone because Dad was talking to his men, and Colt and Ewan left me behind. I told him about hunting and fishing. He listened to me. I love those things, but no one in Boston ever cared except for Colton. He had his rifle and let me shoot. It didn't shock him I was good. Like really good. He was proud of me. No one else there was."

I hate remembering these parts. Or rather, I hate remem-bering how I felt during those trips. I'm fine remembering going to Boston and even the things I did or people I saw. It's reflecting on the loneliness and alienation that I'm not so fond of.

"His wife, Daisy, became a second mom to me whenever I went to Boston. My stepmom, Maureen, was awesome to me, but I clicked with Daisy. I know she regrets ever suggesting her son ask me out. She feels guilty despite how many times I've told her Colt is his own man and made his own choices. They had a cabin in the Berkshires, and they'd bring me along when they took Ewan and Colt out there if I was in town. By then, the guys drove and went off to do their own thing. I hung back. Daisy loves carpentry, so she taught me woodworking. Colton would take me shooting. The better I got, the more challenges he found for me. The distances increased, the angles got sharper, the targets got smaller. I excelled."

"He trained you to be a sharpshooter."

"Yes. I made it more than that."

Sean's hand rests on my hip while his other arm is slung around it. He moves his hand up to my ribs and presses me back against him. The only way I can tell when he gets upset is his heartbeat. It's back to racing. His breathing is even. His body feels relaxed. His touch is light. But his heart is about to pound out of his chest.

"The summer after I graduated high school, I went to Boston for a month. The friends I'd made were my age and just graduated, too. Colton and Daisy let me go out to the cabin with four girls. They're all mob daughters."

Let someone call me a motherfucking mob princess. Show me the fucking castle. Show me the lavish excesses. The only thing making me a princess is my very own Prince Charming, whose lap I'm sitting on right now.

"The entire property has invisible fencing and security cameras. The alarm went off while we were in the hot tub our second night there. Each of us had a guard. Mine was Justin's older brother, Stuart, who was in his mid-twenties. Two of them went out to check while I led the girls to the cellar. I was about to go down with them when a different sensor triggered. This one was way closer than just the perimeter. Stuart knew he couldn't convince me otherwise, so he ran to the gun locker with me. I got Colton's rifle—not the one he hunts with—a box of rounds, and the NVGs."

"He keeps NVGs there?"

"For the same reason he keeps more than a hunting rifle and has invisible fences and cameras. I went up to the loft with Stuart, and we pushed the bed beneath the window. With my NVGs, I had a clear view to the south and east. I saw four men converge on the two guards. The guards took out two intruders, but they didn't make it either. I waited until the men stepped under a tree with a light sensor. I flipped up the goggles and could see the intruders' faces. I didn't know them and neither did Stuart. I picked them both off. I went to the master bedroom balcony, which was on the side where the single guy tripped a sensor. We saw him moving away from the house. I thought he was retreating. He wasn't. He got a gear bag. He lifted out rope, an ax, and some other shit before he took out what Stuart told me were flash bangs. He intended to disorient us when he broke in. He never took a step toward the house."

I inhale until my lungs can't take any more. Then I exhale as though that might be my last breath.

"Were you hurt? Did anything happen to you?"

"No. We told the other girls and guards Stuart took the shots. Once we were back, we let people think it was Stuart and the other guys who died who got all of them. The moment Colton and Daisy got the security alerts, they got in the car. They watched their live feed in the car on their way to us. They both knew there was only one person at the house that night who could take those shots. Neither they nor Stuart ever breathed a word to anyone that it was me."

"Who were they?"

"O'Briens."

Pieces of trash. The O'Malleys pushed their sorry asses out of Boston a few generations ago when they thought they could run Boston and take over NYC. They failed at both. Now they're the O'Rourkes' lackeys in Trenton, New Jersey.

"Why go after you and your friends?"

"Because they knew Rowan's daughter was there. I was the target."

"So those men and Lucy. Anyone else?"

"No. Sean, I'm not proud of what I did if I'm talking about the body count I've racked up. But I'm grateful I can protect the people I care about."

"*Cailín*, I know. I understand better than most."

"That's why I knew I could tell you, and why I could text Justin and talk to Colton in front of you. I definitely wouldn't be comfortable confessing all of this to anyone else in your family. Even your mom. I could with you with me, but not alone."

"What did your dad say when you and the girls got back to Boston?"

"Gave each guard a ten grand bonus. Stuart wanted to give his money to me. I refused. He went to the bank and deposited it into my account. After that, I was gracious with anything he offered me."

"Where's Stuart now? Can't you get him to make Justin back off?"

I look out the window as I shake my head.

"He died at the warehouse ambush."

The one Finn led a few months ago.

"Lina, I'm so sorry. I—"

"From what Ewan told me right after it happened, it was either you or Shane. You guys look so much alike, and my guess is you cover your hair. There's no way anyone could tell any of you apart from a distance. Maybe Seamus and Cormac from the rest of you, but not them apart from each other. You, Shane, Finn, and Dillan could be quadruplets from a distance."

"*Mo stór*, I wish I could have seen into the future."

"What does that mean?"

"My treasure."

Other than little girl, that's the only Irish term of affection he's used with me.

"Daddy, you couldn't have possibly known. I don't hold it against you. You and Stuart were there to do jobs. It wasn't some stupid bar fight. It wasn't some random drive by. You both knew what you faced going there. I doubt either of you had much choice, but you went anyway. I wish it hadn't happened. Stuart was the only person who warned me over and over about Colt. It nearly ruined our friendship, but he stood his ground. Justin tried, but he gave up after I told him to stop. When things went up in flames, I turned to him."

"And your closeness to Stuart didn't bother Justin?"

I close my eyes. It's a reasonable question, and I could give a short answer. But I don't want to hide the truth.

"Remember what I said to Colt about when we broke up?"

"I will never forget that. I doubt my brother will either."

I wince. "There weren't four guys. There were three. Stuart, Justin, and another guy."

"Justin and Stuart shared you?"

"It's not like their swords crossed."

"I love Shane and Finn and would give them the last of everything I have. Except for you. There is no way I would share you with them. I won't share you with anyone."

"Because you and I are in a committed emotional and romantic relationship. I wasn't with them. I was so angry and so hurt. I needed an outlet for all of that, and I trusted those three guys. When I said Justin watched me, it was that night. Some things were collective. Others were not."

I don't think Sean wants me to go into more detail. I sure as fucking shit wouldn't want to hear any of this if he were describing his past with Lucy or any other woman.

"Sean, that was the one and only time I was with either of them. We agreed upon that before we walked into the club that night. It was never brought up until I threw it back in his face today."

We're pulling up to the restaurant. We're late, but I don't care. Let Justin wonder.

"Daddy, he's over there. You can't get out with me."

"I know."

"It won't take long."

"It's already taken too long." He kisses me.

I wish this could go on and on, and somehow we magically arrive in his bed. He controls this kiss, and it's unrelenting. It makes me want to forget anyone other than Sean exists. I want this to be the prelude to something even more exciting.

"Daddy, when this is done, can we go home?"

"Home?"

I hear his hesitation. "You've been calling your place home. I guess I got used to it."

"*Our* place is home. Yes. We can go there, *cailín*."

"I'll be back soon, *nounours*."

I pull out the burner I didn't use to call Justin or Colton and punch in Sean's number. He answers as he taps the window. I lock the screen and put it in my pants pocket. My bodyguard walks me over to where Justin waits.

He pulls open his suit coat and turns. No guns holstered under his arms or at his lower back. He pulls up his pant legs. No guns there either. I pull my pant legs tight and open my purse. I pull out the knife just enough for him to see the handle. He does the same for the two in his pants' pockets.

We both open a door and go into the restaurant next to each other. We're shown to a table that allows us both to have our backs to walls while still seeing the door and windows.

"Justin, please don't do this. Even if you got me away from Sean, you know I'd never forgive you. You know your life would be forfeit to the O'Rourkes or me."

"But he wouldn't be with you."

"Neither would you. I'd leave you, and you'd never find me. Do this, and I'll send you a picture a week of me fucking someone who isn't you. Someone I pick. Someone I want."

"Nikki, don't."

"You know I would. I won't be your Stockholm Syndrome submissive."

"I'm not going to kidnap you."

"But you want to take me away from where I want to be and the people I want to be with."

"To protect you. So, you don't love me. I can accept that.

I've already had to. But I don't have to accept you being with someone who's likely to get you killed."

"It's not your decision to make. Just like you didn't get to decide whether your mom stayed or left."

I'm picking at a twenty-year-old scab.

"Don't do that, Nik. That's not fair."

"But it's the same. You didn't get to decide whether your dad stayed or left Stuart to take care of you while he fucked half the women in the Caribbean."

"Nikki." His voice is getting testier.

"Justin, these aren't your decisions. But you have to live with the outcome. I know that means you're alone, but Ewan and Colt are there."

"Don't be a bitch."

"Justin, follow through with this, and you'll do more than sign your death warrant. The O'Rourkes won't let this go as some loner who acted without his boss's permission. You go after one, you go after them all. One Bostonian goes after them, they'll blame all Bostonians. You will start a war. Ewan won't support you. If you made it out of New York, he'd turn you over the moment you arrived in Boston."

"Ewan won't come near me while you're with me."

"Justin, you know I won't go willingly. If an O'Rourke doesn't stop you, I'll do it myself. Unless you have someone to help you, you're a failure before it starts. Who's going to side with you, knowing they'll be losers?"

His hands are in fists, and his knuckles are white. I have to ease off. I've scrubbed off the scabs, and his festering wounds of abandonment are fresh all over again.

"The O'Rourkes aren't shit in this city anymore. That's why you're more likely to wind up arrested or dead than have some Disney happily ever after. No one respects them. They're shit under every other syndicates' shoes."

"I don't know about that. They look like they're doing just fine."

"Really? Then how'd I get a bratva guy to work for me so easily? He wouldn't have gone near Sean if he didn't think he could report back to Maks with a win."

"But he didn't report back with a win. He's dead. Sean killed him. That looks like an O'Rourke win to me, and a bratva big fat fail. Do you really think Maks is going to work with you again if you already failed once?"

"Maks didn't work with me. I told you Mikhail worked for me. *Me*."

Short of pounding his finger into his chest, he couldn't puff up more.

"Okay. You poached a bratva guy. Who told you to look for Lucy? There's no way you just stumbled upon a woman who happened to be involved with Sean not that long ago. Who made her your mark?"

"You don't need to know that."

"But I do. You want me to believe it's safer to be with you than with Sean? To my ear, it's going to piss the bratva off when they find out you hired one of their guys. Then the guy got himself killed by the mob boss's cousin. Maybe you're not working with Maks if you think this is still moving forward. Albanians? Mexicans? Polish? There are plenty to pick from, but the list isn't endless. We can play twenty questions, or you can tell me, so I don't nag."

"Besides the bratva, there are only two other families who matter in this city. The O'Rourkes aren't one of them."

"The Diazes and Mancinellis. This is about Enrique getting pissed I canceled my meeting with Pablo. He wanted the chance to dick Ewan over in whatever deal I was supposed to make. He's butt hurt because I chose Sean over having a pointless conversation with his nephew."

"No."

"So, Pablo's the butt hurt one? He was a little pissed when Sean and I ran into him the other day."

"Your brother wanted you at that meeting to distract you from the one Colt had across town."

What the hell? Ewan went to Baltimore, and Colt was here? No.

"Justin." I flash my gaze to the ceiling and back to him as I sigh. Fucking idiot. "You're lying."

"No, I'm not."

"Yes, you are. You clench your jaw with the last word of any lie. You've done it since we were kids. Colt wasn't here. You were. You told Ewan you volunteered to guard me. You were at the restaurant when I had lunch with Sean. But you weren't at my meeting with Nishida. You had your own meeting. Salvatore?"

His left thumb just rubbed between his first and second knuckle of his index finger. I'm on the right track, but not quite.

"The underboss?" Wish I could remember his name.

He says nothing, but he doesn't have to.

"Bingo. The don's nephew."

"What?"

"You rubbed your finger, which told me I was close. When you cracked your knuckle, I knew I got it right. Did he act alone?"

"You're barking up the wrong tree, Nik."

"Justin, I'm the only person you have who knows you as well as your know yourself. Everyone else is gone. Ewan and Colt never cared enough about you to learn your tells. I did. I did it to protect you against them when they'd pick on you. It kept you from losing your shit. I know when you're lying and when you're hiding a truth someone is way too close to. Did the underboss work alone?"

"Nik, stay out of this."

"Stay out? You dragged me into it kicking and screaming. Does Salvatore know?"

He glares at me.

"Fine. Don't tell me. But when this inevitably fails, which it will, they'll leave your ass out to dry. You refuse to believe me when I say the O'Rourkes will not let you live. If you fail, the Mancinellis will kill you. Hell, even if you succeed, the moment you got into bed with them, you picked the first syndicate to get in line to kill you. The O'Rourkes, the Mancinellis, the Kutsenkos. Have you done anything to piss off the Diazes yet? Or is that tomorrow's epic fuck-up?"

"Fuck you."

"Been there, done that, didn't want the t-shirt. If, by some psychedelic stretch of the imagination you got me to leave with you, and somehow the O'Rourkes didn't get to you, I deserve to know who's likely to make me a casualty of war. The Mancinelli underboss and who else?"

"His *capo di tutti capi*."

"Fancy. Your Italian isn't that great. You can just call the guy *capo dei capi*. Still means boss of bosses. Who's the third in command in the Mancinellis? There are as many of them as there are O'Rourkes."

"Luca's the underboss, and Marco's the *capo dei capi*."

"They set this up? They targeted me to get to Sean?"

"No. You weren't the target. You were the distraction."

"Convenient. Justin, we're done. I don't want to see you or talk to you again. You're not who I thought you were. You're so much less. We could have remained friends, and now the only people you have are Ewan and Colt."

"You're going to abandon me when all I wanted was to protect you."

I'm pouring salt, lemon, and vinegar in this wound.

"Yes. I don't want you. I want Sean."

His fist slams on the table. I see my guard shift from the corner of my eye. He has a straight line of fire now. I'm sure Sean's getting out of the car if he heard the table rattle.

"Justin, we could have remained friends for the rest of our lives. You've been a great one and an excellent bodyguard. But you went too far. You overstepped. It wasn't your place as just a bodyguard to tell the boss's sister who she can and can't be with. You ended this, not me. You pushed me away. You did this."

The vein in his temple pulses. I know what's coming. I slide out of my seat as he reaches for me. His fingers graze my wrist. I shoot my guard a glare that tells him not to intervene.

"Nikki, don't walk away from me."

I keep going. I get to the door, and I can see Sean getting out of the car. Fuck. Not yet. I push through the doors without facing Sean. Justin grabs my wrist, but I don't stop walking. He tries to pull me to a stop, so I grab his pinky and pull back on it, breaking his hold. I rush to the alley a couple hundred feet away. I fish into my purse and grab my knife. I flip it open because I know what's coming. He can't see me, but I put the handle between my teeth.

His hand goes to my hair and grabs a handful. I reach back, clasp his wrist with both hands, and twist my body down and behind him. I push his arm up his back and grab my knife from between my teeth. The blade goes to his kidney.

"You cunt. Fucking whore. You—"

Sean's fist crashes into Justin's jaw, and the force pushes Justin back into me. I can't keep my balance. Someone behind me catches me as I lurch backwards. I let go of Justin, my knife tumbling to the ground. As he falls past me, I see blood pooling in his mouth. He spits toward me, and a tooth goes with the glob of blood. Before he lands, Sean's shoe kicks upward beneath his chin. Justin's head snaps back before he hits the ground.

"You all right, Nikki?"

It's Seamus. I nod as he steadies me.

Dillan and Shane grab Justin and haul him to his feet as a van backs into the alley. Cormac gets out and holds the two doors open. I guess Finn's driving. I watch Seamus pull on a rubber glove before he grabs the tooth Sean knocked out. He has a bottle of what smells like bleach. He turns the nozzle and sprays it anywhere Justin's DNA might have touched the ground. He pulls the glove off with the tooth still in it, and Cormac hands him a plastic bag. The glove and the bleach go into it.

From me entering the alley to me walking out was maybe five minutes, if that. Then I'm back in the town car and on Sean's lap again.

"Two spankings in one day, little one. Your arse is going to burn tonight."

Chapter Twenty-Four

Sean

My brothers are taking Justin to the station until I can deal with him. Right now, my priority is Lina. I want to get her home where I'm convinced she's safe because I'm not going anywhere for the rest of the day or tonight. We have more to talk about, and my palm itches to spank her.

We ride to our place—mine is definitely now ours since she's said repeatedly she's staying—with her next to me. With my cock in her mouth. She's not sucking me off. Oh, no. This is the beginning of her punishment. She's warming it while I play with her nipple. I roll it between my finger and thumb, sometimes tugging and sometimes pinching. I'm texting with the guys as we start planning our retaliation. We all know this is the Mancinellis' retribution for what we did to Lorenzo and Marco. Justin said Marco's the one who reached out to him.

We targeted them to get the feds' attention off our backs over the O'Briens. Their revenge is justified, but machismo demands we not let them have the last word. That's what most of syndicate rivalries are about. It's posturing. The money, the infamy, the everything else are just the means. The one-upping is why these disputes never end.

Finn will dig into the latest financials he can find, but he doesn't expect to find much. Lorenzo is their accountant, and his computer science degree is equivalent to Finn's. After I kill Justin, it'll be my hacking and intel gathering skills that are most likely to move things forward with whatever plan Dillan devises.

I look out the window as we pull up to our place. I press Lina's shoulder, and she lets go of my dick. I fix my pants, and she covers her tits. I'm hard as a fucking plank, but I can wait to get off. Lina will never be my sub, even though that's something I would have done with one. But we have a dynamic with elements of that.

As much as it might frustrate her when I edge her or how it gratifies me to have her warm my cock, it reassures her we're still in a good place. It allows her to focus on something other than what's going on. It allows her to give me control and reminds her I have it. That I am and will take care of her.

We ride up to our floor in silence, and we head straight to our bedroom. My fingers are laced with hers, so once we pass through the doorway, I tug her hand. She turns to face me, and I wrap my arm around her.

"Are you all right to take your punishment now?"

"It's not that I want to get it over with, but I want us to be back to a good place."

I don't want to let go of her hand, so I cup her cheek with my other palm. I stroke my thumb over her cheek.

"*Cailín*, I told you from the start I will punish you if you risk yourself. I will carry out that punishment. Not because I think you're a child who needs correction. Not because I think you'll forget and need to learn from a spanking. Not even for you to gain my forgiveness. I'm doing it because I promised to take care of you, and you agreed to let me. I promised to take the lead during sex, but also with your safety, and you agreed to let me. You broke that promise, but that's not what bothers me. I still trust you. I'm punishing you because it returns us to our homeostasis. I lead, and you follow when it comes to your protection. You got lucky, Lina."

"I know, Daddy. I don't regret what happened to Lucy or leading Justin into the alley. I'm sorry that to do those things, I put my life at risk, and *that* scared you. I don't want to make you feel that way. You crave control to feel calm because control keeps you and the people you care about alive. I get that you don't want to control all my behavior, but not having control over the risks I take, upsets you. I knew those things would bother you, and I did them anyway. I want the punishment to let you know I recognize I broke my promise. I also want the punishment because I made a promise I can't keep. I'll keep taking punishments for breaking that rule, but I'll keep breaking that rule if it's to protect you or our family."

"You've told me that, and I can live with that because if it were reversed, I would do the same thing. I can't fault your dedication or loyalty. I just wish you'd let me walk beside you rather than catching up. I will disagree with you. I will try to offer alternatives that keep you safer. But if there's no other way, then I would rather I be there to protect you as much as you're protecting me. We do this together, *mo stór*."

"It's us against the world, *nounours*. I know that, and I have to act accordingly."

"That's right. I'm sorry you didn't feel like you could trust my family to do what needed doing."

"Wait, Sean. I told you in the car on the way to meet Justin that I trust your family as much as I do you. That wasn't the issue. The need to do this myself—to be the one who avenged you—was too strong to ignore. Maybe it was impatience. Maybe it was my belief I could do it better. Maybe it was just rage I didn't master. But this wasn't about anyone's shortcomings. At least no one's but mine."

"It wasn't shortcomings. We figure these things out together from here on out."

"Yes, Daddy."

"We are okay already, Lina. I've forgiven you already. Honestly, in a way, this was never about needing to forgive. If we don't go through with this, we would still be okay. I won't hold this against you or anything like that. But I think it's important that we do."

"I agree. I trust you."

I bring our lips together, and it's a tender kiss that makes my hard heart soften. I give her a peck when we pull apart. I let go of her and walk to the drawer with the sex toys and devices. I withdraw the Shibari rope and unwind it.

"Strip."

I lean back against the dresser, my right ankle crossed over my left. My right elbow props up part of my weight on the dresser. The rope hangs from my left hand. She's quick to do it, and I marvel at her beauty. I wonder how I got so lucky. Everything about her—inside and out—draws me to her in a way no one else ever has. I skim my gaze over her, and I want to taste every inch of her.

She stands, naked, with her hands clasped before her. I prowl to her, and I sense a moment of trepidation before she recalls I will never push her beyond her limits. I'll take her to the edge, but I won't abuse her faith in me.

I walk around her, trailing the rope between her tits, around her waist, and up between her shoulder blades. She doesn't expect me to spank her arse with it. I move her arms through some gentle stretches before I raise them over her head, bending them, so her hands clasp behind her head. I skim the back of my fingers along her right ribs before grabbing her arse and squeezing as hard as I dare.

"You are mine, *cailín*. You have been since the moment we saw each other. You know that. I know that. Your cunt belongs to me to pleasure and deny. Your arse belongs to me to worship and punish. Your heart belongs to me to love and cherish. I will do that for the rest of my life. I won't allow you to deny me that. I won't allow you to cut that short. I will always do everything I can to come home to you because you have my heart."

I let go of her arse before I drape the rope over her wrists and make sure the lengths are even. I wrap the ends twice, careful that the fibers don't dig into her skin. I have far too much experience doing this and not for BDSM. I usually do this to inflict the initial pain, but that's not what I want here. I check that I can still slip a finger between her skin and the rope.

"If anything tingles or goes numb, you tell me immediately. If I get this wrong and do you any permanent harm—"

"I know, Daddy. You might forgive me, but you wouldn't forgive yourself. That's the last thing I want. You'd torture yourself, and that thought is agony to me. You say you have faith in me, and I want that to last."

"Thank you, *mo stór.*"

With the rope that's remaining, I create a chest harness. Maybe one day I will take the time to create a dragonfly or some form of a *hishi karada*, or even a large diamond *karada*. They're all intricate ties along her torso that accentuate her tits and can press against the outside of her pussy. But for now, I create a bikini harness. I wrap the rope around her chest several times, above and below her breasts. Then I pass the rope around the top and bottom, tugging just enough to capture the most tantalizing set of tits I've ever seen. A rope end passes over each shoulder before looping through the back a few times, then I knot them.

"How're you doing, *cailín*?" It took nearly ten minutes to create both positions because I kept checking the placement and tightness.

"I'm all right, Daddy."

Her breathy voice is one of anticipation. She longs to know what's next, but I have no intention of telling her. She'll find out as we go. I turn her to face me, checking the harness from the front. The way the rope binds her makes her tits appear to swell. I can't resist the temptation. I lean forward and lick her left nipple before nipping at it with my lips. I catch it between my teeth and give a light tug. I move to her right side and practically suck the entire thing to the back of my throat.

I've never had a preference for size, nor have I been steadfastly a tits or arse guy. I crave all of Lina. She's so slender that her arse fits perfectly in my hands. I cover it and have all of it at once. It feeds the possessiveness I feel. Her B-cup breasts are also the perfect size for my hands to do the same thing. I can nearly swallow them whole. There's no part of them that isn't mine. I will never be so possessive as to stop her doing the things she wants. She's not mine to lock away from the world. I have no wish to dominate her spirit or change even a sliver. But physically, I revel in it.

I step back and return to the dresser. This time I leave the drawer open after I withdraw a Wartenberg pinwheel. I could gather all the things I want, but I don't want her to guess what I'll do. The uncertainty—the surrender to me—that's our give and take right now. I run the tiny, notched wheel around her now sensitive nipples.

I start with the right, encircling it before running over it, top to bottom, then left to right. I move to her left and draw the prongs from the bottom rope to her nipple, over the dart, and up to the top rope. I wheel it around the mound, keeping it close to the ropes. Then I make it creep down her belly until I get to her clit.

I'm super careful not to pinch any skin as I draw it down the crease between her pussy and right hip, across her pussy lips, and up the opposite crease. I turn my hand to pull it sideways over her clit, then push it back over the sensitive bundle of nerves.

Her breathing is faster but deep. Her abs contract as need makes her shift her weight from one foot to the other. I reach around her with my free hand and land a smack that nearly pushes her forward. I return to the dresser, retrieving a crop.

"Widen your feet."

She obeys immediately. She glances down to her cunt, so it makes her shriek when I land the crop on her left tit. I set a pattern she can't predict as I smack her tits, arse, and cunt. I watch the clock on my bedside table, doing this for a minute. I toss the crop onto the bed and untie the ropes. I'm gentle as I move her arms, ensuring they don't grow stiff. I keep the pressure light as I massage her breasts as the full circulation pours back into them.

"How do you feel?"

"Like this can't be done, Daddy."

"Not nearly, *cailín.*"

She breathes easier. I don't know if she wants this sexually, or she doesn't believe the punishment is enough. I kiss her temple because I'm proud of how she's taking this, and I need the moment of affection. She turns her head, and we exchange a light kiss. I wouldn't do this with a sub. It is—it was—a different mindset with a sub. I love Lina. I'm certain of it. Would most people question my feelings because they've developed so quickly? We've known each other nearly three months.

Dillan's sister, Colleen, loved romance novels. She schooled all of us when we teased her about them. If my relationship with Lina were a story, Colleen might have called it instalove. Instalust for sure. But time takes on a different meaning in this world when permanence can last only hours. Where I'm old at thirty-one. I know plenty of men who haven't made it to this age. Some of my bullet and knife wounds threatened to take me to hell much younger. A minute is an hour, an hour is a day, a day is a lifetime.

"Climb on the bed and lie on your side, arms in front of you."

I've given what comes next plenty of daydreaming. I tested it to make sure the logistics work with a few hard tugs. I lift her top leg and bend it, so her left instep rests on the inside of her right knee. I wrap the rope around her legs several times, binding the length of her thigh to her calf. I ease her top knee back to widen the gap between her legs. I step back and toss the remaining rope over my curtain rod, tying the ends to the rope that stretches in the air.

"Try to close your legs."

Her left leg moves just enough that I'm not worried about her hip, but she can't do more than a couple inches. I slipped vibrating Ben Wa balls in my pocket the last time I went to the dresser. They have a remote I keep hidden.

"How does it feel?"

"Good, Daddy."

"We'll see." I waggle my eyebrows before intensifying my gaze.

I watch her suck in a breath that caves her stomach and pushes out her chest. I press the balls into her, rubbing her clit as my fingers withdraw from her pussy. I use the remote to turn them on, and she shrieks again. I put them straight on high. This time her breaths are fast and shallow. I watch her, growing concerned. She sees me, and I can tell she's forcing herself to calm. She doesn't want to upset me.

This is my last trip to the dresser. I grab a foam wand and a blindfold. I slip the blindfold over her eyes. I watch closely for how her body reacts to losing that sense. Now she truly doesn't know what will come next. I shift to stand behind her, but at a distance that allows me to hold the vibrator against her clit while spanking her with the crop.

What we've done has been the prelude to her punishment. I observe her with an intensity I haven't even used with a captive I'm torturing to the brink of death. I know I'm creating sensory overload for her. It's a state of confusion where she doesn't know which sensation to focus on. The vibration on her clit or the vibration on her g spot while her arse burns.

I purposely didn't restrain her hands for this. That would be more lack of control than I want to create. She's clutching the bedding to keep from reaching down to stop me. She moans over and over, yelping when the crop hits a particularly sensitive spot that I've already spanked. If she whimpers—even hints at a whimper—it will all end. I watch her breathe through it all.

"Daddy, I need to come."

"I know. But don't."

"I won't be able to stop it."

"Yes, you will. Do not come until I say you can."

"But, Da—"

"*Cailín.*"

"Yes, Daddy. I'll do my best."

The authority I infused into that one word and her obedience says everything about this. Her tone sounds more relaxed than it has since we started. She's fully given me control, and it eases her mind. I've taken what she's given me, and I'm at peace.

I turn off the wand and put it on the bed. I shift to spank

her pussy, but I keep it light as I unbutton and unzip my pants. I toe off my shoes. I put down the crop to finish stripping. I'm careful as I retrieve the Ben Wa balls. Then I ease into her and just hold myself still. I kiss the inside of her knee since it's almost level with my mouth. My hand caresses her deep pink arse.

"Daddy?"

"Yes, little one."

"Thank you."

"You're welcome. What do you need?"

She smiles at the question. She knows the punishment is over.

"Well, start by fucking me then—"

She presses her lips together before her teeth appear and sink into the right corner of her bottom lip.

"Yes. I'll give you what you need."

I'm certain of what she was going to say. I wrap my leg around her bound leg, leaning forward to cup her breast that's against the mattress. I draw my hips back before slamming into her. I pound my cock into her cunt over and over; her moans filling the room, only slightly muted by my periodic growls.

"Come, Lina."

"Thank God."

"Or just me."

She giggles before she tenses.

"Sean!"

"Good God, you're tight."

I have to pull back before I come and can't give her the other half she needs. I'm quick to get her leg untied while I rock my hips.

"Take your blindfold off."

I shift her onto her back before I pick her up. She wraps herself around me like a koala as I climb onto the bed. I remain sitting as I hold her hips. I guide her to ride me, so she shifts to bend her legs to kneel. Our bodies press together as we kiss. It's erotic and so intimate. We're making love. I can tell the difference. The difference between this and fucking. It's obvious, but we've done both before. I can also tell the difference between all my sexual encounters before Lina and what I share with her. I give her all my heart and probably most of my soul.

"*Cailín*, I love you."

"I love you, too, *nounours*."

"Will you always be mine?"

"Yes."

I pray the next time I ask a question like that, I get the same answer.

It's been a month since my kidnapping and Lina's near double homicide. There really is no other way to describe it. She would have killed Justin if I hadn't found her first. She's had withdrawn moments, and I know she thinks about what happened with Lucy. We've talked about it, and she feels the same way as she did when she killed the men who attacked during her girls' weekend. She doesn't regret or feel guilty about killing. She questions why she doesn't. She worries about the ease with which she's done it in two separate and different situations. I've told her what I can about my early days and how I feel when it happens now. It makes me examine myself and the monster I've become.

I said that once, and she lost her ever-loving mind. We were in the living room, and she jumped off the sofa, sprinted to the bedroom, and came out with a paddle with holes in it. Those hurt even more than a solid one. If she'd been strong enough to pull me onto my stomach like she tried—and she put all her weight into it—she would have spanked me long and hard. She threatened that if I ever said that about myself again, she'd wait until I was asleep, then take the paddle to my arse.

Letting her have that moment of control gave her a chance to show her protectiveness—even if she's protecting me from myself—and it gave me a chance to submit and feel even more loved than I usually do. We understand each other.

But beyond our home, it's been an ongoing source of frustration. Only two things have been satisfying as we deal with our enemies. I used my CI in Baltimore to get photos of Ewan going in and out of Ellie's house. He got photos of them fucking all over the place in there. I sent them to her husband. I feel not a miniscule speck of remorse for her husband kicking her out.

She made her bed and laid in it—with Ewan all the fucking time—so she got what she deserved. Ellie's husband was there the next time Ewan arrived because he planned to help Ellie move to Boston. The guy beat the shite out of Ewan, giving him a broken jaw and two cracked ribs.

That was nothing compared to what I did to Colt. I told Lina I needed to go to Boston, and she deduced what I was going to do. She didn't explicitly ask, and I didn't give her any clues. She knows how I feel about the way Colt treated her. Now he knows too to the tune of four broken ribs, a punctured lung, a busted kneecap, an elbow that will never let him hold a rifle again, and needing his own splenectomy.

I jumped him in the dark and worked him over on my own. There is no proof it was specifically me, but I branded a four-leaf clover right over his arsehole. He can keep taking it up the arse for the Irish—and by that, I mean my family. We are *the* Irish.

"Look, Donatelli's would be a blow Salvatore would never recover from." I'm at Dillan's with the others. "That would send a message the universe would hear, but Mikey doesn't deserve it."

Mikey Donatelli has been Salvatore's best friend since they were kids. He's not *Cosa Nostra*, but he grew up surrounded by it. He owns a restaurant that's like Salvatore's second home. Mikey expanded it and even made a special family dining room just for the Mancinellis.

Everyone knows he's sacrosanct but not just because he's Salvatore's friend. He's an all-around great guy. He runs a food pantry on the weekends, even when he's the busiest. He'll hire homeless people to do odd jobs around the restaurant, and he gives high-school kids their first job, offering benefits to those who need them.

Taking out that restaurant would be a personal blow Salvatore wouldn't recover from. Even though the bratva destroyed the first home my family had when they immigrated to America, and it'd become a central gathering place for our extended family, we have limits to what we'll take from people.

Shocking.

I know.

"Marco didn't order a hit because he knows better than to kill you. But he definitely wanted you fucked-up, and he wanted us to suffer not knowing where you were." Shane's been chomping at the bit to go on the rampage.

My twin held it together while they searched for me, but it all crumbled the next day when we were alone. He came to my place, and we went in my office. Lina stayed at the other end of the condo. We were in there for two hours of extremely unmanly sobbing and hugging. He'd known something was wrong even before he got the call. Lina was sleeping, but he said he had a wave of nausea and broke into a cold sweat. We already know the pattern. It happens to us when one of us gets injured or really sick. When I got tonsillitis, he was the one who couldn't stop puking. He inflamed his throat so much that he wound up getting a tonsillectomy too.

We're so closely bonded that it's a level of empathy I can't put into words. Because our bodies are made exactly the same, and our minds work so similarly, feeling each other's pain isn't difficult to fathom. But the telepathy we have and that other identical twins claim to have has no scientific explanation. How we know something is wrong when we're not together defies explanation, and neither of us questions it.

"He and Liz just bought that house on Grand Cayman. They haven't even spent a night there. He thinks no one knows he's stashing shite there. I'm sure Liz doesn't, but we do." Finn turns his laptop around, so we can see photos of an exquisite villa on a beach that looks more like a painting from someone's imagination than could be real.

Ten minutes after Shane left that day, Finn showed up. Our time locked away was *only* ninety minutes. But it was more hugging and crying. While my bond with Shane is inexplicable on so many levels, it has never felt more significant or stronger than how I feel about Finn. Shane says the same thing. My oldest brother can be a monumental pain in my arse. Even in his thirties, he still likes to flex and make me do things for him. I give in by choice because I love my brother, and it's usually something trivial, like giving him my seat somewhere.

But he's protective of Shane and me in a way I can't explain, either. It's in his marrow that, until Ally came along, no one came before us. I've seen him knock out a three-hundred-and-twenty-pound guy who could have been a Sumo wrestler with one punch because he took a swing at—and missed—Shane.

"What's he got there right now?" Seamus leans forward to see the house better.

"Amyl nitrate." Shane grins.

The shite's a depressant with medical uses for things like angina. But it's become a party drug. People huff it, and some guys use it like a cheap replacement for a little blue pill if they can't get it up or keep it up. It's also highly flammable.

"He's gonna have a fun time explaining to Liz why her wedding present exploded." I'm tempted to rub my hands together like some cartoon super villain.

"What's the product valued at?" Cormac is nearly as tight fisted with money as Finn, so every penny of everything counts.

"The street price is still cheap at ten dollars a vial, but you know the Mancinellis. They'll make their buyer think those Poppers have some magical ingredient that sets them apart. To them, it'll easily go for three times that price. From the pictures we have of the shipment, my guess is about two-hundred grand." Finn shrugs.

In the world we work in, that's chump change. But it'll be inconvenient because the profit is likely already designated to help pay for something way more expensive, thus way more important. I've been hacking their emails and inventory systems to find any hint, but nothing's hit yet.

"When?" Dillan's remained quiet so far.

I laugh. I can't help it. "His birthday is in two days. *Buon compleanno.*" Happy birthday.

"Too bad he won't be there to blow it out. *Tanti auguri!*" Many wishes. Shane's chuckle echoes mine.

"Make it happen." Dillan joins in the laughter, but he appears unsatisfied.

"Do you want us to do more?" My brow furrows.

"Not to the Mancinellis. I'm not satisfied with how things wound up with the O'Malleys. It doesn't feel done enough."

We kept Justin at the station for two weeks. The first four days had him strung up, naked, starving, and dehydrated. We barely kept him alive. When he slid toward unconscious, we'd cut him. Nothing deep enough to make him bleed out or knock him out, but enough for the pain to register and revive him.

I worked him over once a day, and my relatives took turns. Cormac, Seamus, and Shane took turns for the night shifts. The second four days had us taking turns with baseball bats and steel pipes. We learned little because Lina was right. The physical pain did next to nothing to get him to talk. But the last six days were slow emotional torture.

We got into his phone and discovered he'd saved a mailbox full of messages from Lina over the years. I pulled up her social media and scrolled photos of her, lingering on ones where he was in the background, or we knew he was there when it was taken. For each photo I showed him, I told him about what we ate for breakfast together that morning or dinner the night before. I told him what movie we watched or what time we went to bed and what time hours later we fell asleep. I *never* reveal any intimate details. That is for no one but Lina and me. I will never violate our relationship by sharing that stuff.

I reminded him every chance I got that she picked me. That he had no one. That Ewan hadn't tried to negotiate for him. He knew he wasn't going anywhere. That wasn't the point. He knew no one cared enough to try. By day twelve, he was so broken, he shared everything he knew. That's how I arranged for the photos with Ellie and to attack Colt.

It's also how I found out who the gunmen were. The one who shot me, and the one who shot Ewan. Turns out it was Mikhail in a building across the street from the hotel. We hired the guy who almost took out Ewan. He's now a CI.

I hung a photo of Lina and me sharing a lounger beside my parents' pool on the wall in front of where Justin hung most of the time he was at the station. For the last three days of his miserable life, he had his arms stretched over his head and connected to a meat hook. I made sure he couldn't turn his head, and he couldn't spin himself away from that view. We just left him there. No food. No water. Just Lina's and my smiling faces. Just as he was about to die, Shane and I took him down and tossed him into the vat of acid we keep as one of our disposal methods. He screamed just before he drowned, the chemicals burning the skin from his bones.

Nothing about that made me happy, but it was satisfying.

"Ewan's home and still recovering. What do you want to do to him?" I know that because the piece of shite texted Lina asking her to video call him.

Fuck no. She didn't want to give him any sign that would make him think he could manipulate her. If she hadn't refused, I would have insisted she not make the call. He hinted at Colt's condition but didn't describe it. I feared she'd talk to Colton Senior about it. She didn't.

They spoke, but it was about Ewan's accountant. She eventually told me Blake had gotten handsy with her once and tried to box her into a room. She'd gotten past him, but he'd been an arse to her after that. She asked Colton to take him out, and he did. Ewan and all the O'Malley men know she ordered it, but they don't know Colton did it. They just know it was one of them.

"Did Nikki ever share her encryption?" Finn's as curious about how her system works as I've been.

"Yes. She suggested we wipe them out last night. Is that what you want? Empty all of their accounts?"

Yesterday morning, she heard from a woman who dated Blake but can't stand him now. Lina and Suzette are friends, so Suzette told Lina that Ewan only wants to talk to her because he wants her to smooth things over between the O'Malleys and us. Apparently, he was going to tell her that if I love her, I wouldn't keep her in the middle since he's ready to extend the olive branch.

Dillan nods. "Yes. Move all the money that goes into payroll for their legit employees into an account, so they don't get fucked. But take everything else. Finn, you handle where it goes. Hide it all."

Finn has accounts a pack of bloodhounds couldn't find. Accounts buried so deep into shell corporations, behind DBAs, and under stolen social security numbers that we can weather a storm strong enough to need Noah's ark.

I glance at my watch. "I gotta go."

Shane stands when I do. "You got everything?"

"Yup."

I'm more excited than on Christmas. Our parents never got us matching anything for Christmas or our birthdays unless we asked. It was never a case of one of us opened a present and the other wondered which color he got. We've been separate people to them since the moment we were born. I loved opening presents.

"Call us in the morning." Dillan gets up with the rest of the guys.

"Not a fecking chance. It'll be at least three before I plan to talk to anyone besides Lina. Pish off." I know Dillan's fucking with me.

I get to the driveway just as a car pulls up. I wave to Lina and get in when it stops in front of me. From our kiss, you'd think we'd been a part for days rather than hours. I'm like a puppy when I'm away from Lina. I have no concept of time. I'm always excited.

When we pull apart, she realizes we're still on Dillan's street—which connects the neighborhoods with every married syndicate couple our age and those of our parents. Finn and Ally are six doors down from Dillan and Mair. We drive past a house for sale that's next door to Maks and Laura. Definitely not stopping there. We turn onto another road, and we pass

Gabriele and Sinead's house. I internally shake my head and roll my eyes as we pull up to a house four doors past them. There's a for sale sign here, too.

"Sean?"

"I figured we could look around at a few since you keep telling me you like the area."

"I do, but wasn't that a *Cosa Nostra* house back there?"

"Yeah. There are three more between this street and the next cul de sac over. Eight doors down and across the street is a bratva couple."

"If a neighborhood could be incestuous, this would be it." She half mutters as our driver, Tommy, opens her door.

"It's not like we have pineapples out and swap."

"Because that would be a bloodbath. None of you could stop the women from carving each other up if they looked at a man other than their own husband."

"Would you?"

"I've been sharpening my knives since we started talking about moving in around here."

I let her know when Justin could no longer be an issue. We started talking more earnestly about the future and what that would look like for us. Today we're house hunting.

We visit every house on the market in this neighborhood and the one next to it where more syndicate couples live. Mostly the ones my parents' age. We've just come back for a second tour of the third house we checked out.

"Do you really like this one the most, *nounours*?"

"I do. We can make an offer now if you want."

"Really?"

She knows this is going to be a cash purchase. It's not like we need to line up a preapproval first.

"Let's take one more walk through."

There's a bay window on the second floor in the master

bedroom, and she mentioned how she's always wanted a window seat. She walks over to it but looks back at me.

"Sean?"

"Hmmm."

"What's this?"

"Open it and see."

She picks up a gift box with a lid that lifts while still connected to the base. There's a small white envelope that she opens without peeking beneath the tissue paper it sat on.

I hated the sun was out that day. It felt wrong. I haven't had a day without sunshine since I met you. Nothing has felt righter.

She looks up at me now that I'm standing beside her. She pushes aside the tissue paper, and her eyes widen at the smaller box nestled within. I wait for her to lift it out, but her gaze locks with mine. Her lips pull in for a flash as I bend one knee. Then she's beaming as I take her left hand.

"Lina, I love you. Every day, I'm grateful for those early texts. I'm grateful you agreed to lunch. I'm grateful for the peace you bring my life and the happiness I never expected to feel. Will you marry me?"

"*Oui*, Daddy."

Every once in a while, she'll slip into French. We don't notice since I'm fluent and switch easily. She pulls out the smaller box but hands it to me. I flip it open, and she grabs my shoulder with her right hand as her left trembles. I slide the ring on and stand. She launches herself into my arms. It's another first kiss. Our first one as an engaged couple, a couple about to own their forever home, a couple who are soulmates.

"How'd you get this here?"

"I put it down as you were looking at the closet."

"You left it here?"

"I knew we'd be back."

"You knew this was the one I'd like the most."

"Just like you knew this is the one I'd like the most."

"And if I hadn't?"

"Danny was ready to run in and get it."

My third cousin, like six times removed or something like that, is her bodyguard today and was in the front passenger seat.

"Shall we buy a house, *cailín?*"

"We're buying our home, *nounours.*"

Epilogue

Lina

I had video calls with my mom while I briefly lived in Boston and then once I stayed in NYC. Sean met her that way, and he met her in person when he had to make a trip to Montreal to meet with Granddad two weeks before he proposed. It was right after he told me Justin could never interfere again.

That meeting had nothing to do with us, so I couldn't go. My mom joined them for dinner one night, but besides that, it was all business. I don't know the details, and I didn't bother to ask. But Sean was happy when he got home, and it wasn't because business went well. He'd hit it off with my mom, and my grandfather saw him as more than a business associate. I know because Mom and Granddad video called me while Sean was on the flight back.

But today's the first time we're all going to be in the same place together. Mom and Granddad just landed at the private airfield in Jersey. Sean and I are here to meet them. I watch them descend the steps to the tarmac, then I'm hugging them before I know it. Breda's hugs have always been nearly as good as my mom's, but there's just something about hugs from the person you said your first word to. Mine was *Maman*.

"Elise, Jean-Peter, it's good to see you." Sean gives my mom kisses on each cheek and shakes my grandfather's hand.

It's a quiet but cheerful car ride to our new house. We finished moving in two days ago. We're chatting as we enter the house through the garage.

"Surprise!"

Sean has his arm around me, so he pulls me behind him as he reaches back for his gun. My grandfather steps in front of my mother, reaching back too. But it only takes a second to see Sean's family inside. It shocks me to see my mom's older brother, my aunt, and cousins, along with Colton and Daisy, waiting for us. Even my stepmom, Maureen, is here. There's a banner for a wedding shower.

"Whose idea was it to scream surprise to two mobsters?" Sean's grumbling, but he's smiling from ear-to-ear.

The wedding isn't for another six weeks, so I didn't expect this at all. We aren't waiting or anything like that. We aren't making sure this is the right decision. We want an early autumn wedding in Maine. Apparently, the O'Rourkes have some properties along the coast. We'd like to take advantage of the fall foliage and have an outdoor wedding.

I know a Catholic wedding would mean a lot to Sean, but I also know all the men in my family and his feel ashamed going to church when they know the sins they've committed and the ones they are yet to commit. He's told me about his conflicted feelings, and the guilt he has for being a hypocrite. He'll go when he has to for other people's weddings, baptisms, and funerals. But I didn't want to insist and ruin a day that's as much about him as it is me.

"How'd you get all of this set up?" I'm standing with Breda, Saoirse, and Siobhan.

"It was Finn and Shane who organized things with your family, and Colton and Daisy. Dillan took care of the decorations. Cormac took care of the food. You'd never guess most of it is vegan. Seamus helped smuggle in the unhealthy stuff. And the three of us made sure Danny knew he'd die if he arrived too soon. We told him to 'find' traffic." Breda uses air quotes and all.

I learned Cormac is the cleanest eater in the family because of some article he read as a kid about processed foods. He's not vegan, but he owns a small organic grocery store. He says owning it is a tax write off for all the healthy "shite" he eats.

Sean wraps his arm around me again and leans to whisper in my ear. "I had no idea. Did you?"

"None. It's amazing, but it kinda makes me wonder if our skills are slipping."

He laughs. "I thought that too. So much for us being able to detect national secrets."

"I'm glad though."

"Me too. Are you happy, *cailín?*"

"Blissful."

Time passes in a blur as we mingle, laugh, and eat. Good God is there a lot of food here. When I saw the tables ladened with food outside, I wondered how many people Cormac and Seamus thought they were feeding. By the time my fiancé, his brothers, his cousins, their fathers, my uncle, my cousins, and my grandfather plus Colton went through, there were practically crumbs left for the women. I had no idea sixteen mobsters could eat so much. Mair and Ally planned ahead and brought out some dishes they saved for the rest of us.

It's growing late, and I'm tired. It's been a tremendous night, but I'm ready to just be with Sean. We keep darting glances at each other, and I know he feels the same. He excuses himself for a moment and slips out of the living room. It's practically a grand salon in a palace, but we knew we have large families. It was part of the appeal because we can entertain with space for everyone in one room that isn't the dining room.

When Sean comes back in, he sits beside me on the loveseat. Not two minutes later, the O'Rourke men and the Tremblay men reach into their pockets. They pull out vibrating phones, scanning the message that came in. My head spins as people say their goodbyes. My mom, Maureen, Mair, and Ally look confused, but Breda, Saoirse, Siobhan, and Daisy grin and laugh as they hug me.

"What did you do?"

Sean shrugs.

"Let me see your phone." I put my hand out and flap my fingers.

He hands it over, and I tap the text icon. I see a group text with fifteen other names listed.

SEAN

You have 5 mins to get out before I blow something up you have to fix. Say goodnight to my bride.

I look up at his unrepentant expression.

"You wouldn't have really..."

"None of them wanted to find out."

"Sean!"

"Hmmm."

He scoops me over his shoulder before taking the stairs two at a time then carries me to spare the bedroom with a lock on the outside. We've decorated it in a style no one needs to find. Though I suspect Mair and Dillan, and Ally and Finn would appreciate it. I think they're like us. I don't mind everyone leaving in such a hurry. Tonight's full of surprises.

"Strip, *cailín*."

"Yes, Daddy."

When Seamus O'Rourke learns there's a surprise witness he's about to cross examine, he doesn't imagine it'll be a woman with a man's name. A beautiful woman with all the curves he desires. There's one problem: she works for the wrong family. Discover Seamus and Tiernan's story in *Mob Saint*.

Before you go, would you like a *free* extra epilogue with a steamy hotel room scene from Sean and Lina's trip to Montreal?

Subscribe to my newsletter and get this gift from me to you.

Don't miss the next installment

Preorder *Mob Saint* and have it ready when you wake up on release day.

They call me a saint, but I'm really the Devil in disguise.

I'm more than I appear.

I'm smarter than people think.

I like it that way.

Cross me, and you'll soon find out who I really am.

She's mine to love and protect.

And that's exactly what I'll do.

Pleasure awaits her, and I'll be the one to give it to her.

Get between us, and there'll be nothing left but ash.

Meet Seamus and Tiernan

Get a bonus epilogue

Enjoy this free bonus epilogue with a scene from *Mob Princess* where Sean and Lina visit Montreal. Lina has plans to keep them both warm. Join them for the ride home and some kinky sex once they're there.

Check out this extra sexy scene with Sean and Lina. Get your Copy here.

Thank you for reading Mob Princess

Sabine Barclay, a nom de plume also writing Historical Romance as Celeste Barclay, lives near the Southern California coast with her husband and sons. She loves her days at the beach soaking up way too much sun, a good Netflix binge, and a strong hot chai. Her heroines are independent women who can defend themselves but love their Alpha heroes who want nothing more than to protect their soulmates in her Mafia Romances. She's Gen Y/Oregon Trail and loves creating engrossing contemporary romances that will make your toes curl and your granny blush.

Subscribe to Sabine's bimonthly newsletter to receive exclusive insider perks.
www.sabinebarclay.com

Join the fun and get exclusive insider giveaways, sneak peeks, and new release announcements in
Sabine Barclay's Facebook Dubious Dames Group

Do you also enjoy steamy Historical Romance? Discover Sabine's books written as Celeste Barclay.

The O'Rourke Brotherhood

Mob Boss
BOOK ONE SNEAK PEEK

DILLAN

I hate meetings like this. I don't need to wear pants from some shitty off-the-rack suit that are too tight to *try* to make my dick look bigger. I'm secure in my cock size, and I don't need to show how big my balls are for people to know I run this part of the city. I loathe strip clubs too. I'm past the point where naked women make my jimmy do jumping jacks. I can appreciate a hot bod and gymnast level strength, but it does nothing for me. These douchebags? They're practically ready to come in those cheap arse pants. Why am I here? I keep asking myself that. Seamus and Shane are doing just fine with these negotiations. I'm just here to look good. I'm the muscle today. Or rather my name and my position. Who the fuck thought— way, way back in the day —that giving the mob hierarchy nautical names was a good idea? Fucking Skipper. This isn't motherfucking Gilligan's Island. None of these numb nuts are the Professor, even if they think they're fucking Mr. Howell.

But who is that? If this is *Gilligan's Island*, then she's Mary Ann.

I glance at Seamus, but he's focused on the Albanian he's trying not to lose his shite at. Shane smirks at me when I dart my gaze to him. I cock an eyebrow as the waitress walks over. She's definitely not a dancer. She has too many clothes on. But you can barely call the pieces of thread she's wearing clothes. She's got on a bikini top that's barely more than pasties, and the skirt she's wearing would make my Catholic grandmother do somersaults in her grave.

It's the standard uniform for this place, but somehow it doesn't look right on her. Not because she doesn't have a banging body because she does. Not because she's a butter face— but-her-face —as in great bod, not so great face. She's beautiful in a super understated way. That's part of what makes her look out of place. She has next to no makeup on. I think those are even her real eyelashes. The natural beauty is drawing way too much attention.

"'Scuse me."

She tries to step around Zef Hoxha, the *kyre* of the Albanian mafia here in New York. When he reaches out to grab her wrist, I'm out of my seat with my hand around his. He never gets a chance to touch her because my hold is so tight he can't bend his fingers. I keep squeezing until it must feel like I'll snap the bones.

"No touching."

Zef drops his arm as much as my hold allows. I let go and stare at him before I tilt my head toward the waitress. I narrow my eyes, and he knows what I expect.

"I apologize, miss."

"That's all right, sir. Here's your drink."

She's polite as she hands him his glass. Unfortunately, to put down the rest, she has to bend forward, giving everyone a view of her glorious cleavage. Tits and arse are what sell here, and she has them in spades. I'm certain it's why my cousin hired her. If I sit down, everyone will know I'm just as guilty as these fuck nuts because she's made my dick do something that hasn't happened in a strip club since I was like twenty-three. I'm now thirty-three.

Mob Boss
Mob Star
Mob Princess
Mob Saint
Mob Bride
Mob Knight

Do you also enjoy steamy Historical Romance? Discover Sabine's books written as Celeste Barclay.

The Ivankov Brotherhood

Bratva Darling
BOOK ONE SNEAK PEEK

LAURA

As I sit across from the four Kutsenko brothers, I press my lips together to keep from drooling. No four men should be so strikingly handsome. Not all from the same family, anyway. I fight a valiant battle against letting my gaze drift toward the eldest, Maksim, whose ice-blue eyes bore into me. After years of negotiating billion-dollar investment contracts while facing countless ruthless businessmen, I've learned to keep my expression studiously blank. But it's a true struggle today. Instead, I focus my attention on the squirrelly lawyer sitting across the conference table. While he's disingenuous with each comment, he's a good negotiator. But I'm better. How cliché am I?

While I feel Maksim watching me, I focus on Dmitry Yakovitch as he continues to argue the merits of the venture capitalist company I represent, RK Capital Group, merging with

Kutsenko Partners. What he means is the merits of Kutsenko Partners acquiring RK Capital Group, then stripping it and making it another money-laundering shell corporation. While most people in New York have little awareness of the Russian mafia, I do. The Kutsenko brothers' names appear on no titles or deeds anywhere in New York City, but it wasn't difficult to determine which shell companies likely belong to them. Their assumption that I'm unfamiliar with them is proving beneficial to me as they continue to whisper amongst themselves in Russian. I think they may even believe they're convincing me that they don't speak much English.

The senior partners of RK Capital Group know who I'm negotiating with, though they may not know I'm aware of these Russians' more nefarious operations. They've given me the go-ahead to agree to a merger with an eventual acquisition, but only for the right price. A price to the tune of twenty billion dollars. Considering an investment firm like Goldman Sachs is worth nearly one-hundred-and-twenty billion dollars, my clients' asking price appears reasonable.

"Mr. Yakovitch, I shall stop you now." I raise my left hand, pen caught between my index and middle fingers. When I have his attention, I lean back in my chair and casually twirl the pen over my index finger and thumb. "Fifty billion is my clients' asking price. You know that. Your clients know that. RK doesn't oppose the merger. What they oppose is the insulting offer you've made. It's nearly noon, and I'm hungry, Mr. Yakovitch. I have a delicious ham sandwich waiting for me. I even have three chocolate chip cookies waiting for me. If we aren't going to make any progress, I shall let you go, so I can move onto my eagerly anticipated lunch."

I cant my head just enough for me to appear as though my gaze rests solely on the opposing attorney's face, but I can see each

Kutsenko brothers' reaction. My face battles yet again against showing my emotions as I fight not to smirk. Their muted but surprised expressions confirm what I already know.

"Please tell your clients to make a reasonable counteroffer, or I will conclude this meeting and enjoy my ham sandwich and cookies."

Dmitry glares at me before turning to Maksim and his three brothers. In rapid Russian, he doesn't interpret my suggestion. Oh no. There's no need for that. I can't catch every word because his voice is too low. But I catch something along the lines of "The bitch refuses to budge. What now? A fucking ham sandwich. More like a stick up her ass."

Maksim swivels his chair to look at his brothers. In Russian, he says, "Fifty billion is ridiculous. She's not so stupid or naïve not to know that. My guess is they'll settle for twenty billion. We offer fifteen."

"That's barely better than what we already offered," Aleksei, the second-oldest brother, argues. "She'll be eating the fucking sandwich and dipping her cookies in milk before we walk out the door. We need the buildings."

"We offer twenty, Maks," Bogdan, the youngest, insists.

As I watch the brothers discuss, their voices barely lowered, I pull my lunch sack from the black leather satchel by my feet and set it beside my laptop. It's a ridiculously pink floral bag with an embroidered monogram, the L and D overlapping. It's an empty prop, but they don't know that. I watch as five sets of eyes narrow. I offer a smile that would appear innocent in any setting other than this meeting. It's patronizing, and I know it.

Bratva Sweetheart
Bratva Treasure
Bratva Beauty

Mob Princess

Bratva Angel
Bratva Jewel

Do you also enjoy steamy Historical Romance? Discover Sabine's books written as Celeste Barclay.

The Mancinelli Brotherhood

Mafia Heir
BOOK ONE SNEAK PEEK

LUCA

This asshole is pissing me off. We've been going around in circles for five minutes, and the longer we stand out here, the greater the likelihood someone will spot us. I have a sixth sense about these things. It's why I'm still alive at the ripe old age of thirty-one.

"Espinoza, enough already. Either sell to us or don't, but we set the price. Your tequila is good, but it isn't nectar from the gods."

I'm watching Carlos Espinoza, some lackey for the Mexican Culiacán Cartel, try to maneuver me into paying more than the agreed upon price. I know it's so he can skim off the top.

"It's as close as you're going to get. You've upped the order, so the price per case goes up."

My uncle, Salvatore Mancinelli, is the New York don. He negotiated this deal, and I warned him it was a bad idea. But what do I know as his underboss and heir? I'm not backing down.

"Haven't you ever heard of a bulk discount? The more I order the better the price should be. No one else around here is buying from you. You know we're your only choice in three out of five boroughs. You aren't going to the Bronx because you won't get more than pennies there. You aren't going to Queens because you don't want to run into the Colombians. You aren't going to Manhattan because then you face the bratva along with us. And what are you going to do in Staten Island? Sell to us anyway? We control Staten Island and Brooklyn when it comes to liquor stores, so take the money and go."

"Luca, there are plenty of liquor stores in Brooklyn that aren't owned by Italians. I'll go there."

We aren't friends. He's patronizing me by using my first name. Fuck him and the horse he rode in on. I have other solutions for this shit.

"And I'll just take what I want from them for free. That's not a half bad idea. The deal's over. Take your shit with the worm in it and go."

"Motherfucking racist. Not all tequila has a worm in it."

"You're selling Mezcal. It's known for the fucking worm. I wouldn't start calling me names, you *penche hijo de puta*." Fucking son of a bitch.

He has twenty-five crates of stolen tequila that he's trying to offload because he knows he can't sell it at his own liquor store. "What did you call me?"

Carlos takes what he thinks is a menacing step forward, and his two bodyguards do the same. Not smart. Neither of my two bodyguards nor I react, but the three men in each of my cars open their doors. They won't do more than that. It's just a reminder that the Culiacán can try, but the *Cosa Nostra* still run New York City.

"This is the third and final time I say this. Sell or leave."
Every head turns toward the liquor store's back door as it opens.
A gorgeous blonde steps out, and I wish I had the time to
appreciate her beauty, but she's about to die. Carlos and his
men draw their guns and pivot toward her. My men pull their
weapons too, but we keep them pointed at the Mexicans. The
woman stands like a deer in the headlights for a second before
ducking behind the industrial garbage dumpster like a frightened rabbit. Three shots hit the metal almost at the same
moment. That's all it takes for my men and me. The two bodyguards standing with me aim for a guard each, and I set my
sights on Carlos. We squeeze our triggers, and the men fall.
Screeching tires tell me Carlos's driver takes off. I hear more
gunshots as at least one soldier in my cars tries to shoot the
escaping vehicle. Glass shatters, but the sedan keeps going. I
hear more tires squeal as one of my SUVs takes off and chases
the guy. I holster my gun and wave my men to do the same.
I inch forward toward the trash can, but I see the shadow shift.
The woman bolts from the other side. She's still the frightened
rabbit, but I'm the fox pursuing her. She's fast, I'll give her that.
But she has to be at least a foot shorter than me. My legs are a
lot longer and cover a lot more ground with each stride.
She weaves among the cars, most likely believing it's harder to
hit a moving object. She isn't wrong, but I have no intention of
shooting her. I push myself harder and pounce as she darts out
and tries to cross the last stretch of parking lot to reach a better
lit area near a bus stop. I lunge.
"Stop running, *piccolina*. I won't hurt you."
I wrap my arms around her and pull her back against my chest,
but I'm quick to spin her around and put space between us as I
grasp her arms. Of course, she fights me.
"If I wanted you dead, I would have shot at you, too."
"It doesn't mean you won't kill me after."

She's breathless as she continues to struggle. I almost let go to take a step back, insulted at what she implied. But I can't blame her. If I were a woman, I'd be terrified of the same thing.

"I'm not going to rape you. I'm going to talk to you."

"Talk? You are not a man who talks if you just killed a guy."

"To keep him and his men from killing you. I told you, if I wanted you dead, I would have shot at you too. And I wouldn't have missed."

She stops struggling against me, but her eyes continue to dart from one place to another, trying to find somewhere to flee. I know I can keep her in place with only one hand, so I release her left arm. I still have a firm hold on her right one, but I haven't held it nearly as tightly as I could.

"I'm Luca. I know you figured out you interrupted something you shouldn't have. Did that man know who you are?"

"Yes."

"What about his driver? Would he know you?"

"Yes."

"Do you have a name?"

"Yes."

"*Piccolina*, we won't get very far if yes is all you can say. Are you willing to answer me with more than one word?"

"No."

I knew that was coming, and I grin. I can't help it. I wasn't wrong about her being gorgeous, but I doubt she wants to know that's what I think. At least, not if I want her to know I won't assault her.

"Fine. I have more than twenty questions I can ask that you can answer with one word. Do you work at the store?"

"Sometimes."

Ah, an improvement.

"Did Carlos know you were still working?"

"No."

"Do you have a car, or do you take the subway or bus?"

She raises her chin and remains silent. Smart but counterproductive.

"The subway or the bus will get you killed. You're too easy to find and follow. Do you have a car?"

"Yes."

"Can you stay with someone instead of going home?"

She refuses to answer.

"If that man knew you and you sometimes work in the store, then he knew where you live. If he found that out, so will someone in his cartel."

"I know. Let me go. The longer I stand here, the more likely someone is to come back for me."

"No one will touch you while I'm here."

"Arrogant. If he shot at me, he would have shot at you."

"And he would have died, anyway. What's your name?"

"Jane."

"Look, I know you won't get in one of my cars and let me drive you somewhere. In most cases, I would say that's a smart move. But you did nothing wrong tonight except for leave work at the wrong time. I know that, and you know that. But the Culiacán won't see it that way, *piccolina*."

She freezes for no more than five seconds before she trembles so much that I can see it. I don't know what drives me next, but it's the same instinct that's made me call her little girl three times. I pull her to my chest and tuck her head against it. I stroke her hair down to her shoulders, rubbing my hand up and down her back. This is the most inopportune moment to notice she isn't wearing a bra. I will my body not to react.

"What does that mean?"

Her voice is barely more than a whisper, but I know what she's asking.

"It means little girl."

"I should be insulted, but the way you say it..."

"It has nothing to do with your height. I know you're not a child."

God, do I know she's not. She feels amazing. Her tits are soft as they press against me, and I can see she has the most delectable ass. I'd love nothing more than to cup it and squeeze until she goes up on her toes and begs for me to wrap her legs around my waist and fuck her. For fuck's sake. Stop, you disgusting asshole. That is not what you need to be thinking about.

"Why didn't you shoot me? Whatever you were talking about, if it was with a Cartel member, then it wasn't completely legal. Carlos didn't want me alive to talk about seeing you together. Why are you letting me live?"

"I told you. You did nothing wrong but try to leave work. He should have checked the building before starting the meeting. That was on him. The only thing I take issue with is you leaving by yourself and walking into a dimly lit parking lot. I suspect you do that often, and that's too dangerous. Jane Doe, I don't hurt women."

Mafia Sinner
Mafia Beauty
Mafia Angel
Mafia Redeemer
Mafia Star

Do you also enjoy steamy Historical Romance? Discover Sabine's books written as Celeste Barclay.